MISTRUNNER

BOOK 4

MISTRUNNER

BOOK 4

NICHOLAS SEARCY

Podium

Published in 2024 by Podium Publishing
www.podiumaudio.com

Podium

MISTRUNNER

BOOK 4

___

CHAPTER ONE

AN END'S BEGINNING

When I first met Mirabelle Braddock, I knew she would be trouble. I should have killed her, there and then, but I was too selfish to see what she might become. I was too interested in winning our war.

—Alistaris Kargat

I huddled in the corner of my bedroom, my knees clutched to my chest as I stared at what Patrick had become. I was grateful he was alive. Of course I was. But I couldn't ignore the reality of his transformation. Even in darkness, the right side of his face shone with the blue light of his artificial eye. The rest of his cybernetic parts were hidden beneath the blankets, but I knew they were there, all the same.

How could I not?

How could I forget that I was the reason they were necessary? After all, through my actions, millions of people had died. Most of them had been Pacificians—pseudosapient androids built around the blueprints of real people's minds—but there were plenty who'd been killed in the aftermath of their self-destruction. Those deaths were on me. Without my vendetta, all those people would still be alive.

And Patrick would still be whole.

So, I sat against the wall, and I wept for all the evil I had caused. For all the lives I had cut short. And for all the people I had maimed. People like Patrick, but without the possibility of rebuilding their bodies through cybernetics. After all, I knew just how many credits those parts had cost. Not to mention a qualified cybernetic engineer to install them. No—the death toll would climb with every passing day. Some would succumb to their injuries. Others would survive, but for how long? The world wasn't kind to those with disabilities. It was hard enough to survive in the best of times, but adding missing limbs or broken spines to the mix? Few would make it through that, and only those with the money to treat those injuries would thrive.

I knew I should have been grateful for Patrick's survival. His cybernetics weren't the highest quality available, but they were better than most. As such, he could've actually seen it all as an upgrade. In fact, he'd said as much right after he'd woken up.

But still, the guilt remained, and rightly so.

I had done horrible things, and until that very moment, I hadn't had the opportunity to truly wrap my mind around it all. Millions of Pacificians. A huge crater on the moon, visible even from Earth's surface. Tens of thousands of humans. And that wasn't even considering what I'd done back in Nova.

I'd long since come to terms with the fact that I was a killer. A mass murderer. I had my reasons. Of course I did. Even with the benefit of hindsight, I was secure in my choices. I would make them all again, too. However, even if that was the case, it didn't preclude me from feeling guilty about the things I'd had to do.

The people I'd had to kill.

The collateral damage I had left behind.

Like that, I remained for hours. Eventually, my tears dried up, and my thoughts turned from the regrets of the past to plans for the future. I still had open skill slots. The opportunities they represented were nearly infinite. There were skills out there for every purpose, and I knew I'd barely scratched the surface of what was possible. There were two problems, though.

First, I had spent almost every credit at my disposal, so buying new skills from the Bazaar was out of the question. Even if I went to Anaseteramanimix, the lone skillsmith I counted as a friend, I still couldn't afford her wares. With the credits I had at my disposal, I wouldn't even be able to buy a single skill.

Second—and perhaps more importantly—I had no idea what to choose. As far as I knew, there were infinite possibilities, and I had no clue what to pursue. Did I go for something with more combat abilities? I already had more than I could rightly use, but I could easily integrate something useful into my normal repertoire. Did I get something with more utility? I'd seen the sort of things a skilled medic could do. Or a pilot. Or even an engineer. There were hundreds of potentially useful skills out there.

But I couldn't get them all. I couldn't fill every niche. Not only was it implausible that I could find the time to train them, but I also knew good and well what was coming. And as much as I wanted to branch out, I couldn't deny my role in the war of Integration. Becoming an engineer might offer me a chance to branch out, but it would do almost nothing to help keep me alive. Or to win the war I knew was coming.

The one I'd volunteered to fight.

And that dictated that I focus on skills that would help me in combat. Still, there was a choice to be made in that arena, as well. Did I go for something like [Acrobatics], where the bulk of the benefit was in passive modifiers? Or did I seek out useful abilities, like those that came with [Combat] or [Fieldcraft]?

I sighed.

The reality was that I didn't know which way to go, and I wouldn't until I saw what was available.

With that in mind, I established my priorities. First among them was to earn some credits. To do that, I would need to assault some Rift-mining operations. Perhaps I could even raid a Rift or two. Once I had enough, I would buy my new skills. I scrolled back through my notifications until the one I wanted appeared on my HUD:

Warning: You have recently lost three (3) skills. Replace them within sixty-two (62) days (Planet 2341-M) or you will forfeit the potential and any attributes exceeding your new, lower potential.

Unlike the first time I'd seen a notification like that, the time frame with this iteration wasn't really all that onerous. A lot could happen in two months, and even if I failed to meet my goals before the timer ticked down, I would only lose a few attribute points. It would be a loss, but not a devastating one. So, while I intended to try to get things done before time ran out, I wasn't going to do something stupid and put myself in undue danger. Nor would I settle for cheaper skills just so I could save a few attribute points. No—I needed to be smart about this because I knew just how difficult it would be to gain another evolution of my class.

If it was even possible.

I'd had to kill millions of people to reach level seventy-five. Sure, that same feat could be accomplished killing monsters and running Rifts, but that strategy would take decades. What I had just done was not repeatable, even if I was willing to shoulder the burden of guilt that would come with it.

Of course, I wasn't really sure how true that was.

If I'd turned my attention to mass murder, I could have destroyed dozens of cities a year. I would have killed more low-level innocents than actual combatants, but I could have done it all the same. Would that have resulted in the same level of progression?

Maybe.

But my instincts told me that wasn't the case. From everything I had seen, I made far more progress from taking out powerful targets. It just so happened that there were quite a few of those within the population of the Pacificians I'd killed.

Whatever the case, it took much more effort to gain levels the higher I climbed. So, it stood to reason that, going forward, I would see far less progress in that category. In turn, that meant that I might've hit my limit in terms of class evolutions.

Or perhaps I was wrong. The reality was that, despite living with the system for years, there was so much I didn't know. That I would probably never discover.

I moved on from that unproductive line of thought, resolving to ask my friends in the Bazaar about it. In the meantime, I needed to establish the rest of my plan. So, once I'd gathered a nice cache of Rift Shards, I would head back to the Bazaar, sell them, then visit Ana the skillsmith. Hopefully, I would have enough money left over to make some upgrades.

I glanced at the still-sleeping Patrick.

I would get him some upgrades, too. After all, he deserved the best, and I knew precisely what kind of high-end cybernetics were out there. My own Hand of God was a good example of how I intended to outfit him.

Once we had our equipment, cybernetics, and skills sorted out, I needed to get down to the serious business of training. At the same time, I needed to help Alistaris wherever I could as we set out to prepare for the coming Integration. We couldn't prevent it, but there was a lot we could do to blunt the edge of the coming sword.

Sighing, I leaned back against *The Leviathan*'s bulkhead.

There was so much to do, and with the Integration looming less than two years away, it didn't feel like we had enough time to do it. But there was no choice in the matter. The aliens were coming. Nothing I could do was going to stop that. They would descend upon Earth like locusts and devour everything they saw.

Some, like Alistaris, would have fairly benign intentions, but there were enough of them with the opposite philosophy that there was no chance for peace. If they came, they'd pay for every step with blood. Eventually, it would reach the point where the cost-benefit analysis tipped in favor of leaving Earth to its own devices.

It was a long shot.

I knew it. So did Alistaris. Jeremiah had known it, too.

But I was committed now. And what's more, I could no longer stomach the idea of running away. All it took was to remember all the horrors I'd seen perpetrated by various aliens—the Castorix, who'd enslaved people with slave implants and specially made skills; the Pacificians, who'd used people as batteries; or the E'rok Tan, who'd bred people as livestock—to know that, regardless of what I had tried to tell myself, retreat had never been a real option.

For a while, I made and discarded plans until, at last, Patrick rose. I watched silently as the blue light of his artificial eye intensified. He let out a groan, then pushed himself upright. Only a second later, he turned to face me.

"Good morning," he said, his voice still low and raspy from his ordeal. Not only had he lost his legs, arm, and half his face, but he'd also had multiple organs replaced. Even with skilled medical personnel, that kind of thing didn't go off without a hitch. He would be healing for quite some time.

"It's actually the middle of the night," I said, forcing a smile. "You've been asleep for almost twenty hours."

"Oh."

"How do you feel?"

"Weird," he admitted, running his hand through his hair. His fingers stopped when they met the metallic half dome. "That's going to take some getting used to, no doubt about it."

"Patrick, I—"

"If you're about to apologize again, I don't want to hear it," he said.

"But—"

"It wasn't your fault."

"It literally was."

"You couldn't have known this was coming," he said. Shortly after the cybernetic engineer had finished replacing his limbs, I'd explained everything to him. And I hadn't pulled any punches, either, telling him in great detail about how I'd killed millions. And how I was ultimately responsible for what happened to him. Still, from the very beginning, he had insisted that I was innocent of any wrongdoing. I vehemently disagreed.

"I didn't even think about it, though. I was too wrapped up in making them pay."

"And you did. A little collateral damage was always going to happen. Besides, you did what you thought you had to do," he stated. "We're at war, Mira. We have been since the very beginning. And people die in wars. It sucks, and nobody wants it to happen, but it's inevitable. We should do what we can to minimize it, sure, but we're not just talking about money or land or anything like that. We're talking about the freedom of our species. This is about our very survival. We have to do what we have to do, make the sacrifices we have to make. That's just the reality of the world we live in."

"Under that logic, you can excuse just about anything."

He shrugged. "Maybe that's the point. It's not an excuse, Mira. It's a reason. Actions and consequences, right? That's what you always say. With the stakes as high as they are, we can't afford to hold back. We can't let ourselves worry about sacrifices. We just have to do what needs to be done. And if a few innocent people die? Then that's on the aliens for putting us in this position."

I looked away. He'd never spouted that sort of rhetoric before, so I was a little taken aback. However, I could certainly see the logic behind it. If the stakes included the enslavement or death of the entire human race, then whatever we had to do to avoid that fate was justifiable.

"I'm not sure if I can live like that, Pick."

"You already are," he said, leaning forward with his elbows on his cybernetic knees. "Every decision you've made, you've based on that same reasoning. First, it was killing Nora. That was important, so you did what you had to do. You accepted the consequences. It's the same with the Pacificians. Don't even try to tell me you wouldn't make the same choices if you had to do it over again. You would, and you know it."

"Maybe."

In fact, I knew it was true. In each instance, I felt guilt, but I would have still taken the same actions.

"So," he asked, clearly wanting to change the subject. "What now?"

"Training," I said. "You need to get used to your cybernetics, and I need to test some things out. I . . . Uh . . . I evolved my class, so . . ."

"You evolved? Is that even possible?"

"Apparently so," I stated. Then, I told him about the choices with which I had been presented, then explained my reasoning for choosing the {Mist Warden} option, ending with, "It just seemed a lot more powerful than the other options. With those requirements, it had to be. And then it merged half my skills. You should see my modifiers now. I mean, I haven't made many quantifiable gains lately, but I feel like I can probably do twice the damage now."

"That's . . . That's a little scary, actually."

I couldn't really bring myself to disagree with that assessment. I was already capable of untold carnage, and that was before I'd evolved my class. After choosing {Mist Warden} and augmenting my modifiers, I could only imagine the things I could do. Especially after I trained a little.

"Before I can get down to really training, though, we need to earn some credits," I said, not wanting to dwell on the danger my new, evolved skills represented. "I think I'm going to need new weapons, and I need to fill my remaining three skill slots."

He shook his head and gave me a tired smile. "That's insane," he said. "Three open skill slots. You know that's more than most people ever get, right? What are you thinking of getting to fill them?"

"I don't know yet. I have no idea what's even available. But I do know it's going to be expensive. And that's before we worry about you."

"What about me?"

"I think we should look into upgrading those cybernetics, and—"

"No thanks."

"W-what? Pick, those aren't the highest—"

"I have plans for these. I was thinking about it before. You know, right after we got back to *The Leviathan*. This can be an opportunity for me, you know? With the [Cybernetic Engineer] skill, I already get more out of cybernetics than most people. But now that I have so much to work with, I think I can modify these and overclock them. I'm not saying I should never upgrade them," he said. "But I am saying that I want to experiment as much as I can, then get something using higher-quality materials later on. Heck—I might even be able to make my own stuff."

"Really?"

"Yeah. Maybe. I mean, I know I can do it. I just don't know if I can make anything as good as what we could potentially buy. And I won't know until I check things out. Speaking of which—what happened to the workshop?"

"Completely collapsed. You're the only survivor."

He sighed, and his lips sagged into a frown. "Kind of guessed that much, but . . . I mean . . . Having it confirmed . . ."

I didn't interrupt. I'd never really liked Cirilla, but I hadn't wanted her to die. Besides, she and Patrick had been close enough that her death had to have hit him pretty hard.

"We need to dig it all up," he said.

"What?"

"The workshop. The mech suit is still in there. So are the leftover Mist circuits. I won't abandon those," he stated. "They'll be critical going forward. And if that armor can survive having a building dropped on it, it's far more valuable than I expected it to be."

I nodded, and over the next few minutes, we continued to discuss our upcoming plans. Most of it was just a rehash of things we'd both already said, but it was good to focus on taking steps forward rather than looking back at the past.

In the end, we'd established a plan for the immediate future. Now, all that was left was implementing it.

CHAPTER TWO

A FEW MONTHS LATER

It can't be overstated how jarring it is to wake up missing a bunch of parts. Even as I took shelter in the mech suit, I knew I was never going to be the same. However, the extent of the damage to my body far exceeded anything I could've ever anticipated. Now, I vacillate between wondering if I'm a monster and getting excited about all the possibilities my new parts represent.

—Patrick Ward

I leaped, grabbing hold of the bar and using my momentum to swing around, then launch myself to the next platform. I landed with a roll, then sprang forward to the next. The moment my feet left solid ground, I saw a projectile speeding in my direction. I twisted, narrowly avoiding it on my way to the next platform. Then, flaring Balance, I raced across a narrow beam before once again sending myself sailing through the air. I slapped the big red circle before descending to the ground, then rolling to my feet.

I rose, panting as I glared at my HUD.

"Three minutes," I muttered, disappointed. "How the hell did I get slower?"

Patrick, who was busy with his own training regimen, answered, "You've been at it all day. You're tired, Mira. Of course you're going to slow down."

I turned my glare in his direction, but it did no good. His back was turned, so he was incapable of experiencing the full weight of my annoyance. He just didn't understand. Patrick trained as hard as just about anyone else, so he knew a little about how to push himself in pursuit of self-improvement. And his attributes showed it, too. He'd never focused on leveling, but he definitely got the most out of his capability. Usually, he hovered only a few points shy of maximizing his potential.

And for the first time ever, I was in the same boat.

Nearly three months had passed since my class had evolved, and I'd yet to absorb a single new skill. Part of that was due to my lack of funds. *The Leviathan* was a huge expense, so it sometimes felt like every step forward Patrick and I took was soon followed by a couple of steps in the opposite direction. So, while we'd made some progress in accumulating the wealth we would need to purchase my would-be skills, we certainly hadn't reached my goals.

As a result, almost a month past, my potential had readjusted to my new skill total. So, instead of a potential in the five hundreds, it was stuck at two-thirty-five. Which meant that I'd actually lost a handful of attribute points, which was the exact opposite of my goals.

It was probably the reason I felt like I was backsliding.

By comparison, Patrick's performance, while lagging significantly behind mine, had grown by leaps and bounds. Largely, this was due to his acclimation to the cybernetic parts that had replaced the limbs and organs he had lost. One of the abilities that came with [Cybernetic Engineer] allowed him to get a little more out of any artificial parts, so the replacements had actually improved his overall level of power.

And he was getting better with every passing day.

Normally, I wasn't the jealous type, but my competitive spirit certainly balked at the idea of anyone—even the man I loved—outpacing me. So, I'd rededicated myself to training as I tried to eke every ounce of ability out of my attributes. Those efforts had been met with mixed results.

Certainly, without constantly evolving attributes, I'd managed to pinpoint a few holes in my development. Chiefly, I hadn't even come close to reaching my theoretical limits. With my attributes, I should've been capable of so much more. However, I'd learned from Alastaris that my issues were not unique. In fact, he claimed that it often took people years to acclimate to increased attributes. In that way, my constant improvement had been something of a detriment. Sure—my overall power increased, but without the ability to settle into that newfound power, I was only getting, at most, sixty percent of what I should've been capable of.

Which was why I'd continued training so rigorously and why I held myself to such high standards of performance.

I glanced back at the obstacle course we had built. By all rights, getting through it in only three minutes was an accomplishment, but even thinking that felt like I was trying to placate my own disappointment. I was better than my time, and I knew it. I just needed to work harder. I needed to focus more.

Because I knew there would come a time when I would need to harness the entirety of my power.

Sighing, I massaged the back of my neck and said, "I'm going again."

"Mira, it's almost dark. Why don't you . . ."

I didn't listen to the remainder of his suggestion, instead trotting back to the beginning of the obstacle course where I started over. From there, I worked long into the night, but my times didn't get any better. In fact, they consistently got worse until, at last, I missed one of my jumps and hit the ground with a thud. I rolled and quickly rose, but I'd been going so long and so hard that my legs felt like jelly. Robbed of my momentum, I collapsed to my knees, where I remained for a long few minutes, my breath coming in ragged gasps.

I knew I was pushing myself too hard, trying to accomplish the work of years in mere weeks. But time was not on my side. Soon enough, the world would be under siege, and if I wasn't ready by that point, the alien invaders would wash over everyone and enslave humanity.

And that was the best possible scenario if we didn't stop them. The worst was that they simply killed us all and brought their own people in.

Sighing, I looked down at the grassy turf and considered the monumental task before humanity. It didn't look good, no matter how I spun it, and despite my previous resolutions to fight until the very last breath, I questioned whether or not Patrick and I should simply pick up and leave. I rejected it quickly, but the remnants of that thought remained as background noise for my mind.

So, to distract myself, I glanced around at my surroundings. *The Leviathan* stood only a quarter mile away at the base of a rolling hill. Otherwise, the area was almost entirely open grassland. Every now and then, the plains were broken by a low hill or a lonely tree, but for the most part, it was just a flat prairie. I looked up at the night sky, which seemed even more expansive than usual.

For a while, I just enjoyed feeling small and inconsequential. Beneath that vast sky, I couldn't feel any other way. But soon enough, reality caught up, reminding me that I had responsibilities. I had plans and goals. And I would never achieve anything if I let myself lose focus.

So, with that, I pushed myself to my feet, dusted off my knees, then headed back to *The Leviathan*. We'd been in the prairie for almost a week, and before that, we'd spent the previous few weeks going from one Rift-mining operation to the next. Some, we'd hit before. Others were new. But none of them had been nearly as profitable as we'd hoped. It seemed that the aliens had finally wised up to our strategy of robbing the operations themselves, and as a result, they more frequently sent their Rift Shards back to the Bazaar, where they ended up in the hands of whoever funded the operations.

It was inefficient, and it required using humans to get around the restrictions associated with transporting goods off of Earth, but it seemed that, to them, that was preferable to making themselves vulnerable to my assaults.

The following text appears on a torn scrap overlapping the top of the page:

The reality was that we needed a new
rick, but neither of us wanted to tak
Rifts before, and we'd both nearl
in any hurry to put ours

---

strategy. I knew that, and so did Pat- the obvious next step. After all, we'd run died because of it. So, neither Patrick nor I elves back in those situations.

The Leviathan, Patrick wasn't waiting on me as I'd en I went looking, I found him in the cargo bay, which o a makeshift workshop. There were crates full of supplies, inets for his tools, and of course, the giant mech suit we had m the ruins of Fortune. Back then, it had sustained a good deal of al damage, but after a hefty amount of work, Patrick had returned it to e condition.

And it was an impressive machine.

With sleek lines that screamed athleticism, it was roughly the shape of an armored human being. However, it was at least five times the size of any person, painted stark white with gold highlights, and engraved with a variety of esoteric symbols that made it look more like a medieval suit of armor than a war machine. The cockpit was housed in the torso, which was comprised of four-inch-thick armor plating. In short, it was like an ambulatory tank crossed with a chivalrous knight.

So, it fit Patrick well. He was the only person who could operate it, owing to the fact that it was technically a cybernetic paired to his interface. The workings were similar to my Cutter, though a little—but not much—cruder.

But Patrick wasn't working on the armor. Instead, he'd removed one of his legs and had propped it on the table that served as his workstation. He didn't even look up from where he was tinkering with it as he asked, "Finally had enough?"

"Not really. I just couldn't go any longer," I admitted.

"You collapsed again, didn't you?"

"Maybe."

He sighed, then turned to look at me. I must've looked a lot worse than I felt because he just shook his head and said, "You can't keep going like this, Mira. I don't like what it's doing to you."

"If I told you the same thing about your projects," I said, gesturing from the suit to his workstation. "Would you stop? No. Because you know as well as I do what's coming. We can't afford to relax, Pick. We let up, and we'll end up dead."

"Maybe," he said. Then, he glanced around, adding, "Not like I have much room to talk. You're out there pushing your attributes to the limit, and I'm in here working on my cybernetics. Neither of us has taken more than a few hours off since Fortune."

I didn't want to dwell on that point, so I changed the subject by asking, "Any progress?"

"More and more every day," he sta[ted]. [...]
netics earlier. I'd have given up a hand o[...]
these kinds of discoveries."

"Like what?" I asked, crossing the cargo bay th[...]
I had to sweep a few parts out of the way, which I kn[...]
my defense, he should've just put them away when he was don[e...]
them.

"Like I've been looking at cybernetics all wrong," he said. "I mean, understanding the mechanics isn't hard. They're just machines that run on Mist, right? But most of us have a fundamental misunderstanding of how cybernetics connect to our bodies."

"They go through the Nexus Implants, right?" I asked.

He shook his head, saying, "See? That's what I'm talking about. That's how everyone thinks. But it's just not true. Not of the high-quality cybernetics, at least. Like that hand of yours—do you know why it's basically indestructible?"

"Because it's made of Mist-infused titalumiron bones with nano-fiber muscles?"

"No. I mean, yeah. Partially. But none of that would mean anything if it wasn't for the constant Mist connection," he said. "The high-quality cybernetics, they mimic the connections we have with our actual bodies. That way, the Mist keeps flowing through and empowering them. It's impossible without something like those Mist circuits. For the longest time, I had no idea what I was even looking at. It wasn't until I had my breakthrough with the armor that I started to get it. And now that I have my own cybernetics, I'm able to run experiments so I can see how everything interacts."

"And that's going to help you make them stronger?"

"It is. If I can use the information I'm gathering to optimize those connections, I think I can increase the power of my cybernetics by at least a hundred percent. Maybe more."

"Uh . . . Seriously?"

"Seriously. I'm a little ways off from that, though. And I'm going to have to build my own Mist circuits to make it work. I think I'm on the verge of being able to do that, though, so I'm really not as far off as you might think. Maybe six months. A year on the outside. Then, I can get the right materials and . . . Well, I'll build myself some cybernetics that can rival that Hand of God. But with more oomph instead of defense."

"What about the armor?" I asked.

"That's a little further away," he admitted. "Apparently, plenty of people in the core worlds use mech suits. Bots are popular, too. Most of the power without any of the danger, you know? But with the armor, I'm thinking I'm two or three years away from perfecting it. At least insofar as my skill will take me. If I evolved it like you did with your skills, it would net better results, though."

"How good is it now? You haven't even piloted it since we got it loaded up."

Indeed, he'd connected to the giant suit of armor when we'd excavated it from the ruins of Cirllia's workshop, but beyond that, he'd barely even mounted the thing.

"It's hard to tell," he admitted. "But if my calculations are right, I'd say that its durability is equivalent to around two hundred Constitution, give or take ten. Strength is lower, though. So is control. And its Mist consumption is a little higher than I'd like. I can only run it at full strength for around an hour at a time. And that's without any advanced weaponry."

"Two hundred? That's almost as tough as me," I remarked.

"Yeah. My giant suit of armor is almost as tough as my girlfriend," he said with a shake of his head. "When you put it like that . . ."

"No. Seriously, Pick—this is huge," I said. And I meant it, too. Especially if he still had a long way to go before he perfected it. "Do you think it'll be ready when the Integration starts?"

He shrugged. "Maybe. I don't know," he said. "But I'll take it as far as it'll go."

I nodded, then leaned back on my palms. "With that suit, I think we might be able to hit some Rifts," I said. "I mean, think about it. We took a few on before, and both of us were a lot less powerful back then. If you're in that suit . . ."

"Then I won't be a liability."

"That's not what I meant . . ."

"Yes it is," he said. I started to rise, but he waved me away. "You're right, though. I mean, without the suit or these cybernetics, I'm just . . . I'm barely more powerful than a regular person. With it, though . . . I think I could make it work. So long as I don't have to fight any extended battles, I mean."

"You can't run it on Rift Shards like *The Leviathan*?" I asked.

"No. It's a cybernetic. They only work off personal Mist."

"Well, that just sucks."

"Not really. Think about it. If people could use Rift Shards to power cybernetics, there'd be no chance we could fight the invaders," he said. "At least this way the power of a cybernetic is tied to a person's attributes and level."

"I suppose," I said. But I was still a little disappointed. "I was just imagining slapping some high-quality Rift Shards into that thing and letting you go wild."

"If we could do that, then others could, as well," he reminded me.

I nodded, then said, "But the point still stands. We need money. Lots of it, if all of that is as expensive as it sounds."

"It will be."

"And I still need my skills," I said. "*The Leviathan* needs power, too. So, the way I see it, there's only one way to meet our needs. We need to spend the next couple of years running Rifts. It'll help both of us train and let us earn some money so you can work on your projects, and I can upgrade my arsenal."

"If we survive."

I couldn't really counter that small caveat. Some of the most difficult fights of my life had been inside Rifts. They were dangerous and unpredictable, and there was a good reason we'd sworn them off years before. However, my points still stood, and my reasoning remained unassailable. If we were going to meet our goals—or even come close to it—we didn't have much choice in the matter.

"We will."

He sighed. "I hope you're right."

"I usually am," I pointed out.

"Just because you're strong enough to power through mistakes doesn't mean you were right in the first place," he pointed out.

I shrugged. "Same difference. Look, Pick—we need this. I think you understand that as well as I do. But if you don't want to do it, we won't. We'll keep going like we've been going, picking off alien mining operations," I offered.

"It's fine. I'm okay with it. But just because I'm willing to do it doesn't mean I like it. I just . . . I just hope there are no fucking spiders," he said.

"You and me both."

After that, we worked out some of the logistics and set a time frame. In the meantime, I resolved to contact Alistaris so I could establish a series of viable targets. As far as I was concerned, all aliens were potential enemies, but he could give me some context as to who the truly terrible groups were.

So, just like that, we had a plan. I could only hope that it was one we could potentially survive.

THREE CHOICES

I hate Templars. They have so much power, and yet, they choose to allow the occurrence of one injustice after another, always claiming that if they intervened, the consequences would be worse for everyone. And my response is simple: tell that to all the people you let become enslaved.

—Alistaris Kargat

The next day found Patrick and me making our final preparations to move on. The plains had been a good place to train, rest, and plan, but that period had come to an end. Now, we needed to move on. To that end, I spent much of the next morning breaking down the obstacle course and loading it into *The Leviathan*'s cargo bay. For his part, Patrick occupied himself with buttoning up his various projects before erasing any remaining evidence of our presence. He took down the awning we'd attached to the ship's fuselage, buried our firepit, and loaded the various bits of furniture we'd set out.

And just like that, we were ready to go.

As Patrick took his customary position at the controls, I sat in the navigator's seat, then said, "Before we do this, we need to stop and see Al."

"What? Why?"

"Because he's a paranoid asshole, and he wants to give me the files in person," I said. "He doesn't trust me, even over a Secure Connection."

Patrick rolled his eye, then shook his head. "I wouldn't trust you, either, honestly. He knows you're dangerous."

"So is he."

After all, he could have killed me at almost any time he wanted. He'd proved that back in New Cairo, when his team surrounded me. He'd also shown me that he could infiltrate *The Leviathan* whenever he chose to do so. He probably couldn't bring the same kind of destructive power to the table that I could, but that didn't mean he wasn't dangerous in his own way.

Besides, he had an army behind him.

But was that really true? He'd hinted as much, but the little Dengyt had never said so outright. And I'd certainly never seen more than a handful of his subordinates. For all I knew, he only had access to a couple dozen fighters, which would explain why he was so desperate to get me on board.

Regardless, it didn't really matter. I was already committed. The fact that I didn't completely trust him was just one more facet of my working relationship with Alistaris. What I did know was that he'd held up his end of our past bargains, so a degree of trust was probably warranted.

Even if it made me feel naive, like I was going to turn a corner and suddenly discover that I'd been duped.

"So, where are we going?" Patrick asked, choosing to ignore my last statement as inconsequential.

"Place called New York," I said. "It's on the other side of this continent. A bit to the north. I'll input the coordinates."

Then, I did just that. As far as I could tell, it would take a little over an hour and a half for us to reach our destination. We could have reached it in half the time—or maybe less—but going that fast so close to the Earth's surface would burn Mist—or more accurately, Rift Shards—like crazy. And we certainly couldn't afford that.

After I entered the coordinates, Patrick started the Mist engines and directed the bulky ship to lift off. *The Leviathan* was far from the sleekest machine, but it was perfect for our purposes. Not only was it quite roomy for a ship, but it was also practically indestructible by Earth standards. Sure—it wasn't impossible to bring it down, but it would take something truly powerful to do more than leave a few scratches.

For the next hour or so, Patrick and I cruised across the continent. Along the way, we passed in the vicinity of a few cities. One, called Apex, was a shining metropolis that looked like a utopian paradise; I knew it wasn't, though. While the people who lived there did indeed lead nearly perfect lives, they had built their city on the shoulders of thousands of slaves.

Their city—or the poorly constructed slums that passed for one—was nearby, though we'd have had to alter course to see it firsthand.

As we passed it, I couldn't help but let out a sigh, which Patrick noticed.

"What?" he asked.

I shrugged. "It just occurred to me that even if we win, it probably won't do any good for most people," I said. "I mean, look at Apex. Only humans live there. No real alien influence at all, according to Al. But look what they've created. And I'm not talking about that pretty city they built, either."

"Yeah. I got that," he said, still clutching the controls with his cybernetic hand. He hadn't bothered to cover it in artificial skin, so it looked more like a metallic skeleton than anything else. "But look—we can't fix the world's problems, okay? You know that."

"Do I?" I asked. "Then what am I doing? I mean, if I'm not trying to fix the world, then why did I even commit to this war? Especially if I know humanity is just going to fuck it all up in the end. I hate the aliens. Right down to my core. The things they've done . . . It's horrible, Pick. And I want to kill them all for it. But at the end of the day, are we any better? Look at Nova. By all accounts, the alien influence there was minimal. Sure, there was some, but they mostly just left people alone. And you saw how corrupt it was there. Whole swaths of people living in squalor, turning to drugs or living their lives in virtual spaces so they could escape reality. Is that what we're supposed to fight for?"

"No."

"Then what are we doing?"

"We're not fighting for them, Mira. We're fighting for an idea."

"Yeah? And what idea is that?"

"That people deserve to be free to make their own mistakes," he said. "That we shouldn't have to worry about some ultrapowerful alien race coming in and enslaving an entire populace. Or genetically engineering them into something people were never meant to be."

"And what if we end up doing that to ourselves?" I asked.

"Then so be it. At least we would have no one to blame but one another," he stated.

It was a bit of a change for him, that sort of attitude. Before, he'd been only lukewarm on the idea of fighting against the invaders. So had I. But the things we'd witnessed had changed our views. I suspected that, after losing multiple limbs and a couple of organs to the self-destruction of the Pacificians, Patrick was even more committed than I was.

In any case, we only had to fly for another fifteen minutes—which was at least a couple hundred miles—before we arrived at the coordinates. The settlement didn't look much different from any other I'd seen. It featured the same prefabricated structures, a sturdy plasti-steel wall, and a shimmering Mist shield. However, I couldn't ignore the presence of dozens of combat drones and a handful of bulky robots like the one I'd forced to malfunction at the first Dengyt outpost I'd assaulted.

"Do we just land by the gate?" Patrick asked.

Before I could answer, a high-pitched voice came over *The Leviathan*'s communication system, directing us to a small clearing about a quarter of a mile away from the walls. Patrick piloted the ship to the appropriate location, then set it down. After going through his postflight checklist, he engaged *The Leviathan*'s defenses. I supplemented them with Bastion, though I knew that Alistaris, at the very least, could bypass the ability.

"You ready for this?" I asked, glancing at Patrick. He gave me a nod, then a grin before confirming that he was. So, with that, the pair of us disembarked *The Leviathan* and headed toward the settlement. As we walked, I noticed a few figures shadowing our every move. They'd engaged some form of Stealth, but it wasn't capable of outpacing my Observation, especially if I chose to flare it. When I did, I saw that they were accompanied by quite a few camouflaged drones.

They hadn't threatened us, but I knew it wouldn't take much to set them off. So, I made a bare-bones plan to deal with them if things went wrong. As I did, I relayed it to Patrick through our Secure Connection, and he confirmed his part in the plan. He'd cannibalized my supplies—and part of my arsenal—to upgrade his cybernetics, so anyone that attacked us was going to get quite the surprise from his capabilities.

For my part, I was well-versed in dealing with ambushes, so I knew precisely how to combat whatever threat they represented.

However, our stalkers kept to themselves, clearly thinking they remained undetected, as we approached the gate. Once we reached it, I called out for Alistaris, and as a response, someone sent a drone out to scan us. I considered shooting it out of the sky, but I decided to mind my manners. We were guests, after all, and I still needed Alistaris's help if we were going to make the most of our Rift-diving expedition.

It seemed to get what it—or rather, its controller—wanted, and soon enough, the gate retracted, and the Mist shield faded away. A moment later, a red-haired Dengyt scurried out to greet us.

"Welcome!" she said, wringing her hands. "Please, follow me. The commandant is expecting you."

"Commandant? You mean Al?" I asked.

"Al?"

"Oh. Right. Alistaris."

"Commandant Kargat."

"Yeah. Him. Short guy, bushy eyebrows. Kind of shady."

"The commandant is not . . . shady," she huffed.

"Agree to disagree on that one."

I could tell that she had to resist mightily to keep from rolling her eyes. It was curious that expressions could be so universal. In any case, the Dengyt introduced herself as Lieutenant Doryth, then led us into the settlement. And it was very much what I'd expected from what I'd seen from the air. However, I was a little surprised when Doryth explained that it was only a temporary base. Knowing that, the settlement was a lot more impressive.

The Dengyts I saw were dressed similarly to any others I'd seen, which meant that they wore dark jumpsuits. Some had pistols strapped to holsters at their waists, while others were unarmed. All had a military look about them, which would have been a little comical, given their diminutive size, if I didn't know just how dangerous they could be.

Over everything loomed the combat bots, each one capable of wreaking untold carnage.

We covered ground relatively quickly, and soon enough, we reached what had to be the command hub. It was a bland two-story building built along the same lines as every other structure in the settlement. The only difference was that I could feel the Mist swirling around its own shield. I could also sense a web consisting of individual strands of Mist connecting each building as well as the individual Dengyts.

That was one change that had come with my class evolution that wasn't explicitly stated in my status. Before, I could only sense individual systems— like people with Nexus Implants, terminals, or Mist-powered machines—but after I had evolved into a {Mist Warden}, those sense had been expanded to include the actual connections between those systems. At first, it had been a little overwhelming, but my Mind attribute was high enough that I quickly acclimated to the extra sensory input.

I wasn't certain what the use of the new sense was—not yet—but I knew it would be important at some point. In any case, it provided some context for how connected everyone in the temporary base was.

Doryth stepped up to the door, and I saw her Mist flare before a bit of it slid through the connection and into the closest terminal. When it did, the shield deactivated, and the door slid open.

We followed her inside, and as I did, I got a good chance to inspect a few Dengyts more closely, and what I found was that the cloud of Mist hanging off of each one was different. In some cases, it was dense, but in others, it was so diffuse that I could barely sense it.

"Auras," I said to myself.

"Huh?" asked Patrick.

"Nothing. Just figured something out. I'll tell you later."

Before, I'd seen a few skills in Ana's collection with the word *aura* in their names. Back then, I'd had no idea what it meant, and besides, I'd been looking for skills that would be useful in combat. Given that all the aura skills were labeled as noncombat, I'd mostly skipped them over. But now? I was beginning to wonder if what I was seeing was related.

I didn't have much chance to contemplate it as Doryth quickly led us through the facility and to a large conference room where Alistaris awaited. But

I almost stumbled when I saw him because the strength of his aura was almost overwhelmingly dense. To my senses, he was like a miniature blue star, blazing with all the intensity that would imply.

He raised one bushy eyebrow when I missed a step, but he didn't remark on it. Instead, he hopped down from his gnome-sized chair and said, "Thank you for coming."

"Didn't have much choice, did I?" I asked. "You made that abundantly clear."

He nodded, then dismissed Doryth. When she was gone, he said, "Apologies. After what you did, we've had to enact certain security protocols. I'm sure you understand, given your own obsession with . . . ah . . . security."

I rolled my eyes. "Sure. You know Patrick, right?" I asked.

The two had never met, but I was certain that Alistaris knew as much about Patrick as Patrick knew about him.

"Yes," Alistaris said. "It's good to meet you."

"Same," Patrick said. Neither seemed to particularly mean it. I knew that Patrick bore the Dengyt no ill will, but after what he'd been through, he was almost as prejudiced against aliens as I was.

"Right. So, you said you wanted some targets, didn't you?" Alistaris asked.

"Yeah. We've got a couple of options of our own, but I figured we'd ask about it before we committed. Maybe kill two birds with one stone, you know? I don't care about our targets except that we have the chance to make money," I said.

"Do you have some new expenses of which I am unaware?"

"I want to upgrade my arsenal," I said. "And Patrick needs some materials to continue his own development. Not to mention that *The Leviathan*'s a credit sink."

"Ah, yes. That particular model is intended for intergalactic cargo transport," he said. "Military logistics, in fact. It was never meant for extensive use in this kind of atmosphere."

"It works for us," Patrick stated.

"No, no—don't misunderstand. It is one of the best ships on this planet," Alistaris conceded. "It's just . . . as you say, expensive to operate."

"Hence our need for credits. Or Rift Shards," I said, trying to move the conversation along. "We're looking to rob some mining operations blind, then run the Rifts. I think you have a good idea of my capabilities. I figured there's got to be a couple of targets that could help both our causes."

"My cause is your cause."

"Not yet, it isn't," I said. "I told you—I'd fight your war. But until the Integration, I'm going to prepare my way."

He sighed. "I expected as much. So, I prepared a few options for you," Alistaris said. "Two are fairly standard. Typical defenses, low-level Rifts. But the third is different. Not only is the Rift extremely potent, but this group's defenses are quite stout."

"But you think I can handle it?"

"Of course. It will not be easy, but it should be within your capabilities," Alistaris stated. Then, he glanced at Patrick. "Even more so if your partner is going to accompany you."

I nodded, then he passed me a tablet, which I used to access the files on the three targets. The first one was a mining operation manned by a group of humanoid aliens that looked like they'd been painted a deep purple. They had extra eyes in the centers of their foreheads, and instead of hair, they had fleshy tendrils. However, the file detailed fairly advanced weaponry, though it wasn't anything I couldn't handle.

The second camp's occupants looked like a cross between humans and frogs, though they were quite a bit larger. The Rift was located in the center of a swamp—which presented problems all its own—and was slightly more advanced than the first.

Finally, there was the third option, which was quite a bit different than the other two. First, it was located underwater, which meant that, from a logistical standpoint, it presented an extra level of problems. Second, the aliens who ran it were a sort of crab people, complete with bulky shells and bodies that reminded me of insects. And finally, they were the most technologically advanced, meaning that they had many of the same defenses I had seen in the Dengyt camp.

"What makes you think we can handle this?" I asked. "And why should we bother? It looks difficult."

"Not as much as you might expect," Alistaris said. "But I'll give you three reasons you want to hit it. For one, they're allies of the E'rok Tan, and they have similar attitudes about humans. They don't herd them, but the Crutacaans have been known to sample from the E'rok Tan herds. Second, the other two operations have weekly pickups, while the Crutacaans only off-load their Rift Shards once every two months. So, once you take everyone out, you will have ample time to mine the Rift yourself. And finally, the Rift itself is far more advanced than any you've seen."

Patrick asked, "What does that mean?"

"If you complete that Rift, you will gain at least ten times as many shards," he said.

I tapped my lip as I considered it. Then, I sent a communication to Patrick, asking for his opinion. He wasn't really all that helpful, though, because he said that he didn't know enough about Rifts to make a viable judgment.

So, it was up to me.

Which meant that there was no real choice. I knew Alistaris was manipulating me by telling me that the Crutacaans ate humans, but just because it was manipulative didn't mean it wasn't effective. Especially when the file confirmed the assertion.

I said, "Alright. Looks like we're going for a swim, then."

AQUATIC

For most people, losing multiple limbs would be a devastating thing. Even with cybernetics, it's just not the same—no matter what anyone tells you. But for me, it was a boon. It gave me insights into cybernetics I never knew were possible. Still, I would give anything just to hold Mira with my own two hands, just one last time.

—Patrick Ward

I gazed out the window, watching the wispy white clouds whip by as *The Leviathan* cut through the sky. We'd been flying for hours, and we still had quite a ways to go. Below us was the ocean, deep, unfathomable, and home to some of the greatest predators on Earth. If something happened to *The Leviathan* and we ended up crashing into the sea, I knew we wouldn't last long. Even with all my strength, it would count for almost nothing if I found myself on the wrong end of a sea monster.

Over the years, I had seen a few of them. Sea serpents hundreds of feet long, great leviathans that weighed thousands of tons, squid and octopuses that could sink ships with barely an effort—there were so many threats in the ocean that trying to cross it was something akin to harboring a death wish.

Even flying above it was a risk, though one that was mitigated by distance. Still, I had heard of giant tentacle monsters snatching flying ships right out of the sky and dragging them into the depths. So, as we flew, I paid close attention to any potential threats. None presented themselves, though.

"What are you thinking?" asked Patrick, never taking his eyes from his instrumentation as he piloted the ship.

"Huh?"

"I asked what you were thinking," he repeated. "You've been sitting there for hours, just staring at nothing. I know you've got something on your mind. Just tell me. Maybe I can help or something."

"Honestly? I was thinking about giant sea monsters," I admitted. "Probably because we're about to go for a dive. I mean, even closer to shore, there are creatures that can—and will—eat us alive."

"You sound like you know that from firsthand experience."

"I didn't ever tell you about the giant jellyfish that I ran into?" I asked.

He shook his head, saying, "No. I think I would've remembered that."

"Huh," I muttered. I could have sworn I'd told him about it, but there was a chance I was mistaken. There was also the chance that his injuries had muddled some of his memories. He'd experienced a pretty serious concussion, and on top of that, his brain had been deprived of oxygen. For a moment, I found myself worrying about his health, but then I thought better of it. He'd been scanned by multiple doctors and cybernetic engineers, and they'd all proclaimed him as healthy as could be expected, given what he'd been through. I needed to trust their expertise.

But trust didn't come easy for me, especially when the subject was someone I loved.

"I told you about Bayou La Batre, right?"

"Yeah. That was before we met, wasn't it?"

I nodded. I was so naive back then. So weak. If the current version of me met those same challenges, I would have gone about things very, very differently. But my uncle had meant it as training, so if I'd been completely prepared for it and made all the right choices, it probably wouldn't have been very effective.

"It was. Anyway, I got into some trouble, and I ended up having to swim away," I said. "I got like a mile out, and that's when this huge jellyfish—later, I found out that it's called a Portuguese man-of-war—that wrapped its tentacles around me. Or . . . I mean, it didn't really actively do anything. It was just kind of there. Anyway, I got caught up in its tentacles. And it was some of the worst pain I've ever experienced. Like, imagine all your nerves catching fire at the same time."

"Sounds terrible," he said. "I can't imagine something like that. What did you do?"

I cut my eyes at him and grinned. "Same thing I usually do. I cut it to pieces," I admitted. "Then I swam away."

"And you're worried we'll run into something like that when we attack these . . . What are they called again?"

"Crutacaans."

"Right. Crutacaans. You think we'll get hit by sea monsters when we go down there?"

I shrugged. "I don't know. Maybe. Probably not, though. I guess it was just kind of on my mind, if that makes any sense." I sighed, then leaned my head back. "Do you ever wish we had a more peaceful life? Like, we were just normal? I mean, I know it's not possible. Not anymore, if it ever was. But I sometimes think about what things were like back before the Mist. I have some books from back then, and . . . I don't know. The idea of just living our lives without anyone trying to kill or enslave us . . ."

"Or eat us."

"Or eat us," I agreed. "I don't know. It just feels kind of . . . wrong. But right, too. Like, I know I'd be bored out of my mind, but I can't help but wonder what it would be like to live like that for a few days. Kind of like a vacation."

"We could go visit that beach you liked so much. The one on the island near that volcano."

I smiled. We'd visited there a couple of years before, and we'd had a fantastic month where we did almost nothing. But even then, we'd had to look out for wildlings, mutated wildlife, and sea creatures that might crawl out of the ocean. In the end, we'd been forced to leave when a herd of giant crabs had taken over the beach. Perhaps we could have killed them, but their intrusion had stolen the place's sense of peace.

"Pass. We need to get this done," I said. "The sooner I can get some new skills, the better. Plus, I want some stronger weapons. I think I can handle some of the big guns now."

"Like what?"

"Gala has a bunch of energy weapons," I said. "Plus you took my scattergun, so . . . Well, I need to replace that, anyway."

"You never even used it, and you know it," he said.

"Still."

He'd cannibalized the weapon for parts, integrating them into his cybernetics. I still wasn't sure what he was trying to do, but he'd claimed he was successful. Perhaps I'd find out sooner rather than later, considering that he insisted on participating in the assault. He'd be wearing the armor, but I was still worried about his safety.

For another couple of hours, we cruised along until, at last, we reached our destination. We didn't dare land in the vicinity of the Crutacaan mining operation, so Patrick guided the ship to a small clearing about sixty miles to the north. After that, we spent the next couple of hours preparing for our assault. Patrick did final checks on his armor, while I made sure that my arsenal implant was fully stocked with ammunition.

With my class evolution, [Cybernetic Mastery] had become [Mist-Infused Body], and as a result, my cybernetics had become quite a bit more efficient. For the arsenal implant, that meant that the utility slots could hold about twice as much as they had before the evolution. So, I had enough ammunition and explosives to level a city.

Before we left, I glanced at Patrick, who was readying himself to mount the armor, and asked, "Are you sure you want to do this? Things are going to get pretty dicey."

"I'm fine," he said. "This armor can withstand whatever they throw at me."

I wasn't so sure. Two hundred Constitution was impressive, but it wouldn't make him bulletproof. My own exploits were evidence enough of that; I'd rarely gone on a serious mission without getting shot at least a couple of times, and even with my advantages—a seriously inflated Constitution, a high-tech infiltration suit, and subdermal armor—I wasn't completely safe.

But I knew I needed to trust that Patrick could take care of himself because, whether I liked it or not, he refused to sit on the sidelines any longer.

Once he was firmly ensconced within his armor, Patrick went through a series of checks before announcing that he was ready. So, with that, we set off. Given that I was mounted on the Cutter, my pace was much faster than his, but that was by design. By the time he caught up to me, I hoped to have already scouted the enemy position and established a plan. So, as I sped along through the countryside, I went over everything I knew from the file Alistaris had given me.

That didn't occupy me for very long, though. I'd already memorized everything, so my mind was quickly freed to appreciate the surrounding wilderness. The Crutacaan base was nestled just offshore from a sizable island in the northern hemisphere, so the weather was cold and clammy and seemed perpetually cloaked in a persistent fog. But there was an ethereal beauty to it, too.

Adding to that were the remnants of an abandoned civilization. Along the way, I passed more than one ancient moss-covered castle. None of them were huge—not like the palaces I read about in my books—but they were impressive nonetheless, and I couldn't help but appreciate them for what they represented. They'd been built hundreds of years ago, and still, they stood. Would any modern structures persist after a couple of centuries? I couldn't help but doubt that.

Gradually, I covered ground. I didn't speed, largely because the area was completely uninhabited, and so, there were few roads to speak of. I was no stranger to cutting cross-country, but usually, there were the ruins of old highways to follow. That was not the case with this island, and so, I had to take things fairly slowly.

Even so, I reached my destination, which was a steep cliff overlooking the roiling sea, in good time. Once I did, I stored my hover bike away, then crept to the edge of the cliff. Hundreds of feet below, the angry ocean crashed against the cliff in an ongoing battle between earth and sea.

I flared Observation as I scanned for signs of the Crutacaan base, and I quickly found what I was looking for in a small glimmer of metal less than a mile out to sea. I recognized it as the platform the aliens used as a dock for the humans who'd been contracted—or enslaved, I suppose—to take their wares to a rapid-transference node that would send the Rift Shards to the Bazaar where they would either be sold or sent along to whoever had financed the Crutacaan operation.

The fact that it was underwater meant that attacking this base presented some very unique problems. For one, I had no idea if my Stealth would be effective down there. For another, I would very much be at a disadvantage in any physical confrontation with the Crutacaans who were clearly far more at home under the sea than I could ever be. However, I hoped to get past that with a generous application of firepower.

Even so, if I'd had my way, I would've just dropped a hundred bombs on them and let the whole thing sort itself out. However, that came with the significant issue of damaging the Rift aperture. If that happened, we wouldn't be able to access the Rift, which would in turn nullify our entire reason for being there.

Aside from killing a few aliens, that is.

But that was going to happen either way.

In any case, I didn't intend to just swim in, guns blazing. Instead, I wanted to use my very specific skills to my benefit. To that end, I engaged Stealth, then I contacted Patrick through Secure Connection and told him, "I'm going in. With luck, they'll be cleared out in a few hours. But if I call for you, I want you to—"

"Come running at full speed," he said. "I remember the plan."

To conserve power, he was taking it easy on his way from *The Leviathan*'s landing spot to the Crutacaan base. However, if he wanted to burn through his Mist, he could move almost as fast as the Cutter. Hopefully, that wouldn't be necessary.

So, cloaked in Stealth, I started climbing down the cliff. I'd have preferred to access the ocean in a more convenient way, but the sheer cliffs extended for miles in both directions. Which meant I had little choice unless I wanted to spend even more time in the water.

All in all, the climb wasn't terrible. With my attributes and compact body type, I'd always been a good climber. And my training had pushed me even further down that line. The result was that I could move down even that sheer cliff face with alacrity, and I reached the water in only a few minutes.

Then, without further hesitation, I dove in.

And immediately regretted that decision.

For better or worse, I had grown up in a climate-controlled city. Then, I'd spent the bulk of the next few years in a subtropical environment where the temperatures rarely—if ever—approached freezing. So, plunging into that water came with a significant shock. I could survive in some pretty extreme temperatures, but just because I could live through it didn't make the experience pleasurable.

Still, I wasn't going to let it dissuade me, so I quickly swam away from the cliff and into deeper water. With Observation, I could see fairly well underwater, but I still felt like something was going to jump out at me at any moment. When I started to get short of breath, I surfaced, took a few deep gulps of oxygen, then dove below the surface.

Like that, I covered the distance to the Crutacaan base, and when I drew close, I retrieved my respirator from my arsenal implant, placed it over my mouth and nose, then dove down into the depths.

The seafloor was awash in life, largely because of the increased Mist levels common to any Dead Zone. A forest of green kelp stretched as far as I could see, but nestled among that green carpet was what looked like a blue-tinted bubble. I knew from the file that it was the base habitat; the Crutacaans were an amphibious race, so they could survive underwater. However, the Rift aperture could not, so they were forced to come up with a work-around. Thus, the bubble, inside of which I would find the base.

In an effort to maintain my Stealth, I swam forward slowly, then descended into the kelp forest. Once I was there, I allowed myself to speed up slightly, though not enough to ruin my ability. Like that, I progressed until, at last, I reached the line of demarcation between the sea and the dry atmosphere within the bubble.

Then, I pushed through.

I had no idea how it worked, but the bubble was permeable to solid matter. So, I only met slight resistance as I passed into the dry atmosphere. One of the advantages of the bubble not allowing water through was that it instantly dried me out, too, though it was murder on my hair.

Not that I was thinking about that kind of thing. Instead, I turned my attention on my environment, then crept through the maze of buildings until I found what I was looking for.

The Crutacaan was huge. At least three times my size, and that wasn't even including its bulky shell. One of its arms ended in a meaty claw, while the other was more humanoid, though with only three fingers. It had four legs, and to me, it seemed to follow the pattern of the mythological centaur, though it substituted the body of a horse with a crustacean's.

In short, it was a horrifying-looking creature, which made my mission that much easier to stomach.

I reached out with my {Mist Warden} senses and grabbed ahold of its system. In seconds, I'd bypassed its middling defenses and uploaded the latest iteration of *Time Bomb*. Then, I retreated to an out-of-the-way corner of the base and settled in to wait.

I knew it wouldn't get them all. Some of them were sure to have much more potent defenses. However, my efforts would thin their numbers significantly so that when Patrick arrived and we went on the offensive, we wouldn't face overwhelming odds.

CHAPTER FIVE

CARNAGE

The universe is supposed to have rules. It shouldn't just be a capitalist dystopia where all that matters is how much money or influence you can snatch away from the weak and powerless. That's why I do the things I do, fight the wars I fight. Anyone capable of making a difference who chooses otherwise is a coward.

—Alistaris Kargat

'm in position," Patrick said through our Secure Connection. "Just give me the word, and I'll come in, guns blazing."

"That doesn't fill me with a lot of confidence," I muttered, though I didn't let it go through. He wouldn't appreciate any admission that I feared for his safety and wished that he would choose another way to contribute to the cause. Sure, he was wearing a suit of armor the likes of which nobody else in the world could acquire. He should have been protected, provided he didn't completely shut his mind down. But that didn't seem to matter so much when I knew all the ways any battle could go wrong. Still, I couldn't keep him from the fight. He wouldn't allow it. Even if I could stop him, he'd just go off and fight without me. At least this way, I could look out for him.

My Ghost was already nearing the end of its gestation period, so we only had to wait until the bodies started falling, and then we would be free to commence the assault. As such, I had my Pulsar in hand, and I'd positioned myself atop the tallest building. From there, I could see much of the base, though the sight lines weren't as expansive as I might've hoped. That meant that, before everything was said and done, we'd have to fight building to building.

Which was fine, if a little more dangerous than I would've preferred.

In any case, at least they couldn't call for help; I'd already rerouted their communications, so while they could call out, their messages would never reach their intended destinations. It was a necessity so we wouldn't run the risk of being interrupted while we were inside the Rift. According to the file I'd been given, the Crutacaans didn't have any other operations on Earth, but they did have a few allies they could call to for help.

In any case, I continued my vigil until, at last, I saw the first Crutacaan tip over and die. Then another. And another after that. They kept falling until, at last, sixty out of the reported hundred aliens had died to my Ghost.

That's when I opened fire.

Targeting the alien with the densest Mist aura, I used Empowered Shot, then Execute before firing. The round, which was empowered to a ridiculous degree, tore through him with enough kinetic force that it looked like he simply exploded in a shower of shell, white meat, and similarly milky blood.

Then, I sighted in on another one and fired. Even without abilities, my modifiers were immense, and the results were largely predictable. The second Crutacaan went down just like the first, though it remained more or less intact, aside from the gaping hole in its shell. It died all the same.

As it fell, Patrick arrived like a tank on two legs, bursting through the bubble and crashing into a building. It crumpled under the combination of his weight and strength, exposing the Crutacaan inside. It reacted quickly, as befit a creature powerful enough to survive my Ghost, launching itself at him.

I shot it in the torso, but the round was slowed by a personal shield. The alien lived through the shot, then hit Patrick in a flying tackle.

And it was stopped cold as a blue Mist shield bloomed in front of Patrick. It only lasted a brief second, but it kept the Crutacaan's sharp claws from tearing into Patrick's mechanized armor. It also served to rob it of its momentum as it rebounded off the shield and tumbled to the dry seabed.

Patrick rushed forward and aimed a kick at the monstrous alien, taking it in the shield. A loud crack filled the air as the impact sent it flying into a nearby building. That's when I shot it again; this time, I'd taken the time to use Empowered Shot, so when the bullet hit, it did so with predictably explosive force. The creature died instantly as its crab-like head erupted in a shower of gore.

But by that point, the rest of the Crutacaans had responded, flooding out of the buildings to combat the threat they could see. If I'd been alone, they almost assuredly would have taken refuge in the structures. However, with Patrick out there in his shining white armor, he provided the perfect distraction. So, even as they raced toward him, I started firing.

I didn't bother with abilities. Instead, I trusted my weapon and my modifiers as I squeezed the trigger as quickly as I could shift my aim. I wasn't trying to kill anything right off. I knew that was a tall order, what with their clearly advanced Constitutions and thick shells. But I could injure them and slow them down so that I could pick them off at my leisure.

In the past, I never would have put Patrick in such danger. He was too fragile. But with that armor—and the shield he'd somehow built into it—he was more than a match for the flood of Crutacaans. So, even as he set his feet and activated his shield, I fired. One shot after another. Shells shattered. Milky-white blood flew. And flesh scattered across the seafloor. And yet, Patrick remained unharmed as he took shelter behind his shield.

I had no idea how he was powering it. The thing was at least ten feet across and tall enough that he didn't even have to crouch to stay behind it. The Mist requirements for such a thing should have been so steep as to make it impractical. And yet, he was making it work.

For now. Eventually, he would run dry of Mist. And then, he'd be a sitting duck. So, I kept firing until, at last, the scenario I'd feared presented itself. The shield winked out, and the remaining Crutacaans swept in for the kill. One overly large claw took him in the shoulder. Another hit him in the legs. A third went in for his torso.

I screamed, already leaping from the building. I exchanged the Pulsar for my assault rifle, taking aim as I fell. After using Explosive Shot, I squeezed the trigger, peppering the monstrous aliens with one exploding round after another.

I hit the ground hard, then rolled forward to absorb some of the shock before I sprang upright and into a sprint. All the while, I never stopped firing.

But Patrick hadn't stood idle, either. Even as I watched, his right arm extended and unfolded into a blade almost as wide as his torso. The edge crackled with blue energy as he deployed it in a backhanded swing that sliced right through a hastily raised claw. The Crutacaan who owned it screeched and fell back, but Patrick wasn't letting it get off so easily. He stepped forward, rearing back to bring the blade to bear in a powerful overhand attack.

The Crutacaans were no slouches, though, and they adjusted to the new weapon with such alacrity that Patrick had no chance to respond when they swept in and latched their claws on to his armor.

That's when I finally reached the battle; my assault rifle, even with my modifiers and Explosive Shot, was incapable of doing more than minor damage to the Crutacaans, but I certainly had something that would be more effective. So, I exchanged the rifle for my nano-bladed sword and leaped at the rearmost alien.

The blade swept out, crackling with blue energy as it bit deep into the first Crutacaan's shell. I kept moving, using my momentum to my advantage as I aimed a spinning attack at the next-closest alien's thick armored neck. It went through without issue, easily decapitating the creature.

I leaped back, avoiding another snapping claw before whipping Ferdinand II from the holster at my hip. I spun around, aiming it at the back of another Crutacaan's head, then squeezed the trigger. The pistol bucked in my hand, evidence of the powerful ammunition I'd loaded, and a second later, the creature's head exploded.

Or I thought it did, judging by the bits of crab person that splattered against my back as I turned my attention to another Crutacaan. Like that, I continued. With one hand, I lashed out with my nano-bladed sword, and with the other, I wielded Ferdinand II.

Normally, I would have kept my distance, but with Patrick under siege, I didn't have that luxury. Maybe he could stand up to the assault, and maybe he couldn't. But I wasn't willing to test the durability of his armor in its first real outing. He'd proved its viability, and logic dictated that we take it one step at a time.

Still, even as I steadily dismantled the Crutacaan warriors, I was impressed with his showing. Patrick's armor was performing as well as could be expected, but what really surprised me was its potential as a weapons platform. If it had enough Mist to run that shield, then what kinds of guns could we put on it?

It was a fantastic idea, but one that would have to wait until later. For now, I needed to focus on finishing the last of the crab-like aliens. To that end, once I'd thinned the numbers to something manageable, I leaped backward to put some distance between me and the group, then exchanged my weapons for the much more powerful Pulsar.

Taking aim, I resumed my assault, picking off one Crutacaan after another. It was odd. With Patrick there taking the brunt of their attention—and rightly so, given that the armor was huge, bulky, and painted blindingly white with gold trim—I was free to act with virtual impunity. Sure, some of them noticed me here and there, but I could move so quickly and I was so comparatively small that they couldn't really keep track of my movements.

It was a nice change of pace from being the center of attention, and I used the situation to the maximum advantage, switching between ranged and melee combat until, at last, the final Crutacaan fell to my blade. I skidded to a stop, whipping the sword out to my side to clear the milky blood.

And then, suddenly, everything was quiet.

Patrick's voice came over our Secure Connection as he asked, "Is that all of them?"

"You want more?" I asked incredulously as I looked around. We'd killed at least forty aliens—there was no telling without counting them, and that would probably be incredibly difficult considering that most of them were in pieces.

"Uh . . . No? I got six levels there," he said. "Is this why you're so much higher than me? Do you get this kind of progression every time you fight?"

"No. I mean, sometimes? I don't know. It's weird. Sometimes, I can kill one monster and get a whole level, but then I'll kill a hundred without moving the needle."

"Oh. So, I shouldn't get used to this, huh?"

"Probably not. But what do I know? Doesn't really matter, I guess. It's not like we're doing this specifically to gain levels."

Even when I'd asked some of my friends in the Bazaar about leveling, I hadn't really gotten any straight answers. The fact was that nobody really knew what went into how it all worked, except that more powerful kills were more valuable. How much more was up for debate, and it seemed to vary significantly.

In any case, what I'd said was true. Gaining levels was great, but at present, it was more of a side effect than a goal. Perhaps that would change in the future, but for now, we were focused on making money so I could get my skills and we both could buy new equipment and supplies.

With that in mind, the Rift aperture called to us.

Even so, I knew we needed to take care of things outside before we could get to that point. So, our plunder of the base commenced. First, I rifled through the bodies, piling all the weapons and equipment nearby while Patrick headed into the nearest building to do the same. My Ghost had killed plenty of Crutacaans, so I knew it would take a while to sort through them all—a prediction that proved prescient because we didn't finish until most of the day had passed.

Still, the result was a significant pile of weapons that Patrick stored via his Pack Mule ability. He was a little cagey about the limits of that storage space, only saying that it would take something truly remarkable for him to run out of room.

After we'd looted all the weapons, we started in on the storehouses. We went through like a pack of locusts, stealing everything that wasn't nailed down. In the meantime, I also used my Mistwalk to infiltrate every terminal I could find. Once inside, I downloaded hundreds of files, sequestering them into a partitioned portion of my interface.

Overall, the entire looting process took almost two days, and if we'd called it quits right then and there, we'd have still made out pretty well. Normally, we'd have left after that. However, this time was different. We intended to run the Rift.

Which was how we found ourselves standing near the aperture, which was located on the southern side of the base. I looked at it, wondering what we would find on the other side.

"Are you sure about this?" Patrick asked, clearly sensing my hesitation. The last time we'd run a Rift, we'd both nearly died. In fact, every time we'd gone through one of those apertures had ended with similar results. Even going back to my very first Rift—which was fairly low-level, all things considered—I'd come close to dying every single time.

And this one was going to be the toughest one yet.

Until recently, I'd considered all Rifts relatively equal. However, that just wasn't true. Some were clearly deadlier than others. In areas with a higher concentration of Mist, the Rifts were more complex and far more dangerous. And this Rift had been chosen specifically because it was located amid some of the highest concentrations of Mist in the world.

"I am," I said. It was the most efficient way to get what we needed. Certainly, it was possible that I could ask Alistaris for help. He'd probably give me all the credits I needed. But I was more than a little wary of what he'd ask in return. I had no intention of subjugating myself to him any more than I already had, so with that in mind, I didn't see that I had a lot of other options. "Come on."

Having steeled my resolve, I stepped forward and passed through the aperture. A moment later, I felt the Mist swirl around and then through me. And then, I was suddenly somewhere else.

Patrick came through only a few seconds later, the heavy steps of the armor loud in my ears. I barely noticed the sound, though. Instead, my attention was wholly focused on our surroundings.

Before me, a huge landscape stretched out, but it was like nothing I had ever seen before. Crystalline trees, each one the color of a real tree, sprouted from the ground creating a glittering carpet of green. In the distance, I saw a palace stretching toward the sky. It was made of yellow crystal, but even from so far away, I could tell that there was something incomprehensibly different about it.

Still, the bulk of my attention was locked onto the giant golems, each looking like it was made of enormous Rift Shards, moving through the forest. If they were any less than a hundred feet tall, I would have been incredibly surprised.

"Uh . . . Mira . . ."

"I know."

I took a deep, steadying breath before I repeated, "I know."

The Rift was clearly very different from anything I had ever experienced. If I had been alone, it wouldn't have been much of a problem. I was confident in my Stealth and Camouflage abilities. However, with Patrick by my side, I couldn't simply sneak through and hope for the best. I'd need an entirely different strategy if we were going to survive.

Suddenly, I couldn't help but wonder if we'd made a mistake.

I pushed that thought aside, saying, "Come on. We need to find somewhere defensible so we can plan for our assault."

"Assault on what?"

I pointed to the distant palace. "Seems like a good goal, right? I'm guessing that forest there is full of crazy monsters and challenges. So, we're going to need to be on the ball if we expect to survive. For now, though, I need to stash you somewhere out of the way so I can scout things out."

He didn't refute that claim, so we quickly set off out down the hill where we had arrived and into the forest.

CHAPTER SIX

THE EMERALD FOREST

Rifts are dangerous things. No one disputes this. However, there are a multitude of ways to mitigate the danger. Through thorough scouting to Mist diffusion, the universe has farming them down to a science. But on an Unintegrated world, for a native species, none of this is available. They just have to go inside and hope they're strong enough to overcome the challenges. Most aren't.

—Alistaris Kargat

Once I had Patrick settled in a deserted cave, I checked my equipment, then embraced Stealth before heading into the emerald forest. He didn't like being left behind, but he knew his limits well enough to recognize that it was the best course of action. In truth, I think he imagined himself stepping into the Rift and dominating anything that dared stand in his way. And with the power of that armor, he probably could have—in most situations.

But this Rift was different. If it wasn't the most dangerous Rift on Earth, I would have been surprised. Alistaris had certainly thought of it that way, and I had no reason to dispute his assertion. Still, it was telling that he hadn't skipped a beat before sending me into such a deadly Rift. Clearly, he thought I was capable of conquering it, which meant that he considered me one of the strongest people on the planet.

That wasn't surprising. Not really. I knew precisely how much death it had taken for me to reach my level, and while I was aware that there were other, less genocidal methods of gaining levels, none of them were very fast. As such, that path was one that required years—perhaps even decades—of patience as people steadily whittled their way to a high level.

And then there was my Nexus Implant to consider. While I wasn't reaping the benefits of it at the moment—I still had three skills to acquire—I knew that it had accelerated my attribute growth. After all, the higher one's potential, the easier the lower rungs of the ladder were to climb. I'd used that to my advantage with my training so far, and I was looking forward to continuing that route after I bought my new skills.

In addition, my training set me apart. I didn't think there were many people who'd gone through the intense training regimen my uncle had subjected me to. Even if there were a multitude of people who tried, most of those would fall by the wayside as the difficulty overcame their endurance.

And I had been at it for years, never really letting up. Few could boast the same, I was certain.

Finally, there was my class. Even before I'd evolved it to {Mist Warden}, I'd been a {Mistrunner}, which was an exceedingly rare class that gave me a host of advantages. Now, those assets had been further optimized, turning me into something akin to a perfect weapon. I could hit hard and fast, or I could take my time and whittle an enemy down. I could attack in a wide variety of ways, and I could do it with a specialist's power. In short, I was a perfect foil for the coming invasion.

And yet, I wasn't invincible. Even if it was difficult to permanently put me down, I could still be killed. So, before I went down too deep of a rabbit hole, I focused on my surroundings. As I did, I was once again taken aback by the alien nature of the environment.

Up close, the trees were shaped the same as any I'd ever seen. They were just crystalline in structure, though the density of the crystals varied depending on which piece I was looking at. For instance, the trunks were so solid that I couldn't see more than a quarter inch into the brown-gray crystal, even if I flared Observation. By comparison, the leaves were almost entirely transparent, which cast the entire area beneath the canopy in a subtle green light.

Still, it was familiar enough—at least in shape—that I didn't have any trouble navigating through the forest. At least until I stumbled upon a pack of wolves.

Or that was my initial impression of the creatures. Like everything else, they were composed of crystalline chunks that, when I looked closely, only seemed to be connected by thin threads of Mist. In addition, their bodies were rough, like sketches half-finished. And finally, they were clearly deadly because they were standing over a much larger creature, which they were in the process of eating.

Even as I listened to the steady crunch of crystal, I tried to skirt around them. However, there were enough of the creatures around to make that all but impossible. Either I killed them, or I wasn't getting any farther—a notion that was supported by both the ubiquity of the creatures and their obviously sharp senses. The moment I drew within a few feet of them, they looked up, obviously recognizing that an interloper was in their midst. But they were incapable of finding me.

So, I backed away until I was well out of their range, then crouched as I thought things through. The creatures were a problem, there was no doubting that. I considered climbing the trees and bypassing them from above, but I had quickly discovered that that strategy just wasn't possible. The moment I tried, I'd been beset by a pain so intense that I couldn't even maintain a grip on one of the branches.

I had no idea what caused it. There was no swirl of Mist or any other indication of where the pain had originated. But it was there, all the same, meaning that I had little choice but to travel along on the ground. So, I needed to find a way past the wildlife.

I took off on a parallel course, but after a couple of miles, I found that the forest simply ended in a giant cliff into nothingness. Looking over the edge, I couldn't see the bottom—if there even was one. And the line of crystal wolves extended almost to the edge, creating an obstacle that I couldn't simply bypass.

No—if we were going to progress, we'd have to kill the wolves.

And that presented a significant problem, if for no other reason than that there were so many of them. I'd counted hundreds of them along the way, and I suspected that there just as many in the opposite direction. On top of that, even if I could sneak past, there was no way Patrick could do the same. If we wanted to progress, a fight was unavoidable.

So, I retreated to the cave where I'd left Patrick. When I arrived, I found that he'd left his armor and had it open as he tinkered with its inner workings.

"What're you up to?" I asked, startling him.

He flinched, then let out a deep breath when he saw that it was me and not some monster having invaded his little safe house.

"Don't sneak up on me like that," he muttered, wiping his cybernetic hand on a rag at his waist.

I gave him a crooked smile, saying, "I'll stop doing it when you stop reacting."

He mumbled something under his breath, and even though I could've listened in with a little application of Observation, I chose not to. Instead, I decided to just dive into the explanation of our situation, ending it by asking, "So, what do you think?"

"Traps."

"Huh?"

"We set a huge trap," he said. "And if that's not possible, we find somewhere defensible where they can only come at us from one direction." He looked around. "Like this cave. Maybe one with a slightly narrower opening, though."

It was an obvious answer, and one I'd already considered. I hadn't discarded it, either, so it definitely had merit. However, the question remained of what sort of trap we wanted to build. I knew he had the ability to create some high-tech versions, but all of those would require Rift Shards to operate. So, it was probably better if we stuck with low-tech options. After all, a simple pit was often just as effective as something far more elaborate.

"The problem is that we don't know their capabilities," I said.

"That's true."

"And if we make too much noise, those huge golems are probably going to respond," I pointed out. Even if they weren't visible, what with the forest's canopy blocking sight lines, I hadn't forgotten about those enormous crystalline monsters. "So no explosions or gunfire unless we're backed into a corner."

"Can you use your Ghosts like you did with those spiders back in the first Rift we ran together?"

I shook my head. "No systems," I stated. It had been one of the first things I'd tried. "I think those were a special case. Like, they weren't supposed to fully be monsters. I don't know—it's not like we had the ability to really check it all out back then."

"True. So, did you want to do the trap idea? Or the defensible-position plan?"

"Neither of them seems much like a real plan," I said. Indeed, setting a trap felt akin to leading the monsters off a cliff. Effective, maybe, but it certainly didn't feel like some grand plan. It was the same with finding a narrow corridor of engagement; sure, it made all kinds of sense, and I'd used the strategy before, but it seemed somehow inadequate for the situation.

Patrick shrugged. "So long as it works, who cares?" he said.

That was true, too. Sometimes, I got so caught up in trying to create a perfect, elaborate plan that I forgot the universal truth of any battle. Simple was often better than complex. It had been true throughout history, and nothing I had seen would change that. Battle tactics usually boiled down to picking appropriate ground and outflanking the enemy, neither of which were incredibly complicated.

So, over the next half hour, Patrick and I discussed our options. In the end, we decided to use both plans. With that in mind, I went back outside and started scouting for a proper location. Once I found a cave that would work, we got down to the business of digging. The ground was a little crunchier than it was back on Earth, but due to my attributes and Patrick's armored suit, we made quick work of it. When we'd finished, we had dug a pair of holes forty feet deep and half again as wide.

Then, we dug another that ran parallel to the first, creating a narrow corridor of approach to our defensible position. I'd have preferred a proper trap, but we just didn't have the materials to make that work.

Once that was finished, Patrick set himself up at the end of the corridor. He'd said that he had plenty of Mist to power the suit, so his job was to anchor the whole thing. Meanwhile, I was supposed to be the edge of our sword.

I knew it wouldn't work out exactly like we planned, but that was part of fighting any battle. When things went wrong—and they would, I was sure—we'd have to adjust accordingly. The ability to adapt was the measure of a warrior, as far as I was concerned.

Whatever the case, once we'd prepared our ground, I headed toward the line of crystalline wolves. My characterization of the creatures probably wasn't particularly accurate. They didn't exactly look like canines, except on the most basic level. But I needed to think of them as something, so I chose something vaguely familiar.

But for now, I needed to focus on the task at hand rather than what I wanted to call the monsters. To that end, I took a deep, steadying breath, then picked up a rock and tossed it at one of the monsters. Without waiting for it to hit, I turned on my heel and sprinted away. I didn't need to look back to know they were following; indeed, the sound of those crystalline creatures tearing through the forest was loud enough that I questioned my decision not to use firearms or explosives. If that crunching, grinding sound that came from their pursuit wasn't enough to alert the entire Rift, I would have been surprised.

Still, I stuck to the plan and raced across the forest, dodging between the curious trees before, finally, I reached our chosen and prepared battleground. I didn't stop there, though. Instead, I kept going, passing Patrick, who'd planted himself at the end of the corridor between our pits, and dipped into the nearby cave.

The first of the crystalline wolves crashed into Patrick's shield only a moment later, and I wanted nothing more than to whip out my weapon and join him. And yet, I needed to trust him to play his part while I set about my own task. So, I laboriously ignored the clash between the two forces as I let myself slip into Stealth. Once I was sure I wouldn't be detected, I slipped back out into the open and leaped across the rightmost pit.

Even as I did, I couldn't help but notice that Patrick was holding his own. With the massive shield stretching in front of him, he was largely unassailable for the mass of crystalline wolves that had descended upon him. The corridor was working as intended, keeping them from attacking him more than a couple at a time, too. So, everything was going precisely as we'd planned.

Now, I just needed to do my part.

So, without further hesitation, I circled around and waited. As I'd expected, the wolves were incredibly observant, and the moment they'd heard the result of my baiting the first set of monsters, the rest had responded with their own pursuit. A horde of the creatures at least two hundred strong—and probably more—descended upon the location, funneling into the corridor we had created.

A few fell into the pits, and though I knew that wouldn't take them out of the fight, it did serve to keep the creatures hemmed in.

I watched as the flow slowed to a trickle, and all the monsters in the area—at least I hoped that was the case—had arrived. That was my cue to act, and I didn't hesitate to drag my blade out and go to work.

At first, they had no idea I was even there. I hit hard and fast, retreating before they could react. One attack after another, over and over, I sliced into the mass of monsters. At the same time, Patrick held the line, periodically using his shield as a battering ram to get room, then deactivating it just long enough to bring his sword arm to bear. The crystalline creatures were sturdy, but under such an assault, they were incapable of defense.

And slowly, we whittled them down.

It wasn't easy, though. More than once, one of my opponents whipped around and nearly took my head off. But through a combination of my high attributes, the prepared ground that kept them from overwhelming either of us, and my modifiers, they eventually fell.

So, it was probably always inevitable that there would be a lot more to it.

I'd just decapitated the last one when I saw—or maybe *felt* would be a better word—the crystalline corpses begin to vibrate.

"Uh . . . Mira . . ."

"I know," I growled, my mind whirling. I had no idea what was happening, so potential responses were limited. Still, I reacted on instinct and started kicking the corpses away from one another.

It was a good thing, too, because only a few moments into my kicking spree, the piled bodies began to merge into a single mass.

"Oh . . . God . . ."

Seeing what those bodies were turning into, I attacked. But it was too late, and the thing—which already looked like a smaller version of the golems—lashed out with one of its boulder-like arms, hitting me with bone-crunching power. I went flying across the trenches we'd dug and collided with a tree before falling to the ground.

Seeing stars, I shook my head as I tried to clear the cobwebs, and by the time I came back to my senses, I saw precisely what I'd been trying to avoid. All the slain wolves had seemingly merged into one entity, taking the shape of one of the golems. Fortunately, it wasn't nearly as large as the ones I'd seen in the distance.

Not that that was as much of a comfort as it might've been, given that it was at least forty feet tall and almost as broad. Patrick faced it down, hefting his arm—and the attached Mist shield—in an effort to block a rapidly descending blow.

I watched impotently from afar as it fell, crushing him beneath its massive weight.

For a brief second, it didn't feel real. I couldn't think. My brain simply refused to work. But then, that emptiness was replaced with absolute rage. And in that state, I didn't care about making too much noise. I didn't even think about my own life as I pulled my assault rifle from my arsenal implant and took aim.

I pulled the trigger, and mayhem followed.

MASSACRE

Imagine a world. Any world will do. Think of all the various factions, nations, tribes, ethnicities, and every other factor that can contribute to its political landscape. Everyone has their own perspective, and on a scale of billions, the only result is barely restrained chaos. Now, multiply that by thousands of planets, and you'll understand how complex a galaxy's political landscape can be. But even that only tells a tiny fraction of the universe's story.

—Alistaris Kargat

Even as I peppered the crystalline monstrosity with superheated balls of plasma, my mind went white with rage. Shards of crystal flew with every shot, and I didn't even realize that I was screaming incoherently. I just wanted to punish the monster. To tear it apart, piece by piece until there was nothing but glittering dust left.

In the back of my mind, though, I knew that none of it would bring Patrick back. He was gone. Buried beneath that giant golem's massive weight. And there was nothing I could do to change that. Without my fury, I probably would have given in to my grief. Then and there, I would have surrendered everything. But my anger buoyed me. It kept me afloat to exact vengeance.

As the monstrous golem fully formed, my first magazine ran empty. So, I used Instant Reload, then Explosive Shot before resuming my barrage. Each round tore huge divots into the crystalline structure, but they were mere pockmarks for all the good they did. If I was going to take my revenge, I would need a more potent weapon.

The only problem was that my most advanced firearm had been destroyed. Cut in half by a giant-sword-wielding android. At the time, it had probably saved my life, but as I faced off against that crystalline golem, I could lament its loss—at least I would have if I was thinking straight.

I wasn't.

I sprinted forward, emptying my magazine in a tight grouping around its leg. It didn't really have joints, per se. Instead, its limbs were shapeless lumps of crystal, which meant that there really weren't any spots of vulnerability. Still, in my less-than-optimal frame of mind, I figured that if I destroyed one of its legs, I could send it tumbling to the ground. What I planned to do then was a mystery, but I couldn't really be bothered to think about that.

Not when images of Patrick's sudden and unexpected demise kept flashing through my mind.

At the moment, I didn't realize that tears were falling down my cheeks. Even if I had known, I can't claim that I would have cared. I was too focused on destroying the crystalline golem by whatever means I could muster.

My latest magazine ran dry before I reached the monster, so I yanked Ferdinand II from his holster and, at a dead sprint, took aim. In the space of an instant, I was already squeezing the trigger, and to predictable results. The revolver was already loaded with a drum of armor-piercing rounds, so each shot dug a little more crystal out of the crater I'd already created with the generous application of Explosive Shot–enhanced rounds from my R-14. But I knew it wouldn't be enough.

The creature finally finished assembling itself, then turned its attention on me. It swung its arms in a ponderous arc, and I leaped, intending to sail over the crushing attack. But at the apex of my leap, it used an ability.

A sound like the world's largest tuning fork tore across the emerald forest, shattering limbs and felling trees for a mile in every direction. I didn't fare any better as the noise pierced through me, shattering my eardrums and sending blood misting from every pore. More leaked from my eyes, and even my fingernails splintered under the attack.

It was almost enough to get me caught by the monster's next swing, which came at me much more quickly than the first. However, at the last second, I pushed through the agonizing pain, activated Teleport, and instantly appeared in the crater that was the result of my previous efforts. I stumbled to one knee, but I couldn't allow myself to stop; so, still reeling from that aural attack, I yanked a small demolition charge from my arsenal implant, shoved it into the gaping wound, then leaped away.

When I hit the ground, I did so with a roll before finding my feet at a dead sprint. A second later, the crystalline golem's featureless arm crashed down, narrowly missing me. However, it hit the ground with such force that I had to flare Balance to keep my feet and stop myself from careening over the edge of the trap we'd dug.

I juked to the right, then immediately reversed direction. The maneuver worked, fooling the golem into attacking the spot where it expected me to end up. Meanwhile, I dashed in the other direction—directly toward the monster's other leg.

Exchanging my handgun for my assault rifle, I took aim at the middle part of the undamaged leg. Then, I once again used Explosive Shot, draining a good portion of my Mist. However, because of my progression, the cost wasn't nearly so onerous. I hadn't gained any more Mist; rather, my abilities had gotten more efficient. And given that I'd barely even made a dent in the crystalline golem, I knew I would need every scrap of efficacy I could muster.

I continued to fire on the rightmost leg, repeating my previous actions. If there was a scrap of good news, it was that the creature was seemingly incapable of real thought. Instead, it was almost purely reactive, which allowed me to utilize the same strategy I'd used before. I tore a hole in its leg, then raced forward; this time, there was no aural attack, though, so I made it without issue, then planted another charge.

All of that happened in the space of half a minute, and for most of that time, the thing hadn't even fully formed. However, by the time I completed the latest step of my plan and bounded away from its leg, the creature gained the capability to follow. It lumbered after me, its massive weight shaking the ground with every step. I led it away, reaching the end of our little corridor of death and leaping over fallen and shattered trees as I manually reloaded my assault rifle.

I had Mist to spare, but I wouldn't waste it unless absolutely necessary.

The creature followed, and I continued to pepper it with gunfire. Soon, I had stretched my lead enough that I felt confident in switching strategies. So, after vaulting over the crystalline trunk of a fallen tree, I used Vanish, then Stealth. The moment those two abilities took effect, I summoned my Pulsar, then cycled through my most potent abilities.

First came Explosive Shot, draining yet more of my Mist. Then Execute. And finally, Empowered Shot. As I rose from cover, a second passed, letting that final ability charge. And then, I squeezed the trigger.

In the past, when I'd used all three of those abilities in conjunction, I'd seen the resulting shot practically disintegrate less powerful enemies. Even against the strongest foes, it was wildly effective.

But now, with my modifiers having increased by a significant amount since my class's evolution into {Mist Warden}, it was absolutely devastating. The shot took the monster directly in the chest, digging a six-foot crater in the bulky crystal. Then, I repeated the actions, though I left off Execute because it wasn't usable without Stealth.

Still, the results were acceptable, so I kept going, digging six more craters in the golem's crystalline body. Once that was done, I once again charged. I was ready for the creature's aural attack, but that piercing sound ripped through my defenses like they weren't even there. I stumbled midstride, though I managed to recover just in time to avoid being crushed beneath one of its pulverizing attacks.

Mostly.

I still got clipped, and the shock wave sent me skidding across the ground until I hit another overturned tree. But whether by fortune or instinct, I had angled my approach in such a way that my trajectory ended with me behind the monster. So, by the time it lumbered around to face me, I was back on my feet and leaping onto its body.

The first charge I planted in its chest, but in only a few scant seconds, I jammed six more demolition charges throughout its body. Then, I jumped away, narrowly dodging another lumbering attack. This time, I rode the shock wave rather than fighting against it, and when the dust—and crystal—settled, I was almost fifty feet away.

That was far enough.

So, I yanked the detonator from my arsenal implant and ignited the charges.

Once again, my newly enhanced modifiers showed their worth, and the resulting series of explosions—all seven of them—ripped the creature to shreds. If I'd simply planted the bombs on the golem's exterior, it wouldn't have been very effective. That was why I hadn't used the BMAP. But shoving those charges into its body definitely did the trick.

Even as dust and shards of crystal rained down, my grief caught up to me. The monster was dead. I had felt the influx of Mist the moment the bombs went off. However, that was poor compensation for what I'd lost, and now that I didn't have the immediate danger of a towering monster looming over me, my emotions slammed into me with enough force to fell a building.

Somehow, I managed to stagger back the way I'd come. There, in the center of our well-prepared killing field, was Patrick's armored form. I trudged that way, knowing precisely what I would find. He hadn't moved since the beginning of the fight—which was at least ten minutes, but probably more—so the odds that I'd find him alive were slim.

Still, I clung to a thin thread of hope when I saw that his armor hadn't been completely crushed. Sure, the enamel was chipped, and it bore quite a few dents. But after what it had been through, that was the height of expectation.

Perhaps it would be fine.

Maybe he would live.

My mind whirled with that hope, but it was tempered by my many experiences with death. Everyone else I'd ever cared about—really loved—was already dead. Because that was the world in which I lived. And no amount of luck, or in this case hope, would change that. Pessimism quickly pummeled that hope into submission, so it was with a heavy heart and copious tears that I finally reached the mech suit's cockpit.

It took quite some effort to lever it open, which only served to exacerbate the tidal wave of grief threatening to overwhelm me. I pushed it aside, focusing on the task at hand. Patrick deserved that much.

So, with some difficulty, I managed to pry the cockpit open, and when I did, I saw the familiar face of the man I loved. His eyes were closed, making it appear that he was sleeping. Or that would have been the case if it wasn't for all the blood.

It was everywhere, but it was especially thick around his eyes and ears . . .

"Wait . . ."

Hope bloomed anew, and I leaned forward, flaring Observation as I tilted my head, putting my ear only an inch away from Patrick's face. For a long moment, I felt nothing. But then, a second later, a gentle breath tickled my ear. My heart jumped into my throat as Triage came into effect, noting the pace of his heartbeat, the depth of his breathing, and his approximate body temperature.

And it all told me one simple fact. He was alive, if unconscious. Though, aside from the blood, there didn't seem to be any outward indication of what had knocked him out. That's when I once again remembered the aural attack. It had been powerful enough to tear through my defenses, so Patrick's were nothing before it. After all, his armor wasn't soundproof—a vulnerability that neither of us had ever expected to rear its ugly head.

But even that probably wouldn't have been enough to knock him unconscious. There had to be something else.

It was only when my heart slowed down to a normal pace that I started paying attention to the curious senses I'd gained upon evolving into a {Mist Warden}. Usually, a cloud of Mist clung to everyone; I'd come to think of it as an aura, and its density was dependent on a few factors. First, it was a good gauge for how strong someone was. The higher the level, the larger the cloud. But I'd also discovered that a person's attributes affected the density of their aura. So, if someone was like me and they had nearly reached their potential—a temporary thing for me until I filled all my skill slots—then it would be incredibly dense. However, if they hadn't trained themselves, then it was the opposite.

There was one other way to affect the density, though, and that was if someone had exhausted their Mist reserves. So, seeing as how I knew precisely how Patrick's aura should feel, there was only one explanation for why the cloud of Mist around him was so diffuse.

That, coupled with his unconsciousness, told me precisely what had happened. He'd used the entirety of his pool of Mist—probably in an effort to survive the golem's attention—and as a result, he'd reached too far. I knew from experience the consequences for that kind of thing.

More, knowing what was going on made it clear what I needed to do. So, I pulled one of the precious Mist boosters from my arsenal implant, then jabbed the needle into his hip before discharging the payload. Almost immediately, his aura began to recover, and it was only half a minute before his eyes fluttered open.

Relief washed over me as I stared at him. Then, without saying a word, I clapped my arms around him and buried my face in his bloody chest.

His cybernetic hand found my back as he asked, "What did I miss? Did you get it? What even was that thing?"

I didn't answer. Not immediately. Instead, I just hugged him as tightly as I dared—with his apparent infirmity and my enhanced Constitution, I had to be careful not to do too much. In any case, a few moments later, I pulled away, wiped my tears as best I could, then asked him, "Are you hurt? Other than the Mist deficit, I mean."

He shook his head. "I'm in pain. Worst headache I've ever had really. But I'm okay, I think," he said. "That sound . . . I was just about to get the armor back under control when it hit me. I used one of my emergency abilities to cut it down, but it drained the last of my Mist, which was already low after running the armor. But I'm okay. It was enough."

I nodded, then described an abbreviated recounting of the battle I'd fought. Once I finished, he asked, "What about the other golems?"

"Huh?"

"The big ones you saw in the distance. That's why we didn't want to—"

It was at that very moment that I let my mind envelop the sensory input that came from Observation. And I heard something crashing through the emerald forest. It was still a long way away, but . . .

"I think we're going to have a problem. Is your armor still operational?" I asked.

He nodded. "It is, but I need at least an hour to regenerate my Mist," he answered. "I can move it now, but . . . Well, I won't be at full combat capability until then."

"Okay. I'll distract them, then," I said.

"How?"

"You'll see."

When I'd looked before, there had been six of the building-sized golems. So, no matter how I spun it, things were going to be close. They were still miles away, though, so I figured I had plenty of time to prepare a proper welcome. So, after explaining my plan to Patrick, I set off through the emerald forest, my plan at the forefront of my mind.

CHAPTER EIGHT

A WELL-LAID TRAP

I don't know how she does it. Day after day, battle after battle, she never shies away from what she has to do. Meanwhile, I have nightmares about every single fight I've ever been in. It makes me feel like a coward until I remember that Mira's the odd one. Most people can't go from one life-and-death struggle to another and be unaffected.

—Patrick Ward

I let out a deep breath, then wiped my hand across my face. I'd used some of the water I had stored in my arsenal implant—those extra slots were really getting huge—to wash some of the dried blood away, but I still felt filthy. Largely, that was because I'd been scrambling around, setting everything up for the coming conflict. Now I was finished, though, and the golems were still miles away.

It was a testament to their size that I had originally assumed that they were a lot closer. The same could be said for the palace in the distance, which was probably closer to fifty miles away than my original estimate of ten.

In any case, I still had plenty of time to get set up for what I hoped would be a massacre of giant golems. Still, over the Secure Connection, I asked, "Are you ready? You have that—"

"I have it," Patrick said. "But I told you before, I wasn't able to fully repair it. The only reason it works at all is because I integrated it into the armor. It's still going to put out quite a kick, but it's going to drain my Mist fast."

"That's fine. You're just here to help me finish them off," I said as I trotted through the emerald forest. Patrick grumbled about being relegated to the back lines, but I ignored him. The fact was that his armor, while impressive, wasn't ideally suited for the fight ahead. Which just showed how advanced the Rift really was. If we'd gone into the Rift with the spiders as our current selves, we could have ripped through it with ease.

But that was irrelevant.

Because at that moment, I finally reached my destination, which was the highest point within the Rift. That wasn't saying much, but I was hoping that slight elevation would give me the sight line I needed to bring the full weight of my power to bear. So, without further hesitation, I climbed one of the crystalline trees, scurrying up its trunk until I reached the very top. It was painful, but I'd resolved myself to enduring it, if only for a few moments while I scouted the region. By the time I got to the top, I was in agony, but I remained in place long enough to see the glittering canopy stretching off in every direction, and I found myself idly wondering just how big the Rift was.

Not that it mattered, especially with six enormous golems—they each had to be at least three hundred feet tall—slowly lumbering in my general direction. Using Observation, I took a good look at the one in the lead, and I saw that it wasn't comprised of the formless crystal I'd seen from the smaller version. Instead, there were crystal trees growing out of its back, and it actually had hands as well as subtle facial features that made it look like a half-finished sculpture.

Gradually, the horde of crystalline monsters drew closer, and I commenced with the final step of my preparations. First, I settled into the sturdiest firing position I could find before summoning my Pulsar and extending its stabilizers. I hooked one leg around the tree limb, then leaned forward onto my stomach, extending the sniper rifle out in front of me.

It took a few more minutes for the golem to get into range, but when it did, I took a deep breath, then, one by one, activated all my relevant abilities. First came Stealth. Then Explosive Shot. After that, I used Execute. And finally, Empowered Shot. I wasn't sure precisely how much those abilities would modify the damage of my shot, but I knew it was significant—especially with the modifiers associated with my evolved class of {Mist Warden}.

Once Empowered Shot had charged, I squeezed the trigger. The shot took the first golem directly in the chest, hitting it with the force of an artillery shot. Midstep, the giant creature staggered, which, given its size, was quite a feat to have caused. However, as much as I would have liked to see it fall, it quickly righted itself and continued its steady march in my direction.

But by that point, I'd already used Vanish, then reapplied Stealth before going through the cycle once again. The next round hit almost directly where the last had and, though it took the application of Observation to see, resulted in a spiderweb of cracks in its crystalline form.

Over and over, I cycled through the same process, and eventually, I carved quite a crater in its form. However, by the time it was only a mile away, I started to realize precisely what I was up against. Hopefully, my plan would work out; otherwise, Patrick and I were in for a long and exceedingly dangerous series of fights.

One ponderous step after another, the golems crossed the emerald forest. And as they drew closer, I was once again astounded by their sheer size. I had seen plenty of large buildings in my time, but there was something wholly terrifying when something that big was mobile.

Finally, the last crystalline golem crossed the threshold I'd marked in my mind. It was precisely what I'd been waiting on. So, after exchanging my Pulsar for the BMAP, I also took a small detonator from my arsenal implant. Then, without further hesitation, I flipped a switch before pressing a button to ignite the explosives I'd set up throughout the forest.

An instant later, the series of explosions sent waves of billowing force tearing across the emerald forest. Soon, those shock waves—each one the result of a separate explosive charge—were followed by surging blue flames that left nothing but melted crystal in their wake. Even from a mile away, I was soon buffeted by the force of those explosions, and I had to grip the branch even more tightly just to keep from falling free. Fortunately, the flames died well before they reached my position, though. Otherwise, I'd have been melted just like everything else.

Well, everything but the golems.

They weren't unaffected. In fact, a few of them had fallen to the ground, their legs melted into stumps. However, they were far from dead.

But that was okay. I'd expected as much. The problem was that, if I were to create bombs powerful enough to kill those creatures in one shot—a dubious prospect, at best, given my supplies—detonating them would almost assuredly catch me in the blast zone. So, I'd resolved to kill them with a steady onslaught rather than one huge blast.

Which was why I had drawn my BMAP out of its slot in my arsenal implant.

I'd loaded it with the most powerful ammunition I had, which was saying something, considering that I'd spent a veritable fortune on the various types of explosive shells it used. Assembling that collection had been a money sink that could rival operating *The Leviathan*, but I felt it was well worth it. However, even with that commitment to quality, I'd only managed to buy two canisters of this particular ammunition. Not because I couldn't afford it—I really couldn't, but I would have made it work—but rather due to lack of availability. Earth was still a backwater, even among frontier planets. And with the quarantine still in place, good equipment was hard to find. Truly destructive ammunition was even more so.

In this case, the shells in question were made from Mist-infused carbonatium—which was supposed to be incredibly reactive—and the warheads were comprised of depleted Rift Shards that had been saturated in some incredibly reactive substance whose name I couldn't even begin to pronounce. The result was, hopefully, the most destructive ammunition I had at my disposal.

Usually, I couldn't use something so potent because I didn't want to deal with the collateral damage. Or because I would've been in the blast radius. However, in this instance, I didn't have to worry about either.

Taking aim at the fallen golem, I used Shatter Shot, then Explosive Shot to increase the damage of the entire cannister. Normally, I wouldn't use Empowered Shot with anything but my Pulsar, but there was nothing about the ability that said it couldn't be used with my BMAP. It just usually wasn't necessary or feasible. However, this time, I did just that, activating Empowered Shot before using Execute.

Then, I finally fired.

The other issue with the BMAP was that it didn't fire with the force of a true firearm. So, the shell flew slowly enough that I could follow it with my naked eye. More, I'd had to arc the shot so it would cover the appropriate distance. Because of that, it took almost an entire two seconds for the shell to come within range of the golem.

That was the biggest reason I'd had to immobilize it via the previous explosions. Otherwise, hitting the creature would have been annoyingly inconsistent. However, now that it was on the ground, I had no such issues, and as soon as the shell came within range of the fallen monster, it broke apart into five mostly identical copies.

Each of the shell's doppelgängers was a little less powerful than the original, but with all my modifiers and abilities, I didn't think that would matter.

An instant later, the barrage hit home.

Six nearly identical flashes of light preceded the same number of balls of fire. A fraction of a second later, the impact of those six explosions tore across what was left of the emerald forest. But I only had eyes for the golem.

It shattered into a thousand pieces before a thick black mushroom cloud bloomed above it. Amid that smoke were a multitude of blue tendrils of pure Mist, each one looking like a persistent lightning strike.

Via Secure Connection, Patrick said, "Damn, Mira . . ."

I didn't respond because I was too busy cycling through my abilities. The only difference with the second round was that I had to precede it with Vanish, then Stealth. However, the results were similar when I finally loosed the shot at the second golem. It attempted to react, but it was both far too large and crippled from the detonation of the first set of charges.

Again, six nearly identical shells hit it, and with the same explosive results.

I kept going until all but one of the building-sized golems had been completely destroyed. So had most of the landscape, and the once-beautiful emerald forest had become a hellscape of melted slag. However, one of the golems had managed to survive the barrage, and given that I was out of those incredibly powerful shells, I knew that, if we were going to progress, we needed to get up close and personal with it.

Fortunately, it hadn't escaped the bombardment unscathed, and the mountainous monster had been reduced to crawling across the hellish landscape. It was still incredibly dangerous, though. One wrong move, and we would be crushed by its enormous mass. So, it was with immense caution that I descended from the tree.

Soon enough, Patrick—in his armor—joined me.

I looked it over, seeing that the white enamel looked almost completely undamaged. At that, I asked, "Weren't there a few dents before?"

"Mist-powered regeneration," he said, his voice slightly robotic from within the cockpit. "It was functional before, but now it's almost back to peak efficiency."

"Sexy," I said, looking back at him with a smirk. "Nothing gets a girl going like peak efficiency."

I could practically hear his eye roll when he said, "Not the time, Mira."

"If not now, then when?"

He didn't respond, which meant that I had nothing to distract me from the results of my bombardment. Melted crystal was everywhere, the ground had been completely torn asunder, and everything looked like a postapocalyptic hell. Which was kind of accurate, given our circumstances.

In any case, we slowly traversed the mile or so we needed to cover before, at last, the final golem loomed over us. Even prone, the thing was at least a hundred feet tall, and I knew that that thick, grasping arm probably weighed many hundreds of tons. If it hit either Patrick or me, we would be crushed.

"How do you want to do this?" he asked.

"You need levels," I said.

"You think I can hurt it?"

I shrugged. "Maybe. You never know until you try," I stated. Even if he didn't do much damage, so long as he participated in the battle, he would accumulate some Mist. And given how much the golem contained, even a fraction of the credit would probably send him up at least a few levels.

"Alright," he said. "Step back."

"I'll be fine right here."

"Suit yourself."

Then, I saw the Mist of his aura swell, then swirl before the armor whirred to life. A pair of panels on his back opened up, and a familiar shape emerged. The Dragon had been cut in half back in Olympus, and the ensuing explosion had proved to be the edge I'd needed to defeat the red-suited android that had almost killed me on multiple occasions. However, before I'd left that city behind, I'd gathered the pieces. Then, when Patrick had told me he needed a bigger gun, I'd given him what was left of the powerful weapon. He'd since worked his magic, fusing the two halves into working condition, and mounted the result in his armor.

I knew that, during the armor's creation, he'd built multiple such slots into the structure, but seeing the back open up and reveal the rebuilt Dragon was impressive, nonetheless. Notions of what else we could mount in there had me salivating; he could become a walking weapons platform whose only limit was how much money we had to spend on his arsenal.

That was a comforting thought, the idea that all our problems could potentially be solved by simply having more money. I knew it wasn't true. We could throw hundreds of thousands of credits at the aliens, and they wouldn't even consider stopping. Because they were after something far more important. They wanted power for power's sake; wealth was either a means to an end or a simple by-product.

Once it had emerged from his back, the rebuilt Dragon rose to his shoulder. Then, it roared.

I knew it wasn't as powerful as if I'd used it. Not only did Patrick lack my modifiers, but the weapon itself had lost quite a bit of its efficacy. He expected that he could slowly bring it back up to its former glory, but at present, it operated at something around sixty percent effectiveness. Which still made it an incredibly potent weapon, but it was nothing compared to what it had been when I'd used it.

Still, the weapon's issue streaked across the intervening space between our position and the giant golem, and when those rounds hit its bulky body, it sent shards of crystal spraying into the air.

But I knew it was like jabbing it with a needle. Painful, probably. And eventually, it might do real damage. On any sort of timeline that mattered, though, it was grossly ineffective. Even so, it was enough for the system to tag Patrick as having participated in the battle. So, once he'd emptied the Dragon's significant store of ammunition, I said, "Alright. That should be good. Now, it's my turn. You should probably retreat because this is going to get really . . . uh . . . bad."

Before Patrick had a chance to reply, I raced forward with a long, ground-eating stride, and when I got close, I used Engage, springing across the space between us and landing on the monster's head. Once there, I started planting bombs.

Individually, they weren't nearly as powerful as the ones I'd used to bring the column of giant golems to a halt. Those had been built for mass devastation, and in that arena, they had met complete success. These new bombs were slightly weaker—on average—than the ones I'd used against the other, much smaller crystalline monster.

But using them had one clear advantage in that, technically, they weren't just bombs. Instead, they were also equipped with tiny drills that, once placed, would dig through any surface until I stopped them.

I hadn't used them against the first monster because, well, I hadn't really been thinking straight. But now, it felt like they'd been tailor-made for just such a fight. So, without further hesitation, I raced along the golem's body, every now and then having to flare Balance to keep from falling from its struggling form, as I placed almost fifty of the bombs.

Then, I used Teleport to escape its immediate vicinity before running off to join Patrick almost a mile away.

By that point, the little drones had had a chance to drill deep into the thing's bulky body. When I reached Patrick, I said, "This all feels a bit anticlimactic, doesn't it?"

He had his cockpit open, so I could see him shrug when he replied, "I'll take anticlimactic, Mira. We're not here for excitement. We're here to make money for the coming war. So, if we can do that a little more efficiently, I'm definitely on board."

"I guess."

Even as I said it, I couldn't deny my disappointment. Certainly, I didn't want to risk death. Yet, I had to admit that there was a part of me that enjoyed toeing that line. I'd felt it against the first golem, but with the much larger, far more dangerous line of larger creatures, any sense of real danger had been largely absent.

Sure, if I'd made a mistake or two, that would have changed. I knew that. But still, that feeling of slight discontent remained.

I shrugged. "Well, at least I got to blow some stuff up," I muttered. Then, I pressed the button on the detonator. A grin spread across my face as fifty small explosions erupted in the distance, and a moment later, I felt an influx of Mist surge through my body.

CHAPTER NINE

THE PALACE

In my world—or any of the worlds colonized by my people—I am not a popular man. Tucked safely away in the core worlds, they can't understand why I would dedicate my life to fighting on the frontier. To them, these people aren't . . . well . . . people. They're, at best, statistics. At worst, little more than animals meant to be tamed. Or pests to be exterminated. I've spent my life trying to change that perception, but everything is so far away from their comfortable little worlds that they can't make the connections necessary to change.

—Alistaris Kargat

The emerald forest had devolved into a wasteland of multicolored glass, melted by my efforts and reformed as everything cooled. I remarked, "It's actually kind of pretty, in a . . . you know . . . deconstructed kind of way."

"Only you would say that," Patrick muttered from within his armor. "It's just a puddle of glass now."

"Yeah."

"But it was so amazing before. I mean, I know it was full of dangerous and deadly creatures, but you have to admit that all those crystal trees were incredible," he said. "And now? It's all gone."

I shrugged. "It's changed, not gone. Different doesn't mean worse."

But I knew he wouldn't agree with that assessment. Patrick was nothing if not committed to order. He liked it when everything fit together into a cohesive whole. The forest had been like that before. Now, from his perspective, it had all been destroyed. I thought the opposite, and I could certainly find beauty in the chaotic mess I'd created. In fact, I found it even more enticing than before, if only because it wasn't so constructed and clearly contrived.

In any case, we continued on, trekking through what had once been the emerald forest as we made our way toward the palace in the distance. For miles, the landscape was mostly unchanged, and then we reached the edge of the destruction I'd wreaked. Suddenly, the trees were back, towering higher than ever before, but there were no monsters or wildlife to speak of. Sure, every now and again I'd see a crystal squirrel or something of the like, but those weren't aggressive, so they felt more like set pieces than actual creatures.

But that feeling wasn't abnormal. Every time I entered a Rift, it felt less real than the last. Some of that was due to the contrived nature, but now that I was a {Mist Warden} I felt like I could see the underpinnings. I couldn't. Obviously. But there were hints here and there that made me feel like I was walking through someone else's playground.

That feeling persisted as we approached the palace. It was much larger than my previous observation suggested, mostly because it was farther away than I'd thought. So, as we drew closer, I couldn't help but feel a sense of awe, if only at the sheer size on display. However, as with everything else so far, it felt somehow empty. Like I was looking at a photo, rather than experiencing a three-dimensional space.

Or perhaps that was just because I could see the framework of Mist that that supported everything in my line of sight. Even so, I knew just how dangerous Rifts could be. Whether or not the setting was real seemed irrelevant to its lethality. So, I kept my wits about me as we slowly continued on our way.

It was a good thing, too, because if I'd let my mind wander for even a second longer, there's a good chance that both Patrick and I would have died. As it was, I saw the shimmer of a Mist aura only a few moments before the creature pounced, tearing out of some Stealth variant to ambush me.

Having been warned by the thing's aura, I was ready for it, though. So, I met its attack with my hastily summoned nano-bladed sword. Mist-infused blade met crystal, and with a crack that sounded like shattering glass, the blade won. I barely had a chance to see the monster before its head tumbled free, and the rest of its body tackled me to the ground. I wrestled free of the spasming creature, but it quickly became apparent that it was already dead and the movement was merely its death throes.

"What the hell was that?" Patrick asked, his voice breathless.

I pushed myself to my feet, then nudged the twitching monster with my foot. Like everything else in the Rift, it was made of crystal, but in this creature's case, it was pitch-black in color. Otherwise, it looked far sleeker than anything else I'd seen so far, with flesh made of articulating crystals that looked like scales. Beyond that, it had the roughly feline shape.

"Crystal cat," I said.

"That can't be what it's really called."

I shrugged. "Can't say it isn't appropriate, though. It looks kind of like a panther. But, you know, crystal. So, crystal cat."

"You're really bad at naming things."

I tossed a grin his way, then said, "I guess I can stomach not being good at one little thing. Nobody's perfect."

After that, Patrick and I continued on our way, but now, we were both on the lookout for the stealthy crystal cats. A good thing, too, because it felt like we couldn't go more than a few dozen feet without being attacked. So, the rest of our trip took far longer than either of us had anticipated, and by the time we finally reached the glittering palace, we were both exhausted. So, I asked, "Do you want to camp out here? Or inside?"

"Here," Patrick answered. "I need to regenerate some of my Mist, and I don't think it's smart to go into the palace where we don't know what we'll encounter."

I agreed with that, and over the next few minutes, we set out our various defenses. First came a basic Mist shield that created a dome of protection around us. It wouldn't dissuade a determined attacker—indeed, one of those crystal cats could get through it with only a couple of swipes—but it would serve to warn us of any intruders. On top of that, it gave my Bastion ability something to latch on to.

After using that, I deployed a couple of autoturrets; again, they weren't intended to kill potential attackers. Rather, they were only supposed to slow down and distract while Patrick and I responded.

Finally, I set up a decent-quality holographic display that would hopefully camouflage us from anything that might stumble into the camp's vicinity. Individually, none of our defenses were terribly strong. And yet, together, they were capable of giving us the edge we needed to respond to any threats. More importantly, they gave us peace of mind, which would be important if either of us intended to get any sort of rest.

Once the defenses had been deployed, Patrick climbed out of the armor. As always, I couldn't help but notice his cybernetic parts. It wouldn't have been so bad if he'd hidden them beneath faux skin, but he almost wore the bulky, obviously mechanical pieces with pride. More, the lack of fake skin gave him the access he needed to continuously study and improve upon them. So, I couldn't really argue with the logic of keeping them exposed, even if I'd have preferred a different aesthetic.

Or maybe I just hated being reminded that, ultimately, his injuries had been my fault. It would have been so much easier if, every time I looked at him, it wasn't a reminder of the unintended consequences of my actions. Sure, I hadn't meant to bring that building down. When I'd used that Ghost to disconnect the

Pacificians from their local hive mind, there was no way I could have known that they would self-destruct. But that was what had happened. And without my actions, thousands of innocents would have survived.

"What are you thinking?" Patrick asked after he'd finished the inspection of his armor. It had a subtle self-repair function, but it was limited in scope. Thankfully, none of the damage exceeded its capabilities, and it would be as good as new after a few more hours in his storage space.

"Nothing," I lied. That last thing he wanted to hear was me complaining about things no one could change. It was better to keep that to myself. "Just thinking about what the rest of this Rift has in store. It'll probably end somewhere in the palace."

"Probably. But at least we won't see any more of those huge golems in there. I don't think they'd fit."

"I don't think we were meant to kill them," I said.

"Huh? Really?"

"Think about it. Do you think those crab people—"

"Crutacaans."

"Yeah, them. Do you think they fought those golems? No. There was probably another way around," I said.

"They might've had some kind of tech to make it easier."

I shrugged. "Maybe."

I knew good and well that the aliens were equipped with technology meant to streamline the Rift-mining process. For some, it was gear specifically designed to combat whatever challenges the Rifts presented. That kind of strategy required copious scouting and, more often than not, a good deal of sacrifice. But once they were armed with that information, the aliens had the contacts to commission tailor-made work-arounds. And since they'd been at it for decades, they'd long since perfected the process.

We had no such advantages. Even if we could have figured out the Crutacaans' methods, they would have been useless to us, largely because those strategies were only suited for the specific aliens who'd commissioned them. So, we couldn't even steal them and repurpose the technology for ourselves.

It made Rift mining an extremely dangerous process, which I had to admit was probably by design.

I sighed, and after sharing a meal of mostly tasteless travel rations with Patrick, I took the first watch while he tried to get some rest. After a few hours—during which nothing happened—we switched places, and I forced myself to sleep. It was telling that, even in such a dangerous environment, I had no issues with that. I'd slept in much worse situations, after all.

Without a day-night cycle, it was a little difficult to judge time, and without my interface, there's every chance that I would have lost track. But soon enough, it was clear that we needed to move on. We weren't on a timer, per se, but we both wanted to complete the Rift as soon as possible. That way, we could move on to the fun stuff like getting new skills, weapons, and cybernetics.

With that in mind, Patrick and I cleaned up our campsite, gathering the autoturrets, Mist-shield apparatus, and holographic display. He stored it all away, mostly because he had far more space than I did. The extra slots in my arsenal implant had grown alongside [Mist-Infused Body], but they couldn't hold a candle to Patrick's more dedicated skill-attached storage space.

Soon, we were on our way, circling the palace grounds as we searched for an entrance. The structure was enormous, though I was a little disappointed that, even close up, it wasn't very detailed. Like the golems, it looked like someone had only half finished a sculpture. Or in this case, a building. Sure, the basic shape was there, but it was too rough to be considered complete.

Eventually, our search bore fruit, and we found our way to a huge open gate that allowed for access into the palace. So, without further hesitation, Patrick and I stepped inside. The moment we did, the world shimmered. I reached out to grab Patrick's arm, but I quickly realized that he wasn't there.

I admit that I panicked then.

Fortunately, it only lasted a few seconds before he reappeared right beside me.

"What the hell?" he muttered, the fleshy side of his face going pale.

I shook my head. "I don't know."

Then, I looked back the way we'd come, and instead of seeing a gate, there was nothing but a solid wall of crystal. It only took me a moment to surmise that the gate hadn't been a mundane door but, rather, a portal similar to the one we'd used to enter the Rift in the first place. However, because it didn't have the benefit of being stabilized by the mechanical aperture, passage through the portal had been a little disconcerting.

I explained all of that to Patrick, and he nodded along, clearly having come to the same conclusions. I ended with, "Well, I guess there's no way to go but forward."

With that, I looked around, taking stock of the current environment. It looked like the entry hall of a palace, but on theme, it was one that seemed too rough to have really existed. The floor was the only part that wasn't made of crystal and instead was constructed of crude tiles in alternating colors. There were no decorations. No sculptures, tapestries, or paintings on the walls. Instead, it was entirely barren, which made the whole place feel almost like a natural formation rather than something that had been built.

"You'd better put on your suit," I said. "I think this is going to suck."

"You mean worse than it has so far?" he asked, already summoning his armor.

As he climbed inside, I said, "Probably. I mean, they do typically get more difficult."

"I did kind of get crushed yesterday."

"Only a little," I said. "You made it out just fine."

Of course, I left unsaid that, at the time, I'd thought he'd died, and I had gone on a bit of a rampage. But that wasn't something I wanted to revisit. Far easier to simply make light of the situation.

As Patrick mounted the mech suit, then sealed himself inside, I summoned my R-14. Of late, it had become increasingly less powerful, and I suspected that the only reason it remained even moderately effective was due to my modifiers and abilities. With that in mind, I also used Explosive Shot to increase the damage of each round in the magazine. Hopefully, that would go a long way toward alleviating its weakness, but I knew it would be a hole in my arsenal until I earned enough credits to replace it with something better. The same could be said for my Pulsar, and I needed to replace the Dragon, as well. In short, my arsenal wasn't what it once was, and I desperately needed to address the issues.

But that was a problem for after the Rift. For the time being, I had no choice but to work with what I had. In a Rift as strong as the one we'd challenged, that meant I'd have to use multiple magazines to down any foes.

"Stay here while I scout things out," I said.

Patrick didn't argue, instead unfolding the rebuilt Dragon from his back and perching it on his shoulder. On one arm pulsed a blue Mist shield, while the other had transformed into his long blade. He was as ready as he could be for anything that might stumble upon him. So, assured of his relative safety, I embraced Stealth and stalked through the entry hall and to the corridor leading deeper into the palace.

I found the first enemy less than a minute later, and at first, I didn't even recognize it. If it weren't for my {Mist Warden} senses, I probably would have walked right past the pile of crystals. However, because I could see its aura, the thing stood out like a sore thumb. Still, it wasn't until I used Distraction, resulting in a slight clicking sound at the other end of the hall, that I saw it for what it was.

The thing burst forward, a whirling dervish of floating crystals. It was just a ball of dense Mist and crystals, but it moved like a tornado with five different axes. Unfortunately, I didn't get the chance to see how it would attack because, after it seemed to recognize that there was nothing there, it quickly settled back down.

Carefully, I crept past it and continued on my way.

Over the next couple of hours, I saw ten more of the crystal dervishes, though I didn't antagonize any of them. Instead, I focused on mapping the palace as best I could, which proved an arduous task due to the sheer size and mazelike construction of the building. Still, I managed to accomplish the feat after half a day. The whole time, I kept in touch with Patrick, who remained, nervous and waiting, back at the entrance.

Eventually, though, I found a door, which was impeded by a thick Mist shield. Along the frame were twelve slots, each one about four inches across and in the rough shape of a Rift Shard. I tried to use Misthack on the thing, hoping it had some sort of interface, but it was useless.

"Are you sure you found all the dervishes?" Patrick asked via Secure Connection.

"I don't know," I replied, still cloaked in Stealth. "Maybe? I didn't explore the whole palace. Why?"

"Well, you found eleven of them, right? If there's one more out there, that might be the correlation we're looking for," he said. "Maybe those slots are like locks, and when we kill the dervishes, it'll unlock."

I was about to reply that that didn't make any sense, but then I remembered that Rifts weren't like the real world. They featured challenges with clear means of overcoming them. I'd never really cared for puzzles or games, so that probably explained why I didn't really care for Rifts, either.

Or maybe it was the mortal danger.

Either way, because of the contrived nature of the Rifts, Patrick's suggestion made a ton of sense. So, I quickly embarked on a search for the extra dervish, which I found less than an hour later in an out-of-the-way corner of the palace. I didn't stop there, though. I wanted to make sure there were no others before I latched on to Patrick's plan.

"I think you're right," I said after a while. "Which is a problem."

"Huh? I thought solving the puzzle was a good thing," he said.

"Oh, it is. But now we need to figure out how to kill balls of Mist and crystal, right? And without bringing the whole building down on top of us," I said.

"Oh. Yeah. I can see how that might be a problem."

CHAPTER TEN

THE PROBLEM WITH DERVISHES

I've seen dozens of worlds fall. Some were stripped of every resource they had to offer, then abandoned. Left with a dead world, the people had no choice but to become refugees. In other cases, one faction or another chose to destroy a planet simply because they couldn't stomach their enemies winning. I don't want that for Earth, but I don't know if I can stop it.

—Alistaris Kargat

I sat with Patrick, sharing a tasteless meal of travel rations as we both stared at the Mist lamp we'd deployed. The blue-tinted light flickered, bouncing off the crystalline walls to cast everything in a subtle azure glow. Finally, I let out a sigh and asked, "So, any ideas?"

"I don't know," Patrick admitted, fidgeting with one of his cybernetic arms. He had the thing open and had shoved a screwdriver inside. "I was kind of hoping you'd figure it out, if I'm honest."

I gave him a smirk. "Also, don't you think you should do that kind of thing in a more optimal environment?" I asked.

"What?" he asked, a little confused. Only a second later, comprehension dawned on his face, and he said, "Oh. This. Yeah, it would probably be better if I had a proper workshop. But I'm not really doing anything major. Just adjusting some of the servos because I noticed a glitch in the articulation of a—"

"That sounds pretty complicated."

"It's not. Besides, it relaxes me," he stated.

"If you make a mistake, the whole arm's going to be useless," I pointed out. "That would stress me out like nothing else."

"Coming from the girl who makes bombs in place of meditation . . ."

"That's different."

"Yeah, because if you screw up a bomb, you're not the only one affected. If I mishandle one of these servos, one of my fingers stops working. I think *different* is probably an understatement," he said.

"I suppose that's fair," I admitted. "But seriously—any ideas? Because I don't know if bullets are going to do much against balls of Mist."

"They might die if you destroy their crystals."

"They might not, though," I pointed out. "I mean, there's a chance that this place requires specialized equipment."

"The Crutacaans were mining it."

"Yeah. But did they go this deep? I mean, there's every chance that there was a cache of Rift Shards outside. They could've focused on mining those and probably left when the cache was exhausted. After that, they would've just had to wait for it to reset," I explained. In fact, that was how most Rift-mining operations worked. Few aliens bothered conquering the entire Rift. Instead, they took the easy pickings, then exited the Rift and let it reset.

And while that was much safer, it very much limited the profitability of even the most Mist-dense Rifts. If Patrick and I could afford to stay in place for more than a few weeks, we might've used a similar strategy. However, if we did that, we'd inevitably have a fight on our hands. Worse yet, if we weren't careful with the timing, there was every chance that we'd exit through the Rift aperture and find an ambush waiting on us.

No—our only viable strategy was to go in, conquer the Rift, and get out as quickly as possible. Otherwise, we'd end up facing a strong enemy without the benefit of preparation. It had nearly happened after my first Rift, and I had no interest in revisiting that kind of risk.

Besides, the way back was blocked now that we'd entered the palace, so the choice was taken out of our hands.

"I think I might have an idea," Patrick said. "But I'm not sure if it'll work."

"We're not sure anything will work, Pick."

"True."

"So? What is it?"

"Okay, so you know how I've been fiddling with your old scattergun, right?"

"I'm aware, yes."

"Do you know it works?" he asked.

"Not really," I admitted. "Mostly, I just pointed it at stuff and squeezed the trigger."

He sighed, and I could tell that he was about to start a lecture. I had no interest in listening to that, so I cut him off by saying, "Just the high points, Pick. I don't need to know the fine details of Mist circuitry or whatever it is you're about to explain."

He actually looked a little offended at that. I'm not sure if that offense was based on me not being interested in what amounted to his life's work, or if he couldn't imagine anyone not wanting to know every tiny detail about the afore-mentioned Mist circuits.

Still, he said, "Whatever. But don't come crying to me when you don't know why your guns aren't working."

"I will do exactly that. Why else would I keep you around, if not to fix all the stuff I inevitably break?"

"I thought it was my rugged good looks."

I laughed. "Pick, you're a lot of things, but rugged really isn't one of them. Pretty would probably be more appropriate."

"Even with this?" he asked, gesturing to the metal half dome that covered the left side of his face.

"I told you about that lady I saw one time in Nova, right? Her whole face was like a golden mask," I said. I'd seen her on Bourbon Street, and she'd been working as a prostitute. "In fact, I think her whole body might've been like that. People liked it, though. She had a bunch of clients, from what I could tell."

"Are you suggesting that I should replace this with a golden mask and go into prostitution?"

"No!" I said. Then I noticed his smirk and crossed my arms in annoyance. "I'm just saying that it doesn't make me love you any less, idiot. You know that."

He shrugged. "Yeah, sure. But counterpoint—you're really cute when you're annoyed, and it's extremely easy to tease you. So, yeah."

I rolled my eyes. "Weren't we talking about something else?" I pointed out, trying to change the subject.

"Oh. Right. So, I think I can take the scattergun apart and use some of the other parts in my storage to make what I'm tentatively calling Mist anchors."

"You can't just put the word *Mist* in front of another word and think it makes any kind of sense."

He shrugged. "Everyone else does it," he said. "But whatever. The name isn't important. The function is what we care about."

"And what is that?"

"So, the scattergun doesn't really create lightning. Instead, it agitates the ambient Mist. That electricity you see isn't actually electricity. It's more of a side effect as it travels through the air."

"Looks like electricity to me."

"It's not, though. When that effect hits someone or something with con-centrated Mist, the agitation causes a chain reaction, which in turn creates the stun-like effect."

"Or death. For a nonlethal weapon, it kills a lot of people."

"It does have a bit more kick than I expected," he admitted. "But that just works in our favor. So, what I'm suggesting is that I take the gun apart, then use the pieces that agitate the Mist along with some other parts to create these lit-tle . . . anchors. One won't do anything, but if we put them in a circle, they'll cre-ate a web that will hopefully disrupt Mist. If those things are like you described, then there's a chance we'll incapacitate them."

"And if it doesn't work?"

"We throw every other weapon we have at them. Something is bound to work, right?" he remarked.

That sounded more like my kind of strategy than his usual plans, but given what we were up against, I couldn't really come up with anything better. I said as much, adding, "May as well give it a try. What do you need from me?"

"Uh . . . Just . . . I mean, don't take this the wrong way, but I just need you to be quiet and let me work," he said.

"Wow. Just tossing me to the side like that. I see how it is."

"Mira, I'm not—"

"Kidding, Pick. Totally kidding. Do your thing."

He looked like he still wanted to apologize, but then thought better of it. Soon enough, he'd summoned his armor, from which he began to extract the scattergun he'd built into the suit. Like the rebuilt Dragon, it was intended to deploy from within the armor, so it took him a few hours to completely detach it. When he did, he tossed it onto the ground and started to dismantle the weapon.

As I watched, I had mixed feelings about what he was doing. I'd used that weapon countless times, and it had seen me through some tough battles. Now, it was being used for spare parts. Even if everything worked out the way he thought it would, the loss was still poignant enough to twist my stomach into knots.

How, then, would I feel when I had to replace the Pulsar? Or the R-14? The BMAP still had a lot of life left in it—in fact, I wasn't sure I'd ever outgrow it, considering that, with that weapon, the shells were far more important than the platform itself—but most of my arsenal would soon be discarded in favor of more powerful models.

"I think I'm way too attached to my guns," I muttered to myself, though my voice was low enough that Patrick couldn't hear. Or maybe he was just too invested in his own project to notice, which wasn't abnormal. In that way, we were more than a little similar.

In any event, as Patrick worked on the Mist anchors, I busied myself with exploring my new senses. I'd slowly grown accustomed to using them, but I knew I'd yet to plumb the depths of what they had to offer. Being able to see auras was one thing, but I had to wonder if there was more to it. It almost felt like I could simply reach out and manipulate the Mist directly.

Which was absurd.

Everyone had to use skills. That was the whole point of the system.

But then again, was that the case with mystics like the Templars? Was that their secret, that they had adapted to manipulating the Mist without the buffer of the system or Nexus Implants? I suspected that was the case, but I wasn't sure. And in any case, I wasn't one of them. I couldn't do the things they could do.

Yet.

That was the word that kept popping up in my mind. I couldn't do it yet. But who was to say what would happen as I continued to progress? After all, I felt certain that I had reached a higher level than just about anyone else on Earth. My uncle might've been of similar level; he'd killed a lot of people, and he'd once intimated to me that he'd spent quite some time hunting powerful animals, as well. So, there was a good chance that he'd evolved his class, too.

But he wasn't a {Mist Warden}.

Even as a {Mistrunner}, I was special. Few people were afforded the opportunity to acquire such a class. I knew that much. So, given the rarity of the base class, how uncommon was its evolution, especially when the requirements had been so high? I suspected that the number of people whose kill count reached into the millions was fairly low. There was even a chance that I was wholly unique.

So, who was to say that becoming a {Mist Warden} hadn't set me on the path of attaining mystic-like powers? Freddie had said that, eventually, I would go down that road. Perhaps I'd just jumped ahead a little.

Such thoughts occupied my mind until, hours later, Patrick finally finished the first anchor. When he did, he gave a little cybernetic fist pump of celebration as he said, "Nice! I think this is going to work."

"You didn't before?"

"Uh . . . Mostly. I mean, it was better than a fifty percent chance I was on the right track," he said. Before I could respond, he went on: "But the real variable is whether or not the crystal dervishes are built the way we think they are."

"They are," I said. I'd spent more than a little time studying the odd creatures, so what I had described was accurate. "Still not sure if the Mist is holding them together or if it's just a by-product of something else, though. Banking on the former, but I wouldn't be terribly surprised if it was the latter."

"That's reassuring."

"Eh, it can be," I stated. "Think about how boring the world would be if you already knew everything. A surprise here and there is what keeps us on our toes."

"You sound like you want them to be different than what you expect."

I shrugged. "Maybe I do."

But then again, I definitely didn't want to put Patrick in any more danger than absolutely necessary. For my part, I felt confident that I could deal with whatever came my way. Unless it was another situation like the irradiated wildlings that had nearly killed me what felt like a lifetime ago.

After shaking his head in bemusement, Patrick went back to work. The next anchor took a little less time to construct than the first one, and the one after that was even quicker. However, the speed with which he could build them leveled out after that, and the next five took a collective ten hours to put together. I utilized that time by diving into my collection of Ghosts, where I fiddled with the structure of some of the older ones.

That was what I liked about Ghosts. No matter how well-built they were, there was always room for improvement. They could always get a little more efficient. A bit more powerful. Or quicker. So, there was always something to chase, which was good for me because I tended to achieve my training goals at a prodigious rate. In any case, that occupied me until, at last, Patrick announced that he'd finished.

I looked down at eight metallic cylinders, each with tiny legs. "That's it?" I asked.

"Do you have any idea how complex these things are? Plus, look at those legs—they stick, Mira. Like, I can deploy them on the walls!" he exclaimed, clearly excited.

"I could have given you some sticky paper I use when I'm making my demolition charges," I offered.

"But . . . But the little legs . . ."

"I think they're . . . uh . . . very nice."

"Don't patronize me," he muttered. "I think they're awesome."

"They are. I was just joking. You know me. I'm famous for my jokes."

"You're famous for killing millions of people."

"They were robots. They don't really count."

"According to the system, they counted," he pointed out.

"Well . . . Um . . . Whatever. I don't care. Robots aren't people. Besides, your little anchors are great. Really good job. Nobody else could have built them like you did."

"You're terrible at this," he said. "You do realize that, don't you?"

"I'm serious!" I said, picking one of them up. "Very well put together. Sturdy. Like you want your anchors to be, I guess."

He sighed and shook his head as I continued to extol the virtues of his anchors. Eventually, I got the picture and let the compliments peter out, and we set off to find a place to properly deploy them. We couldn't go too far into the palace, or we'd run the risk of attracting the dervishes' attention. Even so, we soon found ourselves at an intersection that Patrick declared was perfect for our purposes. So, I helped him deploy the anchors—one at each corner, then two more each on the ceiling and floor.

Once everything was in place, we both stepped back, and he activated them.

Immediately, the world came alive with swirling Mist. The tempest was contained within the rough boundaries created by the anchors, but even from ten feet away, I could feel the agitation of the Mist affecting me. It wasn't pain—not precisely—but it wasn't comfortable, either.

Patrick had it worse, though, and I could see his cybernetics twitching more violently with every passing second. Finally, he deactivated the trap and let out a relieved sigh. "Well, that's a little stronger than I thought it would be."

"You're not kidding."

"Drains me pretty fast, too. Running that thing for thirty seconds takes as much Mist as running the armor for an hour."

"That much?" I asked. I knew that his cybernetics—which, apparently, included the anchors—were incredibly efficient because of his skills. So, the fact that the trap drained him so quickly was further evidence of the power at play. Hopefully, it would be enough to take care of the dervishes.

"It's not as efficient as the armor," he said. "Which I think is expected, considering that I spent months working on the mech suit, and these anchors are the product of a few hours."

"Almost a day, really."

"Not the point, Mira."

"Sure. I know. Just pointing it out. Don't want you to be too proud of your little invention. Can't have you getting a big head, you know?"

He sighed. I giggled. And after that, we went over the plan of attack. It wasn't complicated, but we wanted to be on the same page. So, once we'd worked out the kinks, Patrick hopped into his armor, and I set off to find the first dervish.

I found it only a few minutes later.

So, from as far away as the hall would allow, I took aim with my R-14, activated Execute, then Empowered Shot, and let loose.

CHAPTER ELEVEN

CONTROL

I wish I knew how to fix it. The world, I mean. Machines are so much easier. I can diagnose the problem, find the appropriate parts, and replace whatever needs to be replaced. But with the world—and people, I guess—everything is so much more complicated. I can't just replace a part or two, and suddenly, everything works the way it's supposed to.

—Patrick Ward

There was an argument to be made that I should have used my Pulsar, enhancing it with all my abilities. However, because I didn't expect it to really do much good—due to the nature of the dervishes—I chose to save the more expensive ammunition used by the Pulsar. With that in mind, I let loose with the R-14, sending a three-round burst of molten plasma to tear into the whirling mass of Mist and crystal.

The results were as expected. The first round hit one of the crystals, cracking it with sheer momentum, but the second passed through the swirling Mist to hit another crystal on dervish's far side. Finally, the third missed the crystals altogether, slamming into the crystalline wall on the other side.

Then, the dervish reacted, whirling in place for a split second before tearing across the corridor in my direction. However, I was already gone, sprinting down the hall, then turning a corner. I could hear the thing behind me—all clinking crystals and rushing wind—but I didn't dare pause long enough to even glance backward. Instead, I used every point of my enhanced attributes to propel me with as much speed as I could muster.

Seconds later, I turned the final corner, sliding across the floor to crash into the wall before bouncing away and continuing my trek. Almost a hundred yards away, I saw Patrick—or, rather, his white-and-gold armor—looming before the wall that had once been the palace's entrance. More importantly, between us was the collection of small cylinders that I hoped would trap the thing.

I reached it within a couple of seconds, then dove through while shouting, "Now!"

Patrick didn't follow my orders. Instead, as I rolled to my feet, he waited another couple of agonizing seconds before he activated it. Skidding to a stop as my momentum dissipated, I whipped back around to see tiny arcs of lightning bound from one anchor to another until there was an entire sphere comprised of a webwork of Mist channels surrounding the dervish.

Even from a dozen or so yards away, I could feel the agitated Mist rattling my every cell, which was anything but a pleasant sensation that made me equal parts jittery, nauseous, itchy, and in pain. But it was barely bearable—especially when I saw the dervish railing against the confines of the Mist trap, and to no avail.

"It's not getting out, right?" I asked, watching the thing slam its crystals into the spherical web of quivering Mist. Over and over, it attacked the trap, but even if it filled the corridor with the screeching sound of shattering glass, it seemed incapable of escape.

"I don't think so," Patrick said, his voice distorted by strain as much as it was altered by its passage through the armor's communications system. "But I can't hold it indefinitely, so you need to figure out how to kill it before my Mist runs out."

That's when I started shooting. I knew it was inefficient, and I missed with a disturbing amount of shots, but over the next thirty seconds, I managed to destroy the vast majority of the crystals. As my first magazine went dry, Patrick grunted, "Can't . . . hold it . . . any longer."

Just then, the trap deactivated, freeing the dervish. With the bulk of its crystals having been destroyed, it had mostly become a formless cloud of Mist. But even as it surged forward, I had to believe that destroying the rest of its crystals would destroy it. So, I continued to fire, one three-round burst after another until it drew within a few feet. Then, I used Teleport right before it made contact.

By that point, Patrick had summoned his broad Mist shield, which he thrust at the cloud of Mist and crystals. It hit with a thunderous impact, stopping the dervish's advance. Meanwhile, I kept firing, and at last, I managed to destroy the last of the crystals.

But it didn't stop.

In fact, the Mist swirled even faster, scouring layers from the floor and the crystalline wall. It also wrapped around Patrick's shield, seeping over the top and extending an amorphous tendril of blue-glowing Mist toward the armor.

Instinctively, I knew the armor wouldn't survive contact with the dervish. And if the armor fell prey to its touch, then Patrick would soon follow. I couldn't allow that. But I also had no idea how to stop it. My weapons were ill-suited to combat the formless creature, and without the ability to Misthack, I had nothing else going for me.

I watched impotently as the swirl of Mist continued its inexorable reach toward Patrick. I wasn't idle. I continued to shoot. But my rounds, as devastating as they often were, proved entirely ineffective against such a formless foe. And with my {Mist Warden} senses, I could see it all so clearly.

Patrick couldn't, though. That was clear enough.

Desperately, I clawed at my own awareness, searching for anything that might make a difference. And suddenly, something snapped. If I could see the Mist auras, perhaps I could manipulate them, as well. Using the same strategies that enabled me to overcome the complex defenses of even the strongest Mistwalls, I focused everything I had on Misthack.

I screamed with the effort.

And suddenly, the world broke.

Or perhaps it was my mind.

Tears traced lines down my cheeks as, unexpectedly, I could see everything so much more clearly. I couldn't just see the auras. I could feel them. More, I was keenly aware of just how densely the Mist infused the very air around me. It was like I'd suddenly developed an entirely new sense, and the strain of so many stimuli was enough to very nearly tear my mind asunder.

But I pushed through it, using the bones of Misthack to reach out to that dense cloud of Mist and latch on to it. The moment my mind touched it, the thing went wild, undulating and spinning with increased ferocity. I ignored it, focusing every ounce of my being on the task at hand.

With a growl, I grabbed hold of a single nanite. It was microscopic, but I could feel it just as clearly as if it had been the size of my fist. Then, with a simple flex of my mind—which was much more difficult than it sounds—I ripped it free. With my {Mist Warden} senses, I watched as the thin tendril of some unidentifiable power that connected it to the rest of the cloud snapped.

That got an even more vivid response from the dervish, but even as blood leaked from my nose, I kept going, targeting the next nanite and repeating the action. Over and over, with ever-increasing rapidity, I tore the cloud apart. There weren't just thousands of them. Millions was an understatement, as well. In fact, there were tens of millions of the tiny nanites comprising the cloud of Mist.

I'd long known that my processing speed was much quicker than that of an average person, but normally, I couldn't really bring that to bear. It showed during Misthacks and Mistwalks, but otherwise, I was incapable of expressing that insane processing speed in the physical world.

But in this instance, I could bring the full weight of that characteristic to bear. And for every passing second, I ripped hundreds of the nanites away. Then, thousands. Tens of thousands. My mind was moving at such a speed as to make the world look like it was going in slow motion. But still, I pushed further. I went faster.

I knew there would be consequences.

How could there not be?

And yet, I also knew that Patrick was going to die if I let up. I hadn't found any other ways to harm the dervishes, and so, I had to focus on what I could do.

Which is precisely what I did, over and over until it started to tremble with instability. I kept going, ripping bigger chunks away with every passing instant, and the intensity of the shuddering continued to mount. Soon enough, its undulations grew wild and unpredictable as it fell from Patrick's shield, only to writhe on the ground.

Seeing weakness, I redoubled my efforts.

Vaguely, I recognized the sharp pain jabbing into my mind. I was also aware that the flow of blood from my nostrils hadn't stopped. Indeed, it had been joined by a similar flow from my ears. Bloody red tears fell down my cheeks, but I ignored it all.

Only about ten seconds passed, but in that time, I ripped millions of nanites away. In the end, I was tearing them free without conscious thought, and even then, it felt like hours had passed. Finally, the last stubborn bit came away, and the dervish died.

If it was ever really alive in the first place.

I fell forward onto my hands and knees, but a swirl of Mist behind me grabbed my attention before I could give in to the consequences of my exertion. I whipped around—awkwardly—and saw the shards of destroyed crystal coalesce into a single prism that took the shape of the holes I'd seen around the exit.

It clattered to the floor.

And I finally collapsed onto my face. Unfortunately, I didn't black out, though. That would've been too easy. Instead, I was forced to endure a sharp, stabbing sensation in my brain that pushed right up to the edge of unconsciousness but kept me from plunging into that relieving abyss.

Vaguely, I was aware of Patrick kneeling beside me, but I couldn't pay him any mind. Instead, I focused on the only thing my addled mind could latch on to. At some point during the fight, I'd received a notification:

Abitlity: Misthack has evolved into Mist Control. Retains all previous characteristics, while gaining the ability to manipulate Mist directly, though with great difficulty. Continued use may result in further evolution.

I felt something jab into my shoulder, and I harnessed just enough control over my body to jerk to the side. However, Patrick's surprisingly strong grip kept me from moving too far, and I heard him say, "Easy, Mira. Just give it a minute. It's only a med-hypo."

"It's dead, right?" I muttered, my voice hoarse. Was that from all the screaming? Or was it something else?

"If it was ever alive, it's not anymore," he stated. "Now relax. I'll keep a lookout for any others."

I wanted to point out that that would do little good; he'd already proved that he was incapable of dealing with the things, after all. However, I couldn't muster the strength to do much more than lift my head.

I made a habit of pushing my limits. That was the part of training I truly enjoyed—seeing just how far I could go before my body—or mind, as it were—failed me. But even with all that experience, I'd never felt as exhausted as I felt at that moment. It wasn't just physical fatigue, though that was part of it. It was like I'd reached all my limits—body, mind, and Mist—all at once, and the result was that I felt as weak as at any time since my Awakening.

I considered using a Mist booster, but when I took stock of my stores, I realized that I didn't really need it. What I had done—whatever that was—hadn't taken an ounce of my personal Mist.

Which made no sense.

Tentatively, I turned my attention to the senses I'd gained upon becoming a {Mist Warden}, and I was surprised to find that they were sharper than ever before. More, I was aware of each individual nanite, and without even really focusing.

Before I even thought about it, I reached out, grabbing a single nanite from the ambient Mist and pulling it to me. I sensed that I could have gotten many more, but I wanted to take it easy. Even moving that single nanite was difficult, though not nearly as straining as what I had experienced while I was dismantling the dervish.

Perhaps my repercussions had been magnified by my insistence on forcing Misthack to do something it was ill-suited to do. Maybe that was why it had evolved. Not because I'd met some sort of prerequisites but, rather, because I'd forced it to do so.

I shook my head—which I regretted because it caused a sharp uptick in the pain—then let out a groan.

"Are you okay?" asked Patrick.

"No. Not really. Maybe? I don't know," I said. Then, as I forced myself upright and shifted to lean against the crystalline wall of the palace hall, I explained what had happened. Patrick asked plenty of questions, most of which focused on my health, and I answered them as best I could. But I didn't know enough to provide more than a few assurances that I was fine.

Probably.

I really couldn't get more specific than that because, according to the health readout on my HUD, there was nothing wrong with me. Still, I wasn't going to trust that over the way I felt.

Over the next couple of hours, I slowly began to recover. At first, the piercing pain simply faded into a pounding headache, which in turn became little more than a dull ache behind my eyes. Eventually, it dissipated altogether. Then, the fatigue went the same way, eventually fading into nothing. Soon enough, that neutrality turned the corner into vigor, and thus, I went back to normal.

It took longer than expected, especially considering that with my high attributes and the advanced state of my Regeneration, I could heal from all but the most serious injuries in a few hours. So, the fact that a headache took most of a day was a testament to how much damage I'd done to myself.

But it wasn't all for naught. I'd evolved an ability, and for the first time, I had done so without it being attached to my class. That had to count for something, and what's more, now that I could more easily manipulate Mist, I felt that dismantling the dervishes would be far less dangerous. Perhaps I could even finish them off before they overloaded Patrick's trap.

"I think I'm feeling alright," I said.

Patrick hadn't moved from where he'd station himself at the head of the corridor. There, he'd remained, his Mist shield deployed and ready to defend me with everything he had.

"Are you sure?" he asked, finally turning to face me. He was still in his armor, though I could tell from its sluggish movements that he was on the verge of using his entire store of Mist.

"I am," I said, summoning a bottle of water and a rag from my arsenal implant. Then, I started cleaning myself up, wiping the blood from my face. It wasn't perfect—I knew I'd missed some—but I'd take a shower when we got back to *The Leviathan*. Until then, I just had to accept that I was going to remain a bit bloody.

"What are we going to do?" he asked, finally opening the suit's cockpit. The chest plate of the armor lifted, revealing a haggard-looking Patrick. "Those things probably require some sort of special equipment to kill. And we don't have it. If we were back in *The Leviathan* with all my equipment and parts, I might be able to cobble something together. But I emptied all but the essentials out of my storage so we'd have enough room for however many Rift Shards we can find. And I don't—"

"It's fine, Pick. The strategy worked."

"It most certainly did not, Mira."

"No, it did. I know that because the monster's dead, and we're still alive. I even evolved a skill. So, that's a win-win. Or maybe a win-win-win. Yeah, that sounds about right."

"Mira, you almost died."

"Not the first time," I pointed out. "Probably not the last, either. Anyway, Mist manipulation is a lot easier now that I have Mist Control. I think I could repeat what I just did without even bleeding from my eyes now."

"That's a terrible gauge of success."

I shrugged. "It'll be fine. Once you get topped off on Mist, let's get the trap set back up, and we'll kill the rest of these little bastards, huh?" I said, pushing myself to my feet. It was a mistake, and I promptly stumbled. I caught myself on the wall, but I couldn't deny that my legs were still a little wobbly. So, I said, "Maybe we'll give it a few more hours, though. I need to get my feet back under me."

A WARM WELCOME

My world is civilized. Or so everyone claims. And yet, I've seen children starve. I've seen innocent people dying for no other crime than being too poor to evacuate before a natural disaster. Worse yet, I've seen my government turn a blind eye as other worlds are stripped of every natural resource then left to die a slow, ignoble death. In the core, that's what civilization means, and I want no part of it.

—Alistaris Kargat

It was nearly three days later when we finally killed the last dervish, and by that point, we had perfected the task. It had been a long, hard road, though, and I would have been more than content to never see another one again. At first, the process had been very similar to my first use of Mist Control; it was a little less taxing on my body and mind, but the building blocks of the method were unchanged. However, after the third dervish, I started to get a handle on the new ability, and by the eighth, I'd learned to wield it with alacrity and relative ease.

Using Mist Control was still fatiguing, but after I'd finished dismantling the dervishes, I wasn't completely exhausted. So, I counted that as a win, and over the final four fights, I managed to improve even more until, at last, I was able to tear the cloud of Mist apart without issue.

"Still sucks," I muttered, letting my shoulders sag as Patrick retrieved the large crystal that had formed after the latest dervish had died. "Maybe I can upgrade it again and make things even easier."

I certainly hoped so. Acclimating to using my other abilities hadn't been nearly as difficult, but I suspected that that was because they had to function with the framework of the system. Mist Control seemed to exist outside of that—at least to some extent—and as such, it was propped up by artificial scaffolding.

In short, using my other abilities was like riding a bicycle with training wheels, while with Mist Control, those aids had been removed. Without them, I was forced to rely only on my own mind and willpower to see me through.

Patrick sent the crystal into his storage space and said, "That's the last one. Do you want to rest before we open the door?"

I nodded. The way forward was clear, but neither of us had any idea what awaited farther into the Rift. For all we knew, we'd have to fight a bunch of those dervishes all at once. I hoped not because, if that was the case, there was every chance that we'd both die. I could dismantle them, but even with all the strides I'd made, it still took quite some time and an incredible degree of focus to accomplish that feat. As such, combating more than one at a time—especially without Patrick's traps—would be far more than either of us could take.

But we didn't have much choice in the matter. I'd explored the entire palace—or at least the area on our side of the door—and I'd found nothing but a bunch of dead ends. The moment we'd stepped inside, our options for getting back to the real world had narrowed down to one.

There was no way out but through.

After that, Patrick and I gathered his anchors, then headed through the palace. Walking those halls without the benefit of Stealth was strange, and it left me feeling completely exposed. However, there were no enemies left alive within the palace, so that was almost assuredly my imagination at work. Even so, it wasn't pleasant, and I was relieved when we finally reached the door, where we both settled down to rest.

It was easy to forget that our strategy to defeat the dervishes was only possible because of Patrick's contributions with the traps, and as such, he was at least as drained as I felt. Once we reached our destination, he sagged against the wall and slid down to the floor, where he sat with his shoulders slumped. For my part, I did much the same, though I endeavored to put on a slightly better front. That didn't go unnoticed, and Patrick said, "I can't believe you're not passing out right now. After that first one, I thought we'd be here for a month."

"It's getting easier," I admitted.

"What's it like?" he asked.

"I don't know. It's hard to explain. I mean, we know that Mist is everywhere, right? Well, if I try hard enough, I can see it. And I can manipulate each individual nanite. It's harder with stuff like your shield, but I think I could still tear it apart if you gave me enough time," I explained. "I can even see the collection of nanites that make up your Nexus Implant."

"What do you mean?"

"That's what they're made of. Nexus Implants, I mean. They're just Mist. I think skills are the same way. Everything is," I said. "I mean, not outside. Mostly. The Mist is in everything. From rocks to you and me. It's not all there is, but it's everywhere."

All it took was a little focus, and I could see—or maybe feel; things got a bit blurry on that front—just how much the little nanites had suffused the entire world. Perhaps they would be less ubiquitous outside of a Rift, but I suspected that wouldn't be the case. I think that was based on what I'd felt since my class had evolved. Before Misthack had become Mist Control, it had only presented in the form of my ability to see auras, but I think that, in the back of my mind, I'd felt the underlying layer of nanites even then.

Now, I had to consciously block that awareness.

Fortunately, with my Mind attribute being what it was, I had little trouble doing just that. Still, it was a little overwhelming, knowing what was hovering below the surface. If the Mist had been hostile, everyone on Earth—and maybe in the universe—would be dead.

"That sounds terrifying," Patrick said, clearly coming to a similar conclusion.

"Yeah. But there's nothing either of us can do about it," I responded, massaging my forehead. Ever since we'd begun our fight against that first dervish, I'd been dealing with a persistent headache. Not surprising, given the sheer volume of sensory input I'd had to deal with. If my use of Observation hadn't already prepared me for dealing with that kind of thing, I might've collapsed into seizures. As it happened, I just felt like my brain was overheating. Not pleasant, but not fatal, either. "Freddie told me before that they manipulate the Mist directly. I think this is similar to that."

"So, you're a Templar now?" he asked. I'd already told him all about my various interactions with Earth's resident mystics, and he'd been right there with me when Zachariah and Isla had saved me from a horde of irradiated wildlings.

I shrugged. "Not really. Last time I saw him, he intimated that as we progress, the gap between mystics and people with Nexus Implants closes," I stated. "And with my Tier 7 implant, it was always going to be sooner rather than later. I think I might've just crossed a threshold or something."

"Think about when you get your new skills and start training again," he said. "Your attributes are going to shoot up."

I nodded in agreement. It was a well-known fact that a person's progress was more than just a limit to their potential. It was that, but I'd learned firsthand that, with higher potential, it was easier to raise attributes. The bigger the gap between a person's actual attributes and their potential, the more easily they could increase their attributes.

In my case, once I filled all my skill slots, my potential was going to shoot through the roof. And as such, my attributes—all of which were in the mid-two-hundred range—would respond better to training, increasing at a prodigious rate so long as I put in the work. That would slow down as I drew closer to my potential, but not before I grew a lot more powerful. It was one of the reasons I was so eager to fill my skill slots, because at present, I was all but maxed out. And I missed seeing the results of my training reflected on my status.

In fact, I hadn't bothered looking at my status in almost a month, and that wasn't going to change until I went up to the Bazaar and bought some new skills. That thought brought me back to our current predicament, and once again, I found myself hoping that we would make enough credits in our current Rift that we could afford whatever we needed.

For the next few hours, Patrick and I rested while I daydreamed about all the things I was going to buy. The skills, I was unsure of—that was up to what Ana had available—but I knew I needed a couple of weapons, too. First on my list was a replacement for the Dragon, but I wanted to upgrade everything else, as well. The only weapon I felt confident wasn't going anywhere was my nano-bladed sword, which was just as useful as it had always been.

For Patrick, I hoped we could obtain some high-quality parts so he could continue to upgrade his cybernetics. If I'd had my way, we would have replaced them altogether, but he insisted that he would get more out of slowly tinkering with the ones he already had. And considering that he was the expert, I had no basis on which to disagree.

In any case, I knew he needed parts to implement all his plans, so I figured that would be the best use of whatever credits we spent on him. Plus, he needed some new weapons to integrate into his armor, and the Dragon's rebuild was still ongoing. At present, it could only function at a fraction of the power it had once displayed, and I knew that, if we were going to meet the challenges ahead of us, we'd need to do a lot better than that.

And if we had anything left over, I intended to look into upgrading *The Leviathan*'s weapons systems. Right now, they were adequate for earthbound threats, but once the Integration began and the aliens were freed to descend upon the planet, the threshold for adequacy would shift out of reach.

I sighed.

"What?" asked Patrick, who'd begun to perk up a little. He was still low on Mist, but he was well on his way to recovering the full extent of his power.

I shook my head, saying, "I don't know. There's just a lot to do. It feels a little overwhelming. Like, we're just two people. How the hell are we supposed to fight a whole army of aliens?"

"It's probably multiple armies."

"That doesn't make it any better, Pick. It feels hopeless."

"Tell that to the Pacificians."

I tilted my head back and closed my eyes. "That wasn't on purpose," I breathed. And it hadn't been. I'd killed millions, and I hadn't even meant to.

"That's my point, though. If you can do that by accident—and I'm not even going to mention the moon thing—think about what you can do if you really set your mind to it," he said. "I mean, do you know how insane it is that you've been picking these whirly crystal things apart with your mind? Extrapolate that for, like, two seconds. Think about where that's going. One day, you might be able to tear those aliens to pieces without lifting a gun."

I knew I was a long way off from that—if something like what he described was even possible—but still, I appreciated that he'd say it. I didn't often need him to cheer me up, but he was always there to say the perfect thing, anyway.

For the next couple of hours, neither of us really spoke. Instead, we both focused the whole of our attention on our individual recovery. For my part, that meant that I just sat there, eyes closed, while I tried to ignore my pounding headache. And as the hours passed, the pain eased until, at last, it dissipated altogether. Even so, it took another hour or two before Patrick had entirely recovered.

Once he did, we took a while to ensure that we were as prepared as possible for what we both hoped was the final phase of the Rift. For me, that meant reloading my weapons and readying my various grenades. For Patrick, preparation took the form of doing various checks on his armor as well as making certain that its built-in weapons were functioning properly. Apparently, he'd tied the Dragon's magazine to his own storage space, so he had tens of thousands of rounds at his disposal. He wouldn't be able to fire them all in one burst—the barrel would overheat if he tried—but he could definitely bury something under a hail of gunfire.

Finally, we were both ready, and after a couple of last checks, I started sliding the crystals into the slots surrounding the door. They all fit perfectly, telling me that they'd always been meant as keys, and when I slid the twelfth into place, the powerful Mist shield flickered, then faded. A moment later, the crystalline door dematerialized, exposing the chamber behind.

I tried to get a good look at what was inside, but it was entirely dark. I used Observation, but it did no good. I could see nothing.

"Night vision isn't working," Patrick said from within his armor.

"You have night vision? Seriously?"

"We don't all have fancy abilities," he replied.

"Fair enough."

"So? You want to go first? Or should I?" he asked.

"You're the one with the big, fancy shield and armor," I pointed out.

"Counterpoint," he said. "You're basically indestructible. And way faster. And you're practically invisible when you want to be."

"I don't think that'll work," I argued. "But whatever, you big baby. I'll go first."

"I'm not saying I won't go first. I'm just saying—"

I didn't wait for him to finish the thought. Instead, I embraced Stealth, then stepped through the door. The moment I did, I felt my ability stripped away, completely exposing me. The next thing I saw was that the darkness had faded, showing me a giant circular room full of crystal statues.

And in the center of the room, a gargantuan creature stood. On the surface, it took the shape of some sort of avian, with definite birdlike wings. However, it differed from a bird in a few key ways. First was the long serpentine neck and reptilian head that resembled that of a snake. Second, it was equipped with sturdy, muscular legs tipped with huge talons. And finally, it was made almost entirely of white crystal.

In the center of its chest pulsed a purple light, but it had yet to move an inch.

"Is it clear? I lost sight of you when you stepped through the door?" asked Patrick.

"It's fine," I said, inspecting the closest crystal sculpture. It looked like a miniature version of the golems we'd defeated in the forest. "Just a bunch of statues."

I looked back to see nothing but a wall, but soon enough, Patrick simply appeared beside me. Clearly, it was a similar situation to what had happened when we had entered the palace. Which left me more than a little nervous, considering the difficulty we'd had with the dervishes.

I turned back to study the statues, and I saw the same Mist I always did.

"Odds these things are going to come alive after we trip some alarm or whatever?" I asked.

"Uh . . . Pretty good? I don't know."

I continued to study the chamber, but the only additional feature that jumped out at me was another wide hall on the other side of the room. Beyond that, my first impressions seemed fairly accurate.

"So, what are we going to do?" he asked.

"Stealth won't work," I said. Indeed, I'd tried to reapply the ability the moment I'd entered the room, but it hadn't worked. Unsurprising, considering how easily it had been stripped away, but it was still more than a little disappointing. "So, I don't think we can use the same strategy we've used so far."

"Fair enough."

Then, in his armor, he stepped forward.

I don't know if it was the sudden movement, or if he'd passed some ephemeral threshold. But I do know that it was a big mistake because the weird crystalline bird dragon at the center of the room suddenly moved. The motion was confined to its serpentine head, but when it locked its eyes on Patrick's huge white-and-gold form, the message was clear.

It had seen us.

The purple light in its chest flickered. Then, without preamble, the thing arched its neck, opened its mouth, and spat a column of purple fire that would have engulfed us if I hadn't been warned by that tiny intensification of purple light in its chest.

Instead, that small warning was all I'd needed to erupt into motion, tackling Patrick and his suit of armor to the ground. We skidded across the floor, crashing through a pair of statues before coming to rest almost twenty feet away.

I glanced back to see a hellscape of melted crystal and dancing Mist.

"Do not move," I muttered through Secure Connection as I glanced back at the creature in the center of the room. It had settled back down, as if it thought that a single burst would be enough to kill us.

"What the hell just happened?" asked Patrick.

"This is really going to suck is what happened," I said. "Now, when I get off you, you're going to have to push that armor to its limit and get out of the way. Got it?"

"What are you going to do?"

"I'm going to kill a crystal dragon-bird thing."

CHAPTER THIRTEEN

AMBIGUITY

Challenging Rifts is a fool's errand. Even with proper precautions, it is potentially lethal. And yet, across the universe, there are droves of idiots willing to risk their lives for power, glory, and of course, monetary gain. The universe depends on these ill-fated and often desperate adventurers. Without them, the universal economy would collapse. Perhaps that would be a good thing.

—Alistaris Kargat

As I hefted my sniper rifle, I flooded Vanish with Mist, disappearing entirely. The moment the ability took hold, I embraced Stealth, then cycled through my abilities. However, the second that Vanish's effect dissipated, my Stealth fell away. I never even had time to shoot before I was once again visible.

I scanned the area to see if I could figure out what had canceled my ability, but my first glance yielded no results. It wasn't until I looked a little closer that I saw a subtle glow coming from the multitude of statues.

"Shit," I muttered, freezing in place as I prayed that the crystal dragon—that was the only way I could really describe it—wouldn't respond to my movement. Fortunately, I hadn't crossed whatever threshold existed for a response, and it remained completely inert. I knew that wouldn't last, though.

"What?" asked Patrick through Secure Connection.

"The statues. That's what keeps canceling my Stealth."

"Can you pick them apart like you did with the dervishes?"

"No," I answered. "I mean, yes. But it would take too long. Plus, I could only get the ones in our immediate surroundings before I had to move into the crystal dragon's range."

"It's more like a wyvern," Patrick said. "Because its arms are part of the wing structure, and—"

"Not important, Pick."

"Right. Sure. So—what are we going to do?" he asked.

I racked my brain. If it was just me, I would've just blanketed the whole area in powerful explosives—either planted or shot from my BMAP—but with Patrick there, I was hesitant to do so. He didn't have the benefit of Blast Shield, which, to a degree, protected me from the power of my own explosions. So, anything I did that would destroy the statues or the crystal wyvern—I hated that I couldn't think of it any other way after he'd pointed it out—would almost assuredly put Patrick in mortal danger.

So, it looked like I wouldn't be able to use Stealth.

"Okay," I said. "How sturdy is that armor? Do you think it can stand up to that purple fire?"

"So long as my shield stays active," he answered. "Won't last long under that kind of barrage, though. Maybe twenty seconds if what we saw a minute ago is the best it can do. Why? What are you thinking?"

As usual, I felt that simple was probably better. If we'd had time to plan, and all my abilities were available, perhaps I could've thought of something better. However, I felt like the moment we crossed into the crystal wyvern's range, all hell was going to break loose. And with Patrick there, my options were even more limited.

No—a straight assault was probably the best-case scenario. I just needed a little distraction.

So, I told Patrick what I wanted. For his part, he took to the plan with gusto, largely because it hinged so thoroughly on the operation of his armor. For better or worse, he'd always felt like he was holding me back. It wasn't true. He served a vital role in our relationship, both tactically and socially. However, no matter how many times I made that clear, a bit of an inferiority had persisted.

But now, he was needed, and he couldn't contain his excitement at that turn of events. Even if, by all rights, he should have been terrified of the literal monster whose attention he was supposed to get.

I knew I was, but not for myself. Rather, I was afraid for him.

And yet, I had no real choice in the matter. Our backs were to the wall, and as far as I could tell, there was no way to completely shield him from the dangers of combat. So, once Patrick was ready, I kicked off the ground and raced forward. Meanwhile, he unfolded the Dragon from his back and opened fire.

The wyvern reacted immediately, and it turned its purple flames in his direction. At the same time, he pelted it with the Dragon's weakened issue; in my hands, it was a weapon capable of tearing down buildings. In his, it was the antipersonnel weapon it was always meant to be.

Unfortunately, the wyvern was made of seemingly indestructible crystal, and so, even though the rounds hammered home, the result was only a few chips in its crystalline body. At the same time, though, it bathed Patrick in purple fire, and I knew the clock had begun to tick. Soon enough, his Mist would be exhausted, and then, there would be nothing to protect him from being cooked inside his armor.

So, before that could happen, I raced across the chamber, weaving between the scattered golem-shaped statues. Each one reacted to my passing, flashing with purple light, but before that action could bear fruit, I was already gone.

Never before had I moved so quickly, and I propelled myself forward with every point of my exaggerated constitution. At a dead sprint, each step covered almost ten feet, and before a few seconds had passed, I was leaping into the air, my nano-bladed sword held high in a striking position.

It fell before the wyvern could react, and the blade bit deeply into the thing's wing. I let my momentum take me past the monster in a tumbling roll that ended a few feet later.

And that's when things started to go wrong.

The moment I gathered my feet under me, I felt a tide of Mist coming my way. Without thinking, I embraced Teleport and appeared twenty feet to my right. But it wasn't enough to allow me to avoid the wave of purple fire that swept over that side of the chamber. I screamed as it washed over me, then instinctively lashed out with Mist Control.

Years of pitting myself against increasingly difficult puzzles during my training paid off, and I tore through the building blocks of that fire—nanites that weren't so different from the clouds of Mist that comprised the dervishes—with a blistering pace. It wasn't enough to completely protect me, though. I felt my skin blistering under the heat even as I pushed myself to the limit. But it could have been much, much worse, and by the time the fire faded, I was still alive and on my feet.

And I was pissed off.

With a roar, I launched myself at the wyvern, hacking at it with my nano-bladed sword. I got in six attacks before it swept its wing in my direction and sent me stumbling backward. I turned that stumble into a roll, and when I found my feet, I leaped high into the air and summoned my R-14.

Shooting an automatic rifle with one hand is an ill-advised tactic. I knew that. However, with my Constitution as well as the size and relative proximity of the enemy, I felt I could handle it. So, with my assault rifle in one hand and my sword in the other, I embraced Explosive Shot before emptying my magazine into the crystalline wyvern.

It took the shots well, but with my modifiers as well as Explosive Shot, I could put an incredible amount of force behind each round. Crystal splinters filled the air as I dug deep craters into the monster's body. However, by the time I had emptied the entire magazine, I realized that the damage was only cosmetic.

Activating Instant Reload, I finally hit the ground only a few feet in front of the monster. I hacked at its legs, hoping to repeat the tactic I'd used to take down the first golem. Via blade and bullet, I dug a deep groove into its knee, but when I placed an explosive, I got yet another surprise when the thing's entire body burst into purple flames, destroying the charge with a wave of burning Mist.

But more urgently, whether it was an ability or a signal, that pulse of flame awakened the golems. Light burst forth from their chests as they surged into motion, racing in my direction. I leaped, kicking off the wyvern's crystalline claw and landing atop its head. There, I continued to hack at its glassy flesh.

Meanwhile, Patrick shouted something incoherent before turning the Dragon on the swarm of golems. He was incapable of hurting the wyvern, but the same couldn't be said for its minions. Even the weakened Dragon was more than a match for those smaller golems, and in only seconds, he cut a swath of golems down.

That was enough to get their attention, and my heart leaped into my throat as they lumbered toward him. But that was all the attention I could spare because the wyvern hadn't spent those few seconds idle. I twisted, narrowly avoiding a giant spike of crystal that erupted from its shoulder, then leaped aside as another came from the side of its head. Even as I dodged, those spikes retracted before being replaced by more.

I danced, putting every point of my enhanced Mind and Constitution to the test as I twisted and turned in an effort to avoid being impaled. At the same time, I continued my attacks, targeting the same spot as often as I could.

I was just starting to get the hang of it when the monster spread its wings and leaped into the air. Before I knew what was going on, we were airborne, and I was forced to dismiss my rifle as I hung on for dear life. But the spikes had never stopped their assault, and in that brief second of surprise, I was pierced through by three spear-like protrusions.

I screamed in mingled pain and frustration as I redoubled my focus.

At the same time, I tossed out grenades—not my best, but good enough—peppering the golems with explosions. The wyvern beat its wings, gaining altitude until it slammed its back against the ceiling.

Unfortunately, I was caught between a wyvern and a hard place, and in addition to the burns and other wounds I'd sustained, I felt bones crack with the impact. Still, I held on for dear life, but when it pulled away, my sword fell from my broken hand. I watched as it clattered to the ground.

Far below, Patrick continued to defend against the horde of golems, filling the air with shattered shards of crystal. Still, they persisted, and I knew he'd run out of ammunition well before he destroyed them all.

I needed to do something.

And even as I continued to cling to the monster's back, I knew that my options were limited. So, I once again reached out with Mist Control, hoping to pick the creature apart in the same way I'd torn the dervishes to pieces.

That was an absolute mistake, as I discovered a moment later when my interrupted attention almost got me thrown free. As powerful as Mist Control was, it required unmitigated focus. As such, it couldn't be the solution to all my problems. So, I abandoned that line of attack and committed to a more familiar path.

Activating Combination Punch, I grabbed hold of one of the wyvern's ridges, then reared back with the Hand of God. Harnessing every ounce of strength I could bring to bear, I smashed the cybernetic hand into the nigh-invulnerable crystalline surface of the wyvern's head.

The first attack did almost nothing. But due to the nature of Combination Punch, the second did much more damage. And the third was even more impactful. By the fourth, I'd started to make a dent. Normally, that was where the string of punches would end, but my influx of levels as well as my increased pool of Mist meant that I could use two more attacks.

The fifth punch, which was twice as powerful as the fourth, tore a huge crater into the wyvern. For the first time, it screeched in pain, and it tucked its wings close to its body, prompting a dive. Hanging on for dear life, I hit it again, extending the string of punches to the maximum.

At my best, I could hit damned hard. I'd tested it a few times, and I could put almost six thousand pounds per square inch worth of force behind each punch. And given that each attack in the string associated with Combination Punch doubled the power of the previous blow, that sixth attack came with almost two hundred thousand pounds of pure impact. Add to that the previous punches, which had already undermined the integrity of the crystalline wyvern's glassy flesh, and that final attack very nearly tore its head from its shoulders.

I'm not sure what the thing's plan for the dive had been, but my punch had torn its attention to pieces, and as a result, we slammed into the ground with the force of a falling meteor. A dozen golems shattered at the point of impact, and one of the wyvern's wings broke free. For my part, I leaped from my position and used Teleport to arrest some of my momentum before hitting the ground in a roll that highlighted just how much I'd already been injured.

But I didn't have time to wallow in my pain. So, I summoned my R-14 and pushed myself to my feet just in time to see Patrick—in all his armored glory—laying waste to the remaining golems. He'd stowed the Dragon away—probably because he'd used all his ammunition—and had replaced it with the long blade extending from his arm.

On his other arm was a smaller, mobile version of his Mist shield.

I'd seen Patrick fight often enough to know that he could handle himself. However, still, I was more than a little surprised with the level of technique and power he brought to bear. He didn't move quickly, but his every motion screamed efficiency as he slammed golems to the side with his shield or shattered them to pieces with his enormous sword.

It was absolutely glorious.

And I admit, I had trouble focusing on anything else for a few seconds. But then, the moment passed, and I remembered that, despite his combat prowess, he needed my help. So, taking the R-14 in hand, I started firing.

One three-round burst after another, I tore through the ambulatory statues. At first, I concentrated on their legs, removing their ability to walk. However, after a few moments, I realized that they were far weaker than expected. So, I adjusted my aim and started firing on their torsos or heads, killing one with each burst of fire.

Gradually, Patrick and I whittled them down until, finally, the last one fell.

Only then did I let myself feel the full weight of my injuries.

The silhouette on my HUD glowed almost entirely red, with a few spots of orange, telling me just how extensive my wounds were. So, without further hesitation, I yanked a med-hypo from my arsenal implant and jabbed it into my hip.

Immediately, the pain I hadn't let myself acknowledge began to fade. But I knew I wasn't out of the woods. Not yet.

Vaguely, I was aware of Patrick calling my name, but I couldn't focus on that. Instead, now that the adrenaline of battle had begun to fade, I needed every ounce of my attention on the task at hand. So, with some degree of difficulty, I dragged another item from my arsenal implant.

I jabbed the needle for the Mist booster into my hip about an inch below where I'd injected the med-hypo. Then, as Mist flooded my body, I focused on Mist Control.

When [Cybernetic Mastery] had first evolved into [Mist-Infused Body], I'd been disappointed by the reduction in potential cybernetic slots. However, after looking at the skill's description, that disappointment reversed course into elation:

[Mist-Infused Body]—Allows for increased performance from up to five (5) cybernetics. In addition, the Mist-Infused Body can utilize Mist to repair damage to organic tissue. Frequency of use limited by Mist attribute. Current: Once per seventy-one (71) hours (Earth or Planet 2341-M).

The ability to regenerate via Mist hadn't activated like all my other abilities. Instead, it had required me to use my {Mist Warden} senses to prompt activation. However, now that Misthack had evolved into Mist Control, I had far more influence over the process. I used it to guide the Mist into the worst of my injuries, then let [Mist-Infused Body] take over from there.

I screamed as the nanites jolted my body back to some semblance of health. Old, burned skin flaked off, then regrew in the space of seconds while my broken bones wrenched back into place and mended. A hundred other, smaller injuries healed in the space of moments, and by the time Patrick reached my side, I'd been almost entirely rebuilt.

I looked up at his armored form and said, "That was incredibly unpleasant."

"You're bald."

"Huh?" I muttered, reaching up to feel my head.

"Like, no more hair."

"Oh God . . ."

"I think it's sexy," he said in his semirobotic voice. "In a weird, alien sort of way."

"Ugh."

I didn't really have room to complain. After what I'd just been through, I probably should have been dead. Or at least horribly scarred. Once again, I'd been bailed out by strange new abilities.

And I didn't like it.

I was used to the world making sense. I understood how all my skills and abilities worked. It was right there in my interface. But there was so much more to Mist Control. And the regeneration associated with [Mist-Infused Body] wasn't even listed as an ability. Was that how mystics like the Templars did things? If so, I wondered how they ever managed to progress.

"Are you okay?" asked Patrick.

I shook my head. "I don't know. Just thinking about how much I took clarity for granted." I pushed myself to my feet, then said, "So, you think that was the last monster?"

He pointed with his armored finger, and I followed the gesture until I saw a huge crate in the center of the room. It was at least the size of a train car, and the moment I laid eyes—or more accurately, my {Mist Warden} senses—I knew it was full of Rift Shards.

"I think that answers that," Patrick said.

"Can you fit it all?" I asked.

He answered, "I don't know, but I'm damn sure going to try."

And with that, we went to collect our hard-won loot.

CHAPTER FOURTEEN

BACK INTO THE BAZAAR

I don't know what's happening, but it feels important. Every time I turn around, Mira does something unbelievable, and I feel like she's becoming less human with each passing day. I'm trying to keep up, but no matter what I do, she just keeps getting further ahead.

—Patrick Ward

Exiting the Rift was anticlimactic, especially after the battles we'd endured in the emerald forest and the palace. However, when we did step back into the real world, both Patrick's and my storage spaces were absolutely packed full of Rift Shards. In addition, we each carried large, full packs on our backs, and Patrick carried an enormous crate he'd filled with those valuable crystals.

In short, we'd looted more Rift Shards than either of us had collectively seen before. Suddenly, we had more wealth than we could accurately calculate. In short, the operation had been an unmitigated success, which meant that we had a good chance of accomplishing our goals. More importantly, it meant that we wouldn't be forced to run multiple Rifts just to rearm or resupply.

Not anytime soon, at least.

I was well aware of our expenses, though. Just keeping *The Leviathan* in the air was expensive enough, and that wasn't even considering the cost of ammunition and other supplies. No—for the short term, we were fine, but that wouldn't necessarily be the case in a few months. So, there was every chance that we'd be forced to run another Rift before the dawn of the Integration.

Which was a little more than a year away.

In that time, Patrick and I—as well as anyone else willing—would have to ready ourselves for war. Because that was what was coming. And I knew it would be a bloody one, too. The aliens weren't likely to give up without a sig-nificant fight, so I had to prepare myself for a long, violent conflict that could very well leave Earth in ruins.

And yet, that was better than the alternative.

Those thoughts accompanied me as Patrick and I stepped through the Rift aperture and back into the Crutacaan stronghold. Unfortunately, not even that went as planned, and I quickly found myself swept away in a strong current that pulled me through the small settlement. My mind swirled as I rocketed past submerged buildings, and more by instinct than as a result of conscious thought, I reached out and grabbed hold of the corner of a structure. The fin-gers of the Hand of God dug into the plasti-steel surface, barely arresting my momentum before I was swept out to sea.

Even as the current tugged against me, I retrieved the respirator from my arsenal implant and slapped it over my face. Once my own oxygen supply was assured, I took a moment to search for Patrick.

And I found him standing just beside the Rift aperture, his white-and-gold armor practically glowing in the scant light. He'd thrust his arm blade deep into the seabed, anchoring him in place. However, I suspected he'd only managed to do that much because he was weighed down by the sturdy armor.

"What the hell?" I muttered through Secure Connection. "How heavy is that thing?"

"A few thousand pounds," he answered. "Are you okay?"

"I'm fine. Just took me by surprise is all," I said. "What happened?"

"The shield keeping the water out probably ran out of juice," he answered. "I bet it was a resource hog."

That made sense. Running a Mist shield—especially one powerful enough to keep out millions of gallons of water—was expensive, and since we'd killed all the Crutacaans, there was no one to recharge it. Either way, it didn't really mat-ter; we were done with the settlement, so there was nothing keeping us around.

"May as well get out of here, then. Watch out for sea monsters. I'll meet you back at the cliffs," I said. I wanted to stick around, but the current was far too strong. With that reality hanging over me, I let go of the building and kicked my way to the surface. As I did so, I had to fight against the riptide that wanted nothing more than to pull me out to sea, but with my attributes, I managed it well enough. Fortunately, the current weakened as I got closer to the sur-face, and after I finally broke through the waves, I had little trouble swimming toward shore.

Still, by the time I reached the cliffs, I was already tired of being in the water. So, I wasted no time before latching on and climbing to dry land. Once I reached the top of the cliff, I flipped over and basked in the weak sunlight of an overcast day. That was how, almost twenty minutes later, Patrick found me.

I felt him before I even opened my eyes—Mist Control continued to grow stronger with every passing moment, it seemed—and when he drew closer, I asked, "Have a nice little swim? Or was it a stroll along the seabed?" I opened one eye to see him standing over me in his dripping armor. "You can't swim in that thing, can you?"

"Nope. Thanks for waiting up."

"You didn't expect me to swim along beside you, did you? You've proved you can handle yourself just fine. You don't need me to be your bodyguard."

That much was true. While the armor was too big and bulky to be completely without weaknesses, it—and by extension, Patrick—had proved powerful enough that I didn't think I needed to worry about his safety quite as much. Still, I knew I'd never completely leave that anxiety behind.

Thankfully, he didn't argue, and soon enough, we were on our way back to *The Leviathan*. When we reached the ship, I swept it for tracking devices—my experiences with Alistaris had shown me that people could bypass whatever security measures we had in place—and after finding none, we finally let ourselves relax.

Patrick left his armor in the cargo bay, where he clearly intended to work on it sometime in the near future, while I took a long, hot shower. It was telling that Patrick didn't even consider joining me. We were both too exhausted for that kind of thing, and as soon as I was clean and comfortable, I headed straight to bed. Just before I fell asleep, he joined me.

The next couple of days were spent in recovery. For my part, the regeneration associated with [Mist-Infused Body] had healed me completely, but it had done nothing to allay the pervasive lethargy that had built up over the course of delving the Rift. Some of it was physical, but the bulk of that exhaustion was the result of stress and mental fatigue. Because of that, we both took our time ensuring that we were in the best possible condition before moving on.

Even so, a few days later found us flying to the least contentious town that had a Bazaar access point. Curiously, it wasn't a particularly large settlement. During a previous visit, Patrick and I had discovered that only around fifty thousand people lived in Montreal. Apparently, it had once been much larger, but a catastrophe had struck a few decades after the onset of the Mist, killing the bulk of the residents. Since then, they'd rebuilt, but they'd yet to regain their former glory.

"Did you ever find out what exactly happened here?" I asked, looking out the window at the island city, which was situated at the confluence of two large rivers. There were other waterways nearby, as well, and I could see the tops of ruined buildings poking above the surface of a sizable lake.

"Monstrous beavers."

"What?"

"Beavers. You know, rodent-like creatures that build dams."

"Yeah. I learned about them in school. But they're not supposed to be dangerous, right?" I queried.

As he guided *The Leviathan* to a dock, he shrugged and said, "Well, when they're the size of hover cars, apparently that changes. Not many people left who know the whole story, but last time we were here, I talked to this old man who said that thousands of them came pouring out of the river, overwhelmed their Mist shields, and then swarmed the whole city. Killed plenty of people on their own, but most of the casualties happened when they dammed one of the rivers and flooded the town."

"Doesn't look flooded."

"That's because a group of settlers came and took it back," he explained. "The guy said it took almost ten years to get rid of the beavers, then another couple to drain it."

"Why'd they bother? Just move somewhere else."

As he guided *The Leviathan* closer, he gave a small shrug before saying, "I don't know. People get attached to where they live."

"That's stupid. One place is as good as any other."

But I knew I was a little abnormal in that sentiment. Most people couldn't just pick up and leave, and even if they were capable of doing so, they usually wouldn't choose to. Back in Nova, it had taken an ongoing gang war to get people to abandon the city. And those people had terrible lives. I couldn't imagine what kind of sentiment might come along with a city that treated its citizens well.

Perhaps that was the sort of place Montreal had been.

Now, though, it looked little different than dozens of other cities I'd visited. It was clearly built on the ruins of something much older, and some of those ancient buildings remained. However, most of the old city had been replaced by more modern buildings reminiscent of the megabuildings back in Nova. They were much smaller, but the layout was similar enough to prompt a wave of nostalgia.

And guilt followed close on its heels. I pushed both aside and focused on the dock, which was a series of tall platforms rising above the river. Supported by single pillars, most were too small to accommodate *The Leviathan*, but there were a few appropriately sized berths. Patrick expertly navigated to one such platform, then set it down.

I took a deep breath, then said, "You ready? We have everything, right?"

"I do. Did you contact that guy who buys Shards?"

"Everything's set up. All we have to figure out is the price, which is your department," I said. We'd already counted everything out and sent Borack, the insectoid who always bought my Rift Shards, an inventory detailing the entire stock of crystallized Mist. And he'd given me a rough value, though I intended to let Patrick negotiate. He had some abilities associated with haggling, so he was far better at it than I ever could be.

"Fair enough. You think we'll have enough for everything?"

"That depends on Ana's prices. Skills aren't cheap."

He shook his head. "Not a bad problem to have, though. Think of all the possibilities. You've got three open slots. That's as many as most people have altogether."

I was well aware of how unique—or nearly so—my Nexus Implant was. However, because I hadn't spent a ton of time researching possible skills, I wasn't really sure what direction I wanted to go. Thankfully, Anaseteramanimix was good at her job—at least as far as I could tell—and I trusted that she would steer me in the right direction.

Before that, though, we needed to pay the dock fee, traverse the city, and enter the Bazaar via the obelisk that would send our consciousnesses to the space station in question. One day soon, we wouldn't have to go through such a hassle, and as soon as the Initialization's quarantine was dropped, we'd be able to take *The Leviathan* into space and dock with the station directly.

But that was still a little ways off, so for now, we needed to jump through the same hoops as everyone else.

So, after we disembarked and Patrick paid the dock fee, we took the Cutter into the city. The hover bike had been damaged during the fight in Olympus, but Patrick had repaired it to almost perfect condition. I still felt a slight wobble in the steering, but he assured me that it was all in my head. Either way, it was still more than serviceable, which was all we really needed for the time being.

Montreal turned out to be a fairly normal town, and I was too excited to notice much more than the bare minimum. We reached the building containing the access point for the Bazaar about twenty minutes later.

It turned out to be one of the few pre-Initialization buildings in the city, and it was characterized by a large green dome atop a squarish main structure made of white stone. Otherwise, it was set apart by a long set of stairs that cut through an expansive lawn out front.

"Lots of wasted space," I remarked.

"I think it looks nice. It—"

His sentence was cut short by the chiming of bells. For my part, the sudden noise prompted a sudden reaction as I yanked Ferdinand II from the holster at my hip. Only a second later, I realized that I might have overreacted because no one else in the vicinity had even flinched.

"Sorry," I said, holstering my weapon. "Still a bit jumpy."

Indeed, after everything I'd been through over the past few years, it had become incredibly difficult to turn my combat instincts off. Sometimes, it meant waking up in the middle of the night, having been dragged out of unconsciousness by a stray sound. Other times, I had to endure a formless dread that I was on the verge of being attacked. Rationally, I knew it was all just a result of spending weeks at a time behind enemy lines, but that didn't really help me deal with it any more easily.

"It's okay," Patrick said in an understanding tone. He reached out and squeezed my shoulder. "It's fine."

I sighed. I hated showing weakness, even to him. But to Patrick's credit, he never judged me for it. In fact, he'd only ever wanted to support me as best he could. It was one of the reasons I loved him.

"I'm alright."

Then, we continued on our way, climbing the steps until we reached three sets of doors. We entered through the middle pair. The interior of the building reminded me of some of the ancient churches I had seen throughout my travels. The vaulted ceilings and arched halls were certainly impressive, either way.

Soon enough, we found our way to a large chamber that must've been beneath the dome. At the end of that cavernous room stood the red-and-black obelisk that would allow for access to the Bazaar. There were a few people waiting for their turn, but the area was a lot emptier than I would have expected. Only two others stood guard, though they didn't seem altogether necessary, given the placidity of the people in line.

Patrick and I found our way to the back of the queue, and though the person directly in front of him did let her gaze linger a bit on Patrick's exposed cybernetics, there were no real issues until we finally reached the front of the line almost two hours later.

The moment one of the guards told us the cost associated with accessing the obelisk, I understood the reason there were so few people there. Still, we didn't have much of a choice in the matter. Neither of us wanted to go elsewhere, and for a variety of reasons, not least of which was that all the other access points were located in cities where we'd already worn out our welcome.

Or I had, at least. Patrick usually flew under the radar.

So, we paid our fees, then stepped forward to join the other four people with their hands currently on the obelisk. The moment I touched its surface, I was prompted to pay the system's fee. It was exorbitant, but that was true of every time I'd accessed the Bazaar. So, I paid yet another fee, then let the system whisk my consciousness away.

At first, it was much like it always was. I felt like a ghost being pulled upward, first through the dome, and then into the atmosphere. However, only a few seconds into the journey, my {Mist Warden} senses awakened. When they did, I let out a scream of surprise as I beheld the dense column of Mist leading from the access point and disappearing into the sky.

I rode along that river of Mist—more of a pipe, really—until, finally, I stumbled onto the Bazaar's metallic floor.

At first, everything looked the same, but the moment I glanced up, I saw that most of the people were nothing but blobs of Mist. In retrospect, that made perfect sense. We were all just projections. But even so, I was definitely taken aback.

"Mira? Are you okay?" Patrick asked, his voice coming from a blob of blue Mist right beside me.

"Uh . . . No. No, I'm not."

"What's wrong?"

"Not here," I answered. "Let's . . . Let's go see Borack. Then, we have some shopping to do."

CHAPTER FIFTEEN

SKILLS AND EVOLUTIONS

Once it was harnessed by the system, the Mist should have been a gift to the universe. With it, miraculous things are possible. I know the science behind how it works. I've read all the research. And still, it often looks like magic to me. Even so, there are times when I wish we'd never tamed it.

—Alistaris Kargat

Borack's little village of insect people had grown in the years since I'd last visited. With its stone huts, oddly colored trees, and alien animals, it looked like the strangest interpretation of a medieval village imaginable. Borack himself was clearly from another world, though, and he could best be described as a curious amalgam of man and insect.

He also didn't seem very happy to see me. Standing in front of his door, he scowled in my direction as he growled, "Thought we agreed you wouldn't visit. It's not safe, and you know it. If the wrong people see you here . . ."

"I'm sorry," I said. "It couldn't be helped. If we tried to send everything via rapid transference, it would've cost an arm and a leg."

That certainly got his attention, and he perked up. A little. He still looked grumpy, but his greed had taken the edge off. "So, you got a good haul, then? You said as much earlier. What do you have for me?" he asked.

"Patrick?" I said, gesturing in his direction. I tried to see past the Mist that made up his illusory form, but it wasn't easy. Thankfully, Borack was physically present, which made looking at him a lot easier.

Still, I couldn't help but notice when Patrick's cloud of nanites flashed, then extended a tendril to the insectile man. Borack's own much more subdued cloud flickered as he accepted the connection. I already knew what was happening, so it wasn't difficult to make sense of the exchange. Still, seeing a communications request being accepted was an odd experience.

As he perused the document Patrick had sent, Borack said, "Ah. Oh. Uh . . . This is a lot."

"I know," Patrick stated. "Can you handle that many Rift Shards?"

Borack puffed up and crossed his arms. "Of course I can. Who do you think I am? Some two-bit Shard hustler like Treyachian? I can buy this and more. Much, much more!"

"Good. If you have such enviable buying power, you won't have to try to convince me that you can't afford to pay what this is worth," Patrick stated. "I was thinking three billion credits."

"Three billion?! Preposterous!"

Patrick shrugged. "You know prices are going to go up after the Integration," he said. "What with the quarantine being lifted and all, nobody's really going to need you. They'll just ship the Shards home themselves. No need to go through a broker, right?"

I wasn't really sure how it all worked, but according to everything I'd heard from my allies like Alistaris and Gala, the price of Rift Shards tended to rise once a newly Integrated planet's quarantine lifted. So, even if Borack overpaid a little for our current stash, he still stood to make quite a profit once Earth progressed past the Initialization.

And Patrick was perfectly willing to use that to our advantage. With that hanging over the proceedings, the negotiation began. I watched as the cloud of nanites that constituted Patrick's illusory form ebbed and flowed, flashed and flickered throughout the process. I knew he had some abilities associated with negotiation, though seeing them in action was definitely an eye-opener.

In the end, they settled for a bit less than the three billion Patrick had initially sought, but I knew from our previous conversations that we'd still gotten quite a bit more than either of us had expected. Such was the power of Patrick's negotiation tactics. Or perhaps it was the fear that we would take our business elsewhere. After all, Borack wasn't the only merchant in the Bazaar who traded in Rift Shards, and he'd never developed a personal relationship with either of us. So, given that our dealings were only about business, that was all he could lean on.

Even though the negotiations went well, by the time they were finished, I was more than eager to move on. So, it was with some anticipation that we headed to the first item on my list.

Ana and her premises were much the same as they always were. That meant that she was tiny and green, with huge black eyes. She also wore a silvery jumpsuit and was festooned with, in my opinion at least, way too much jewelry. However, she had always been kind to me, and I had come to consider her a friend. She greeted us with quite a lot of enthusiasm, hugging us both—we had to bend down so she could reach—before ushering us inside her shop.

Inside, the walls were covered in posters of various boy bands, though there were also a few shelves bearing memorabilia like tiny plastic statues of cute young men. I just shook my head at her obsession.

After I told her that I was looking for three new skills, she pressed a button on the wall. The posters disappeared a second later, revealing dozens of racks of skill crystals. There were far more than I'd seen during my last visit. When I said as much, Ana responded, "I'm preparing for the Integration. When the quarantine drops, we should see a marked increase in business up here. No more exorbitant access fees. We can just run shuttles back and forth instead of relying on the projections. It won't be a huge demand at first—no, it'll have to build over years—but I like to be prepared. Besides, it's good practice, making skills. Simulations are nice, and they provide steady growth, but nothing works like the real thing. I'm sure you know that better than most, given how much you've grown."

I narrowed my eyes. "And how would you know how much I've grown?" I asked.

"Relax," she said, holding up her hands in surrender. "I have an investigative ability."

"Must be a good one," I said. I had one of those, too. But from what I'd seen, the version of True Sight I had gotten was next to useless. I'd yet to find anyone it actually worked on, and after a month of trying, I'd all but forgotten the worthless ability. It was strange, too, because Gunther Gunderson had possessed an ability with the same name, and he'd gotten quite a lot of information out of it. Perhaps there was more to abilities like that than I knew.

"It is," she said. "It helps me assess the needs of my customers."

"Oh? And what would you suggest for somebody like me?" I asked.

She reached up and tapped her delicate chin as she gave it some thought. A few seconds later, she said, "{Mist Warden}. A unique class, I think. Oh—Mist Control. Does that do what I think it does?"

"Probably," I said, not willing to give away more information than necessary. I trusted Ana; she was a friend. But I still didn't want to reveal all my secrets.

"Interesting. Tell me—do you see the Mist, then? It is an exceedingly rare capability. Rarer still to be able to control it. Unheard of in most circles. In fact, I've only known of three people in history to have possessed such an ability."

"I'm not saying I do have that kind of capability," I said, hedging my bets. "But if I did, what would you suggest?"

"Three skills. One slot," she muttered. "Yes . . . It should work. And if it doesn't . . . No, it should."

"What?"

"You have merged skills before, haven't you?" she asked. "Before, it was the result of class evolutions. But now that you have reached your current level, you are at the end of that road."

"I won't evolve again?"

"Not due to level," she said. "But perhaps if you managed to meet certain criteria. What those are, I have no idea. But it's possible. Yes, for you, it is the only way you can progress further on your current track."

I asked what she meant, and she went on to explain that, while I could certainly continue to gain levels and increased my attributes, as well as progress my skills, I would never experience another automatic class evolution. However, it was still possible to advance to another more powerful class, though not without meeting certain stringent requirements.

"That is not what I'm suggesting, though. At your level, skills can evolve independently of your class, and there are ways to promote specific evolutions. Chiefly, if you choose secondary skills related to the one you intend to evolve, you will have the chance to merge the two together and evolve the base skill. So, in your case, you would absorb a skill that compliments your Mist Control ability. If it works properly, you will have the chance to merge the new skill with the aforementioned ability and create something much more powerful than either."

"Okay . . ."

It was all a little much for me, but I'd chosen to trust Ana's judgment. She knew what she was doing.

"And then we'd do it again. And again after that," she said. "Three times. Three skills absorbed into a twice-evolved ability. It will become a top-grade skill the likes of which this world can scarcely comprehend, much less defend against."

"Wait . . . What?"

"You absorb one skill, level it to the fifth tier," she said. "Then it will hopefully absorb into the base ability, evolving Mist Control into something better. When that happens, we do it again. And again after that."

"Uh . . . What are the downsides to that, and why doesn't everyone do it?"

"There are only a few skills and abilities with that kind of synergy, but this strategy is nothing new in the wider universe. It's how most people evolve skills and abilities."

"Why don't they just level?"

"How many kills did it take you to reach level seventy-five?"

"Good point," I said, catching her drift. I'd had to kill millions to get to level seventy-five, and I knew that most people would have neither the ability nor the stomach for that kind of thing.

"As to the downsides, there's every chance that it won't work. The new skills will still be useful, but if it wasn't for the potential for evolution, I would not suggest any of the three. And due to the nature of evolutions, you will only be able to use one at a time. So, you're looking at a good deal of focused training if you want to follow this path. Otherwise, I have other options available."

I sighed and shook my head. It was a high-risk, high-reward sort of situation. If I chose to take her advice, I stood a chance to gain an ultrapowerful, world-breaking sort of ability. However, if it didn't work, I'd be stuck with something that, according to Ana's judgment, would be suboptimal.

It was probably smarter to play it safe. I knew that. However, with what the world was facing, I also knew that safe wasn't going to save anyone. I needed to be special. I needed to be better than the aliens. And Ana had just offered me that opportunity. I would have to have been a fool to refuse.

"What are the skills?"

"The first is called [Aura Manipulation]," she said. "It's typically used by stealthy types to hide from Mist-enhanced senses and surveillance systems meant to combat concealment skills."

"Sounds useful," I said. If I'd had something like what she had described, then the final leg of the Rift would have been much easier. Perhaps my Stealth wouldn't have been cancelled in the chamber with the crystal wyvern.

"Once it's been raised a tier or two," she admitted. "But it only gives one active ability and no modifiers. As such, it takes training to get anything out of it."

"What would be the next one?"

"It's called [Shielding]," Ana answered. "Another one with only a single ability. It functions as a low-quality Mist shield whose viability is based on your Mist attribute. For you, it would likely be quite powerful—at least until you ran out of Mist, which would happen in seconds."

That sounded a lot like the shield I'd almost bought from Dex before I'd purchased my subdermal armor. Back then, I'd chosen the other route simply because I thought the Sheath would be useful in a wider variety of situations. And I had never seen a reason to regret my choice. However, the skill Ana had described seemed like it would let me have the best of both worlds.

"And the last?"

"It's called [Recovery]," she stated. "This one also gives you a single ability called Rejuvenate. It puts you into a meditative state that will let you rapidly recover your Mist. If your stores of Mist are full, then it will use the excess to regenerate your body."

I narrowed my eyes. That wasn't so different from what I'd done back in the Rift. If the [Recovery] skill would allow me to do that more efficiently, it wouldn't just be useful. It would change everything. After all, I'd been injured often enough that I'd been forced to spend quite some time in recovery.

"Those all sound kind of amazing to me. Why can't I just take those three and rank them all up at the same time?"

"Because it would affect the end result. If you did that, you would almost assuredly gain an evolved ability. However, it would be weaker than if you ranked them up one at a time."

"Why?"

"I have no idea. That's just the way it is."

I didn't like that explanation one bit, but I didn't think Ana was holding anything back. If she said she didn't know, I was prepared to believe her.

"Okay. So, what do you think, Pick?"

"I think that I'm not touching this with a ten-foot pole. This is your decision, Mira. I'm not going to be the person to tell you how to handle your own progression."

I rolled my eyes and muttered a couple of choice words that he pretended not to hear. But I understood his reasoning. He didn't want to stick his nose into my development because, if he turned out to be wrong, I would have a hard time not blaming him at least a little.

"Fine."

"But I will say this—go with your instincts. They're usually right."

"Aww," said Ana, clasping her hands in front of her chest. "That's so cute!"

I sighed. "And moving right along—what else do you have for me? I need two other skills."

"You said you wanted some sort of piloting skill, right?" said Patrick.

"Yeah. I hate being bad at flying *The Leviathan*. Plus, not being able to pilot a ship almost got me killed a few months back," I said, remembering my difficulty flying the ship out of the moon base. Then, I'd had issues when I escaped Olympus.

"I have [Navigation]," Ana said. "It has a Pilot ability built in, but it's mostly there for . . . well . . . navigating the galaxy. There are some spatial-awareness modifiers, too. Assuming you get the most out of it, which I think is safe to expect."

That sounded good, so I agreed to buy that one. As Ana went to the wall and collected the crystal, I asked her what else she suggested.

"Two choices. One meant for combat, and the other is a little more utilitarian in nature. Though it could help in combat."

"What are they?" I asked, already expecting to choose the combat option. We weren't quite at war yet, but it wasn't far off.

"The combat option is called [Enhancement]," she stated. "It has two abilities. The first is Reinforcement, and it uses a trickle of Mist to provide a slight increase to your Constitution."

"How slight?"

"Five percent," she said.

"With my attributes, that isn't really that slight," I said. And given that I expected to go into intense training for the next few months—once my potential rose to previous levels—it would only get more impressive. "But what's the second ability?"

"Called Surge. It allows you to increase your attributes by almost sixty percent, though at a steep cost, both in terms of Mist and the condition of your body. Using something like that for more than a few seconds will result in torn ligaments, broken bones, and possible death."

"Steep cost indeed," I muttered, though I could certainly see how such a skill could help me. The near-passive increase to my attributes would be a godsend, and the Overcharge ability represented the ability to flip a battle on its head. "What's the other one?"

"[Multimind]," she said. "It provides only one ability, but it's one that can completely change everything about how you fight and train."

"What does it do?"

"At F-grade, it allows you to split your mind in two," she said. "Your collective cognitive ability won't increase. That is tied to your Mind attribute as well as the limitations of your brain. However, it will give you the ability to focus on multiple things at once. Each successive grade will double the number of minds at your disposal, and when it reaches S-grade, you would have one hundred and twenty-eight interconnected minds at your beck and call. Most people would never use so many, but with your high Mind attribute, there's a chance that you could leverage those minds into something truly special."

"Damn," I said, impressed. [Multimind] sounded amazing, but was it better than being able to increase my Constitution? Perhaps. What if it would allow me to break down Mistwalls even more quickly? I could also build Ghosts more efficiently. And that wasn't even considering what it would do for my training. Focusing on multiple things at once would almost have to raise my attributes as well as the tiers of my skills that much more quickly.

It didn't take much more thought for me to realize that I'd already made my choice. "[Multimind]," I said.

"Are you certain?" Ana asked.

I nodded. "It's the best fit," I stated with confidence. "Nobody ever complained about too much brainpower, right? So, I need [Multimind], [Navigation], [Aura Manipulation], [Recovery], and [Shielding]. I'll let Patrick figure out the cost, though. He's a lot better at that kind of thing than I am."

CHAPTER SIXTEEN

ALL THE BEST TOYS

My preference is to build my own equipment. It's probably not better, but with my skills giving me significant modifiers for self-made gear, it's close enough for the distinction to not matter. Even if that wasn't the case, I would do it, anyway. There's just nothing like building your own weapons and using them to protect someone you love.

—Patrick Ward

Do you need to know anything about your skills?" I asked. Just after he'd completed work on his armor, he'd actually gained his class, {Combat Engineer}. When that had happened, his skills had all evolved, but none had merged like mine had. Still, he'd told me a little about his modifiers and new abilities, and I had to admit that I was more than a little impressed by his progression. However, that didn't mean he couldn't learn a thing or two from Ana.

Surprisingly, he shook his head. "No offense to Ana, but I prefer to figure it all out on my own," he said.

"That is usually the case," the small alien skillsmith said. "Self-discovery is always preferable, though there is something to be said for knowing the optimal path. If you need anything in the coming months, please—don't hesitate to ask."

"You know what's coming, right? You know what I did, don't you?" I asked.

"I do."

"And you're okay with it?"

"With mass murder? Not usually," she said, shaking her head. It was a human affectation she'd picked up during her time observing humans from the Bazaar. "But I understand why you did what you did, and I don't condemn your actions. The Pacificians are a scourge upon the universe, and they deserve extermination."

"What about the war I intend to fight?" I asked. "I'm not going to give the planet up without taking my fair share of invaders down."

She nodded. "That is your right. It's how the universe works. You keep what you can. Most of the time, it's precious little, but perhaps you will be different. Maybe you can do better than my people did, so long ago."

"Your planet was invaded?"

"Every planet is. Or was. The core planets may be different, but I don't think so. I think that's just how the universe works. There is always someone waiting in the wings to take what they believe is theirs by right of strength. And it is on us to resist. In some cases, we may even win, but that's not the point, is it?"

"No."

Indeed, the point of resistance wasn't to win. That might have been the goal, unrealistic though it probably was. However, the point was to make the invaders and colonizers pay a horrible price for taking what wasn't theirs. If we could do that enough times, then maybe, we—meaning the poor people at the mercy of the more powerful—might one day turn the tables on our oppressors.

It was a pretty dream, but one I knew stood very little chance of coming true. The deck was stacked against us, and even making the aliens pay for their intended invasion was a tall task. Still, that was the path I had chosen.

After we arranged for the shipment of the skill crystals back to Earth, Patrick and I left Ana's shop. It wasn't until we'd turned down an adjacent hallway on our way to Gala's shop that I realized something that shouldn't have seemed so important. But it did, so I said, "She didn't talk about boy bands or soap operas."

"Huh?"

"That's Ana's thing. She usually won't shut up about them. Last time I dropped by, she practically begged me to go to a concert with her once the Integration began," I explained.

"So, what does it mean?" he asked after a moment.

"I don't know. Nothing good, though."

But in the back of my mind, I had a good idea why Ana had been a little more subdued than usual. Either she thought we were doomed, which meant that she had already begun to mentally sever herself from relationships with earthlings. Or she disapproved of what was coming. Of what I had done.

I had no idea what the culprit really was, but I didn't like either option.

Patrick and I continued on in silence, and soon enough, we reached Gala's premises. Fortunately, the minotaur woman showed none of Ana's reticence, and the moment her door slid open, she wrapped both Patrick and me in a hug. That was normal enough, but it was comforting, nonetheless. However, I couldn't ignore the way her Mist aura flared when she embraced us. Clearly, it was an ability activation, though it was odd seeing such a thing in a benign context.

She pulled away, then put her giant furry hands on my shoulders and said, "I can't believe you're alive. What you did . . ."

"Is probably best not discussed with your door open."

"Right," she said, flipping her hair out of her eyes. "Come on in, then. I suppose this isn't a social visit."

As she spoke, she let us inside, and the door slid shut behind us. When it did, I saw another flicker of Mist, announcing that she had either activated another ability or she had used some sort of security measure. Probably the latter, given the context, but I wasn't ready to rule anything out.

Either way, it was still more than a little disconcerting, my awareness of Mist. With a thought, I knew I could disrupt whatever defenses she'd just enabled. More, I suspected that if I chose, I could have ripped the cloud of Mist that was Patrick's projection apart.

"I guess you want to talk about it, huh?" I asked.

"Did you mean to do it?" was her responding question. "Or was it an accident?"

I shrugged. "A little of both, if I'm honest. I meant to kill some, but not . . . quite as many as ended up dying. Why? Is it a problem?" I asked.

"For me? Not even a little one," Gala stated. "But for you, that's a different story. I hear things, Mira. They're coming for you as soon as the Integration starts. Gomari death squads. Whole armies. They're willing to scour the whole planet if it means they get you."

"The feeling's mutual."

"So, you're fighting? I thought you intended to fly away on the beast you call a ship."

"I did, too," Patrick interjected. "But things change."

"Do they?"

"It's our planet, Gala. You don't know what they were doing down there," I said. "You have no idea the things I've seen."

"I know more than I want to know," the minotaur said, leaning against her counter and resting on the palms of her hands. "I've seen so much more than most. I have a good idea what kinds of things have been going on down there."

"Then you understand why I'm not going to turn my back on Earth," I said.

"I do. What I don't understand is why you're working with the Ark Alliance. A bunch of warmongering idealists who do more harm than good."

I shrugged. "I don't get the luxury of picking my allies. Their enemies are mine, and as odd as it sounds, I trust the guy in charge. Mostly."

"Kargat? S'pose he's as upright as they come. True believer, from what I've heard. But he's only in charge until someone higher up the food chain decides this fight is more important than originally thought. When that happens, some big shot will swoop in and take over. They'll just—"

"I'm aware of how small we are, Gala. I'm not stupid. And if it looks like things are going sideways, I'll jump ship. Patrick and I can get off that planet anytime we want after the quarantine is lifted," I explained. I didn't think it would come to that. In the kinds of battles I usually fought, absolute commitment was a necessity. And once you crossed that line, retreat turned into an impossibility. However, I wasn't going to tell Gala that, even if I suspected she knew the truth of it better than I did.

"Good," she said. "So, what do you need."

"What makes you think I need anything?" I asked with a smirk.

"Past experience," she responded. "No offense, but you're even more businesslike than your uncle. Must run in the family."

"You should try living with her," Patrick said. "Getting her to stop training for more than a day is like pulling teeth."

The two shared a laugh at my expense, and I even found myself grinning slightly. It was so rare that I could talk to anyone but Patrick without looking for an underlying motive. But there was no one I trusted more than Gala. She'd helped me more than once, and what's more, my uncle had given her his trust. That was enough for me.

Finally, I said, "I need some guns, Gala."

"Then you've come to the right place," she said. "If there's anything I've got, it's guns. What were you thinking?"

"Um . . . Don't get mad, but I kind of . . . Uh . . . I kind of blew up the Dragon," I admitted sheepishly. Before she could respond—and there was definitely a response coming, judging by the expression of budding anger building on her face—I held up a hand and said, "But it wasn't my fault, okay? There was this guy with a giant fuck-off sword, and if I hadn't blocked it with the Dragon, he'd have cut me in half. So . . . Uh . . . It gave its life for a good cause."

"If it helps, it's not completely destroyed. I fixed it," Patrick added. "Mostly."

"Mostly?" Gala asked.

He shrugged. "I can run it up to around sixty percent power. But I'm still tinkering with it. I feel pretty sure that if I have the right materials, I can even improve on the design."

"If you do that, kid, there are some people who are definitely going to want to meet you."

"Why?"

"To offer you a job, obviously. Do you have any idea how difficult it is to improve on something like a DR-4 EMG? That's a premium weapon that was designed by one of the top weapons manufacturers in the galaxy. Only core weapons are better."

"Uh . . . Then that might make my request a little . . . I don't know. But I need something better, Gala. A lot better if you can do it."

"I'm sure I don't have anything like that," she said, her bovine eyes flicking back and forth.

"That's an obvious lie."

"Mira, I can't . . ."

"Sure you can," I said. "Believe me when I say that my life depends on whatever weapons you sell me here. You know what's coming, Gala. Help me survive it."

Gala huffed. Then, her Mist flared far more strongly than the previous flicker. Then, it washed over the entire shop before solidifying.

"What did you just do?"

"Made sure nobody could hear us," she said. "You're playing a dangerous game, Mira. There are rules as to what I can sell to earthlings."

"And you're about to break them, aren't you?" I guessed.

"I am. A little. It's only a few months early."

By my count, there were still close to nine months until the Initialization ended, but I wasn't going to point that out. Instead, I asked, "What do you have for me? I need a replacement for the Dragon, for one. And I could use a new assault rifle. Not because the one I have is broken or anything. It just feels a little outdated. Oh, and a better blade, too. I know there's one out there. And if you have a better sniper rifle, I'll be—"

"You want an entire arsenal?"

"If you have better than my current weapons, yes."

"And you have money for that? I'm willing to break the rules. I can even give you a good deal. But I'm not running a charity here."

"We have money," Patrick said. "I'm pretty sure it'll be enough for whatever you have."

She narrowed her eyes—an odd expression, for a woman with a face like a cow—and asked, "You didn't make a deal with the Dengyts or something, did you?"

"I made a deal with Al. But the money's from something else," I stated.

"Al?"

"Alistaris Kargat."

"And you call him Al?" she asked. Then, she chuckled and said, "Bet he loves that, huh?"

"He may have expressed some annoyance at the nickname," I admitted.

She huffed again. "Fine. First thing's first—the Dragon replacement. I'm sorry to say that I don't have another one. But I have something better."

"I thought you said the Dragon was the best you had. That's what you said last time I was here, at least."

"And it was true. I couldn't sell the HIRC back then. Against the rules of the quarantine."

"Herc?"

"H-I-R-C," Gala corrected. "Stands for high-impact rotary cannon. Here. Let me show you."

She turned around and went behind the counter. Like she'd done once before, she pressed a button, and the wall opened up to reveal a large variety of weapons. However, it only took one glance for me to recognize that these were far more powerful than any I'd seen in my previous trips to Gala's shop. They all—each and every one—practically hummed with unspent Mist.

She reached out, grabbing a huge weapon that was at least seven feet long. The bulk of the casing was round and about ten inches wide, but the length came from the barrels. There were seven of them, all around two inches in diameter and arrayed in a circle around a much larger barrel. Like the Dragon, it was clearly meant to be fired from the hip.

"Oh . . ."

"Wish she'd look at me like that," Patrick muttered.

"This is the HIRC," Gala said. "Fifty-thousand-round spatial magazine. Easy reload via cybernetic. You'll have to install that yourself, but with him there, that shouldn't be a problem."

"What kind of punch?"

"The first incarnation was mounted on the nose of a 327 Banshee-class fighter ship," she said. "Since then, it's been through countless iterations. Never got any smaller, but it hits as hard as anything I've ever seen. Fires Mist-infused explosive rounds, too. And that's just the first mode. The second is arguably more powerful, even if it's less practical."

"What does it do?" Patrick and I asked at the same time.

"You have cannons on that ship of yours, right?"

"We do."

"It's like that. But about ten times more powerful. You hit something with that, it'll explode. Shells are a pain to source, but it just so happens that I have a crate in the back. I'll throw it in. Same with the first two magazines of rounds for the other mode, too. Can't sell you a gun with no ammunition, can I?"

"You have some idea of my modifiers, right?"

"A basic notion, yes."

"What will this weapon do for me?"

"You could bring down ships with it. And not those dinky little things you have planetside, either. Real ships. From proper factions. The sorts you'll see once the quarantine is lifted."

"And everything else?"

"You find something that can stand up to the HIRC, you run away. If you can."

"That sounds like exactly what I need," I admitted. Then, I turned to Patrick. "You're up."

"Let's just negotiate at the end," he said. "It'll be easier than piecemealing everything together."

"Fair enough. Better have the money if you're making me go through the sales pitch, though," Gala said. Then, she pressed another button on the wall, and the previous racks of weapons slid away, revealing much more compact firearms. Gala grabbed one that was about three feet long, including the snub-nosed barrel poking out from the sleek casing. Along both sides ran two sets of three nodes, all of which glowed with blue light. Otherwise, it looked much like any other assault rifle I'd seen.

"Seems small."

"Small," Gala said. "But potent. This is the Stinger."

I hesitated for a moment, waiting for her to tell me what that stood for. When she didn't, I asked, "No acronym?"

"Nope. Just the Stinger. This is the standard-issue weapon of the Erdikar Dreadnoughts, one of the most feared military units in the entire universe. If the wrong people knew I even had this weapon, they'd hunt me down, drag me back to the Erdikar Citadel, and flay me alive. Then, they'd have one of their healers bring me back to life just so they could do it again."

"Is it that powerful?"

"Truthfully? No," she said. "Make no mistake—it's the strongest assault rifle I have, and not by a little bit, either. See these nodes on the side? Those infuse any round with extra power, similar to how your modifiers work. Holds a thousand rounds. Spatial magazines again. Fully automatic or burst-fire modes. It's universally regarded as a perfect weapon. But it's not worth killing over, in and of itself. It's the symbol it represents, though. The Dreadnoughts don't like it when anyone steps on their toes, so to speak. They're fanatics who take their jobs very seriously."

I raised an eyebrow. The term *perfect weapon* definitely appealed to me, but her story was a little troubling. I certainly didn't want to be hunted down just because I carried some fancy gun. But on the other hand, it did open Gala up for another negotiation tactic. So, I said, "I'm sure you're eager to get rid of it, then. I bet that'll factor into the price, huh?"

She snorted. "You wish."

"Mira, let me do the negotiating," Patrick said.

I threw my hands up in surrender. "I've said it a million times that I'm not good at this kind of stuff. Just point me at what you want blown up, and I'm your girl. But this? Ugh."

"Does this mean you want it?"

"Obviously I want it."

"Good. Because I don't have anything else that's as close to this quality, even with the issues that come with owning it."

"Alright—that's two down. I need a replacement for the sniper rifle, the nano-blade, and something for close-range. And none of that nonlethal stuff this time like the scattergun."

"Oh, we're way past that," Gala said. Then, she shuffled her wall to yet another display—this one of blades—and retrieved one that looked solid black. She set it on the counter, but she didn't explain it. Instead, she shuffled the wall again, stopping at one featuring a bunch of bulky short-nosed weapons. She chose one, then repeated the process before stopping at a display studded with sniper rifles. At this one, she stopped and waited for a few seconds, tapping her chin as she considered it. Finally, she picked a long, sleek weapon with a square barrel and a smooth plasti-steel shell. The only ornamentation was a thin slit that ran along the length of the weapon, but I couldn't see anything inside.

She set it down on the counter, then pointed at the blade. "That's called an interdiction blade. Run a bit of Mist through it, and it'll wear down defenses. Including Constitution. With enough time and Mist, it'll go through anything."

"Nice."

She pointed to the stumpy weapon with a big barrel. "This one's called ADS. Affliction delivery system. It shoots these little shells that burst when fired. Inside each shell are hundreds of tiny norcite pellets that, when they lodge inside of someone, start draining their Mist."

"I have that with Ferdinand II."

"Sure. But the ADS enhances the effect while feeding that drained Mist back into the wielder."

"Like a minibooster?"

"Like hundreds of miniboosters all at once."

"Damn."

"Indeed," Gala agreed, giving me a flat-toothed smile. Finally, she pointed to the sniper rifle. "This is an Emperor, mark seven, and in your hands, it will probably be the most powerful single weapon on Earth."

"Uh . . ."

"Seven shots. All Mist enhanced, just like with the Stinger. But with seven nodes instead of three," she explained. "All seven rounds are linked, and so long as you meet the Mist requirements—which are steep—every successive round that hits a single target will be three times as powerful as the last. You hit something with all seven shots, and that something will be destroyed. As will anything in its general vicinity. This weapon isn't a sniper rifle because distance will give you a tactical advantage. It's so you won't be in the blast radius of that seventh shot."

I did some mental calculations, and my jaw dropped. With my modifiers, as well as abilities like Empowered Shot and Execute, I could easily see how powerful such a weapon could be.

"Two downsides," Gala said. "First—those seven shots take an incredible amount of Mist, both from the shooter as well as the weapon. Because of that, you can only fire a full magazine once a week."

"There's no way to cut that down?"

"Not that I know of."

"What's the other downside?"

"Money. Not just for the weapon. The rounds aren't just expensive. They're practically priceless."

"So, you're saying that Patrick has his work cut out for him, huh?" I asked. Then, I turned in his direction and said, "I think that's your cue."

CHAPTER SEVENTEEN

GEEKING OUT

The quarantine of any Initialization is supposed to give the natives a chance. With a hundred years, they can progress and grow so that they can stand up to the wave of invaders and colonizers that will come with the Integration. And yet, we all know it's little more than a joke. Even if they had twice that time, there's almost no chance any native population could stand up to civilizations with millennia—and sometimes eons—of development behind them.

—Alistaris Kargat

Patrick did his best negotiating with Gala, and I think she even cut us some slack. However, she was still in business to make money, so there was only so far she was willing to go. And in the end, she wouldn't accept a single credit less than a billion. So, Patrick reluctantly made the arrangements for the transfer while I eagerly looked forward to trying out my new weapons. Fortunately, Gala included quite a lot of ammunition—both full-power and practice rounds—so I wouldn't have to worry about that anytime soon.

Just before we left, she added, "Don't hesitate to order more ammunition. It shouldn't be difficult to resupply after the quarantine lifts, but if you run out before that—unlikely, but possible—make sure you order via that Secure Connection. Most of this stuff is restricted, and I don't think either one of us wants to be sanctioned by the system this close to the Integration."

"Right. I'll keep that in mind," I said. "Thanks, Gala. Really. I know you're stepping out on a limb here, and—"

She wrapped her huge arms around me, saying, "I owe it to you."

When I pulled away, I asked, "For what?"

She shook her head. "Did I ever tell you how your uncle and I met?" she asked. When I told her that she hadn't, she went on: "My little brother went down there. It's one of the reasons I'm here. I was following him across the galaxy, and I didn't catch up to him in time to keep him from going down. He'd joined a mercenary group as a Rift miner. Stupid, but he was always like that. Anyway, things inevitably went wrong, and he ended up on the wrong side of the mercenary leader. They kept him captive, only letting him out to fight for their amusement. Well, I found out where they were, and when I met your uncle, I asked him to intervene.

"And he did. Killed that whole camp and freed my brother. He's been lying low since then, and the moment the quarantine lifts, I'm going down there, picking him up, and taking him home. But I'll never forget what Jeremiah did for me. For my brother. So, I owe him, and that debt transfers to you."

"You're leaving?" I asked.

"Soon as possible," she stated. "I can't afford to slum it in this part of the universe anymore. I'll set up a colleague to keep you supplied with ammunition, but the shop won't have near the quality of gear once I go. That's another reason I sold you those weapons."

"So, you're some kind of big shot?" I asked.

She shrugged her massive shoulders and said, "According to some people, sure. Maybe. But I'm just a gunrunner."

I didn't believe that for a second. Every interaction I'd had with Gala suggested that she was special, and now that she'd revealed a little more about herself, I felt even more strongly that she was one of the most powerful people I'd ever met.

After a bit more back and forth—during which nothing of import was really said—Patrick and I left Gala's shop behind. I couldn't help but wonder if that was the last time I would ever see her. If she was heading back . . . to wherever it was that she called home, then that was almost a certainty.

It occurred to me then that I'd never asked her about her origin.

"What's wrong?" asked Patrick as we made our way toward our next destination.

"Nothing."

"Come on. I know that expression. You're upset about something."

"Not really upset. Just disappointed in myself," I admitted. "I mean, I've known Gala for a while now. Close to ten years. I've visited her dozens of times."

"You're thinking about missing her?"

"No. Yes. But that's not really what I was thinking about," I admitted. Then, I asked, "Do you think I'm a selfish person, Pick?"

"What? No. Of course not. Why would you ask that?"

I shrugged. "Because in all the time I've known Gala, I've never really asked her about her life. I don't know where she's from. I don't know who she really is, other than that she's the person I buy my guns and ammo from. I didn't even know she had a brother, much less one that lived on Earth. It just . . . That's not normal, is it? Am I so self-centered that I don't even think to ask my friends about who they are?"

He didn't answer.

"Oh, God . . ."

"Look, Mira—it's not that you're selfish, okay?" he said, clearly trying to cushion the blow. "You've just got a lot going on."

"That sounds like an excuse."

He shrugged. "Maybe it is," he said. "But here's the thing—you have plenty of time to change, right? Who you are now doesn't have to be who you are next week. Or next month. Or next year. If you . . ."

I stopped listening to him because I'd just noticed someone who was paying far too much attention to us. The halls of the Bazaar were never empty, but almost everyone went about their business without bothering anyone else. But just behind us, I could feel someone who'd been following us ever since we'd left Gala's shop.

It took a little focus to see past the cloud of Mist that comprised their illusory form, but when I did, I saw an unremarkable human woman. She wasn't looking at us, but I could tell that she was paying close attention to every word that passed between Patrick and me.

And I wasn't going to stand for that.

Normally, it was impossible to affect someone's projection. The first and only time I'd seen anyone do it was with Gala, and she'd never turned it into an attack. More, I'd begun to suspect that she was much more powerful than she had first appeared. In any case, I was in no mood to let impossibility stand in my way, so I embraced Mist Control and turned my attention in our follower's direction.

A second later, I ripped the cloud apart.

Doing so was so much easier than it had been with the dervishes, and the resulting pain was slight enough that I could easily ignore it. The same couldn't be said for the woman, who let out an agonized scream before the Mist dissipated into the air.

"What the . . ."

"Sorry," I said to Patrick, who'd whipped around to see the origin of the scream. By the time he did, there was nothing left. "We were being followed."

"What just happened?"

"I dealt with the problem."

"Do you mean you used your . . . you know . . . new thing?"

"I did."

"Do you know what happened?" he asked. "Like, when you tore them apart, did it affect them back on Earth?"

I shrugged. "Not really concerned with it, if I'm honest," I admitted. Of course, in the back of my mind, I had to acknowledge that there was a possibility I was mistaken. Maybe she hadn't been eavesdropping. In that case, there was a chance that I'd just killed someone who didn't deserve it. Or maybe I just severed her connection. There was no way for me to know, and I wasn't going to spend too much time thinking about it.

After that, Patrick and I spent the next twenty minutes heading toward Dex's shop. I didn't really need any new cybernetics, but Patrick wanted to buy some parts. Moreover, we needed to find someone to sell us some heavy armaments for *The Leviathan*. We'd asked Gala, but she was incapable of referring us to anyone, so I hoped that Dex could point us in the right direction. Otherwise, Patrick would have to build them himself.

When we reached Dex's premises, we found his cube-shaped shop empty. After asking his neighbors as to his whereabouts, we discovered that Dex had been exiled for reasons unknown. A quick call back to Gala told me that his exile was related to his relationship with me. The Gomari Confederation had pulled some strings and had him kicked out of the Bazaar. As it turned out, everyone I knew had been threatened, but Dex had been the only one without enough backing to resist.

"Shit," I muttered. "I hope he's okay."

"He's fine," Gala answered. "I made sure of it."

"T-thanks," I said, a little dumbfounded about how to further respond. "I . . . I didn't mean for it to happen."

"Consequences, Mirabelle," she said. "For every action, there is a reaction. This was theirs. You're fighting a war. There are going to be casualties."

I sighed. I had always understood the reality of the struggle, and yet, it never ceased to surprise me when someone else paid the price for my actions.

"Do you know anywhere else we can get parts? Patrick needs materials. As high-quality as we can get," I said.

"There's a dealer I know," Gala said over the Secure Connection. "Sending you the location. But be warned—earthlings don't usually go there."

"Wouldn't be the first time I've gone where I'm not wanted."

She sent the file, which I slotted into my HUD's map. So, after thanking Gala, we set off. As we did, I kept my eyes, ears, and more importantly, my {Mist Warden} senses trained on my surroundings. Fortunately, we didn't pick up any more observers, but I maintained my vigilance as we traversed the space station.

At first, there were plenty of other pedestrians, but as we went, the crowd thinned until, at last, we were almost entirely alone as we walked through the wide corridors. More than once, we passed clumps of those stacked, cube-shaped shops and domiciles, but no one tried to obstruct our passage. That was fortunate because I'd already proved that Mist Control was more than capable of affecting people on the space station, and I was fairly positive that it would be just as effective against the aliens who lived there and the projections people sent from the surface.

The nature of our surroundings changed, as well, and the corridors grew more worn with every step. In addition, we left the huge chambers filled with stacked cubes behind. Instead, each new chamber was just a huge open space. Sometimes, they were filled with crates and alien workers—some of whom drove exosuits to assist with the execution of their jobs—but other chambers were entirely empty.

"This isn't creepy at all," I muttered to myself as I looked around the latest iteration of the latter. "What do you think this is for?"

Patrick answered, "I have no idea. Storage, maybe? Or it could be for use when the quarantine drops. Everyone says the Bazaar is supposed to get a lot busier then."

That was true, and it was easy to imagine that the workforce required to run the space station would need to be much larger to accommodate the increased traffic. Still, even knowing that didn't mitigate the unease I felt at being in such a cavernous and empty room. So, Patrick and I didn't tarry, instead quickening our pace until we finally reached our destination.

To the untrained eye, it looked like a junkyard. Just piles of disparate pieces of robotics, cybernetics, and every other bit of trash one could imagine. However, we'd only taken one step before Patrick's eyes alighted on something sticking out of the closest pile. He rushed to it, then went to yank it free. He came away disappointed, though, because in his projected form, he couldn't touch anything.

"Ye got a good eye, kid," came a rumbling voice.

I jerked my gaze in the voice's direction, and I was surprised to see what I first thought was a human. Yet, when I took a closer look, I saw a few subtle differences.

Like the fact that he was at least twice as tall as any human being I'd ever met. Or that he had only one eye located in the center of his forehead. Otherwise, he wore a pair of what looked like denim overalls with no shirt beneath them. In fact, he wasn't wearing shoes, either, which revealed a pair of massive feet that matched his other proportions.

"How much?" asked Patrick without even looking back at the cyclops. Instead, he was bent down, his face only a few inches from the . . . item . . . he was looking at. To me, it just looked like a piece of trash, but he certainly seemed excited by it.

"For that'n? Four thousand. Not a credit less, or I won't b' able ta feed my chitrens."

"Chitrens?" I mouthed.

"Deal," said Patrick without even haggling, which definitely wasn't like him.

The cyclops grinned widely. "Know ye had a good look 'boutcha," he rumbled. "C'mon, den. Les getcha all settled."

That was when Patrick finally looked up, though he was clearly hesitant to let the item out of his sight. Still, he blanched a bit at the size of the cyclops. He didn't let that dissuade him, though. Instead, he said, "Gala sent me here. She said you had a lot of parts available, and if what I just saw is any indication, she was right."

I didn't miss the cyclops's change of expression. He paled as he asked, "Gala sentcha? Did I say four thousand? Meant two, I did. Musta misverbalized it."

Patrick straightened to his full height and said, "Oh? Awesome. Let me send you a list of what I need, huh? You can tell me what you have, then we can come to an arrangement for everything."

"Uh . . . Any frienda Gala's is a frienda mine. Stand-up bovine, she is. Never met a better one, no I didn't."

After that, Patrick transferred his list to the cyclops, whose name turned out to be Bilibog, before they set about exploring the pile of junk. I had little interest in that kind of thing, so I left them to it. In the meantime, I started to devise a training program that would let me maximize my skills as quickly as possible. I had no idea what grade my new skills were, but if [Acrobatics] and [Demolition] were any indication, it wouldn't take much concerted effort to train them to their maximum tiers.

Especially if I really focused on their progression.

I wanted to advance [Navigation] and [Multimind], but I was more worried about the skills I intended to merge with Mist Control. Because I'd gotten a glimpse of how powerful it could be, and I wanted more.

After all, if it turned out to be as potent as I thought it was going to be, then it could potentially make the difference necessary to see Earth through the coming invasion. If not . . .

Well, I didn't want to think about that.

As I waited on Patrick to complete his shopping spree, I decided to consult Alistaris about my training, as well. He came from a race that had lived with the system for eons, so it stood to reason that he might know how to get the most out of my time. If I had a way to contact Freddie, I would have done that, too. As a Templar, he probably knew Mist as well as anyone, so I felt that it was probably a good assumption that he could help me with Mist Control.

Nearly two hours passed while I made and discarded plans until, at last, Patrick and Bilibog returned. The cyclops looked cautiously content, while Patrick seemed incredibly excited.

"All done?" I asked.

"Got more than I expected," Patrick answered. "A lot more. I think I have enough to do some really cool stuff with the armor."

"Awesome." I said. Then, I turned my attention to Bilibog and said, "I don't think I need to caution you against running your mouth, do I?"

He shook his head, which shook his jowls unpleasantly. "No, ma'am. Don't have to worry 'bout me none."

"Tell me something," I said. "Why are you so afraid of Gala?"

"Uh . . ."

"You can tell us, Bilibog. We're her friends."

He retrieved a cloth from one of his pockets and mopped his forehead. Finally, he leaned close. "Ye didn't hear this from me, ye hear?" he rumbled in the loudest whisper I'd ever heard.

"Sure."

"Well, you know she's Erdikar, right? Used ta be, at least. One of them Dreadnoughts. I never seen her fight, but I heard stories, I did. Don't wanna get on her bad side, ye see."

"Oh," I said. That certainly made sense. Had she sold me her old weapon, then? That meant the Stinger was even more valuable than I'd first anticipated. It made me appreciate it more than ever, and I couldn't wait to put it to use. "Thanks, I guess."

With that, Patrick and I left the confused cyclops behind. As we headed back to the exit, I couldn't help but wonder about Gala's past. Had she left the Dreadnoughts before her brother had headed to Earth? Or after? More importantly, how strong was she if even someone the size of Bilibog feared her?

None of those questions had answers—at least not that I was going to get. Still, they occupied my mind until we finally reached the exit. As we laid our hands on the exit pillar, I pushed those extraneous thoughts out of my mind. I needed to put myself in the right frame of mind because, now that I had the proper equipment, I had a war to prepare for.

CHAPTER EIGHTEEN

A PRELUDE TO TRAINING

Training is one of the most hotly contested subjects in all the universe. Some believe that hyperfocusing on one aspect of a person's development is the key. Others think that a well-rounded approach is better. Still others resort to methods that more resemble torture than training. But the reality is that there is no perfect solution because the most important facet of a person's development is their own persistence.

—Alistaris Kargat

Picking up our equipment proved easy enough, though that was probably because of the presence of a storage node that let Patrick access his own spatial storage without using his own Mist. Otherwise, we'd have looked a bit odd carrying the enormous crates of parts he'd bought from the cyclops junker. He claimed it was all valuable, but no matter how I looked at it, it all looked like trash to me.

But at least it wasn't terribly expensive.

Either way, it wasn't long before Patrick and I were on our way out of the city. It took a little while to traverse the space, mostly because the traffic had increased considerably. In addition, we stopped and enjoyed a late supper at a restaurant we'd noticed on our way in. It wasn't complex food, but the cook was skilled enough to make the simple fare stand out.

Besides, I knew it was probably the last time we'd have the opportunity to splurge on such a meal. Money wouldn't be a problem—we still had a significant fortune, even after our shopping spree—but time was going to be a factor moving forward. After all, we only had nine months left until the end of the quarantine. When that happened, we'd be going to war. So, that time would have to be spent in training.

Our backs were already against the wall, and there was no way I was going to let myself wander into a war without positioning myself as well as possible. Anything else would spell disaster.

And given that I had a lot of new toys to play with, I was more than a little eager to get going. First, though, we needed to get back to *The Leviathan* and find somewhere appropriate to set up a training program. I had some ideas about where to do just that, but I wanted to run them by Patrick before I finalized any plans. So, when we reached *The Leviathan*, I finally broached the subject.

"I want to go back to Mobile," I said.

"What? Why?" he asked.

"Two reasons," I answered. There were really three, but I was keeping one to myself. "First, it's isolated enough that we should be able to train in peace. The closest city is what's left of Nova, and the people that live there aren't in any position to range that far."

He narrowed his eye, and I saw a slight flicker in his cybernetic on the other side. That was new. Or maybe he was just starting to make it his own. Either way, it was a little disconcerting, though I took great pains not to show my discomfort. He was already self-conscious enough that I had no intention of adding my issues to the mix. Besides, it wasn't that big of a deal. Or at least that's what I kept telling myself.

"Okay. What's the other?"

"I know the area, and it's not far from a Dead Zone where I can put some of my training to work," I said. As far as I knew, there were two parts to any training regimen. The first was simple—just repetition of exercises meant to increase a person's attributes or familiarize them with a skill. The second part came from putting that training to use in real situations. That was where the Dead Zone would come in.

They were well-known for harboring powerful creatures, including wildlings. And if I outgrew the one where I'd encountered my first Rift, then I could always head toward the crater where I'd nearly been killed by a horde of irradiated wildlings. It would feel nice to wipe them from the face of the Earth while getting some much-needed training in.

But just as prominent as having a place to hunt was the fact that Mobile held a certain degree of nostalgia for me. It was there that I'd learned to separate myself from everyone else, at least in terms of power. But I'd also made my first real friends, too. I'd spent most of my life in Nova City, but the Dew Drop Inn was my first home.

And now that everything was on the verge of changing again, I desperately wanted to go back.

Thankfully, Patrick didn't have any issues with that. For his part, he only needed somewhere to set up shop, and he would be happy enough. Sure, having some mutated and monstrous wildlife on which to test his creations was nice, but he wasn't as dedicated to raw advancement as I was.

And that was okay.

He could play his role well enough, and that was all that mattered. Still, I hoped he wouldn't neglect his combat abilities altogether. There was still a war coming, and we were destined to find ourselves right in the thick of things.

Before we got going, though, we spent the night in Montreal's dock, where we pretended that we didn't have the weight of the world on our shoulders. And it was nice. Better than that, if I'm honest. The only thing keeping it from being perfect was the knowledge that it was only temporary. That simple fact cast a pall over the evening, but it also gave it an urgency that otherwise wouldn't have existed.

But soon enough, we fell asleep in each other's arms. That night, I dreamed of drowning. Nothing else. Just being stuck in the middle of an endless sea. No surface. No seabed. Just the crushing expanse of water.

I didn't need to be a psychologist to understand the meaning behind it, but after waking the next morning, I pushed it all out of my mind. I had other issues that demanded my focus, and I had no interest in examining the pressure bearing down on me.

After sharing a breakfast of bacon and eggs, we were on our way back to where everything had all started. The trip wasn't nearly as long as the distance would have implied, and we reached familiar territory before nightfall.

"Set it down in what's left of the city? Or do you want to land farther out and go in on foot?" he asked as we hovered in place.

"Land first. I want to absorb my new skills, arrange my arsenal, then check things out from the ground," I stated. "If it's clear, I'll find an appropriate place to set up. Then, I'll guide you in."

"Sounds good."

It was telling that he didn't even offer to come. I was well aware that he wanted to protect me just as much as I wanted to do the same for him, but he knew that he would only slow me down. More than that, he trusted me to take care of myself just like I'd had to force myself to trust him to do the same.

After that, Patrick found an open field where he landed *The Leviathan*. Then, we both went our separate ways. While he headed to the cargo bay to catalog and organize the parts he'd bought in the Bazaar, I retreated into my training room. But I wasn't there to train with my Mistrunning program. Instead, I settled down and retrieved the skill crystals from my arsenal implant.

Two of them—[Shielding] and [Recovery]—I set aside, but I set the three others in front of me. The first one I absorbed was [Aura Manipulation]. Next, I pressed the crystal for [Navigation] to the back of my neck and let it dissolve into my Nexus Implant. And finally, I absorbed [Multimind]. I did them all in quick succession, which was a mistake.

Unlike the first time I'd absorbed a skill, the effect of my new skills was immediate and briefly overwhelming. Suddenly, I was more aware of Mist—both ambient and the nanites concentrated across every inch of the ship—and that sudden increase definitely threw me for a loop.

It wasn't so bad, though, chiefly because I had grown progressively more accustomed to sensing the Mist. However, when that was accompanied by my mind suddenly splitting in two separate awarenesses, it became more than I could bear. I let out a gasp and very nearly lost consciousness as my brain tried to make sense of the disparate threads of thought.

I squeezed my eyes shut and threw every ounce of focus I could at the problem, which was saying quite a lot. I'd spent years training my cognition, and that practice certainly paid off as I wrangled my two minds into submission.

Still, that wasn't to say that it wasn't a long, drawn-out process. It was. Hours passed as I slowly acclimated to the twin streams of thought. However, I was far too stubborn to give in, and eventually, I managed the feat.

Once I had things under control, I navigated through my interface's menus and brought up my status:

NAME	Mirabelle Lisa Braddock		
CLASS	MIST WARDEN		
LEVEL	75 (2%)		
CONSTITUTION	308/535		
MIND	301/535		
MIST	310/535		
SKILLS	7/7		
SKILL NAME	Skill Tier	Modifiers	Abilities
MIST-INFUSED BODY	Tier 1 (7%)	600% Efficiency of Cybernetics	5 Cybernetic Slots Reformation
WARFARE	Tier 1 (19%)	+350% Damage (All) +75% Fewer Bodily Requirements +125% Recovery Speed	Empowered Shot (D) Double Shot (D) Combination Punch (D) Pummel (D) Engage (D) Mark Target (E)

| | | +50% Medication Effectiveness
+100% Endurance
+150% Explosives Yield
+100% Effectiveness (Combat Focus) | Barrage (E)
Explosive Shot (E)
Multishot (E)
Shatter Shot (E)
Instant Reload (E)
Riposte (E)
Execute (E)
Teleport (D)
Triage (D)
Basic Explosives Handling (C)
Combat Focus (C)
Pain Tolerance (D)
Resistance (D)
Foraging (D)
Improvisation (D)
Regeneration (D)
Universal Language (E)
Bastion (D)
Tinkering (F)
Share Map (D)
Waypoint (E)
Combat Map (D)
Secure Connection (C)
Ignore Injury (E)
Blast Shield (C)
Focused Will (D) |
| ESPIONAGE | Tier 0 (72%) | +150% Infiltration Abilities
+200% Mistrunning Abilities
+100% Processing Speed | Stealth (D)
Camouflage (D)
Deception (D)
Mimic (D)
Observation (D)
Charisma (E)
Interrogate (E) |

		+100% Damage (All)	Distraction (E) Vanish (E) Chameleon (D) Sense Deception (E) Mistwalk (C) Mist Control (C) Mistwall (C) System Redirect (D) Disable Cybernetics (D) Overcharge (D) Surge (E) Plague (E) Backlash (D) Mental Fortress (E) Assassinate (F)
COMBAT MANEUVERS	Tier 0 (98%)	+150% Proprioception +50% Movement Speed	Balance (C)
NAVIGATION	Tier 0 (0%)	+50% Spatial Awareness	Navigate (F)
MULTIMIND	Tier 0 (0%)	+25% Cognition	Split Mind (F)
AURA MANIPULATION	Tier 0 (0%)	+50% Aura Strength	Manipulate Aura (F)

I couldn't deny that I was very pleased with how the skills had been integrated into my system. For one, I hadn't expected the modifiers associated with each new skill. For [Navigation], I'd gained a full fifty percent modifier to my spatial awareness. Already, I felt more cognizant of my surroundings, and I hadn't even had the chance to acclimate to the modifier. Surely, once I did, it would be even more powerful.

I probably shouldn't have been surprised to see a twenty-five percent increase to my cognition associated with [Multimind]. Without that, a normal person who absorbed the skill would have been too overwhelmed to function. I wasn't nearly as affected by it—likely due to my high Mind attribute—but it was still a welcome addition to my already stacked modifiers.

For [Aura Manipulation], I'd gotten a fifty percent increase to my aura strength, though aside from a line on my status, I wasn't sure what the effect really was. I certainly didn't feel any different, but I supposed that might change once I had a chance to train with it. Until then, it would probably remain mostly inert.

Other than that, the rest of my status looked much the same as it had before the trip to the Bazaar. My attributes had almost reached their maximum, but now that I'd regained three skills, my potential was much, much higher. I hoped to leverage that to my advantage via copious training. I knew that potential wasn't just the limit of a person's attributes. It was that, sure. But the larger the gap between a person's potential and their current attributes meant faster progression, as well. So, given that I now had a pretty good ways to go before reaching my potential, I expected to make rapid gains in my attributes.

I was also sure that I would need that going forward if we were going to survive.

I did notice even after three months and running a Rift that I'd barely moved the needle on my progress through the level, though. Two percent. That was it. Clearly, it was going to take something monumental to take me past level seventy-five, but given what it had taken to get that far, that should have been expected.

Still, it was a little disappointing.

As far as my other skills were concerned, I'd made some progress, even reaching Tier 1 in [Warfare] and [Mist-Infused Body], gaining some increases to my modifiers in the process. I hadn't really tested anything out, but I hoped that increased power would come in handy.

After looking over my basic status, I moved on to the individual skill trees. First up was [Warfare]:

Tree	Warfare: Tier 1 (19%) <Focus for Modifiers>			
Branch	Arms: Tier 1 (2%)	Explosives: Tier 0 (77%)	Fieldcraft: Tier 1 (11%)	Command: Tier 0 (12%)
Tier 1	+25% Damage (All)	+50% Explosives Yield	+100% Endurance	Ability: Planetary Defense
Tier 2	+25% Damage (All)	+50% Explosives Yield	+50% Effectiveness (Combat Focus)	+100% Effectiveness (Planetary Defense)

Tier 3	+50% Reload Speed (Firearms)	Ability: Selective Explosion	+150% Effectiveness (Regeneration)	+100% Effectiveness (Planetary Defense)
Tier 4	+50% Rate of Fire (Firearms)	+100% Explosive Radius	Ability: Stasis	Ability: Aura of Command
Tier 5	Ability: Overclock	Ability: Replicate Charge	+200% Defense	Ability: Orbital Strike

Three of those branches were fairly self-explanatory, especially when it came to advancing their tiers. However, I still wasn't sure how to affect the progress of the Command branch. I'd made some headway, but it had yet to narrow down the reasons why. I hoped to make some progress in that arena because abilities like Planetary Defense and Orbital Strike certainly sounded useful.

Otherwise, I'd picked up some extra modifiers in damage and endurance, though I hadn't really felt any differences. That was how those modifiers tended to work, though. By this point, adding an extra twenty-five percent damage didn't represent much in relation to the total modifiers from all the skills that had evolved into [Warfare].

Tree	**Espionage: Tier 0 (72%)** <Focus for Modifiers>			
Branch	Infiltration: Tier 0 (97%)	Mist Manipulation: Tier 1 (3%)	Reconnaissance: Tier 0 (62%)	Assassination: Tier 0 (61%)
Tier 1	+25% Infiltration Effectiveness	+50% Mist Abilities	+25% Effectiveness (Observation)	+50% Damage (Stealth)
Tier 2	+25% Infiltration Effectiveness	+25% Mist Abilities	Ability: Sensory Mask	+50% Damage (Stealth)
Tier 3	+50% Infiltration Effectiveness	+100% Mist Abilities	+50% Effectiveness (Observation)	Ability: Sense Weakness

Tier 4	+100% Infiltration Effectiveness	Ability: Mist Spike	+25% Effectiveness (Observation)	+15% Damage (Stealth)
Tier 5	Ability: Mist Cloak	Ability: Mist Deprivation	Ability: Perfect Recall	Ability: Target Weakness

[Espionage] had experienced decidedly less progression, though I was pleased to see that the Mist Manipulation branch had reached Tier 1. I could only hope that things would go a lot more quickly once I could devote all my time and energy toward training. On the one hand, nine months seemed like a long time. I only had to think back to after I'd first gained my Nexus Implant to remember how much progress I could make in that span. However, on the other hand, I knew that it was far too little time to accomplish all my goals.

Still, even if I managed to reach those standards, I'd only move on to the next challenge. That was my curse—I couldn't just rest. I always needed to be working toward something. But curse or not, it was also my largest advantage.

After I'd finished absorbing my new skills, I spent some time arranging my weapons in my arsenal implant. It could now hold five weapons, so I threw the Stringer in the first, followed by the ADS, Emperor, and the HIRC. I finished it off with the BMAP; despite the additions, the weapon still served a purpose, and I didn't intend to leave it behind.

I admit that I was a little sad to leave the R-14 and Pulsar behind. Both had served me well, but my time in the Rift had driven home just how outdated they were. Even with my modifiers, they were just incapable of packing the sort of punch I'd need to dispatch the powerful enemies I was sure to make.

I did keep the nano-bladed sword, though I shifted it into one of the generic slots in my arsenal implant. It was just small enough that I could pull it out with only a little Mist expenditure. The interdiction blade I sheathed on my back. Of course, I also kept Ferdinand II holstered at my hip. He wasn't any more powerful than the weapons I'd replaced, but the pistol had a few advantages they didn't—chiefly that he could fire a wide variety of ammunition. Much like the BMAP, Ferdinand II served a wide variety of purposes, and with the right ammunition—which I'd bought from Gala—he could still pack quite a punch.

Besides, I was more nostalgic for that weapon than any other.

Thus armed, I turned my attention to my infiltration suit and my subdermal armor. The infiltration suit was still the best of its kind, so I couldn't replace it. The armor, on the other hand, had received a new upgrade module that increased its kinetic absorption, meaning that it would take a lot more force to penetrate. And considering that it was my last line of defense before things started ripping me to pieces, that was an attractive upgrade.

Once I'd gotten all of that sorted, I left the room behind. As I passed through the cargo bay on my way out, I bade farewell to Patrick—who was predictably tinkering with his armor—before leaving through one of the side doors.

The humidity hit me like a brick wall, bringing with it a wave of nostalgia. As I processed that, I got the first taste of how useful Split Mind could be. One strand of thought latched on to Observation, keeping track of everything around me, while the other handled my {Mist Warden} senses. I could see everything all at once, which was why I wasn't even surprised when an oversize cougar leaped out at me.

I whipped the interdiction blade out of its sheath and, in the same motion, swept it through the animal's neck. I felt almost no resistance as I stepped aside to avoid the creature's momentum.

Even as two separate thumps announced the fall of both parts of the cougar's body, I realized that I'd never lost track of my surroundings.

"I'm going to like this," I said to myself before setting off toward one of the roads I knew was in the area. When I reached my destination, I mounted my bike and set off toward the only real home I'd ever known.

CHAPTER NINETEEN

THE RUINS OF CONTENTMENT

I think Mira always wanted to go back. She has so many regrets that she just can't leave behind.

—Patrick Ward

The wilderness surrounding Mobile was both familiar and not. It felt like I was looking at a landscape that I should have known like the back of my hand, but none of the details were right. The terrain was populated by the same wildlife and thick vegetation that had overcome the signs of long-gone civilization, but I didn't recognize any of the landmarks.

Of course, it had been years since I'd been back to Mobile, so I shouldn't have been surprised that the wilderness had begun to reclaim the region. Still, it almost felt as if I was walking through a parallel world as I made my way to the closest road. When I reached that destination, I saw yet more changes. The road that had once been so meticulously maintained by the Amigos and their crews was so overgrown that the path was only vaguely recognizable.

As I summoned the Cutter and mounted the hover bike, I was beset by a wave of regret and nostalgia. The first because I was reminded of how my time in Mobile had ended. I wasn't so self-centered that I still believed I could have done anything to stop it. Not anymore. And yet, some degree of guilt persisted, as if my emotions simply refused to take logic into account.

The nostalgia was more justifiable, though. I'd experienced a lot of firsts in Mobile, and I looked back on those memories with fondness. Even the worst parts of my training regimen had taken on a rose-colored sheen, though that was probably as much to do with my obsession with progression as it was because of some misguided reminiscence.

In any case, I mounted the hover bike and took off along the overgrown road, dodging trees and bushes along the way. As I did, I kept one half of my mind on the road while the other remained trained on the results of Observation. I'd been attacked—and without warning—often enough that I knew that just because I was moving, it didn't mean I could avoid predators. Fortunately, though, nothing assaulted me as I made my way, and after only an hour, I reached the outskirts of Mobile.

Unsurprisingly, it was entirely abandoned. The city's location had never been ideal, and once it had been destroyed, there was no reason for anyone to rebuild or reoccupy. Still, I couldn't help but lament the loss as I passed the abandoned ruins of the old city. Along the way, I saw a few wildlings and other local fauna, but none of them took notice of me. I counted myself lucky in that respect. I had no compunctions about killing, but I didn't want to waste my time fighting battles that offered so little to gain.

Eventually, I arrived at the new city, and I was once again beset by a wave of regret as I looked upon the destroyed remnants of the buildings that had once housed the city's population. Most of the wall was still intact, though many of the old cargo containers had succumbed to the elements and fallen from their perch. Without the Mist shield, there was no protection against the harsh storms that ascended from the warm Gulf waters to the south.

As I passed through a large gap in the wall—which was how the Enforcers had breached the city's defenses—that feeling of near familiarity returned, taunting me with the subtle differences. A destroyed building here, an overgrown square there—it was all just left of my memory, and it left me feeling incredibly disconcerted.

And that feeling came crashing home when I saw the remains of the Dew Drop Inn. It had never been a particularly noteworthy building. In fact, in the context of the city, it had been the epitome of normality. However, to me, it represented something I'd never really experienced. It was home in a way the penthouse back in Nova had never been.

And now it was gone.

Just like everything else that had made Mobile mean anything to me.

"Why am I here?" I muttered to myself as I stared at the building where some of my most treasured memories had taken place.

I was self-aware enough to at least recognize that the reasons I'd given Patrick were, at best, excuses. At worst, they were blatant lies. I could have gone anywhere to train. There were powerful Dead Zones throughout the world, and some in more hospitable locations. No—I had chosen Mobile because, in the back of my mind, I knew that my odds of survival past the onset of the Integration were slim.

Sure, I made a habit of defying the odds. Plenty of my accomplishments had far exceeded what anyone could expect. And yet, I had some notion of what kind of enemies were in my future, and I recognized that the chances I'd win were fairly short. I still intended to survive. I wanted to defeat the aliens and ensure Earth's freedom from the oppression they would bring with them. However, I'd also come to accept the limits of my own mortality.

That was why I had insisted on coming back to Mobile. I just wanted to bask in a few good memories while I prepared for the difficult path ahead. That realization made me feel more human than I'd felt in a long, long time, and not in a completely good way.

After coming to that conclusion, I set out through the city so I could ensure that it wasn't populated—by humans, aliens, or wildlife—and I found that, aside from a few overgrown rodents, it was entirely abandoned. I also discovered that the old training building where I'd spent so much time had survived intact. It was just as overgrown with vines as anywhere else in the city, but the interior was mostly clear. With only a few days of work, I could return it to its former glory.

The same couldn't be said for anywhere else in the city. A few buildings remained standing, but for the most part, what hadn't succumbed to the Enforcers' bombardment had been taken down by a combination of time, the local flora, and weather. Fortunately, I did find a mostly empty lot next to the training facility that I thought would make for a perfect dock for *The Leviathan*.

So, I used Secure Connection to contact Patrick, telling him what I'd found. He seemed a little distracted, likely due to keeping busy with his work, but he took the news well and vowed to join me as soon as he finished his current task.

That left me to start the cleanup alone. So, I summoned my nano-bladed sword and got to work on the exterior of the building. Certainly, the interdiction blade was much more advanced, but for cutting down a few vines, the nano-blade was more than sufficient. Besides, it felt a little wrong to use my brand-new weapon for such a mundane task.

Over the next few hours, I gradually circled the building and acted the part of a groundskeeper. It wasn't exciting work, but it certainly gave me a sense of satisfaction when I looked back on the product of my labor. In any case, it needed to be done, so as I always did, I put my head down and did the work.

Patrick arrived a few hours into my task, though instead of joining me, he turned his attention on the lot where he'd landed *The Leviathan*. Though it was flat and unobstructed by any buildings—crumbling or otherwise—it was just as overgrown as the rest of the ruins. So, it required quite a lot of attention before it would meet our standards.

The next week was occupied by much of the same, but by the end of it, we had a nice little training ground that could function as our semipermanent residence while we prepared for the difficulties to come.

And that's when I got down to the serious business of training.

For my physical regimen, I donned the suppressive bands I'd used during previous training sessions. Without them, everything was just too easy, but cranking them up to their maximum power restricted my attributes enough to render me mostly normal. I was still superhuman in terms of strength and agility but not so far above normal human potential that I couldn't properly structure a training program.

Thus restricted, I spent most of each morning lifting weights, running sprints, or utilizing the obstacle course that had somehow survived years of abandonment. After the first week, I added a few extra levels to that course, and the second week saw me expanding it even farther. By the end of that month, it was more than a quarter mile long and wrapped around the inside of the building's outer wall.

Still, I found it too easy for my taste—at least until Alistaris showed up and gave me a new pair of suppression bands.

"How did you find me?" I asked.

"It's my job to know where you are," he said cryptically.

"There's still a tracker in *The Leviathan*, isn't there?"

He didn't answer. Instead, he initiated a data transfer, which I accepted. When I opened the file, I saw that it described a training program. In a lot of ways, it wasn't much different from the one in which I was currently engaged. However, it differed in enough ways that I could easily see how it would improve my results.

So, after scanning the ship once again—and discovering that Alistaris's trackers gave off a subtle Mist signature that made finding them incredibly easy—I continued my training.

Each afternoon was devoted to weapons practice, though with the way I did it, it probably looked little different from my normal physical training. I rarely stood still, instead opting to use obstacle course runs to increase the difficulty. And it worked, too. I noticed a marked increase in the rate of my progression. It was small, but even a tiny difference would be noticeable over time. I just had to keep at it.

For Patrick's part, he trained, as well, though he spent most of his time tinkering with his armor or cybernetics. And just like me, he progressed, too, though not nearly as quickly.

As I trained, I used Split Mind to practice with Manipulate Aura. Barely a moment passed when I wasn't trying to suppress or expand the cloud of Mist that followed me everywhere.

Days passed into weeks, and weeks became months as we single-mindedly pursued our progression. And soon enough, we both saw marked improvements. However, I knew that simple training wasn't enough. I needed to put everything into practice. So, after three months of constant training, I set off for the Dead Zone.

That's when I discovered the true power of my new arsenal. The Stinger hit almost as hard as my old Pulsar had, though with a much higher rate of fire. Meanwhile, the HIRC was even more powerful than the Dragon, and never was that more apparent than when I used it to rip a wildling alpha to shreds.

The ADS was a bit less damaging, but that wasn't its purpose. The shotgun-like weapon was meant to be supplementary, and the draining effect it created was more than a little useful.

But the real star of the show was the Emperor. If I had to compare it to the Pulsar, I would say that its first shot was about twice as powerful as its predecessor, and it only grew more deadly with each subsequent shot. However, it was a real Mist hog—though I did discover that, with Mist Control, I could siphon some of the ambient Mist into the weapon, lessening the load.

That made it a little less punishing, and it gave me the opportunity to practice my ability.

The lone time I used all seven shots in the Emperor's magazine, it looked like a miniature version of the explosion I'd caused on the moon. I'd fired from a mile away, and even then, I felt the shock wave of that final shot. And when I went to inspect the damage, I saw only a hundred-foot-wide crater where the target had once been.

Of the enormous hog I'd shot, there was nothing left.

"Damn," said Patrick, standing beside me at the edge of the crater. "I was kind of hoping we could have pork for dinner."

"I didn't expect it to . . . just vaporize it," I muttered. Indeed, the creature had been the size of a hover car, with giant metal tusks, and it had taken the first six shots fairly well. But that last one? It was like I'd strapped a series of bombs to it.

"What now? More training?"

I shrugged. "Yeah. We're down to a little more than six months," I said. "I've made progress, but . . ."

"But you're afraid it isn't enough," he finished for me.

I nodded, saying, "We get closer every day, and even with all these toys, I don't know that it'll be enough."

"Then we train harder," he said. "We go longer. We get stronger. That's all we can do, right?"

I let out a sigh, but I didn't answer. Inside, though, I knew that there was only one viable response. My commitment to the fight hadn't wavered, and yet, I wasn't certain how I was going to do the things I needed to do.

"Did you figure out that new ability?"

"No. There's nothing out there about it," I answered. "Besides, it's not like I'm any closer to progressing that branch. Right now, it looks like I'll never gain access to Planetary Defense."

"That branch is called Command, right? Maybe you have to lead people into battle or something," Patrick suggested. "That would make sense."

He wasn't wrong, but there was one glaring problem. I had no one to lead. Even if that was how the Command branch of [Warfare] was meant to progress, I simply didn't have the means to facilitate it.

By comparison, [Aura Manipulation] had already gained two tiers. It didn't move quite as quickly as something like [Acrobatics], but with the way I was training, it was flying through the ranks. At that pace, it wouldn't be long before I merged it with Mist Control and started in on the second phase of my skill strategy.

After that brief excursion, we headed back to our training grounds and continued as we had. However, I added a few extra hours of swimming to my daily regimen. Within a week after our return, I was spending close to sixteen hours of each day working toward progression. Sometimes, I exceeded that by a fair bit.

And it had a multitude of effects on me.

First, my attributes skyrocketed under such intense training. Barely a day went by when I didn't gain at least a point in each category. Sometimes, I managed to raise the total by quite a bit more than that. This I attributed to my intense and well-optimized regimen, but it was also due to the application of [Mist-Infused Body]—or, rather, the regeneration associated with it.

At first, it only allowed me to fully regenerate my body every seventy-one hours. That was powerful enough on its own, but as my Mist attribute rose, so too did the cooldown shrink until, after three months, it was down to once per day. And I knew it was only the beginning. Once I reached my potential, I hoped it would be usable with even more frequency.

Regardless, each time I used the ability, it refreshed and regenerated my body, obviating the need for rest. That, in turn, made my training that much more effective.

"That ability feels like cheating," Patrick said after I'd regenerated one time.

I gave him a smile and responded, "Wouldn't you rather I be the one cheating instead of our enemies?"

"You have a point there," he said.

It was in the fifth month that I finally reached Tier 5 with [Aura Manipulation], and true to Ana's prediction, that's when I got a new notification:

Synergy detected! Merging skill [Aura Manipulation] with ability Mist Control.

I was only barely able to read it before I was beset by agonizing pain that ripped through both of my minds. For the first time in a long time, I couldn't think. I could scarcely even breathe, the pain was so intense. I collapsed to my knees, clutching my head in my hands as I desperately tried to acclimate to the pain. Fortunately, it only lasted for a few seconds before it disappeared altogether. Following that was another notification:

Skill [Aura Manipulation] successfully merged with Mist Control. Skill lost. Mist Control has evolved into Mist Authority. Progress reset at F.

"Whoa," I breathed as my {Mist Warden} senses went wild. Suddenly, the auras I'd begun to take for granted became vastly more detailed. In addition, the subtle undercurrent of Mist that suffused everything in the world became more noticeable. However, it wasn't nearly as distracting as that might suggest, largely because I shunted the sensory input into my second mind.

Not for the first time, I found myself sending a silent thank-you to Ana for suggesting [Multimind] to me. Without it, there's no way I'd ever get the most out of abilities like Mist Control.

Or Mist Authority, as it had become after the evolution.

That, as much as any other advancement since I'd begun my training prodded me ahead. With that success under my belt, I was even more committed to the regimen than I'd ever been before.

So, with that in mind, I pushed myself to my feet and resumed my routine.

CHAPTER TWENTY

PAYBACK

Mira has been through a lot. I've lost count of the number of times she's almost died. But none of those instances have affected—or continue to affect—her quite like the time she went up against a horde of irradiated wildlings. It wasn't until that moment, when someone else had to rescue her, that she started to recognize her own mortality. And that has stuck with her ever since.

—Patrick Ward

A month later, I felt confident enough with my new abilities and arsenal to really put them to the test. However, I had no intention of assaulting a Rift-mining operation or other alien enclave. Instead, I wanted to throw myself back into the fray against the opponents who had tested me most completely.

So, Patrick and I loaded ourselves into *The Leviathan* and set off across the landscape in search of the crater where I'd encountered the irradiated wildlings who had nearly killed me the first time around. Of course, this time, I wouldn't have a friendly group of Templars to pull me out of the proverbial fire—as confirmed when Patrick and I reached the site of that battle and saw that there was no human presence for dozens of miles around. The closest settlement was almost a hundred miles away, and even that was sparsely populated, with only the barest hint of advancement.

It reminded me of Bayou La Batre or, rather, what that small town would've been if it hadn't had its shrimping industry to prop it up.

"What are you thinking?" asked Patrick as we banked and circled the settlement.

I shrugged, watching the town so far below. It looked so small. So fragile. But I knew it wasn't. Nobody could survive so close to the Dead Zone without significant ability to defend themselves.

"Nothing," I said. "I was just wondering about all the little towns around Mobile."

Indeed, in the few months since we'd set up shop in the ruins of the city, we'd made a few forays into the wilderness. There, we'd found the remnants of a handful of towns. All had been destroyed or abandoned, likely because, without Mobile to supply and protect them, it was too difficult to maintain those villages. For us, that meant we didn't have to worry about them stumbling on our campsite, but it was also a reminder of the consequences of my actions. I hadn't invited the Enforcers to attack Mobile, but they wouldn't have come if it wasn't for me—or the Tier 7 Nexus Implant I'd absorbed—so I still felt partially responsible.

But aside from the initial destruction of Mobile—and then Nova City—there were far-reaching consequences I'd so infrequently considered. The entire region had been decimated, with only a fraction of the inhabitants being unaffected. Without me, they would have continued living.

"It's not your fault, Mira," he said.

I just nodded, knowing that his statement was never intended to be factual. Instead, it was Patrick's attempt at soothing my guilt, and though I wanted to believe it, I knew better than to absolve myself.

In any case, I continued to ponder the ramifications of my actions as we swooped around and scanned the area surrounding the crater. When we reached the site itself, I saw the same giant reptilian skeleton, which was surrounded by the war machines of a bygone age. Tanks and trucks, all painted in camouflage patterns, were scattered across the crater. Some were more or less intact, but others had been blown to bits. None had escaped completely unscathed, though, and the ravages of age were more than evident.

The biggest difference from my last visit was more attributable to my augmented {Mist Warden} senses. With the naked eye, the entire crater looked all but deserted. A few irradiated wildlings were visible, but the bulk of the horde were buried belowground. Since my first encounter, I'd learned that there was a warren of tunnels and chambers beneath the crater, and that was where the creatures lived. They usually only left to hunt, coming and going from the tunnels via disguised exits.

But with my new senses, which were further augmented by Observation, I could see the evidence of an enormous population. Even through ten feet of solid earth, the creatures' auras were entirely visible. Some were weak—barely denser than a low-level human—but others looked like raging storm clouds, thick and ominous. And finally, there were a handful of auras that clearly rivaled even my own, which was the only real context to which I had been exposed since developing the ability to sense auras.

"There must be hundreds of thousands of them," I said.

"So many?" asked Patrick, keeping his own eyes on our progress. He couldn't see what I saw, but the Dead Zone had more denizens than wildlings. It wouldn't be out of the ordinary for some winged beast the size of a spacefaring ship to attack us. So, he kept his attention where it belonged.

"Al said that wildlings are sometimes attracted to these Dead Zones. It's a way to accelerate their own development, and they're instinctively drawn to it," I said. "They've also had almost a century to breed down there."

Indeed, Alistaris and I had shared more than a little communication during my training, and he'd given me some insight as to what had happened in those areas. Dead Zones were already hot spots when it came to Mist accumulation, but it seemed that humanity's use of nuclear weapons had exacerbated the situation by quite a lot. As such, the Mist had reacted to the resulting radiation—mostly to clean it up—and that adaptation of the Mist had tainted the environment. Without the Mist's intervention, the region would have been uninhabitable for hundreds of years. Now, it had already been rendered safe, though with the result being a unique evolution of the natives.

And that evolution was why the wildlings were so much more powerful than normal. Based on previous experiences, I put their average power level at something around the alphas I'd fought in the past, which meant that the irradiated alphas were a good deal stronger than any other wildlings I'd ever encountered. Then, there were the strongest among the horde to worry about; as far as I could tell, they were the most powerful creatures I'd seen on Earth, and if I'd had to guess, they would have been on par with Edrax Kel Tanimvan, the android with the huge sword whose copies I'd fought on the moon and in Olympus.

Maybe even stronger, considering that a good deal of his power was wrapped up in having multiple copies.

Which meant that the crater represented the perfect opportunity to test my new abilities, higher attributes, and expanded arsenal. In addition, I had Patrick to back me up and assure our retreat if something went wrong. So, we were as prepared as possible.

Still, I wasn't above cheating a little, so I said, "I think it's time."

"Alright. I'll circle it five times, then set *The Leviathan* down where we talked about," he said, turning his attention to business. Though he hadn't seen the horde firsthand—except for a brief glimpse—Patrick knew what it had done to me in the past. So, he was ready for a tough battle.

After rising from my seat, I gave Patrick's shoulder a reassuring squeeze before heading back to the cargo bay. There, I found that he'd already opened the back hatch, exposing me to a blast of cold air. We weren't high enough for it to become truly frigid, but I was a self-avowed tropical person, and as such, I didn't enjoy freezing temperatures. Still, I endured it as I crossed the cargo bay, thanking my Balance ability along the way, until I reached a handful of huge crates.

Normally, I kept my grenades and other explosive charges in my arsenal implant, but I didn't want to waste so much space when I had a perfectly good cargo bay at my disposal. So, when I reached the first stack, I unlatched the lid, then flipped it open to reveal fifteen square charges.

I retrieved the first handful, then started tossing them out of the open hatch. Knowing our general air speed, I threw one every couple of seconds. Then, following that pattern, I kept going until the first crate was finished. After that, I started in on the second. Then, the third. Within a few minutes, I'd placed more than a hundred powerful demolition charges throughout the crater. They weren't perfectly spaced, but it was close enough that I didn't think I'd have to worry about missing any.

"I'm done," I said via Secure Connection.

"Ten-four," Patrick responded before guiding *The Leviathan* to the landing zone from which we had agreed to launch our assault. As he circled back around, I could sense the Mist of my explosive charges, which was quite a bit different than before. I think that was the biggest difference I'd noticed since Mist Control had evolved into Mist Authority. My ability to manipulate the Mist was mostly unchanged, but I could sense subtle differences in a way I never could have before. Without the evolution, I'd have only seen a giant blob of Mist—the horde of wildlings—with a few hot spots here and there to represent the more powerful among the population. Now, though, I could see individuals, even from an elevation of more than a thousand feet. I could also see my own charges clearly, which told me that I'd spaced them out properly.

For a moment, I was beset by a desire to detonate them. If I did, the resulting explosion would kill all but the hardiest of wildlings. However, I chose not to for two reasons. First, I wasn't there to exterminate the population. Sure, it would hopefully be a nice side effect, but the goal of the excursion was to test my abilities and provide Patrick with the opportunity to gain some levels. So, not only did I need the chance to actually bring my expanded arsenal to bear, but I also needed to do so in a way that allowed Patrick to affect the battle and gain experience.

The second reason was a little more personal. I very much enjoyed blowing things up, but there was just something visceral about using my other weapons. And given the state the horde had left me in after our first encounter, I wanted nothing more than to see the effects of my weapons up close.

Or as close as possible.

As we landed, I mentally checked my preparations. The bombs were armed, my weapons were all loaded, and I was about as protected as possible. In addition to my Sheath, which had recently received another upgrade module courtesy of Gala, who'd remained on the lookout for anything that would boost my defenses, as well as my infiltration suit, I had also absorbed the [Shielding] skill.

Using it was a little frustrating, largely because, even after rapidly progressing from F-grade to D-grade, I only had two ways to use it. The first was as a passive defense, which used my Mist aura to block attacks. If I'd had to guess at its efficacy, I would have put it somewhere between the defenses provided by my infiltration suit and the effect of my Sheath. So, it was a very potent ability, though not quite the impenetrable defense that I'd hoped for.

The second mode was not really part of the skill but, rather, a way for me to eke a little more power out of it. Using Mist Authority, I could harden my shield even further, augmenting the more normal effects at least tenfold. However, that came with the downside of rapidly draining my personal Mist reserves, so I could only keep it up for a second or two. I hoped that it would become less costly as my abilities progressed, but even now, it provided strong innate defenses as well as a powerful emergency ability.

Still, it wasn't quite as strong as I'd hoped for, which was the source of my frustration.

In any case, that had never been the point of absorbing the skill in the first place, so I counted any extra defenses as a bonus.

Once I'd triple-checked my arsenal and Patrick had done the same, we both exited through the back hatch of *The Leviathan*. After that, I used Bastion to ensure it would remain secure before we set off through the wilderness. We'd landed the ship a few miles away from our intended battlefield, which meant that it was close enough to provide a means of retreat but far enough away that it wouldn't become collateral damage. So, it took us a little less than an hour to hack our way through the tangled wilderness; we probably could have gone faster, but there really wasn't any reason to.

Finally, we reached our destination, and Patrick summoned his armor from his own spatial storage, then mounted it. Soon enough, he was enclosed within his cockpit, and I'd summoned the HIRC. I set up on the lip of the crater, taking aim at the most concentrated cloud of Mist signatures. Then, I said via Secure Connection, "Get us started, Pick."

He'd set up a few dozen yards away, but the thunder of the assault rifle he carried—it had taken parts of my old Kicker as well as my R-14, creating an amalgam of both that was far more powerful than either had been alone—cut through that distance to ring in my ears. Immediately, clouds of rock and dirt and pieces of vegetation kicked into the air.

His target—a cluster of comparatively weak wildlings—took the fire well. One went down with a dozen gunshot wounds, but the others were almost entirely unaffected. Immediately after his spurt of gunfire ceased, the swollen-bellied creatures whipped around and charged in our direction.

But I wasn't concerned with them. Patrick didn't have my innate power, but he made up for it with the strength of his weaponry. I knew his guns weren't nearly as strong as mine, but they were far more potent than most. Couple that with the fact that each one of them counted as a cybernetic—his class applied significant modifiers—he could more than hold his own on the field of battle.

As such, he could easily deal with that small group.

My attention was on the rest of the horde, which I saw had already begun to surge. Their Mist signatures spun with ever-increasing fervor, but they were still too far away for me to enact the first part of my plan.

That changed before Patrick's targets had even covered half the distance between us. Even as they tore across the crater, vaulting over the ruined machines of war, Patrick filled them all with holes. Meanwhile, the rest of the subterranean wildlings erupted from a hundred small tunnels, adding their bulk to a growing horde.

When that army of mutated creatures grew into the thousands, I hefted the HIRC to my hip, took aim, and let loose.

The results were, in a word, volatile.

The Mist-infused rounds, which were enhanced by both Explosive Shot as well as my significant modifiers, slammed into the front lines, the impacts prompting a dozen small explosions that tore my victims apart. The weapon didn't have the Dragon's rate of fire, but it didn't need it, either, and I felt a smile spread across my face at my increased firepower.

Once, those creatures had stretched me to my limits. But now? My new weapon—and more powerful abilities—made quick work of them. Their fall would have been even faster if I hadn't reined myself in so Patrick could add his own contribution. Doing so would let him gain more experience, which in turn would push his progression further.

Like that, we took care of the first wave, but even as we cut those first couple of hundred down, I could see that thousands more were on their way. And that wasn't even considering the ones deeper within the crater; they were far more powerful, and those would provide me with a lot more context as to the strength of my new arsenal.

Before I'd used even a tenth of the HIRC's magazine, I stowed the weapon away and switched to the Stinger. The assault rifle was sleek and compact, especially when compared to the much larger HIRC, but it felt incredibly appropriate in my hands. Switching it to burst-fire mode, I took aim at the largest cluster of Mist signatures; they were still underground, but I could see that they were on the verge of bursting through.

A few seconds passed, and Patrick continued his own onslaught on the smaller groups. Still, I waited until the first group of elites—they were stronger than the ones we'd killed so far, but I didn't feel comfortable calling them alphas—burst through. I used Explosive Shot on the Stinger's entire magazine, which drained a significant amount of Mist, then let loose in a series of three-round bursts.

Each burst destroyed a wildling. Some went down with the first shot, their chests exploding in green blood and chunks of pale flesh. However, most took at least two shots before their torsos were destroyed. The strongest among them didn't go down without three shots.

That was a testament to their durability.

But a scattered few took multiple bursts. I considered those on the verge of being alphas, though I knew the real battle had yet to even begin. That, more than anything, hammered home just how close to death I'd come during my first encounter with the irradiated wildlings that called the crater their home. Back then, I thought I'd been on the verge of winning the battle, but now, I knew I'd never had a chance.

Even so, seeing how easily I was cutting the creatures down gave me some context as to how much I'd grown. The real challenge, though, was yet to come. I could see much more powerful Mist signatures underground, and already, some had begun to burst through the earth.

Soon enough, I would see how my new arsenal and abilities would stand up to a real threat.

CHAPTER TWENTY-ONE

A HINT OF WHAT'S TO COME

Sometimes, Mira frightens me. I know she would never hurt me, but she has so much power and so little regard for consequences. She once murdered millions of people without even trying, and that's not considering what she did to the moon. What if something goes wrong and one of her abilities goes out of control? It's not outside the realm of possibility that she could destroy the entire world on accident. That keeps me up at night.

—Patrick Ward

The BMAP thumped as I discharged one explosive cannister after another. They were new ammunition, and I wanted to test them out in a less-than-desperate situation before I used them when it really mattered. The shells flew through the air, arcing high above the battlefield before descending toward a cluster of irradiated wildlings. Just before the first hit, the shell exploded into a cloud of Mist-laced gas. A second later, the next one did the same. And the next after that. By the time the final cannister erupted, a hundred square yards of the crater had been bathed in the blue-sparking gas.

That's when the wildlings' excited screeches began to take on a different tenor. Instead of expressions of eagerness, they became the aural equivalent of pure terror and abject misery. Flaring Observation, I watched as the blue gas clung to the wildlings, melting their flesh and eating through their bones. From afar, their bodies looked like melting wax, and in only seconds, all but the hardiest of wildlings in that area had fallen.

"Damn," Patrick said over the Secure Connection.

Indeed. The shells themselves hadn't been terribly expensive, and the base gas was cheap enough, as well. The real trick was the Mist infusion, which was one of the ways I'd found to practice Mist Authority. I knew it wasn't terribly efficient, and the Mist only lasted for a few days before it began to dissipate. However, if I used them before that, the result was obviously deadly.

I knew it wouldn't have been possible for most people to do the same. Tinkering, Basic Explosives Handling, and Mist Authority were all necessary to make it work, and even if someone was capable of replicating the cannisters' construction, they would never have gotten so much out of them. I had my modifiers to thank for that.

In short, the ammunition was personalized to take advantage of my abilities, skills, and modifiers, and it used that specialization to great effect.

The cloud of Mist only lasted a half minute, but during that time, the wildlings were forced to go around. Hopefully, the ability to temporarily block an enemy's intended path would one day come in handy.

I had a dozen more cannisters in my arsenal implant, but I chose not to use them. Instead, I swapped the BMAP out for my Stinger, then laid into the wildlings who tried to skirt the Mist-infused cloud of deadly gas. Due to their relative lack of intelligence, they never even thought to swing wide. Instead, the wildlings all took the same track, racing in my direction as soon as they cleared the cloud. That served to line them up perfectly, and I mowed them down with little difficulty.

"So far, so good," said Patrick over the Secure Connection we shared between us.

I sighed. "Really, Patrick?" I muttered with a shake of my head.

"What?"

"You just had to say it, didn't you?"

"What are you talking about?"

"You don't say stuff like that. You'll jinx the whole thing!"

"That's . . . That's stupid," he scoffed.

"It's real. Just watch. Everything's going to go wrong any second," I replied. I wasn't sure if I actually believed that; usually, I wasn't superstitious. However, there was no reason to so blatantly tempt fate.

Sure enough, only a few seconds later, a few giant figures burst forth from the ground. In some ways, they looked similar to the other wildlings, with limbs that were far too long and massively bulging bellies. However, these were at least twice the height of the already tall wildlings, and I could see that their Mist auras were significantly denser. That suggested much greater levels of power.

"See?"

"You already saw those coming," Patrick argued. "What I said had nothing to do with it."

I shifted my aim to the closest. It was still a couple hundred yards away, but the Stinger was more than capable of reaching that far. And with Observation as well as my modifiers, that distance barely even affected my aim. I fired, one three-round burst after another, hitting the creature in its bulbous stomach. The rounds thudded home with a trio of small explosions that tore into the layer of fat, but they did little real damage.

I couldn't help but smile. Finally, we'd caught the attention of some truly durable monsters. Of course, my perception was a little skewed; it wasn't that long ago when I'd nearly been killed by the more normal irradiated wildlings. Back then, if I'd come up against one of these new larger creatures, I would have died.

Fortunately, I was much stronger now.

So, I flipped the Stinger to full auto, reestablished my aim, then squeezed the trigger. In anyone else's hands, that steady stream of explosive rounds would have sent the weapon bucking, but in mine, with my enhanced Constitution, it was trivial to hold it steady. As a result, the rounds flew true, hitting in a tight grouping in the center of the monster's bulbous stomach. The next few did little more damage than the first three shots, but each impact tore a bit of protective fat and muscle away until, twenty shots in, the creature's innards were entirely exposed.

I kept firing, tearing a hole through the monster, but even as its guts spilled free, it thundered ever forward. I continued firing until, at last, the collective damage sent it stumbling to the ground. That was when Patrick took aim with his modified Dragon and fired at a rate of two thousand rounds per minute on a collision course with the creature's skull. Ten seconds in, its skull exploded, coating the area in wriggling brains and bone.

By that point, I'd already moved on to the next monster. However, this time, I took a page out of Patrick's book, and I aimed for the head. Normally, I chose to target center mass, largely because, even with my abilities and modifiers, hitting a moving target wasn't easy. So, to mitigate the chance of missing, I typically took aim at the most prominent part of the body. Usually, that was the torso, and with the giant wildlings, the protruding stomach took that label as its own.

In any case, when I took aim, I set my sights on the comparatively smaller target of the wildling's head. Predictably, I missed with every fourth or fifth shot—especially when it realized what was going on and started jerking back and forth in an effort to avoid my fire—but with the power I could bring to bear, it didn't matter much. Soon enough, it dropped, its head exploded, as well.

"Aim for the legs," I ordered Patrick. "Slow them down and I'll finish them off."

"Do you want to use the big gun?" he asked, adjusting his aim.

"Not yet."

Over the next few minutes, we systematically tore the wildlings to pieces. Patrick disabled them with his rebuilt Dragon, while I aimed for their heads. Once they were on the ground, my job got a lot easier, so we made good progress. Still, a couple made it through.

Patrick retreated while I darted forward, exchanging my Stinger for the ADS. I fired from close enough that the norcite pellets didn't have much of a chance to spread. As a result, every single one of them hit the creature's bulbous stomach. Even as it lunged for me, I leaped into the air, kicked off its shoulder and somersaulted past it. Even as I flew toward the next in line, I took careful aim and unleashed another spread of norcite pellets.

As they tore into the monster's shoulder, I hit the ground, rolled, then came to my feet at a dead sprint. It swung its fist in an overhand blow that narrowly missed me. Instead, its hand crashed into the ground with the force of a sledgehammer, and the shock wave threw me off-kilter. I flared Balance, then found my equilibrium a second later—just in time to pepper a third monster with the ADS's issue.

Already, I could feel the Mist swirling as it flowed from the wildlings and to me. That was the power of my new scattergun. It wasn't meant to do damage; rather, it was there to tear the Mist from my enemies and feed it to me.

The first one stumbled. Then, the second. Finally, the third fell flat on its face. That's when I pounced, yanking the interdiction blade from the sheath on my back. After dismissing the ADS, I took a two-handed grip and descended on my first victim. It wasn't quite prone, but its head was in easy range.

Or, rather, its neck was.

I lashed out with a horizontal strike, pouring Mist into the blade. It flared with blue light a second before it met wildling flesh. Meat parted easily, and the bones of its vertebrae followed soon after. One swipe, and its head toppled free. However, that one attack had taken a massive amount of Mist—maybe half of my stores. Fortunately, I could already feel the effects of the norcite pellets replenishing my reserves.

So, I wasted no time before repeating my attack on the other two creatures. They tried to put up a fight, but against the interdiction blade, they stood no chance. Only a few seconds later, another pair of heads rolled free, joining the first as I defeated my enemies.

"That was quicker than expected," said Patrick, who was still tearing into the larger crowd of wildlings.

"I'm going to try something," I said, watching the largest cloud of Mist ascending from below. If it kept the same trajectory, it would surface about three hundred yards away. Hopefully, I would have time to finish the others off before then. "Make sure they don't get to me before I finish."

Patrick acknowledged that, then raced forward. Vaguely, I was aware of his stomping footsteps as he thundered in my direction. However, I didn't even devote one of my minds to noticing him. Instead, I used one mind to embrace Mist Authority while I used the other to latch on to the auras in my perception.

Then, I started ripping them apart.

Pain lanced through one of my minds, but I kept it quarantined there so that it couldn't affect my actions. And those actions were incredibly effective. Before, I'd struggled to pick the dervishes apart. Now, though, I felt positive that those amalgams of Mist and crystal wouldn't even slow me down. And by comparison, the wildlings were even more vulnerable. The results were predictable.

I didn't need guns or bombs.

Not when I could tear the motivating energy from their bodies with my mind. Hundreds fell in the space of seconds. Then, those hundreds became more than a thousand. But still, I kept going. I knew I was pushing my limits, as evidenced by the blood pouring from my eyes, ears, and nose, but the heady excitement that came with so much power was intoxicating. I held the power of life and death in my hands, and I wasn't eager to relinquish that authority.

And I didn't.

Not until one of the giant blobs of Mist surged upward, breaking through to the surface in a shower of earth that sent the smaller wildlings tumbling away. I stupidly tried to pick its Mist part, and for the first time, I was rebuffed. The backlash sent me reeling, and if I'd only possessed one mind, I probably would have passed out. However, [Multimind] quickly reaffirmed its worth; one of those minds went dark, but the other remained entirely cognizant.

Pain slammed into me, sending me stumbling backward. But pain I could deal with. I'd long since learned to cope with enough torment to send most people tumbling into insanity. So, I maintained my grip on consciousness and kept my wits about me as I beheld the newcomer.

It was at least twenty feet tall and almost as broad. The other wildlings were thin to the point of emaciation—outside of their bulbous bellies, at least—but this new arrival was, to put it lightly, obese. Huge rolls of fat cascaded down its swollen body, ending in overlarge hands and feet. Its head was nestled somewhere between its shoulders, though even with Observation, it was difficult to see where its face ended and its fatty shoulders began.

More important than its appearance, though, were the waves of Mist roiling all around it. I'd never seen anything so powerful, and I questioned whether I would survive long enough to change that.

"Pick! Run!"

"Mira, it's not—"

"Run, damn it!"

Even as I shouted, I sheathed my blade and yanked the Emperor from my arsenal implant. I barely took the time to aim before letting loose with the first shot. Even with my massively enhanced Constitution, the weapon kicked hard enough to nearly dislocate my shoulder. The round hit the monster directly in the chest, digging a massive crater at the point of impact. Then, it exploded, sending a shower of flesh and blood billowing out from there.

However, when the air cleared, I saw that the creature hadn't even broken stride. There was a hole in its chest, exposing its rib cage, but it still wasn't fazed. So, I squeezed the trigger again. This time, the kick sent me stumbling backward, though I caught myself before I fell. The resulting impact was even more massive than the last—twice as powerful, if Gala was to be believed—and yet, even though it resulted in another crater only a few scant inches from the first, the enormous wildling remained upright.

So, I regained my balance and took aim—making sure to brace myself properly—then fired again. This time, the kick tore my shoulder out of its socket, ruining my aim. The round still found its way into the monster's bulbous body, but because it was only a glancing blow, its impact was minimal. Somewhere behind the creature, an explosion of fallen wildlings, dirt, and rock erupted into the air with the secondary impact.

Cursing, I switched arms, then slammed my palm against my dislocated shoulder, knocking it back into place. I felt certain that every ligament had been torn by the violent injury, but I couldn't afford to let it derail me. Not with the monster progressing ever closer by the second. Its long strides covered a dozen feet at a time, so I knew I only had a few more seconds to take it out.

And three more shots, though I wasn't certain if my body could take it, much less my Mist reserves. So, I reluctantly stowed the Emperor, once again retrieving the ADS from my arsenal implant. Then, I raced forward, firing the bulky weapon one-handed the moment I came within range. Most of the pellets missed, but a few managed to lodge themselves in the creature's obese body.

I fired again. And again.

Then, finally, I came within its reach, which, as it turned out, was a mistake.

It swung its arm in a backhand that moved so quickly that there was no chance I could dodge it. So, without any other option, I solidified the Mist around me, which served to blunt the immediate impact. The Sheath protected me, too, but even then, the blow hit with nearly bone-shattering force.

Thankfully, my Constitution proved up to the task of keeping me from splattering, but it could do nothing with the momentum of the attack, which sent me skipping across the battlefield for nearly a hundred yards. Each time I hit the ground, I felt bones crack, but fortunately, when I skidded to a stop, I was more or less whole.

That's when I noticed the distinctive sound of the Dragon's fire.

"No! Patrick, don't—"

But he couldn't hear me. I watched, aghast as he unloaded his entire store of ammunition into the massive creature. The balls of superheated plasma did little damage to the monster, but it did serve to get the thing's attention. It lumbered toward him, its gait deceptively quick due to its long strides. Knowing that I needed to either put it down or get its attention, I once again pulled the Emperor from my arsenal implant and took aim.

Fortunately, the ADS's norcite pellets had done their job, draining it of Mist and sending it into my reserves, so I had plenty of Mist available to fuel the fifth shot. Still, when I squeezed that trigger, it felt like the life had been sucked out of me.

More distressingly, I felt my collarbone shatter under the recoil.

I screamed.

The round tore across the battlefield to rip a new crater in the back of the monster's rib cage. No—not a crater. The entire side of its torso had been destroyed, exposing broken ribs, organs, and corpulent flesh in large amounts. But it didn't stop moving.

So, the moment I had enough Mist—most of which had drained from the giant wildling—I fired a sixth time. This time, the already shattered bones in my collarbone were ground to dust, and my arm was very nearly ripped away from my body. However, the effect more than made up for the pain I felt.

The round took the creature directly in the back, sending it tipping over onto its face. I yelled at Patrick to run, and I saw the gleam of his white armor retreating into the forest. And yet, I knew that the enormous wildling wasn't dead. Nor would it die if I left it as it was.

So, without giving it any more thought, I took aim with the Emperor, propping myself on nearby rock. Then, I fired the seventh and final shot.

I went flying backward, which, in retrospect, was probably a good thing. Otherwise, I wouldn't have been outside the blast radius when that last round landed in an explosion that rivaled one of my most powerful demolition charges. But there was more to it than that. The Mist whirled, ripping anything in the immediate area apart.

That included the giant wildling.

And the area within a hundred yards of it.

Fortunately, I was just outside the blast zone, though only barely.

I lay there, basking in the agony lancing through my body as well as the influx of experience that told me I had killed the thing. However, when I tried to move, I realized that none of my joints worked quite how they were supposed to. I flopped around—painfully—for a few seconds before I gave up.

Taking a deep, agonizing breath, I embraced [Mist-Infused Body], flooding my body with Mist and guiding it to my copious injuries. Bones snapped back into place, joints came back together, and my skin—which had been broken in numerous places—mended. In seconds, I was back to being fully healthy.

But I wasn't happy about it.

I hadn't intended to use the regeneration associated with [Mist-Infused Body]. The fact that I'd been forced to do so meant that I chalked the whole excursion up as a failure. Angrily climbing to my feet, I looked around. There were plenty of wildlings on which to vent my frustrations, but that wouldn't do any good. So, I took another deep breath, then retreated.

"You tag most of them, Pick?" I asked, sprinting away.

"I think so," he said. "At least the ones I could reach."

"Alright. Then meet me back at the ship."

"So soon? I thought you'd be out here for hours yet," he remarked.

"There's nothing else I need to do here," I answered. Then, I thought better. "Or maybe only one more thing, but I can do that from the ship."

"Alright. See you there."

The trip back to *The Leviathan* was uneventful, and before I knew it, we were back in the air. Patrick guided the ship over the battleground, where the wildlings were still milling about.

"You ready for some fireworks?" I asked, forcing a grin I didn't feel.

"Light 'em up."

I retrieved the detonator from my arsenal implant, then pressed the button. Instantly, a hundred charges went off, bathing the entire area in destruction. Thousands of wildlings died instantly, with many times that being destroyed in the conflagration that followed. The most powerful—the ones on the level of the corpulent wildling I'd fought last—survived, but that wasn't unexpected.

I was tempted to go back down and finish them off, but I thought better of it. There wasn't much to be gained by doing that. The monsters were contained to the crater, so they weren't a danger to anyone. And now that I'd put my arsenal to the test against powerful opponents, I had enough data to inform the second phase of my training.

"Let's go home," I said, tearing my eyes away from the carnage. "We still have a long way to go."

CHAPTER TWENTY-TWO

HONING SKILLS

Some people have a talent for battle. All those split-second decisions just come naturally to them. Others have a knack for training. It's a combination of willingness to push themselves to the limit, over and over again, and the willpower to keep at it long after others would have given up. Mira has both, which, given her other talents, makes her an absolute monster when it comes to progression.

—Alistaris Kargat

The next three months passed without much in the way of variation, and I was once again reminded of my first stint in Mobile. There, I'd laid the groundwork for so much of what I would become. Certainly, the training itself was important, but the habits fostered by the routine foisted upon me were even more critical to my current situation. Back then, I learned to work. To push myself far past the point where other people would have fallen by the wayside. I was forced to realize that limits were as much about mindset as about physical endurance. And those lessons continued to apply as I pushed further and further into territory no one else on Earth had ever seen.

My uncle was powerful. I knew that, and his reputation supported that characterization. However, I suspected that, by the end of that second three-month period, I had surpassed him, and by no small degree.

"What are you thinking about?" asked Patrick, looking up from where he'd had his tools buried in an arm he'd detached from his armor. Throughout our time in Mobile, he'd been tinkering with his creation to the point where he'd replaced more parts than remained from the old version. In addition, he'd thoroughly reworked his arsenal, and I was eager to see how much devastation he could bring to bear.

I let out a slow exhale, then leaned my head against the cargo bay's bulkhead. I let four threads of thought—I'd recently upgraded [Multimind]—go silent. One had been focused on constantly flaring Mist Shield, which was the ability that had come with [Shielding], while another had been cycling through a new Mind-training program I'd bought from Gala. The other two trains of thought were concentrated on building a new series of grenades. Well, one of them was, at least. The other had strayed into thoughts of my uncle.

The sudden stillness in my mind was even more distracting than when it was busy.

I opened my eyes, then asked, "What makes you think I was thinking about anything? I'm training."

"Because your nose scrunches up when you're lost in thought," he said, gesturing with a tiny wrench. He grinned. "It's cute."

"I was also working."

"That's a different nose scrunch," he said.

"There can't be that many nose scrunches."

"Seventeen last time I counted," he said without hesitation. "Though admittedly, three of those are variations on the concentration nose scrunch."

"That's . . . a lot of nose scrunches," I muttered, baffled that he would pay so much attention to such a minute expression. Suddenly, I felt a little self-conscious about it.

"That's a new one," he said. "What's that one mean?"

I looked away, forcing the expression from my face. "Shut up," I said.

"Oh. Judging by your blush, I'm guessing embarrassment. Or is it self-consciousness?"

"I said shut up."

"You still didn't answer me," he stated. "What were you thinking about?"

Eager to move on from any line of discussion focused on my expressions, I said, "I don't know. Just my uncle. He spent almost a century fighting and getting stronger, but I think I'm already past him now, and I've only had my Nexus Implant for a little less than a decade. It seems kind of surreal. I mean, pretty much everyone acknowledged that he was one of the strongest people around, right? And everything I saw from him supported that. But in comparison, I'm probably a lot stronger than he was when he died."

"What are your stats up to now?"

I looked at my status:

NAME	Mirabelle Lisa Braddock		
CLASS	MIST WARDEN		
LEVEL	76 (27%)		
CONSTITUTION	481/542		
MIND	402/542		
MIST	498/542		
SKILLS	7/7		
SKILL NAME	Skill Tier	Modifiers	Abilities
MIST-INFUSED BODY	Tier 2 (96%)	1000% Efficiency of Cybernetics	5 Cybernetic Slots Reformation
WARFARE	Tier 3 (12%)	+400% Damage (All) +100% Fewer Bodily Requirements +200% Recovery Speed +75% Medication Effectiveness +125% Endurance +200% Explosives Yield +150% Effectiveness (Combat Focus)	Empowered Shot (B) Double Shot (C) Combination Punch (B) Pummel (C) Engage (C) Mark Target (C) Barrage (C) Explosive Shot (B) Multishot (C) Shatter Shot (C) Instant Reload (B) Riposte (C) Execute (B) Teleport (B) Triage (B) Basic Explosives Handling (A) Combat Focus (A) Pain Tolerance (B) Resistance (B) Foraging (B) Improvisation (B) Bastion (B) Tinkering (C) Share Map (C)

			Waypoint (D) Combat Map (C) Secure Connection (A) Ignore Injury (B) Blast Shield (B) Focused Will (C) Selective Explosion (F)
ESPIONAGE	Tier 2 (15%)	+175% Infiltration Abilities +215% Mistrunning Abilities +150% Processing Speed +125% Damage (All)	Stealth (A) Camouflage (A) Deception (C) Mimic (A) Observation (A) Charisma (B) Interrogate (D) Distraction (D) Vanish (B) Chameleon (B) Sense Deception (B) Mistwalk (B) Mist Authority (C) Mistwall (A) System Redirect (C) Disable Cybernetics (C) Overcharge (C) Surge (C) Plague (D) Backlash (B) Mental Fortress (B) Assassinate (B) Sensory Mask (F)

COMBAT MANEUVERS	Tier 3 (98%)	+175% Proprioception +60% Movement Speed	Balance (B)
NAVIGATION	Tier 2 (61%)	+100% Spatial Awareness	Navigate (D)
MULTIMIND	Tier 2 (7%)	+75% Cognition	Split Mind (D)
SHIELDING	Tier 3 (18%)	+25% Passive Shielding	Mist Shield (D)

I had made fantastic progress, especially considering that I'd already taken [Aura Manipulation] to Tier 5. It helped that I could focus on multiple tasks at once; it wasn't a one-to-one multiplier in terms of rate of progress, but it definitely sped things up. Barely an hour went by that at least two of my trains of thought weren't focused on pushing my abilities or skills forward. Even when I was working on my physical training or weapons' progression, I was always working on something else.

And it showed.

"My attributes are creeping closer to the five hundred mark," I said. "Gala said that was a big one. She said that only a fraction of a percent of people ever approach that, and even those are usually focused on only one attribute. The fact that I'm getting there with all three is a big deal. According to her, at least."

She'd once joked about me needing five hundred Constitution to wield the best blades in the universe, but I'd since discovered that that was usually only achievable with dedicated cybernetics or armor suits like Patrick's. Those usually came with a significant cost—in terms of credits as well as to the user's body—so I knew I was far ahead of almost anyone I was likely to meet.

Except the aliens, and whatever technology they might have at their disposal. I felt fairly sure I could stand up to just about anyone, but I was very aware of just how little I knew about the universe. For all I knew, there were people out there who were twice as strong as me.

"Damn. You're shooting up there," he said. "And here I was happy about clearing seventy-five in Constitution and Mist. If I could just get to a hundred, I could really boost the armor."

That was the chief limiter for the armor. It put quite a strain on his body, and though much of that was mitigated by his skills and modifiers, it was still what was holding him back. I couldn't help but regard that as a silver lining, though. If there were no limitations on that kind of thing, then any mook could just buy the best armor and match the results of my hard work.

I'd even asked Gala about getting a mech suit of my own, but she claimed that the materials necessary to make something equivalent to my attributes would be almost impossible to find. And if they were available, they would be used for something more important than boosting a single warrior.

But on the other end of that spectrum, I wanted Patrick to be as sturdy as possible. I'd already come close to losing him once, and I wasn't eager to repeat that experience. Thankfully, his class, {Combat Engineer}, gave him a significant advantage in that his cybernetics—which included his armor—were far more effective for him than they would be for most. He was a little cagey about the actual percentages, but I'd seen enough to suspect that, in his armor, his effective Constitution was at least tripled. Unfortunately, it didn't affect his Mist reserves or his Mind, but then again, he didn't really need those attributes as much as I did.

"How are your individual skills progressing?" he asked.

"Pretty well. I'm still barely progressing in that Command branch," I said. Indeed, the fourth branch of my [Warfare] tree was still stuck at Tier 0. I suspected that it was because I wasn't actually exercising it. By comparison, my others had progressed nicely, and I'd even picked up a couple of new abilities. I was still trying to integrate them into my tool kit, but trying to remember to use my glut of abilities was always going to be a struggle. I just had so many that, even with four threads of thought working on it, I often forgot some of them even existed. "You?"

He beamed. "I'm rolling through tiers," he said. "It's insane how much more I can take with that armor."

Patrick had integrated quite a bit of hunting into his routine, even taking *The Leviathan* on a few excursions alone. That was quite a difference, considering that, before, he'd actively avoided combat. Not surprising, given how comparatively vulnerable he had been, but it was definitely a nice change of pace.

Obviously, that had borne fruit. He still wasn't a particularly high level, but that was mostly because he had no way of mass killing. It had taken me millions of kills to reach my level, so it wasn't surprising that the pace of his progression was a lot slower than mine. Still, he'd grown, and that was all either of us could ask for.

But that wasn't really what was on my mind.

We only had a few more months before the world changed, and I wasn't sure whether or not either of us—let alone the rest of the world—was going to survive what was coming.

"Do you think we've got a chance?" I asked.

"I do," he stated. "And if it looks like things are spiraling out of control, we'll just leave. Once the quarantine is lifted, we can get out of here."

"But what about everyone else?"

"We'll try to save them, but if we can't . . ."

That had been our deal. Originally, Patrick had been all for escaping Earth as soon as the Integration dawned. By comparison, I wanted to stay and fight. The compromise was that we'd cut and run the moment things started looking dire.

We both knew that would never happen, though. Neither of us was good at quitting, after all.

A long silence stretched between us before, finally, we went back to our respective tasks. I focused on using [Shielding] as well as Mist Authority, while Patrick reattached the arm he'd removed from his armor. Like that, we remained for the next few hours until the monotony of training was broken by Alistaris, who'd contacted me via an unsecured connection.

"Hold on," I said before using Secure Connection. Once it took hold, I said, "What's up, Al?"

"Need you persist in calling me that? My name is Alistaris Kargat. You may use either of those names. Conversely, my subordinates also call me Commandant."

"Not your subordinate, Al. At best, I'm a mercenary. At worst, I'm somebody who owes you a couple of favors."

He let out a long-suffering sigh. "Very well. One of those favors has come due," he said. "I need you to meet me at the following coordinates tomorrow afternoon."

He sent me a message containing said coordinates. Using my Combat Map, I established that they led to a location half a continent away and nestled in a range of truly impressive mountains.

"What's going on?"

"We're going to fire the first shots in the impending war," he stated. "I won't say more over any connection, even a secure one. This is important, Miss Braddock. I trust you will take it seriously."

"When do I not take things seriously?" I asked, feigning innocence.

Alistaris did not answer that. Instead, he said, "Tomorrow afternoon. I will see you then."

After that, he cut the connection.

"What?" Patrick asked, obviously having noticed something in my expression. I could hide those silent conversations from most people, but not from the person who knew me better than anyone else.

"Our gnomish friend just called. Apparently, we've been summoned."

Then, I sent him the coordinates. He took one look at them, then said, "We should probably get going before long. It's going to take most of the night to reach the area, and I'm sure you're going to want to scout things out before you walk into any meeting."

"We probably need to discuss strategy, too."

"For a meeting?"

"Al said we're about to start the war," I said. "That means we're probably not coming back here anytime soon. More importantly, we need to be ready for whatever 'starting the war' really means."

Presumably, it would involve assaulting locations held by the aliens, but there was no way to be sure until Alistaris revealed the scope of the mission. Moreover, I felt entitled to know exactly what we could expect afterward because I wasn't so naive as to assume he'd let us just go back to training. Once the war started—which was coming sooner rather than later—I didn't expect it to end until we were dead or the aliens had been repelled.

"So, it's starting."

"I think so."

"Do you think we're ready?" he asked.

I shrugged. "I have no idea," I answered. I knew I was much stronger than I'd ever been. The last six months of training had been well spent, and for both of us. However, without more information on what was coming, there was no way to know if we were positioned to win the impending war. We could just as easily have been delusional.

Judging by how all the aliens in the Bazaar had reacted to the coming Integration, that seemed likely. That, as much as anything else, twisted my stomach into knots of anxiety. I forced myself to ignore it, offering Patrick a smile as I said, "Think about it, though. We could win this thing and be free, right? Then, we can go off and explore the universe without worrying about leaving a dead world behind."

"You make it sound so easy."

"It might just be," I said.

"Somehow, I doubt that. But then again, you'll probably kill them all by accident, right?" he joked.

"That was one time."

"Kind of twice," he said. "Or did you forget the moon incident?"

"That was only half accident. I wanted to blow them up."

"The crater you left behind is visible to everyone on Earth," he stated. "It's at least six hundred miles wide."

"I overdid it a little."

"A little?"

"Okay, a lot. But I learned my lesson. Don't mix unknown Mist-infused materials with high explosives. Or don't do it unless you want to blow a hole in a moon. Or a small planet. Earth would probably be fine, though. Mostly."

"That's not as reassuring as I think you think it is."

I shrugged. "Best I can do."

After that, we went our separate ways as we gathered our things. Without the restrictive bands I used during my workouts, collecting my weight set was incredibly easy. The only limiter was how awkward the burden ended up being. Still, I managed it well enough, depositing everything in *The Leviathan*'s cargo hold.

Once everything had been piled into that space, Patrick put it away in his spatial storage. One of the upgrades for *The Leviathan* we'd recently bought was a portable storage node that allowed Patrick to access his spatial storage without using his own Mist. In addition to that, we'd upgraded the cannons as well as installed a new Mist-shield generator that would hopefully protect us from whatever the aliens could throw at us.

When we'd put everything away, I found myself standing before the still-open cargo hatch and looking down on Mobile as *The Leviathan* lifted into the air. The city still held some nostalgia, but it wasn't nearly as powerful as it had been. During the past six months, I'd come to realize that the place in my memory was gone, and now only ruins remained.

With a sigh, I hit the button to close the hatch, then headed to the cockpit where Patrick was seated.

"Say your goodbyes?" he asked without looking away from his instruments.

"Unnecessary," I said. "We'll be back one day. And maybe we'll rebuild it even better than before."

"Maybe" was his noncommittal response.

With that, he hit the accelerator, and *The Leviathan* jumped forward. Soon enough, we'd cross the continent, meet with Alistaris, and learn his plan for repelling the aliens poised to invade the moment the quarantine was lifted.

CHAPTER TWENTY-THREE

PHASE ONE

She is volatile, unreliable, and selfish. Despite that, she represents Earth's greatest chance for survival. I wish it were otherwise because I believe Mira is just as likely to destroy the world as save it.

—Alistaris Kargat

Magnificent mountains, each one wearing a cap of snow, rose to prominence all around us. I'd never felt smaller than in the presence of those giant natural edifices. Patrick piloted *The Leviathan* through the valleys, keeping low so as to avoid detection. The ship had some antidetection capabilities but none that compared to using the natural terrain for concealment. Most people couldn't have flown such a large ship so adroitly, but Patrick was no normal pilot.

As he focused on his task, I practiced my [Navigation] skill. So far, it had been something of a disappointment. It gave me unmatched spatial awareness, and with it, I could read maps like nobody's business. However, that didn't really translate to any ability to pilot *The Leviathan*. So, in that area, I was no better off now than I had been before absorbing the skill. Still, I didn't regret it, largely because it was still useful.

Besides, I had Patrick for all my flying needs.

"We're almost there," he said, cutting between two prominent pillars of rock. "After that, it'll be about two hours on foot before we reach the rendezvous point. Unless you want to just land there. Which, for the record, I'm a hundred percent on board with that plan."

"Afraid of a little walk?" I asked with a slight smirk.

"Out there, yes. Have you seen the temperatures? It's ten below zero. It's right in the middle of a Dead Zone, too, and I've picked up quite a few biological signatures."

"Really?" I asked, looking out the window. The area looked as desolate as any place I'd ever been, and even with Observation, I couldn't see anything but rocks and mounds of snow. "Looks pretty desolate to me."

"The scanner doesn't lie," he said, tapping one of the screens in front of him. Pointedly, I had no idea what the squiggly lines and dots even meant, probably because I lacked the skill and experience necessary to operate the thing. And that irritated me. I was used to being completely self-sufficient, so being confronted with something I simply could not do was more than a little annoying. But I suppressed that feeling and forced a smile.

"Suppose I'll just have to trust you, then," I said. "But no. There's no way I'm going in without scouting things out. You're welcome to stick to the ship, though."

He shook his head. "Not happening. I have a new mode I want to test on the armor," he said.

"I'm skeptical that thing is ever going to be effective in stealth."

"So little faith," he muttered. "I think I've got it perfected, but I'll make you a deal. Once you've seen it in action, if you still don't approve, I'll stay back. If you admit it works, you owe me one."

"One what?"

"To be decided later."

"An open-ended bet? That doesn't seem very fair."

He shrugged, shifting slightly to the right as he guided the ship to the intended landing spot. Then, he said, "You'll enjoy it one way or the other, I'm sure."

"So certain of yourself, huh?" I asked.

"I am."

I saw his smirk and said, "Fair enough."

Patrick's smile only grew broader, but he didn't say anything else. Instead, he slowly guided *The Leviathan* into place, setting it down atop a cliff that was miraculously devoid of snow. Once he'd established that it was secure, we headed to the cargo bay where we completed preparations for our excursion. For my part, I donned my infiltration suit as well as a fur-lined white outfit that would aid both Camouflage and Stealth. After that, I checked my ammunition and weapons, ensuring that my entire arsenal was loaded and ready for battle.

Meanwhile, Patrick went through a similar routine, dressing in a similar battle suit before summoning his mech suit from his spatial storage. He went through a few checks before climbing into the cockpit and firing it up.

"Still don't know how you expect anyone not to see that thing," I said, looking the enormous suit of armor up and down. It was twelve feet tall, bulky, and though it was white enameled, it was still shiny and trimmed in gold. There was almost no chance it would escape anyone's notice.

"Have a little faith, Mira."

I shrugged. "Faith is for people who have to depend on hope. I prefer to rely on something more concrete. Like my abilities. Or lots of bombs."

After that, Patrick activated one of the suit's features. Suddenly, it shimmered, then disappeared. Mostly. I could still see it easily enough, but that was largely because of Observation's high grade. Without it, he would have been entirely invisible. So, I said, "Impressive. What did you do?"

"Localized holographic display hooked to a series of cameras. It just takes in images, then projects them. There are a couple more steps, but that's the gist of it."

"Nice. Not as good as Stealth, but it'll probably get the job done."

He agreed, and after I established Bastion to protect the ship, we exited via the cargo hatch. Once outside, he remotely activated *The Leviathan*'s innate defenses. So, with the ship protected, we set off toward the rendezvous point.

And I immediately regretted it.

It wasn't the cold that bothered me. Instead, it was the snow drifts that were deeper than I was tall. Eventually, Patrick took the lead, breaking a trail through the snow. I followed, though with the sides of the trail piled high with snow, I felt more than a little claustrophobic.

Fortunately, we quickly descended far enough down the mountain that it wasn't a problem anymore. However, that also came with quite a bit more danger, as was evident when a shaggy-furred humanoid creature burst from the snow and attacked us. I had my interdiction blade out and swinging before Patrick even knew what was happening, and all it took was a slight pulse of Mist to empower it to the point where slicing through the monster took almost no effort.

Red blood splashed onto the white snow as the bisected monster fell apart. I leaped away, avoiding getting that blood all over my white outfit. Patrick wheeled around, one of his guns erupting from his forearm, but it was pointless. The monster was already dead.

"See? I told you there were monsters around."

"I didn't say there weren't," I pointed out. Then, I looked at the thing. It was shaped like a person, with two arms and two legs, but it was covered in white fur. Still, there was something familiar about its features. "What do you think it is?"

"Wildling."

"That doesn't look like any wildling I've ever seen," I said. And that was true, too. I'd fought and killed enough of them that I thought myself capable of recognizing the creatures better than most.

"They evolved up here," he said. "Grew fur. They're basically a different species now. It's not uncommon. One of those files Gala sent us went over it."

"But they're just wildlings."

"That's what the Mist does. It's like rapid devolution followed by just as rapid evolution, though with the Mist. That's how the first planets that were engulfed by the Mist survived. At some point, one of those species advanced enough to create the system and Nexus Implants. There's a whole faction of people who think it's immoral. The system, I mean. They believe that planets should be allowed to evolve however they're meant to without any intervention. Of course, there's the fact that without the Initialization period and the quarantine, none of those species would survive, but they're not concerned—"

"Enough of the history lesson, Pick."

"It's interesting, though."

It wasn't to me, but I didn't admit that. Instead, I said, "There might be more of them around. We don't need to be distracted."

He huffed, but he didn't continue his lecture. So, after we both adopted Stealth—he had recently earned a variant by advancing his skills—we advanced. Despite remaining hidden, we were still attacked a couple of times along the way to the rendezvous point, but neither of us had any difficulty dispatching the furry wildlings. We reached the location about an hour and a half later.

I knelt on a sharp cliff, looking down on the valley below. There, I saw three ships that I recognized as Dengyt designs. More, the little gnomes had raised a temporary base, complete with a reasonably powerful Mist shield, a series of autoturrets along the top of the wall, and an entire cadre of powerful combat bots.

"It's a fortress," I said through Secure Connection.

"You see the humans?" he asked, our conversation silent.

I had. I didn't recognize any of them—which wasn't surprising—but I'd already counted ten of them. They all looked like tough customers, and they were armed to the teeth. Mercenaries, unless I missed my guess. Or maybe they were powerful combatants Alistaris had recruited for the coming war. There was no way to tell without getting closer, and I wasn't quite ready to do that.

I trusted Alistaris to a certain degree, but I would've had to have been a fool to blindly walk into such a dangerous situation. I knew precisely how deadly the Dengyts could be, and I wasn't going to underestimate them again.

So, we watched and waited, and to my surprise, I caught sight of something unexpected.

"Do you see that?" I asked Patrick.

"What?"

"The invisible gnomes."

"If they're invisible, of course I didn't see them."

"You know what I mean. They're using some kind of stealth variant. But I can see their Mist auras," I said. "It's subtle, but . . ."

"I can't see auras, Mira," he reminded me.

"Oh. Right."

I had gotten so used to seeing auras that I sometimes forgot that others couldn't do so. I spent the next few minutes watching the definite outline of a pair of gnomes as they approached our position. I pretended I wasn't aware of them, banking on their inability to detect me. My own Stealth had grown since the last time I'd encountered gnomes, and I hoped that growth would be enough to keep them from noticing me.

A few seconds later, one of them appeared with her weapon pointed at Patrick. In a high-pitched voice, she said, "Please disembark the combat suit and—"

I pressed Ferdinand II to the back of her head and extended the interdiction blade to the throat of the other as I said, "You need to rethink your position if you think you get to order us around."

The gnome beneath my blade flinched, but I kept the interdiction blade at his throat.

"Mirabelle, I presume?" asked the woman.

I ignored her, addressing Patrick as I said, "See? I'm famous."

He said, "You blew up the moon and killed millions of androids. I'd be disappointed if they didn't know who you are."

"I think it's my good looks and winning personality that everyone remembers."

"Yeah. That's it," he deadpanned.

"Commandant Kargat is expecting you," said the female gnome. She seemed calm enough, which was impressive, given my reputation for killing aliens. "You need not have hidden out here in the cold. You are more than welcome to join the others before the briefing."

"Were you in New Cairo?" I asked.

"I was."

"Then you can probably guess why I'd be a little hesitant to just waltz in there," I said. Back then, I had very much been outclassed, and the gnomes had used their advantage to stealthily surround me.

"You've grown," she said. "We didn't detect you at all."

"Yeah. I'm special like that. Take your eyes off me for even a minute and I'll pass you right by."

"Indeed," she said. "Now, are we going to stay out here in the snow? Or will you come inside where it's warm? The bulk of your team has already arrived."

"Team?"

"Yes. No one can fight a war alone."

"I beg to differ," I countered. "But fine."

I yanked my sword back, sheathing it while holstering Ferdinand II at the same time. The male gnome—who was in the most adorable little infiltration suit—rubbed his neck, but I'd been careful not to draw blood. I hadn't run any Mist through it, so it probably couldn't have cut him, anyway.

"Was that an interdiction blade?" asked the female.

"Maybe."

She turned to Patrick and said, "And that armor is more advanced than should be available here."

"It's a work in progress," he said.

"Interesting."

After that, she turned and strode off, followed by the male gnome. He was clearly nervous putting his back to us, but he showed discipline by not glancing back. I had to respect that, at least.

I turned to Patrick and said, "Told you they'd see through it."

He let out a groan, but he didn't respond. Instead, he stomped along after the two gnomes. For my part, I followed soon after him, though I kept a smug smile on my face.

The trip down to the temporary fortress was uneventful, but I saw a handful of Mist signatures along the way. Hidden Dengyts all, though some of the auras were significantly more subdued than others. I wasn't sure if that meant they were higher-level but with more control, or lower-level with more scattered auras. Whatever the case, I felt confident that I saw them all.

As we approached the wall, I was tempted to rip through the Mist shield. I felt confident that I could do it, though I wasn't certain if I would have to do so via the methods I'd used with Misthack or if I could tear it to pieces through sheer Mist Authority.

I refrained from doing so. I had to keep reminding myself that the Dengyts, though they were aliens, were my allies. For now. I still didn't trust them completely, however, so I kept my guard up. Normally, when I entered a new situation, I'd have done it cloaked in Mimic, but that wasn't possible now.

"It's okay," said Patrick via our ongoing Secure Connection. "Just breathe. It's fine."

"I'm okay."

"You're not, and that's okay. Just remember that if anyone screws with you, we can blow this whole place up without skipping a beat."

That soothed my anxiety a little. I still didn't like being exposed, but the notion that I could just kill them all if they stepped out of line was oddly comforting.

Inside the fort were a lot more gnomes. However, I noticed that our arrival garnered quite a few curious looks from the humans inside. All of them looked a little rough around the edges and, more importantly, a lot older than Patrick or me. I couldn't help but wonder if they knew whom they were looking at.

The gnome soldier led us to the largest plasti-steel building, and when the door slid open, she stepped inside. I went to follow, but we quickly found a problem. In his armor, Patrick wouldn't fit. So, with an annoyed sigh, he climbed out, then dismissed it into his storage space. That definitely got some attention from the other humans—and a few of the gnomes, as well—but we both endeavored to ignore it as we followed the two gnomes into the building.

Once we were inside, I saw a familiar face.

"Al!" I exclaimed, ignoring all the others inside. "So nice of you to send the welcoming committee to greet us!"

With a long-suffering sigh, Alistaris ran a hand through his white hair and said, "Hello, Mira."

I slapped my hands together and looked around the room before saying, "Alright. Why don't you introduce me to your ragtag group of adventurers?"

"Reel it in, Mira," Patrick said via Secure Connection. "Too strong."

"You sayin' you don't remember me?" came a familiar voice. I glanced in that direction, and I saw an expected broad-brimmed hat.

"Rex. I thought you'd have gotten yourself killed by now," I said.

"Not yet," he drawled.

After that, Alistaris cut in and asked us to sit. I once again looked around the room, which was clearly some sort of command center. There was a large round table in the middle of the room and a series of terminals on one side. Around the table sat a dozen unfamiliar men and women. There were only two open seats, so Patrick and I navigated to those chairs and sat down. Every eye followed us as we did so.

"Thank you," Alistaris said, pushing himself to his feet. He stood atop the chair so that everyone could see him. "I've gathered you all here because you're the best Earth has to offer. Each one of you has the capability to contribute to the planet's defense, and today, I'm going to go over exactly how that starts."

"You mean to tell me that a pair of children are the best of the best?" came a raspy, yet feminine voice. I looked in that direction, and I saw a tall, whip-thin woman with a mechanical hand. She had a sword strapped to her back, and she wore a set of nondescript robes.

Alistaris, who'd obviously expected such an objection, said, "Yes. Mira is by far the most dangerous person in this building. And that assessment is based on the last time we met. I suspect she has only grown more powerful since then."

"Preposterous," the woman spouted.

Even as she spoke, one of the others—a short man with a pudgy face—leaped from his seat and yanked a pistol from a holster at his belt. Or at least he tried to. He barely got a hand to the grip before I ripped the Mist from his body.

He fell forward, his head hitting the table before he slid to the ground. Without even checking, I knew he was dead. I'd used Mist Authority to do the same to plenty of wildlings and animals over the past six months, so I was well-versed in just what my most recently evolved ability could do.

"Anyone else have a problem with me?" I asked. I'd never even moved a muscle, which probably made what I'd just done even more horrifying. That was precisely my intention.

CHAPTER TWENTY-FOUR

THE FIRST SHOTS FIRED

Loose cannon. A bomb waiting to explode. An uncontrollable agent of chaos. All those descriptors apply to Mirabelle Braddock. And yet, that is precisely what this world needs if it's going to survive what's coming.

—Alistaris Kargat

A dense fogbank covered the entire valley, obscuring my view and hiding the alien outpost down below. However, I could still see the tower that extended high above the fog, stretching toward the sky like some mechanical finger. A ring of lights marked the tip, which was nearly five hundred feet from the ground. It was only a few dozen feet higher than the position I'd taken, though it was still hundreds of yards away.

"I could blow it all up from here," I said over the Secure Connection. "Just a few shots from the BMAP, and it'd all come tumbling down."

Patrick responded, "It has a Mist shield, Mira."

His words came out as a sigh, a signal of his fatigue. Some of that was my fault. I'd been complaining since getting my orders—partially because I didn't like being told what to do, but mostly because the plan seemed overly complicated and unnecessarily conservative—and Patrick was clearly tired of it. But he'd also spent the past couple of hours laboriously trekking through the wilderness to put himself in position, so some of his exhaustion was physical in nature.

"Like that would stop me," I said.

"Then you'd have to get a lot closer. Which would preclude the use of your grenade launcher."

"It's a mobile artillery platform," I said. "That's what the MAP of BMAP stands for."

"Looks like a grenade launcher. Works like a grenade launcher. I'm calling it a grenade launcher," he said.

"Whatever."

"You're just mad because the whole plan doesn't hinge on you acting like a lone wolf," he pointed out.

And he wasn't wrong. Not that I was going to say as much, but I knew I could probably accomplish the other groups' tasks more easily than they could. That, as much as anything, was the source of my irritation. However, I knew Alistaris's reasoning, and I agreed with his assessment.

Even if I found it frustrating being relegated to the sidelines.

Or as overwatch, as he'd put it to the others, which was why I had the Emperor out and was lying flat, with the weapon trained on the foggy valley. So long as I flared Observation, I could see through the fog, but I'd also found that my {Mist Warden} senses, which let me see Mist auras, were even more effective at keeping track of everything.

I watched as Patrick snuck down the alley alongside a handful of others. I knew him well enough to easily recognize his aura, especially when he was in his armor. I could also pick out Rex, but the others were unidentifiable by aura alone. Oddly enough, even though Alistaris had claimed that the people he'd recruited were among the strongest in the world, none of their auras were markedly stronger than Patrick's. Of course, that was with him in his mech suit, which amplified the density of the cloud of Mist around him, but even so, it was indicative of just how far he'd come. There was a time when he'd been basically defenseless, but looking at his strong aura, I recognized that those days were long gone.

Ironically, Rex was the weakest among the group, though that was understandable. He was there because of a very specific skill set, not due to his overall strength. Of course, I could do that job better than he ever could, but apparently, that wasn't my role. Instead, I was there in case things went wrong. Because of my unique skill set and obvious strength, I was best suited for rescue operations and to plug any leaks that might appear.

Which was incredibly boring and felt a little counterintuitive to me. I could see Alistaris's perspective, though. If I went in first and got in trouble, there probably wasn't anyone that could save me. However, if the others went in and met with that same situation, there was a good chance that I could hit the aliens hard and fast and rescue the others.

Or, as Alistaris had pointed out when we were alone, I could tear everything down if it looked like the rest of the team had failed and were impossible to save.

I hated the pressure that put on me, but I also hated that he was absolutely right. Of everyone he'd recruited, I was the only one who didn't need help in order to do what needed to be done. I just wished that sending me in alone had been the primary plan, rather than a contingency.

"I bet he can't even get you through the shield," I said, referring to the other so-called Mistrunner. I knew he didn't have the class, but according to Alistaris, the man's skill was one of the most advanced in the world. It was all I could do not to laugh when the gnome told me that. "You'll probably get there and be forced to just stand around while—"

"You're not the only person with skills, Mira," Patrick pointed out.

"No—I know. I'm just saying . . ."

"I know what you're saying. You don't trust anybody to do anything important. That's why you usually work alone," he said. "But Alistaris is a smart guy. He wouldn't send us in here if he didn't think we could accomplish the mission."

I didn't respond. The mission in question was simple. They were supposed to go in and rescue someone important. Once the package—which was how Alistaris had referred to the hostage—was secure, Rex was supposed to blow the place up. To do that, Alistaris had sent a team of nine, including Patrick. I was the tenth, and I was there to provide overwatch. Or pick up the slack if they failed.

If Patrick hadn't been with them, I would've been a lot more worried.

And if I didn't feel like I owed Alistaris for everything he'd done for me, I would have simply ignored him, went in by myself, and completed the mission alone. However, he clearly wanted things done his way, and I felt obligated to help him. After all, he'd already taken care of the human livestock, and he'd gone to quite some trouble to get me into Olympus. On top of that, he'd saved me from certain death by picking me up on the moon.

So, I suppose it wasn't so onerous to let him take the lead, at least until everything went wrong. Once it did, I would swoop in and save the day.

Or blow everything up.

The jury was still out on which way I'd end up going. In either case, I had little choice but to do my job for the time being. So, I concentrated on the group's progress as they approached the Mist shield. Beyond, I couldn't really see any other auras, mostly because of the interference provided by the shield itself. If I'd been a little closer, perhaps I could have, but from so far away, it was impossible.

Suddenly, I saw the shield flare, then flicker, and finally, wink out. The moment it did, I saw a hundred auras bloom into being. A second later, the sound of gunfire rang out, filling the valley. I couldn't properly see anything other than auras, but I still managed to follow the exchange as Patrick and his allies tore through the alien defenders.

According to the packet Alistaris had passed along, the aliens were humanoid reptiles whose name I hadn't even bothered learning. One enemy was the same as any other, so I didn't think classifying these particular creatures was particularly important.

As the battle went on, I continued to scan the surroundings, but no new threats presented themselves. I was tempted to pick off a few aliens, but I'd agreed to follow Alistaris's plan, so I restrained my murderous impulses and trusted the others to do the job. And to my surprise, Patrick and the others managed to send the aliens into a retreat.

"Commencing phase two," came a voice over the communications channel. It was secure, but not nearly as impregnable of a signal as my ability would guarantee.

I watched as my so-called allies spread out, searching the compound. The aliens had barricaded themselves in a fortresslike panic room, just as Alistaris had predicted. That gave the assault team free access to the rest of the facility, including the building that contained the person they'd come to rescue.

However, as they spread out, I saw something out of the corner of my eye that garnered the whole of my attention.

"Incoming!" I hissed over the channel. "Seven. No, eight ships. Big enough to carry hundreds of warriors."

Indeed, each one of the ships I saw swooping into the valley were two or three times the size of *The Leviathan*. Suddenly, I saw a flare of Mist that, at the last second, I recognized for what it was.

"They're about to fire!" I shouted, leaping to my feet. The Emperor would do no good against those ships. Doubtless, they had shields of their own, and even if they didn't, it would be the third or fourth shot with the sniper rifle before I could bring enough force to bear to bring them down.

One thread of thought raced to think of a plan, but I discarded potential strategies, one after the other. None of my weapons were appropriate. The BMAP probably packed enough punch, but hitting a moving target with those slow-moving projectiles was incredibly difficult. Even with my aim, it was no sure thing.

The HIRC would probably do the trick, so long as I used Explosive Shot, but I questioned whether or not it would get through the Mist shields in time. After all, they were built specifically to combat gunfire.

My other weapons—like the Stinger—didn't even bear considering.

No, I needed something else. Something they had no reason to suspect.

I ran forward, summoning my Cutter along the way. In seconds, I'd mounted the bike and was speeding toward a cliff. Or more importantly, I was heading straight at the lead ship, whose cannons were still spinning up. The time that had already elapsed suggested they were aiming to demolish everything in the valley, and I knew I couldn't let that happen.

Patrick's armor was strong, but it wasn't enough to stand up to heavy artillery like those cannons.

It was rare that I really let the Cutter loose. Normally, the terrain couldn't accommodate the sort of speed it could attain. However, with what I had in mind, I needed every ounce of acceleration it could muster. So, I pushed it to the limit, and the hover bike leaped forward, accelerating to more than a hundred miles an hour in less than a second. But I didn't stop there. I continued to pour on speed until, after a few more seconds, I reached the edge of the cliff and sailed into the air.

My momentum took me dozens of feet before I started to fall, but it was just enough to get me in range of the first ship. So, I dismissed the bike, then used Teleport to appear on top of the ship an instant later. I hit the hull hard enough to shatter most people's bones. Mine held up well enough, and I turned the collision into a roll as I came to a stop just before reaching the edge.

I took a deep breath, then put all four threads of my mind to work.

I battered through the ship's Mist shield, targeting the dense aura I sensed at the center of the fuselage. That was the engine, I was certain, and I started ripping nanites away. At first, the Mist was quickly replaced, but I soon began to outpace what it could generate. Even as the ship lurched, I used another thread of thought to upload a Ghost meant to disable its weapons systems.

When I'd accomplished that, I turned my attention to the next ship, which was the only one in range, and I started in on its defenses, as well. Those fell even more quickly than the first, leaving me with only six more ships remaining.

I sprinted across the hull, then leaped to the second ship. I barely made it, but even then, I didn't break stride. Instead, I continued running, then jumped again. This time, I had to use Teleport to close the gap, but due to my training, I had Mist to spare. On that ship, my task went much the same as it had before, and I quickly moved on to the others, crippling their engines and uploading Ghosts to disable their weapons systems.

By the time two minutes had passed, I was leaping away from the eighth ship. The fall was brutal, and I hit the ground hard. However, because of my high Constitution, falling a few hundred feet wasn't going to injure me. Sure, it hurt, but it did no permanent damage.

The same couldn't be said for when the ships fell.

It took a few more minutes, during which Patrick and the others continued their mission—after I assured them that I had it all taken care of. I couldn't help but think that, if I hadn't taken care of the man who'd attacked me in that first meeting, they might have disputed that claim. But they had some inkling of what I could do, so I suppose they were willing to trust me when I said I could take care of it.

The first ship crashed into the ground a couple hundred yards away from where I'd landed. By that point, I'd found my way to a safe zone, but even so, I felt the shock wave. The next seven came down with similar results, which I'll admit, filled me with a significant degree of satisfaction.

"Are you okay, Mira? We've got what we were looking for," Patrick said. "We're headed back to *The Leviathan*."

"I'll catch up. I have things to do."

"Mira, I don't—"

"You know I'm going to do this, Pick. Just leave me to it."

He sighed, then said, "Fine. Do what you need to do."

As if I needed his permission. Still, his acquiescence would at least save me an argument. In any case, I strode forward, summoning my Stinger as I approached the first ship. It was larger even than I had expected, and I could sense hundreds of auras inside.

I probably could have simply ended their lives with a Ghost. Or by simply picking them apart with Mist Authority. However, there were two problems with that. First, my Mist reserves were getting low after using Teleport so many times. And second, I wanted something a little more visceral.

After all, these aliens had come to conquer my planet. They deserved much worse than the clean and relatively painless death that would come if I ripped their Mist away.

So, I advanced, using Mist Authority to open the hatch. A reptilian humanoid stood on the other side, surprised at the sudden opening. I fired a three-round burst that ripped through them.

"We are noncombatants!" hissed someone from inside.

I didn't care. I continued to fire as I boarded the ship, cutting the reptilian aliens down without hesitation. If they were on Earth, they'd designated themselves as the enemy. I couldn't afford to think anything else.

Over the next few minutes, I slaughtered the aliens. In a way, it was anticlimactic. I was so far beyond them that they couldn't stand up to my assault rifle's fire. And whatever resistance they offered was far from up to the task. So, I swept through them without any difficulty whatsoever.

And when I was finished, I moved on to the next ship. By the time I found my way to the third, the occupants had figured things out, and they'd abandoned the ship. I hunted them down without mercy, using Mist Authority to rip the Mist from their bodies. They died screaming—not from pain but, rather, because they had no idea what was even happening.

It was music to my ears.

I don't know how long I spent hunting the reptilian aliens down, but it was well past dark before I'd found them all. They tried to hide. Most attempted to run. But with my ability to sense auras, I tracked them all down easily enough.

And in the end, I killed them all.

That's when I started in on the outpost.

I lost myself to the killing. To the power. I ripped through that fortress without hesitation or mercy, killing everything I found. And when I'd finished, hundreds . . . thousands had perished.

I had barely even lifted a finger. It was little more than an inconvenience, killing so many.

I opened a Secure Connection with Alistaris and said, "Threat ended. You can send your people in to clean up the mess."

"Affirmative," he answered.

"This is what you wanted, isn't it? You knew they'd send those ships."

"I did," Alistaris stated.

"That's why you left me out here. You wanted to make a statement."

"Which was precisely what you just did. They know this planet isn't going to go down without a fight," he said. "Now, we can get down to fighting the real war. Things are going to get much worse from here."

"I expected as much," I answered. And I had. I knew the coming war wasn't going to be pretty. I was going to do horrific things—the sorts of acts that normal people couldn't even fathom—but I intended to save the world even if I had to become a monster to do so. I cut off the connection without any more conversation, then opened a separate line to Patrick. I said, "I'm coming in."

"What happened?"

"I did what needed to be done. I need a shower," I said. "I'll see you in a few minutes."

And with that, I summoned the Cutter, then set off toward where we'd left *The Leviathan*. I didn't even look back at the carnage I'd wreaked.

CHAPTER TWENTY-FIVE

FIGHTING THE GOOD FIGHT IN ALL THE WRONG WAYS

On every world, and in every instance, war is ugly. So it has always been, and so it will always be. But when Mira fights a war, even battle-hardened veterans blanch at her commitment to atrocity. Such horrors are necessary if we want to win such a lopsided war.

—Alistaris Kargat

I sat atop *The Leviathan*, staring at the horizon as the sun set behind the mountains. The fading light cast the expanse in a majestic cascade of blue and orange. The undeniable beauty stood in stark contrast to the day's actions. I wasn't ashamed. Nor did I feel guilty. However, I couldn't escape the reality of what I had done.

I had killed plenty of people in the past. Millions of them, in fact. However, I'd never engaged in such blatant slaughter before. The aliens I'd killed weren't innocent, but many of them weren't combatants, either. As such, they'd been entirely incapable of fighting back. Certainly, they'd tried. I'd been shot hundreds of times, and yet, their efforts were for naught. Few shots had gotten through Mist Shield, and the ones that did were robbed of much of their momentum. As a result, none had even gotten past the thin armor of my infiltration suit. So, I was entirely unharmed.

The same couldn't be said for my enemies.

And more than anything, I felt tired. Not physically. I could keep going for days without rest. And mentally, I was still just as sharp as ever. Maybe more so. However, from an emotional standpoint, I couldn't quite outrun the implications of my actions. So, hours later, Patrick found me still sitting atop the ship and staring out at the abyssal darkness that was only possible in the wildest of places.

His footsteps were loud as he closed in on me, though I didn't look his way. Not even when he settled in beside me. Our shoulders touching, we beheld the black landscape together.

Then, a few minutes later, he asked, "Do you want to talk?"

"Not really."

"I think you might need to," he said, putting his arm around me and pulling me close.

"I know," I responded, though I didn't follow that statement up. To his credit, Patrick didn't break the silence. He knew me well enough to know that I would talk when I got ready to talk and not a second before that. Finally, a few minutes later, I said, "I don't think killing should be that easy."

"It's not."

"I don't think you understand," I said. "With a thought, I can tear the Mist from a person's body. I can agitate it. I can move it. With Mist Authority, I can probably make someone spontaneously combust if I wanted to. I have limits right now, though. It still hurts, and if I try to do it against really powerful people, I'll end up like I did in the Rift. But I'm moving past those limits a little more each day. Eventually, there won't be anything holding me back."

"Good."

I glanced in his direction, horror etched on my face. "Nobody should have that much power."

"No. They shouldn't. But people do. We have no idea what these aliens are capable of. So, if we're fighting that kind of threat, I want someone like you on our side."

He didn't really understand what I was going through. I was never afraid to kill. I'd gotten used to living in a world where such a thing was just a part of survival. And I wasn't even that concerned with killing innocents—largely because I didn't consider any alien worthy of such a moniker. Even Alistaris and his people were invaders, and if they stepped even a toe out of line, I would throw them in with all the other would-be oppressors.

Yet, when I thought about my recent actions, I couldn't deny the anxiety twisting my insides into knots.

It all came to one simple fact: I was terrified I'd let my power run away from me. I'd done it before, and often enough that it could easily be called a pattern. In Nova, I'd done it willingly, but on the moon—and with the Pacificians—I had simply underestimated my own abilities.

And millions had died.

With the further development of my powers, I was terrified that I'd make the same mistakes. And at the scale of my capabilities, I wouldn't just be destroying a city or a few million alien androids. No—if I kept going, it was feasible that I could kill everything and everyone on the planet.

It was a terrifying level of power, and the responsibility of possessing that capability was daunting.

I leaned into Patrick, and for the longest time, neither of us said anything. "I'm afraid, Pick. I know what I need to do. I know what it's going to take for us to win the coming war. The aliens are ruthless, and so we have to be ruthless, too. But I'm afraid . . . I'm afraid of what it's going to do to me. To us. Even if we win . . ."

"We will," he said after I trailed off. "Because the alternative is enslavement, right? That's what we've seen. We can't live in that kind of world, so we only have two options. We run, or we fight, and with everything we have. Half measures won't work. We can't afford to have lines we won't cross. Because they don't. You can't win wars by following rules, especially when the two sides are so lopsided. So, if we stay, if we fight, we have to embrace what we'll end up becoming."

He sighed. "But for the record, I advocate running. I know you don't, though. And I see the value in staying and fighting. But I know you. I can predict what this is going to do to you, and I don't want to see it. I'll stay, though. I'll stay and fight and support you because it needs to be done, and you are the only person who can do it."

I looked up. "You really think that? There are a lot of powerful people out there . . ."

"Not like you."

I knew that, of course. Maybe I'd fooled myself into believing that there were others who could do the things I could do, but that just wasn't the case. As far as I'd seen, I was probably the most powerful individual on the planet, and I wasn't sure if the next person on that list was even close. If Earth was going to win the coming war, I needed to push my misgivings aside and do what had to be done.

"I hate this," I said. "I wish we could just live our lives without having to worry about war and death and oppression."

"We can. We can go right now. We'll spend the next couple of months out in the middle of nowhere, and then we'll leave as soon as the quarantine drops," he said. He sighed. "But I know that's not what's going to happen. You can't leave this behind. You feel like you're responsible for the whole world."

I didn't dispute that. Ever since I'd made my choice to join Alistaris, I had resolved to accept my share of responsibility for Earth's fate. Now, given the rapid increase in my power, I felt that weight even more keenly. Earth needed me. That was obvious and inescapable. However, I needed it, too. I wouldn't be able to live with myself if I left it to be plundered and pillaged by a bunch of unscrupulous aliens.

"I wish I could just leave."

"But you can't. I don't think I could, either," he admitted, running his cybernetic hand through his hair. It had grown longer, almost as if he wanted to compensate for his half-metal face. He'd so far refused to cover his artificial parts with synthetic skin. I wasn't sure if he looked at those parts as a badge of honor, or if he'd been telling the truth when he'd told me that he kept them uncovered so he could tinker with them. "The idea of looking back on a dead or enslaved world and knowing I could have done something to prevent that . . . I don't know if I could handle the guilt."

"Me, neither."

After that, the conversation died out, but we continued to sit there atop *The Leviathan* where we enjoyed the comfort the other provided. Hours passed, and eventually, we migrated back inside where we found our way to bed. Sleep didn't come quickly, though, and by the time morning came, I greeted it with bleary eyes and an exhaustion that had little to do with my lack of sleep.

That's when Alistaris contacted me. I sent the call to the ship's communications apparatus so that Patrick could hear, and I asked, "What's up, Al? You going to try to trick me again?"

"I didn't trick you."

"You definitely hid things from me," I said. "How about you play it straight with me from now on? I'd hate for something like dishonesty to come between us."

I wasn't actually angry with him for keeping me in the dark. It was more annoyance than anything else. But still, I didn't want him to think he could get away with withholding information that might save lives. If I'd known that those reptilian aliens had multiple warships nearby, then I would have set things up quite differently.

"I wasn't certain that they would come," he stated. "And even if I had been, I needed things to play out precisely like they did."

"Why?"

"Shock. Awe. You were clearly caught by surprise, and yet, you still ripped their warships from the sky, and in only a few minutes," he stated. "They will have seen it, and they will know precisely what it means."

"And what's that?"

"That you've begun to break free of the system," he stated. "What you just did is the domain of mystics, and not untrained ones, either. That will frighten them. For some factions, it will make this planet and its resources much less attractive. Some will do the math, then decide to leave well enough alone and move on to the next planet."

"You think that'll work?" asked Patrick. "And just so you know, I don't enjoy being used as bait."

"Noted," Alistaris said. "As to whether or not it will work, I don't know. It is only the beginning of the strategy."

"How about you tell us the rest?" I asked.

After that, he went on to explain his plan, which hinged on me killing a lot more aliens. However, instead of simply taking positions or exterminating the interlopers, the point was to make the planet seem a lot more dangerous than it was. To do that, I would adopt a variety of different identities via Mimic, then repeatedly display the same power I'd shown against the reptilian aliens.

"With any luck, they'll think Earth has at least a handful of powerful mystics," he said. "That will give them pause. For some, it will deter their invasions altogether. As I've stated, this is not a war of ideologies. Not for the invaders. It is a simple business venture, and when the cost begins to outweigh the benefits, we will win."

I wanted to dispute the viability of that claim, but I couldn't. So, I asked, "What's the next step, then? Where do you need me?"

"The next fort is smaller," Alistaris answered. "No more than a hundred combatants. Maybe fifty support personnel. But their defenses are second to none."

He went on to describe the outpost. Like every population center, it was surrounded by a wall, but it was also protected by a host of drones and combat bots whose number and relative power rivaled the Dengyt settlement I'd infiltrated what felt like a lifetime ago. Back then, I'd had some serious issues with the mission, but with my current progress, I knew it would be much simpler.

After he described the defenses and sent over a packet of information concerning the base, Alistaris said, "You had better get going. Over the next few weeks, you're going to crisscross the globe. Each target is going to be thousands of miles away from the last so as to enhance the perception that it is the result of multiple mystic-level defenders."

With that, we said our goodbyes and got underway. Patrick wasn't convinced that we were on the right track—I could see it in his face—but he pointedly didn't say as much. Instead, he only asked me if I was sure about it. When I told them I was, he dropped his dissension.

I would like to say that the following campaign was exciting, but the reality was that it was ugly, tedious, and ultimately boring. That first outpost fell without any real defense. The moment I got through their Mist shield and disabled their robotic defenders, they gave up. It did them no good, of course. I wasn't there to take prisoners. I slaughtered them all—except one—without even moving a finger.

Was I proud of it?

No.

It was disgusting. But in a war for my planet's survival, I couldn't afford mercy. The one survivor was allowed to live so they could spread the word. Of course, that story had been carefully manipulated—mostly, by the fact that, with Mimic, I had taken on the visage of a short and muscular male—but the survivor didn't need to know that.

After that first salvo, I proceeded with Alistaris's plan, and Patrick and I spent the next month going back and forth across the planet. In the process, we killed more types of aliens than I could count. From more of the reptilian sort to giant blobs that moved like slugs, I slaughtered them all.

It got easier, too. With every passing day that saw me slaughtering more aliens, I lost touch with the part of me that found it objectionable. Increasingly, I just saw enemies.

Not people.

Not lives lost.

Not families left without their loved ones.

Just faceless masses of dead enemies.

That helped with the guilt. I also found that it was even more helpful to focus on their Mist auras. Those were just globs of nanites instead of living, breathing people. And in that way, I dealt with the trauma of doing something nobody should ever be asked to do.

"I think that makes it worse," I said on the thirtieth day after Alistaris's campaign had begun. I was sitting in the ship's living area, just staring ahead at nothing. That day, I'd swept through two separate alien installations, leaving only a couple of survivors behind. Those were meant to spread the word.

"What does?" asked Patrick, who was busy fiddling with one of his cybernetic legs. Lately, he'd been talking about adding rocket boosters so he could fly, but he'd yet to figure out a means of stabilization. He was convinced he could do it, though. And I hoped for his success, not least because I would've loved the ability to fly. That wasn't on my mind at the moment, though.

"I don't know," I said. "I want to feel guilty, but I don't. I've lost count of how many aliens I've killed, but I don't really feel bad about it anymore. Now, it just feels like a tedious task that needs to be done. I'm just afraid of what that says about the sort of person I am. Of the kind of person I'm becoming."

"It's worth it."

"Do you really think that?" I asked, looking up and searching for confirmation that I was doing the right thing. Maybe I was going about it in the wrong way, but I had to believe that the cause was just.

"I do," he said without a hint of doubt. I appreciated that, though I wasn't certain if I really believed him.

Before we could get into it any further, I received a communications request from Alistaris. I let it come through, applying Secure Connection without a second thought.

"We have a problem," he said.

"What kind?" I asked.

"The kind that could derail everything" was his response. "We need to meet, and as soon as you can arrange it."

We were still scheduled to hit another couple of bases in the next few days, so I knew that it had to be something serious if Alistaris wanted us to abandon those plans. So, I said, "Send us some coordinates and we'll be there as soon as possible."

After that, I let Patrick know what was going on—or at least what I knew of it. Then, we headed up to the cockpit. Only a few moments later, Patrick joined me and fired up the engines. Once he'd gone through his preflight checklist, he had *The Leviathan* in the sky, and we were speeding toward the coordinates.

It only took us a few hours to reach Alistaris's location, which was a vast savanna where he'd landed his own fleet of ships. Only a few of them were of a size with *The Leviathan*, but there were a dozen smaller vessels nearby.

"Think this is everything he's got?" Patrick asked.

"I don't know. But it doesn't bode well for us that he's out in the open like this," I answered. "Something must really be wrong."

"Well, nothing for it but to land and find out."

With that, he took *The Leviathan* in and landed about a hundred yards away from the other ships.

CHAPTER TWENTY-SIX

THE ENEMY

Bit by bit, we're losing her. I see it every time she comes back from one of her missions. They're sucking the humanity right out of her. We both know it, too. She can feel it happening. But neither of us can see another way.

—Patrick Ward

That looks intimidating," Patrick said as he stared at the holographic display in the center of the room. All around us, Dengyts worked at various terminals, coordinating various teams who were engaged in various missions. At the same time, more gnomes raced through the room on one task or another, making the entire room feel chaotic. But I knew there was a pattern to it all. Alistaris and the other Dengyts were organized right down to the smallest detail, and as such, the chaos was more illusion than reality.

The holographic display showed a huge ship that, to the naked eye, rivaled the Bazaar in size. However, it was much sleeker, and it was bristling with cannons.

"That's a Gomari warship. Class DST-X-109. It's called *Infinite Conquest*," Alistaris explained. "And it is well named."

I studied the ship. From an aesthetic standpoint, it was quite striking. Dark blue, with gold filigree decorating the nose, the ship's hull was sharply pointed, and four symmetrical wings extended from the middle to end in circular modules that I suspected were used as additional housing for the crew.

"What makes it so special?" I asked.

"Everything."

"Elaborate," I prompted.

"Its armor is second to none, making it a perfect platform from which to launch an invasion. More importantly—especially to you—it was created by a race of mystics who'd never been Integrated into the system. So, it is more resistant to your abilities and skills than anything else you have or likely ever will see," Alistaris explained.

"Including Ghosts?" I asked.

"Yes."

"Damn."

I didn't have much context for what mystics were capable of. I'd only met a handful, and I'd only gotten a glimpse of the way they fought. However, I knew enough to recognize that they were vastly different, in terms of the nature of their power, than anyone else I'd gone up against. My own power, which was still less developed than I wanted it to be, was a testament to that. I was no mystic, but I'd been told that I was beginning to walk that path. My experiences supported that notion.

"The only saving grace is that its inherent combat capability trends more toward defense than overt destruction," he said. "However, it does feature a fleet of smaller fighter ships that are likely more advanced than anything this world has to offer."

"What are you doing about it? You've got your Alliance backing you up, right? Don't they have a warship that can counteract this *Infinite Conquest*?" Patrick asked.

Alistaris shook his head. "My organization is not committed to this planet's defense," he said. "It's a cost-benefit situation, and with Earth, the cost of fending off the Gomari Confederation far outweighs any benefit we might see to our overall efforts. What you see here is the extent of what we can offer."

"So, just enough help to give us hope, but not enough to actually do anything," Patrick remarked. Normally, his personality was as steady as anyone I'd ever met, but woe unto anyone who truly made him angry. "Great."

"I'll remind you that I am here," Alistaris said, his voice even. I knew him well enough to recognize the underlying anger that placid tone camouflaged, though. "I am in the same situation as the natives of this world. The Gomari Confederation will kill me the same as all of you. It is no different for my subordinates. Everyone here is risking their lives for a planet that is not their own. I suggest you acknowledge that sacrifice, even if you don't respect it."

Patrick clenched his fist, but quickly subdued his own annoyance by saying, "I'm sorry. I shouldn't have said that."

"Think nothing of it."

I could understand Patrick's irritation. The fleet of ships we'd seen upon arrival was impressive, but not in the context of a planetwide battle. And given the size of *Infinite Conquest*, I suspected that the fleet it housed was far more extensive and exponentially better suited to the task of fighting a global war.

In that context, it was difficult to feel any level of appreciation for what looked like the bare minimum the Alliance had offered.

Still, I wasn't going to let myself get caught up in thinking like that. I'd known all along that if Earth was going to survive, it would be on the backs of its native population. The aliens—even Alistaris and his organization—only wanted to exploit the planet for their own means. For the Ark Alliance, that meant they could fight their enemies on a battlefield so far removed from their own territory that its destruction would be meaningless. Perhaps they also cared about our resources, and maybe a few were like Alistaris and actually cared about humanity, but the fact was that our planet was just a convenient setting for their war.

I needed to keep that in mind, lest I become blinded to the reality of Earth's circumstances.

"How many enemies are up there? And what's their relative power level? Also, what species are we dealing with?" I asked.

Alistaris's answers were more than a little disturbing. He claimed there were at least a hundred thousand warriors inside, but that wasn't including the support personnel or crew. On top of that, he informed us that the warriors included a dozen mystics, each one on the level of a full-fledged Templar. Finally, the population of the ship—which was more of a spacefaring city than a mere means of conveyance from one point to another—was varied enough that trying to classify them by species was largely pointless.

"So, what do we do?" I asked.

"The presence of mystics opens a new possibility," Alistaris said. "You have some relationship with the local Templars, right?"

"How do you know that?"

"It's my job to know things, Miss Braddock," he stated.

"That doesn't answer my question."

"You're aware of most of our surveillance. Leave it at that."

I sighed. He and the other members of the Ark Alliance who'd come to Earth had been watching me for a long time. Well before our first meeting, they'd known who I was and had been keeping tabs on me. So, it wasn't a surprise that they knew about my meetings with various Templars like Freddie.

"Fine. Where do I find them? I haven't exactly kept in touch with the ones I know," I said. There had been a Temple back in Nova City, but I'd never had occasion to visit. Not that I could have without significant subterfuge, given that it had been located in the affluent Lakeview district. That alone had kept me from satisfying my curiosity about the Templars. "And do you honestly think they'll help us?"

"That depends."

"On what?" asked Patrick, inserting himself into the discussion.

"On how persuasive she is," Alistaris answered. "Templars are not our allies. There is always tension between the Ark Alliance and their organization. However, on occasion, we have joined forces to combat rogue elements. They see themselves as peacekeepers dedicated to opposing other, less scrupulous mystic factions. So, there is a chance that they will join our cause, if only as long as it takes to defeat their counterparts."

"And why don't you go? If the Alliance has a history of—"

The Dengyt commander interrupted Patrick by saying, "I am not my organization, and in this instance, I would make for a poor representative for the Ark Alliance. I have history with the Templars."

"And we're supposed to just waltz in there and get them on our side?" Patrick asked.

"Essentially."

Patrick looked like he wanted to respond, but he was dumbstruck by Alistaris's confirmation. So, I cut in, saying, "Fine. Just tell us where to go and we'll do what needs to be done. If they help, they help. If not, well . . . I'll just have to do it all myself."

"This is a much more extensive threat than the Pacificians."

"And I'm a lot more dangerous now."

"Not that dangerous," Alistaris pointed out.

I shrugged. "We'll just have to see, I guess. We've got a short span here. We need to get this done before the quarantine lifts, right?" I asked. "So, we don't have any time to waste. Just send me the coordinates and we'll take it from there."

"Very well," Alistaris said. Then, he followed through, sending me a packet containing a brief summary of the location as well as its coordinates. A glance told me that it was half a world away on a volcanic island on the edge of the planet's largest ocean. "Be wary, though. The Templars are a rigid people for whom respect is a core tenet of what amounts to a religion. If you offend them, you will bring the weight of their entire order down on your head."

"Don't insult the space wizards," I said, snapping my fingers. "Gotcha."

"They are not . . . space wizards."

"Close enough," I said with a shrug. "Patrick agrees. Right, Pick?"

"They're not . . . not space wizards, I guess."

"See, wholehearted agreement," I said with a grin. I didn't really feel it, though. Instead, most threads of my mind were focused on exactly how dire Earth's situation was. If *Infinite Conquest* was as powerful as Alistaris had claimed, it had the capacity to end the war before it really got started. A hundred thousand powerful alien warriors made for a force that would sweep through Earth without any trouble at all.

That frightened me, though I had no intention of letting Alistaris see my fear. He probably knew, anyway. He wasn't stupid, after all.

"What happens when we get them on our side?" Patrick asked.

"We integrate them into our plans," the Dengyt answered.

"Which you still haven't shared."

"Operational security."

"You keep saying that," I pointed out. "What do you think is going to happen? It's not like we're going to go running to the people who want nothing more than to kill us. They wouldn't believe a word we'd say, anyway. And besides, they want to destroy our planet. Neither Patrick nor I want to see that happen."

Alistaris's eyes shifted to his subordinates, and I got his meaning. He wasn't afraid that Patrick or I would share his secrets and ruin the battle plan. Instead, he was worried about his own people. Paranoia was probably a good thing, given that the Gomari Confederation would almost assuredly make a lucrative offer for any actionable information.

It was a poignant reminder of how overmatched we really were.

"The good thing is that, with the combination of *Infinite Conquest*'s arrival as well as our efforts over the past month, our enemies have consolidated. Anyone who isn't part of the Confederation is preparing to leave," Alistaris said. "Or they're already dead."

"That's a good thing, right?"

"It is. It means that instead of fighting against a hundred or more different forces, all with wildly different agendas, we can focus on a single enemy," he said. "They will have a plan for subjugating the planet, though. It won't be down to a ground war. It'll be something else. I have people looking into it, but we've yet to find anything else of note."

"Fair enough. So, for now, Patrick and I need to head to . . . Japan," I said, reading the name of the island off my packet. "We'll try to get the Templars on our side, but what happens if they refuse?"

"What do you mean?"

"If they're not with us, they're against us, aren't they?"

"Are you proposing to kill the Templars?"

"Uh . . . Yeah? Maybe. Why? Is that such a bad thing? I mean, I liked Freddie, and those others saved my life once. But if they're humans and they won't step up against something like this, they're better off dead."

"You will not do anything of the sort."

"What? Why can't I—"

"Never mind that if you tried, you would get a rude awakening as to your actual place in the hierarchy of the universe," he stated. "But you would bring the Templars down on us at the same time."

"Thought they were enemies of these enemy mystics . . ."

"They are. But they will not tolerate attacks on their Temples. You mess with the Templars, and you'll find out why everyone in the universe is terrified of letting mystics run free."

"Fine."

"I need to hear you say it, Miss Braddock. Tell me you won't antagonize or attack them."

"I promise. I'll be a good girl."

"I am not reassured," he stated.

"Don't worry. I'll keep Patrick in line," I said.

"I wasn't . . . Ah . . . Never mind. I see that you were joking. Poorly."

"Ouch."

"It really will be fine," Patrick said. "We're not going to start a war with the space wizards."

Alistaris just shook his head at that. Afterward, he took a few minutes to ensure that we knew where we were going before he filled us in on the details of what the other teams were up to. At present, they were conducting raids on various Rift-mining operations, where they were seizing anything they could get their hands on. In addition, another team had been tasked with assaulting a few key resource-gathering locations.

"That reminds me—you still owe me my cut from the Pacifician mine," I said. After I'd killed the majority of the androids on Earth, the remainder had abandoned their mine. I'd passed it on to Alistaris with the understanding that I would get a percentage of any profits they managed to generate.

"That ore is going to building weapons to defend your planet," he said. "High-quality ammunition is not cheap to make."

"Touché, I guess. But you still owe me. I expect that when all this is over, we'll settle up."

"You'll get everything you deserve," he said. "My people are keeping copious records."

"You sounded really creepy when you said that, Al. Just letting you know," I said. "A more suspicious person might assume that you're going to try to screw me out of what I'm owed. Or kill me. But given my experiences with aliens so far, that wouldn't be so surprising. I think you know how that kind of thing usually ends up going, though, so I'll just choose to believe that I'm being unreasonable."

That definitely wasn't the response he expected. In truth, I didn't really think he intended to double-cross me. Not because he didn't have the capacity but, rather, because he didn't really have much to gain from it. If he'd wanted me dead, he would have just left me on the moon.

After that, Patrick and I excused ourselves and returned to *The Leviathan.* As always when I came in contact with Alistaris or the other gnomes, I spent the next few hours going over the ship with a fine-tooth comb. I found no trackers or listening devices, though, so I reasoned that we were finally getting past the distrusting phase of our relationship.

Once our privacy had been assured, we took off, and Patrick guided the ship a couple of hundred miles away before he set it down. There, we settled in to discuss what had happened. As far as either of us could tell, everything Alistaris had said was accurate, which did not bode well for Earth's survival. Still, we had a plan of attack, and that was all that mattered. Hopefully, we'd figure the rest out along the way.

In the meantime, we set off toward Japan. The trip required us to cross the ocean, which was a dangerous prospect even in the best of times. However, to my surprise, we managed to make the crossing without any major incidents. Sure, we were assaulted by a flock of giant predatory birds, and we also had to dodge a series of weaponized waterspouts that had originated with a pod of whales. But other than that, the trip was uneventful, and about six hours after we'd set out, we saw the island that was our destination on the horizon.

The island itself was mountainous, but the landscape was dominated by a single enormous snowcapped peak. As Patrick piloted *The Leviathan* closer, I saw a walled city at the base of the mountain, but that was not our destination. Instead, we circled the island, coming in from the north. Soon enough, we saw our goal.

Strangely enough, the town was not circled by a wall. Nor did it have a Mist shield. Instead, it was entirely open. The architecture was all sweeping roofs and wooden structures, but what truly impressed me was the expansive gardens that seemed even more ubiquitous than the buildings.

A few white-robed men and women looked up at our approach. On the surface, they didn't look terribly extraordinary. Even with Observation flared, I saw nothing to suggest that they were dangerous. None of them were even armed. And yet, when I looked upon them, a sense of deep unease spread through my mind. For a long moment, I couldn't place why I felt that way, but then it hit me.

"They don't have auras."

"What?" asked Patrick.

"These people, they don't have Mist auras," I said. It was then that I began to understand one of the things that set Templars apart.

CHAPTER TWENTY-SEVEN

DECEPTION

Power without intention is the worst sort of sin.

—Alistaris Kargat

Templars had a reputation.

Even on Earth, which was as isolated of a backwater as existed within the universe, everyone knew about them. Stories as to who they were and what they represented differed, though. To some people, they were looked upon as religious leaders—even when the Templars themselves eschewed such labels. To others, they were mystical warriors who followed strict codes and saved the helpless.

There were hundreds of other stories about them, most of which I knew to be blatantly untrue. The Templars weren't villains, but they weren't saviors, either. Not on the scale that people liked to attribute to them, at least. Certainly, individual Templars had saved people. That was indisputable. I'd experienced that myself. Yet, as a group, they were almost pacifist, and they refused to commit themselves to a path that would set them against anyone that mattered.

From Alistaris and the other aliens with whom I was on speaking terms, I knew that was because they had a different mission, which was to combat mystics who would use their powers to oppress and dominate those around them. The Templars were a neutral peacekeeping force, and anything outside that purview was immaterial to their mandate.

Which was both frustrating and respectable, as far as I was concerned.

Commitment to a mission and a refusal to waver from that purpose was laudable. However, when that meant you and your organization ignored the plight of people you could have otherwise helped, it passed into the realm of frustration. It was even more upsetting because I knew precisely what kind of difference they could have made. My own recent efforts were an example of the sorts of things they could have accomplished.

All that and more swirled in my mind as Patrick settled *The Leviathan* into place. The landing zone he'd chosen was just a wide clearing about half a mile from the Templar settlement, but it served our purposes well enough. After he set it down, he went through his postflight checklist before turning to me and asking, "You ready for this?"

"I don't know. If they're hostile . . ."

"We'll deal with it," he said.

I nodded, though with what I'd seen from the Templars in my previous encounters, I didn't think I had much of a chance if it came down to a fight. Perhaps I could take out one or two of them, but a battle against an entire village of Templars was a mountain I felt certain I couldn't climb.

But I couldn't shirk the responsibilities I'd taken as my own. According to Alistaris, we needed the Templars' help, and if we didn't get it, things were going to get very bad, very quickly. So, I didn't have a choice. Not if I wanted Earth to survive.

So, I took a deep breath, squared my shoulders, and said, "You're right. If they're a bunch of assholes, we'll just deal with it."

He gave me a crooked grin. "So, normal day?"

"I guess so," I agreed.

After that, we readied ourselves for a potential battle. For me, that meant ensuring that all my weapons were loaded, and I had plenty of ammunition in my arsenal implant. Meanwhile, Patrick spent a few minutes checking that his armor was in peak condition before we both donned our respective combat attire. Over my infiltration suit, I wore black fatigues, while Patrick wore a long coat that reminded me of a certain demolition expert.

"You get that coat from Rex?" I asked, looking him up and down. "Tell me you don't have a hat, too."

"I don't have a hat."

"What are you holding behind your back?"

I sensed a surge of Mist, then he spread his hands wide, saying, "Nothing. Seriously, Mira, you need to start trusting me more."

I just shook my head as a slight smile spread across my face. Soon enough, though, I had to put my game face on because we were both ready. So, we headed toward the exit hatch. Upon leaving the ship, I used Bastion while Patrick engaged *The Leviathan*'s native defenses. Once that was done, we headed toward the settlement.

It was only a few hundred yards away, so I didn't bother summoning the Cutter.

"It's beautiful here," Patrick said as he gazed out across the landscape. The Templar village was located in the middle of nowhere, so forested wilderness stretched all the way to the horizon. Meanwhile, the settlement itself was situated on the side of a terraced hill where each step played host to a serene garden.

Even from a distance, it was magnificent.

"Sure," I said. "But it's all a lie."

It was a facade meant to hide the Templars' apathetic existence. They held themselves apart from the rest of the world as they tried to pretend its fate had nothing to do with them. So, I wasn't fooled by the beauty on display.

"You don't know that. Wait until you hear what they have to say for themselves before you judge them."

"What they say doesn't matter nearly as much as their actions, Pick," I said. "They've had a century to prove they care about Earth. But they're right here, living in their little paradise while everyone else scrambles for whatever freedom they manage to scrounge up. You've seen some of the things I have, Patrick. The Templars are well-connected and informed. They have power. They could have done more."

"So could we."

"At least I've tried. They haven't lifted a finger to help the people of Earth."

"They helped you," he reminded me.

I took a deep breath. "They did," I admitted. "And I'm grateful for that. But saving one person because it doesn't really make you go out of your way isn't what I'm talking about. You know that."

"I do. I just think you need to take a deep breath and look at it from their perspective," Patrick stated. "You heard Alistaris. The Templars are there to fight against rogue mystics. If they commit to a war like this without that to spur them on, it'll throw everything into turmoil. There will be wars. Whole planets will be destroyed. And all these other factions will set themselves against the Templars, which will make their mission impossible. The bad mystics will rise up, and there will be no one to stop them from doing whatever they want."

"So, they're choosing the lesser of two evils? Is that it?"

"I think they're doing what they can without setting the universe on a collision course with a war that kills everyone."

"Maybe," I acknowledged. I wasn't stupid. I could connect the dots as well as Patrick could. However, like Alistaris, I still couldn't help but resent the Templars for fighting within the rules they had set for themselves.

In any case, we had a job to do, and I wasn't going to let my personal reservations stop me from at least trying to make things work. For all I knew, the Templars would be a lot more amenable to our shared circumstances than I anticipated. Especially given the arrival of *Infinite Conquest* and its cadre of affiliated mystics.

So, without further discussion, Patrick and I set off across the landscape, passing through what felt like a curated forest until we reached our destination only a little while later. To my surprise, we weren't greeted by a contingent of powerful warriors. Instead, a single man stood in our path, barring our way into the village proper. Beyond, the other white-robed Templars continued on with their days as if we weren't even there.

Or that was what they wanted us to think.

With Observation, I could see every furtive glance cast in our direction. Most of those originated with younger Templars that I assumed were trainees or apprentices, but a couple of older men and women let their facades slip, as well. More importantly, this close to the village, I could finally sense the Templars' auras. They were tightly controlled, and as such, they were only barely noticeable, but I'd spent the past few months constantly exercising my senses. So, even if I couldn't see the men and women tasked with the village's defense, I still knew they were there, just out of sight. But not out outside the range of my {Mist Warden} senses.

"Greetings, Mirabelle," said Freddie, the Templar I'd met on two other occasions. The fact that he was in Japan, so far away from where I'd last seen him, was definitely a source of alarm. However, he looked much the same as both the other times I'd seen him, which was to say that he was an average-sized man with wild hair and a great bushy beard. "You've grown."

"And you're a long way from home. How's Brad?" I asked.

"On the contrary," Freddy said. "This is my home. And my apprentice is engaged in his pilgrimage. He will not be joining us."

"So you were just slumming it halfway across the world?"

"Something like that," Freddie answered. "Do you mean us harm?"

I shrugged. "Not really" was my reply. "I didn't come here to fight. My mission is diplomatic in nature."

He let out a soft chuckle. "Forgive me. That does not seem like your forte," he said.

I shook my head, saying, "Can't really argue with that, Freddie. I'm more of a blow-everything-up kind of gal, but I suppose you can say I'm trying to branch out. Learn new skills, so to speak."

"Oh, you have certainly learned some new skills. Gained some levels, as well. Your aura is interesting. Well controlled, but still very powerful," he said. "I suspect that you are on the edge of the Threshold."

I cocked my head to the side. "The Threshold? What's that?"

"A matter best discussed over tea," he answered. "I will ask you again—do you or your partner intend to inflict harm upon the people of this village?"

"No."

I saw the Mist of his aura swirl, though it wasn't what I normally saw when someone activated a skill. Instead, it was both more controlled and wilder—a contrast that, on the surface, didn't make much sense. But it was the only way I could make sense of it.

"Very well," he said. "Come. We will discuss this inside."

Without another word, he turned around and started strolling through the village. Patrick and I exchanged a quick glance before hurrying to catch up. As we followed Freddie through the settlement, I was once again taken in by the peaceful ambiance of the stepped gardens and simple, yet distinctive architecture.

"What's the name of this place?"

"Serenity," Freddy answered.

"Fitting," I acknowledged.

"Most of the time, yes, it is," he said without turning to face me.

We climbed a few sets of wide, worn stairs before we finally reached the step that was our destination. Freddie took a left turn, leading us farther into the village. As we progressed, I couldn't help but notice that the fearful glances I received from the Templars were a bit unnerving. As before, they tried to hide their expressions, but by virtue of [Multimind] as well as Observation, I saw them all clearly.

They weren't just wary. They were terrified. And that put me on edge, as well.

Finally, Freddie led us to a tall three-story building with a sweeping roof. It had been constructed mostly of wood, though with a stone foundation that raised it a foot or so from the ground. In addition, it had been painted a subdued red.

Inside, the decor was much as I'd come to expect from that style of architecture, which meant that it mostly eschewed walls in favor of paper or cloth partitions. Patrick and I followed the Templar into a room with a low table that was surrounded by cushions.

He knelt on one side, then gestured to the other. Patrick and I sat on the cushions, and a moment later, a white-robed young man entered with a steaming kettle. Another young woman placed a pair of cups in front of Patrick and me, while setting another in front of Freddie. After that, they proceeded to make tea in what looked like an elaborate ceremony. I paid attention with one train of thought, but despite the obvious importance of the act, it didn't hold my attention. Instead, I focused on the auras of the two servers.

Both were subdued and almost entirely contained, with only a hint of the power I would have expected from a pair of Templars.

"They are not even apprentices yet," Freddie said, almost as if he could read my mind. Before I'd developed my aura senses, I might have suspected that he used the Templar equivalent of a skill. But the tightly controlled aura hadn't even quivered. "In all likelihood, they will become wildlings soon enough."

"Is it rare for someone to survive the . . . inoculation period?" asked Patrick.

Freddie answered, "Very. One in a hundred, if we're lucky. Less, usually."

"Then why do it? Why not take Nexus Implants like everyone else?"

"Those Nexus Implants are shackles," the Templar stated, taking a sip of his tea. He let out a sigh of appreciation. "They hinder the natural order. What do you think happens to worlds that experience the onset of Mist but never feel the touch of the system?"

"Do those exist?" Patrick asked.

"Of course. Thousands of inhabited worlds are enveloped by the Mist each week," he answered. "Only the most promising are granted the system's dubious protection."

"Without the system, billions of people would die."

"As is the point," Freddie stated. "Evolution is not a painless process, but without that struggle, none of us can reach our full potential. The Nexus Implants are a crutch. A stopgap that, admittedly, saves lives but also sentences each of its victims to abject mediocrity." He sighed. "But you are not here to talk philosophy. You came for a different purpose."

"We did," I said.

"Care to share it?"

"First, I have a question," I ventured. "You once told me that I would eventually close the gap with people like you."

"I did, and it seems that you have made good on that prediction."

"So, I'm, like, a Templar now?"

"Yes and no," he answered. "The paths we travel matter. How you experience the Mist is fundamentally different from the way we do. However, there are enough commonalities that, to many, the differences become less apparent. I sense that you are . . . capable of terrible things, Mirabelle. You have power unlike anyone else on Earth."

"I'm stronger?"

"Than all but a few? Yes. Including Templars. But your power is also different," he stated. "That makes you even more dangerous."

"So, I'm unique?"

He laughed mirthlessly. "Nothing in this universe is truly unique. But you are rare. Exceedingly so. There is a name for people like you, though. A dubious label given to those rare individuals whose power exceeds easy categorization."

"Yeah? What is it?" I asked.

"World killer."

I burst out laughing. "Really? Isn't that a bit . . . dramatic?"

"No."

His sober answer drew me up short. "Wait, really? You think I can just snap my fingers and kill a whole world?"

"I believe you have that potential, yes. And I think that's the fate some people have been pushing you toward," Freddie said. "This world, it has garnered a lot of undue interest. Factions that should not care about such an inconsequential place are here, influencing and guiding events. Your friend—"

"Alistaris is here to pick up—"

"Gala. Do you know who she really is? What about Anaseteramanimix? Both should be in the core worlds, living lives of luxury. And yet, they are both here, living in relative poverty on a frontier world of almost no consequence. Tell me—do you truly know where that Nexus Implant inside of you came from? What of the skills you take for granted? You have been manipulated since the very beginning. Guided to become a weapon. Your uncle was a powerful man, but that implant was not something he ever should have had access to. No one should. It was an experiment. The result of centuries of research and development."

"What are you saying?"

"That you were never meant for mediocrity, Mirabelle. Whatever Jeremiah told you, it was a lie. His acquisition of that implant was a calculated attempt to create a superweapon. And you have exceeded even those expectations," Freddie stated. "By quite some degree. I sense that one of your abilities is in flux, as if it is only half-developed."

I already knew that Gala had a past and that she was far stronger than she appeared. However, I'd never considered the possibility that Ana was more than she seemed to be. However, in retrospect, the fact that she always seemed to have the perfect skill should have been a clue.

"Is Alistaris part of it?"

"I don't know," Freddie admitted.

"Are you?"

"I am not, though our first meeting was not a coincidence."

"I thought you were there for your apprentice."

"I can do two things at once," he stated. "But you didn't come here for conspiracies and plots, did you? You came for something else."

"I'm not done talking about that first part."

"I am."

The teacup I'd been holding—without drinking from it—shattered in my grip. Patrick flinched, but Freddie didn't even blink. His aura remained just as tightly controlled as ever. If he was frightened of my reaction, he was very good at masking it.

Moreover, that brief moment gave me the opportunity to rethink my own anger. Freddie wasn't my enemy. Nor was his explanation necessary. Now that he'd opened my mind to the possibility that I'd been manipulated into becoming a weapon, I was more than capable of investigating the matter by other means. If worse came to worst, I could head up to the Bazaar and demand answers in person.

So, with that in mind, I said, "Fine. The reason I came here is because there's a huge ship that just showed up. Called *Infinite Conquest*. According to Alistaris Kargat—he represents the Ark Alliance, by the way—they have enough firepower to subdue the entire planet. More relevantly to you, they also have a contingent of mystics on board. So, given your order's stated purpose, he thought you might want to rally the troops to do your fucking job."

"Interesting."

"Interesting?"

"Indeed."

"In what world is that an appropriate response?" I demanded.

"Oh, no—I wasn't talking about your outburst," he said.

"Then what were you talking about?"

Just then, the sound of an explosion echoed in my ears. An instant later, the building shook from a shock wave.

"That," he said. "Come. We must defend Serenity."

With that, Freddie pushed himself to his feet. Suddenly, a long-bladed spear appeared in his hands.

CHAPTER TWENTY-EIGHT

BROKEN PEACE

Ours is a universe of obvious intention. The mighty crave power so they can maintain their wealth and influence. The weak need to grow stronger so they can throw off the yoke of oppression. Peace is a temporary illusion because war is both the means and the end of all things.

—Alistaris Kargat

Freddie jogged ahead of me, his gait unhurried but his aura, held so close and controlled, roiled with obvious agitation. I could scarcely see it, but what I could see felt like a series of carefully contained explosions. There was power there, and even though I knew that an attack was underway, I was eager to see how his strength manifested.

All around, white-robed people—some of whom had been serving us tea only a few minutes before—sprinted away on one task or another. None of them were panicked, which told me that they had endured plenty of attacks through the years. Meanwhile, Patrick and I followed Freddie, and soon enough, we burst through the door to see a huge ship hovering over the town.

The sleek ship was smaller than *The Leviathan*, if only just, and even from so far away, I could feel its cannons charging. So could Freddie because he wasted no more time before rocketing forward almost too quickly to track and planting himself in the ship's line of fire. So, when it let loose with a huge blob of roiling Mist, he found himself directly before it.

It bore down on him with inevitable destruction, but Freddie didn't immediately react. Instead, he waited until the last possible moment before thrusting out with his long-bladed spear.

That was the moment I first saw Freddie's true power.

He unleashed a wave of pure Mist that crashed into the cannon fire and tore it apart. But it didn't stop there. Instead, the expression of his power ripped through the sky, leaving a wake of tiny rippling explosions before it slammed into the ship. A blue Mist shield rippled, then tore, leaving a jagged wound that, only a moment later, mended. At the same time, the ship rocked backward under the blow. It only went a few dozen feet, its sharp nose tilting toward the sky before it righted itself, but even that small result was worth noting.

That was when I summoned the Emperor.

After using Explosive Shot to enhance every round in its magazine, I used Empowered Shot, took aim, then fired. The resultant shot sent a ripple across the ship's Mist shield, but that dissipated within only a few feet. However, that was precisely what I had expected, and I repeated my actions, sending another shot into the ship's shield. This time, the ripples were more widespread, and with Observation combined with my {Mist Warden} senses, I could see a few cracks.

I fired again, and they widened.

But more importantly, I finally felt the impact of the Mist drain. Over the months of my training, I'd grown more accustomed to the cost of using the Emperor, but it was still harsh enough to be distressing.

So, I'd created a bit of a work-around.

Using Mist Authority, I cast tendrils of my will in every direction. However, instead of picking something apart, I grabbed at the ambient Mist and dragged it into the Emperor. I used that to partially fuel the fourth shot. By that point, the weapon's issue was powerful enough to rip a small hole in the ship's Mist shield.

But it wasn't enough.

So, dragging even more Mist into the weapon, I fired again. This time, the ship rocked backward like it had when Freddie hit it with his Mist spear. But I had more in me, so I fired a sixth time.

The Mist shield ruptured like a burst bubble, exploding into motes of Mist that rained down on the town below.

However, the cost had grown even more onerous, and I fell to a knee as the Mist deprivation washed over me. I didn't let it stop me, though. Instead, I summoned a Mist booster from my arsenal implant and jabbed it into my hip. After that, I used Vanish, then Stealth before activating Execute.

Then, after using Empowered Shot once again, I fired the seventh and final shot in the Emperor's magazine. I tried to mitigate it by dragging more Mist into the weapon, but it was a trickle compared to the flood the weapon required, and all the Mist I'd just recovered rushed out of me, leaving only a desert in its wake.

But it was enough.

Even as the ball of Mist-infused death tore through the air, the ambient Mist ignited and swirled. The ship tried to employ evasive maneuvers, but it was far too slow to avoid the pure devastation bearing down on it.

When it hit, the sky erupted into a wave of blue fire that swept in every direction. The sound of that explosion was deafening, and the shock wave tore the roofs from nearby houses. For my part, I was thrown backward, and I saw that Patrick suffered a similar fate. Notably, Freddie endured by virtue of a series of thick ropes of Mist lashing him to the ground. I only got a brief glance before I hit the ground and skidded backward into the wall, but even then, the sight gave me all sorts of ideas.

I was thinking too small with Mist Authority.

Ripping things apart was great. So was using it as a means to spread my Ghosts. But those were unimaginative, and confining myself to those was ultimately going to hold me back. I needed to expand my scope.

I blinked as my vision cleared, and I saw the fruits of my efforts. The ship listed to the side, a third of its fuselage missing. A series of fires raged across its exposed interior, and I saw a couple of aliens fall from the hole in the hull. More importantly, its cannon was entirely gone, and the ship seemed incapable of remaining in the sky much longer.

Unfortunately, the Emperor was spent for now. Otherwise, I would have begun the process anew. But even with it recharging—or recovering from the strain; I wasn't certain which was applicable—I had plenty of other weapons at my disposal. So, as I pushed myself to my feet, I summoned the HIRC and took aim.

But then, Freddie was beside me. He placed his hand on the enormous weapon I held at my hip and said, "No. If you attack it with that, the ship will crash inside the town. Give them the ability to land elsewhere, and we will save our people."

"But—"

"They won't get far," he stated. "Besides, there will be plenty to do in the meantime. Look."

I followed his pointing finger to see that those people falling from the ship were not falling at all. Instead, their descent was controlled. Still, it wasn't until I heard an eruption of gunfire that I realized that they'd sent a team of soldiers in to finish the job they'd started.

By that point, Patrick had regained his feet. As he dusted himself off, he said, "That thing really packs a punch."

"It does," I agreed, watching the ship drift away from the town. It was slowly losing altitude, so I knew Freddie was right. It was going to hit the ground soon enough, with or without my additional input. It was better to fight the invasion that had already begun instead. So, turning to Freddie, I asked, "Plan?"

"They will target the uninitiated. Then the trainees. Any apprentices they can find. Only when everyone else is dead will they converge on full Templars."

"How many do you have here?"

"Seven," he answered. Then, he cocked his head to the side, and I saw a pulse of Mist spread across the town. It only lasted an instant before it dissipated, but when it did, he said, "Six. Laris has fallen. The Adjudicators are efficient and deadly, and they are well-versed in dealing with our methods."

"Shit," I muttered. If someone could kill a full-fledged Templar, then they were a serious threat. "Okay. Patrick and I will focus on saving as many people as we can. Do you have somewhere safe?"

"The Bulwark," Freddy said, pointing to a small building across the square. "It's underground and features the stoutest defenses of anywhere in the village. Most of the uninitiated know to go there."

After that, we agreed on a plan of attack. Patrick was the least mobile among us, so he was best used to secure the Bulwark. While he did that, Freddie and I would sweep through the village and rescue as many people as we could. It wasn't a perfect plan by any means, but it was the best any of us could come up with, given the objectives. So, with that, we set off through the village.

It wasn't long before we encountered the first so-called Adjudicator. The entity was dressed all in pitch-black armor that, as far as I could tell, was entirely sealed. More importantly, when I reached out with my {Mist Warden} senses, I saw absolutely nothing. A quick attempt to rip the soldier's Mist away was similarly useless.

So, I summoned the Stinger and fired.

At the same time, Freddie leaped forward, positioning himself between the Adjudicator and the three white-robed civilians the soldier had been about to attack. The black-armored warrior drew a black sword. Notably, it didn't have a hint of Mist running through it, but even I could tell that it was no ordinary blade.

My fire took the soldier in the chest, and it stumbled. However, the impact was not nearly as dramatic as I'd expected. I continued to fire in a staccato of three-round bursts. Meanwhile, Freddie brought his spear to bear, aiming for the Adjudicator's legs. The warrior danced out of the way of the sweeping attack, but my continued fire threw it off just enough that Freddie's next attack speared them through the chest.

Most of the impact was absorbed by the curiously sturdy armor, but Freddie's long-bladed spear still managed to find flesh, and when he ripped it away, it came free with a spray of blue blood.

But that wasn't enough to stop the Adjudicator, and he leaped forward, but not at Freddie. Instead, his intent was to kill the relatively unprotected civilians. Seeing that, I did two things at once. First, I dismissed my Stinger and drew my interdiction blade from the sheath on my back. And second, I used Teleport, putting myself directly in his path.

I met his blade with mine, then used a front kick to send him stumbling backward. That's when Freddie swept in, his spear clipping the back of the Adjudicator's leg. It cut deep, and the man staggered. I kept up the pressure, rushing forward to remain in range. As I did, I aimed one attack after another at the off-balance Adjudicator, but in a staggering show of swordsmanship, he managed to block each blow.

Barely.

But even barely counted, and I grew increasingly more frustrated with every passing moment. I was so focused on the battle at hand that I didn't even notice Freddie creeping in behind the soldier until I saw his blade erupt through the black breastplate. The Adjudicator went stiff, but only a second later, he tried to wrench himself free.

That's when I saw a bit of Mist leaking out of the crack in his armor. With instincts born of months of practice, I reached out with my Mist Authority, grabbed ahold of that thin trickle of Mist, and yanked it away. The moment I did, it was like a dam had broken, and the Mist came pouring out of his chest in a torrent. I dove into it, ripping it away with reckless abandon.

It only lasted a few moments, but in that time, I tore my way through more Mist than should have been possible. And then, suddenly, the flow ceased, and the black-armored Adjudicator fell forward on his face.

I nudged him with my foot, but I already knew he was dead.

"What the hell was that?" I demanded, turning to Freddie. The Templar was already kneeling next to the Adjudicator's would-be victims. "What was with his Mist?"

"Adjudicators are specially trained warriors whose purpose has and will always be to kill mystics," he answered. "Your Mist-manipulation abilities will not work against them unless you breach their armor. But you've already discovered that much."

"What is it made of? Is it valuable?"

"A norcite alloy. And no. It is bound to them in a way that prevents anyone from reusing it or repurposing the materials. Watch," he said.

I did, and I saw that the armor had already begun to smoke. In seconds, it dissolved completely, dissipating into fumes. That revealed an ordinary, blue-skinned alien corpse.

"Damn," I said.

"Indeed" was Freddie's response. After that, he left to guide the civilians to the Bulwark. I caught a glimpse of Patrick standing before the door, his massive Mist shield deployed as he aimed the rebuilt Dragon at anything that came close. Fortunately, he wasn't up against any Adjudicators but instead fought ordinary soldiers. Still, even though he held his own, it clearly pushed him to his limits.

But I had to trust that he could handle himself.

So, I turned away and raced through the town, gathering men and women as I went. In that way, Freddie and I swept through the village, saving as many as we could. Along the way, I found plenty of casualties. Most were civilians, but I came across two full-fledged Templars, as well. They'd been ripped to pieces, but I recognized the distinct cut of their robes.

Neither had gone down without a fight, and the corpses of their enemies were piled high all around them. Still, despite their power, they'd been killed, and that was a grim reminder of how pressing the danger really was.

There were plenty of fights, too. However, Freddie and I quickly learned to work together, and so long as we didn't make any mistakes, killing even the Adjudicators became routine. The only problem was that we were grossly out-numbered. Everywhere we went, there were more Adjudicators, and they usually didn't come alone. Instead, they were often accompanied by a host of other, more ordinary soldiers that made dispatching the true threats that much more difficult.

But we made progress, and that was all that really mattered.

I'd just beheaded a particularly resilient Adjudicator when Freddie whipped around. He started to say something, but before he could get a word out of his mouth, a surge of Mist ripped him from the ground and threw him across the street. He hit the wall of a nearby building, then went through it like it was made paper. Additional crashing sounds told me that his momentum had taken him deep into the building, perhaps even out the other side.

"Surrender," came a tinny voice. I turned to see a red-robed man. Outwardly, he looked mostly human, though his skin was pale gray, and his head was devoid of hair. He carried a white metal staff that had been etched with fanciful designs. At each end were carved claws clutching rubies that glowed with bloody light. His mouth was covered by some sort of metallic half mask. He stepped forward, adding, "Give up and you may yet live to serve Justice. Resist and you will surely perish."

From his tightly controlled aura, I knew he was a mystic. The other hint was that he'd picked Freddie up and tossed him aside with nothing but a wave of Mist. Ever since I'd seen my first Templars in action, I'd wondered how I would fare in a fight against their kind. Now, it looked like I was going to get my chance.

And I wasn't going to underestimate this newcomer.

So, without answering, I summoned the HIRC from my arsenal implant and let loose. Like its predecessor, it roared as it bathed the mystic in a tidal wave of deadly fire. And yet, I knew it wouldn't be enough. So, even as one of my minds concentrated on sending as many bullets downrange as was possible, another focused on manipulating the Mist. I reached out with Mist Authority and slammed my will against the mystic's aura. I chipped a little away, but it was like throwing myself against a brick wall.

Fortunately, that wasn't my primary objective.

With a third mind, I continued to form an evolving plan of attack. It was a good thing, too, because the mystic burst forth holding his staff before him and deflecting my fire with a sheer expression of Mist.

So, he never saw the pair of grenades I'd rolled in his direction.

Not until it was too late, at least.

They exploded, sending him flipping backward through the air. I tracked him with the HIRC, but he continued to swing his staff, batting aside my fire with his hastily constructed shields of Mist.

So, I switched gears and flipped the HIRC to its secondary fire mode. A moment later, a glob of molten Mist tore across the village. It met the mystic as he hit the ground in a skidding slide. He'd managed to land on his feet, and what's more, his white staff had never stopped moving. However, there was a marked difference between blocking a few hundred bullets and trying to stop a roiling ball of boiling Mist—if only because the explosion that came from the latter was accompanied by quite a bit of momentum.

The resultant shock wave sent the mystic flying farther backward, and I dismissed the HIRC in favor of the more versatile Stinger. As he arced through the air, I continued to fire, peppering him with further fire. I had to use Observation to aim properly, given how far he'd flown, and yet, my training proved up to the task. Finally, a few rounds managed to pierce his defenses, and I was rewarded with the sight of misting black blood.

I didn't let up, though, and I bent the entire weight of my multiple threads of thought to the task of finishing him off.

That was probably why I never even saw his partner coming.

Suddenly, my entire world seized. The Mist inside my body froze, and my body followed suit. I couldn't even breathe as a feminine voice caressed my ears. "Oh, you are an interesting one, aren't you? I would so like to study you."

CHAPTER TWENTY-NINE

IN OVER MY HEAD

Mira almost never encounters something she can't simply over-power, but when she does, it spurs her forward like nothing else can. She doesn't like to lose, but I think it's more than that. It's about strength. And weakness. Her abject loathing of failure. That's what makes her who she is, for better or worse.

—Patrick Ward

I felt the foreign Mist writhing around me like living bands of iron that squeezed my chest until I couldn't think, much less breathe. Somehow, I managed to flick my eyes in the direction of the voice I'd heard, and I saw the blurry outline of a person slowly come into focus.

She was a woman, but she was unlike anyone I'd ever seen before. Part of it was her physical appearance. In most ways, she looked human, and in fact, I expected that if she were to have presented herself in a different context, she could have passed for one. However, I didn't have to flare Observation to recognize that everything about her was just a little off. Her shoulders were too narrow, her arms and legs too long. Her waist was too slim, and her lips too thick. From a stylistic perspective, her hair was the most normal part of her, but it stood out due to the sheer volume and bloodred color.

But even with all that, it was her eyes, which were like deep pools of milky white, that set her apart more than anything else. By comparison, her pink skin was practically commonplace.

She wore a thin white dress that did little to hide her exaggerated curves—or anything else, come to that—and if I hadn't been immobilized by her Mist, I would have blushed and looked away from some of her more obvious characteristics. On one hand, she wore a set of long and thin white-enameled claws. They rippled with Mist, and yet, I could tell they weren't part of her.

"Do you like what you see, little pet?" the woman purred, circling around me. "I find your species disgustingly thick, but you aren't so bad. Perhaps when I'm done studying you, we can have a little fun."

Her aura flared, wild and roiling, yet perfectly controlled, as well. It was a study in contrasts. Inside of her locus of authority, it moved unpredictably, but she refused to let it extend farther than a few inches past her skin. It smacked of an expression of vanity, especially given that I had seen how tightly controlled Freddie's aura was.

"I'll have to politely decline. Thank you for the offer, though. It means the world to me," I managed to grunt. "Now, if you'll just let me go . . ."

She let out a chiming giggle before clapping her hands together. "Oh, how delightfully insolent!"

She stepped forward, then ran one of those white claws down the center of my chest and to my navel. And that was about all I intended to take of that. So, without further banter or discussion, I flexed Mist Authority to the fullest extent of my ability. And given just how much I'd been practicing, that was quite a bit.

For a moment, I thought I was going to escape. The bands of Mist wrapped around me cracked and shattered, and I started to slip away. The woman's eyes widened, her lips parting into a perfect circle of surprise. It only lasted for a second before she reasserted her will. Instantly, the bands firmed, and whatever progress I'd managed to make in my escape attempt fell away like the useless trash it was.

Still, I fought against that grip, which further delighted the woman. She tightened her control, squeezing me to the point where I felt like my bones were on the verge of cracking. And yet, I did not yield. I refused to give in. And slowly, I started to see the cracks in the woman's resolve. It showed in the gaps in her expression of Mist control, in the boiling sea of Mist that was her aura.

I couldn't push any harder, but I could apply my effort more efficiently. With every passing instant, I threw the weight of Mist Authority against her grip, but with another strain of thought, I slipped my own aura into the cracks. And then, when I'd managed to fill every gap, I flexed.

Instantly, the bonds of Mist shattered, and I fell to the ground. The woman screamed, and I rocketed forward, yanking my interdiction blade from the sheath on my back. I slashed downward, harnessing every bit of strength I possessed. But just before I made contact, she recovered. Without hesitation, she swept her claws out, knocking my blade aside. My hands stung from the sudden impact, and the sudden change in momentum sent me spinning. However, I was no novice to battle, and I used that to my advantage, aiming a round kick at the woman's face.

And I connected.

It was like hitting a wall. I rebounded, feeling the bone in my heel crack as I landed ten feet away. And yet, despite her obvious endurance, the kick had sent her stumbling backward. I counted that as a win—right up until she lashed out with her claws. She was well out of range, but that didn't seem to matter. Blades of Mist erupted from those claws, slicing through the air as they bore down on me. I was briefly surprised, but I kept my wits just enough to spring high into the air, avoiding the unorthodox attack.

But then she met me in the air, having jumped at the same time. Her foot connected with my jaw, shattering the bone and sending me tumbling backward. I landed almost fifty feet away, rolling to a stop in the rubble of one of the village's buildings. It was far and away the hardest I'd ever been hit, and I didn't even think she'd put everything she had into it. I pushed myself to my hands and knees, then spat blood and a couple of teeth. Then, I felt my jaw; it was broken. I knew that. But with every passing second, I could feel the nanites that comprised the Mist working to mend the cracks.

It would take some time to get back to normal, but my jaw would be functional in mere minutes.

In the distance, I saw the woman land lightly. Her aura had escaped her control, and she struggled to rein it in. As she did, I summoned my Stinger from my arsenal implant, used Explosive Shot, then opened fire. The first burst took her by surprise, knocking her backward in a spray of blood, but the next missed entirely when the Mist shimmered and she was suddenly a few feet to her left. I adjusted my aim and continued to fire.

It was useless.

Without the surprise of that initial burst, she was more than capable of dodging whatever shots I sent downrange. But that didn't mean I was going to stop shooting.

I filled the air with a hail of gunfire as the clawed woman slowly advanced. My shots were perfect, but I didn't land a single additional bullet. She didn't even bother dodging. Instead, she repeated the first mystic's tactic by extending her Mist aura to intercept any shots that would have hit her.

But even as I shot, one thread of thought searched for a solution, and by the time she came within fifteen feet, I only had one viable option. So, without ceasing fire with the Stinger, I summoned the ADS and fired.

The spray of norcite pellets slammed into her shield, same as all the rest. However, instead of being knocked aside, they bored their way through and tore into her exposed flesh. She screamed, but I fired again.

And again after that.

The woman staggered backward, but not from the force of the shot. Rather, her aura had gone completely out of control, fluctuating wildly as she clawed at her chest in an attempt to remove the pellets.

So, I fired again.

I kept going, filling her with hundreds of norcite pellets, until the ADS ran dry. At that point, I commenced with Stinger fire. Only this time, I went fully automatic. The weapon wasn't capable of the kind of fire rate associated with the HIRC or the Dragon, but its rate of fire was more than acceptable.

I tore her to pieces.

But to my horror, her flesh wriggled back together an instant after the Stinger's rounds ripped her apart. It was a horrific and daunting sight, but I didn't flinch. Nor did I blink. I knew there had to be some limit to her powers, and I was on a mission to find precisely where that lay.

With her control over Mist restricted by the norcite pellets, she was incapable of recovering completely, and I continued to pepper her with a hail of gunfire. At least until, at last, the spatial magazine ran dry. That left me with two options. I could either use Instant Reload, or I could change tactics altogether.

I chose the latter and exchanged the Stringer for the HIRC. By my count, it still had close to half its store of available ammunition left, and I quickly engaged in a quest to put every single one of those rounds in the mystic's chest. The world came alive with the roar of gunfire; it drowned out my screams of anger and frustration, as well, but in the back of one part of my mind, I knew I was fighting a losing battle. If things kept going as they were, there was no way I could win.

My only hope was to exhaust her self-healing capabilities. And to do that, I had to keep up the pressure at a rate of a thousand rounds a minute.

But inevitably, the battle shifted, and not in my favor.

Because I hadn't killed that first mystic. I'd hurt him, sure. And I'd knocked him clear across the island. But I hadn't put him out of the fight. He made that abundantly clear when he came screaming back into the mostly destroyed village, his staff held high.

I began to shift my fire, hoping to ping back and forth between them, but then, something huge and metallic came barreling out of a side alley to collide with the staff-wielding mystic.

"Patrick!" I screamed, but he obviously couldn't hear me. Not with the roar of the HIRC still heavy in the air. But even though I wanted nothing more than to help him, I couldn't let the female mystic regenerate. So, I forced myself to focus on the only way we were going to live through the fight.

Meanwhile, Patrick rammed his retractable sword into the mystic with the force of his charge. At the same time, the Dragon added its own growl to the auditory mix as he aimed it at the still-struggling female mystic. I hadn't known he could split his focus like that, but I was more than a little grateful for it as he continued to stab the male mystic.

But it wasn't enough.

That gray-skinned man had taken everything I'd thrown at him, and he'd come back for more. And regardless of how far Patrick had come, he couldn't really compare to me. Not in combat. So, it was inevitable that the mystic would turn the tables.

And as it always did, the inevitable came to pass when he swept Patrick's armored feet out from under him, then pummeled him with the tip of his staff. Out of the corner of my eye, I could see flares of Mist with every blow, but I had no idea if that was coming from Patrick or the mystic.

I was just about to sweep the HIRC in their direction when the weapon went dry.

"Goddamn it!" I growled, yanking my pistol from his holster. I fired on the still-prone female mystic, but I knew Ferdinand II just didn't pack enough of a punch. No—I needed to get in closer. I started forward, still pulling the trigger as quickly as Ferdinand II's rate of fire allowed. But then, someone grabbed my shoulder.

I wheeled around to see Freddie standing there. His white robes were ripped, and he was bleeding from a hundred different wounds. But he seemed healthy enough. "Where have you been?"

"There were others," he said. "I'll finish her off. Go save your friend."

I didn't ask any further questions because I knew Patrick needed me. So, I raced in his direction, leaping over a pile of rubble before yanking the ADS from my arsenal implant. As I sprinted across what had become a battlefield, I reloaded the ADS, took aim, and fired. The norcite pellets hit the mystic in the shoulder, and before he could even think to recover, I shot him again. I emptied the entire drum of shells into him, and he stumbled away from the prone Patrick.

That's when I fell on the alien with my interdiction blade.

I didn't use any fancy techniques. Nor did I hold back. The invader was almost entirely incapacitated by the norcite rounds, and as such, he couldn't even begin to defend himself. So, all I needed to do was hack him to pieces.

It was grisly work, and it took far longer than I would have expected. While the other mystic had possessed an incredible ability to regenerate from whatever damage I could dish out, the male's gifts seemed more inclined to simple durability. As such, each hacking attack only shaved a bit of his body away.

But I was persistent. And the interdiction blade was capable of cutting him. So, it was only a matter of time before I put him down.

Even as I hacked away at the mystic, Freddie fell upon the female with his spear. By that point, she'd mostly recovered, and the fight that followed was brief but action-packed. Even with all my gifts—and I was one of, if not the most powerful person on the planet—I could scarcely follow their combat. They didn't just move quickly. Their speed defied all logic and the laws of physics.

But even more disturbingly, the Mist danced around them like a well-orchestrated ballet.

I was in awe, and yet, I couldn't spare more than one thread of thought to watch. Even that was enough to show me how little I knew about manipulating Mist. The fight between the two mystics barely resembled what I called fighting. They moved as if they already knew what was coming, and they effortlessly avoided attacks that should have killed them. And all the while, I hacked away like a gruesome lumberjack.

My way was effective. I could acknowledge that. But it certainly wasn't nearly as elegant as the battle between the two mystics. That was fine, though. I wasn't one of them. Sure, I would learn. I would try to take what I could from Freddie. However, at the end of the day, I had my own style. I had my own advantages. And I intended to use those to match whatever those two could do.

Eventually, Patrick managed to recover, and he lent his own efforts to the endeavor, and after a few minutes of that, we finally slew the male mystic. He died with a gurgle, and a surge of Mist told me that he was, at last, gone. I sighed in relief, but I knew I wasn't finished. So, I turned my full attention to the other fight.

And now that I had a few moments to concentrate, I wanted to try something I was almost certain wouldn't work. However, there was a chance that it would, and I was willing to give it a shot. So, without further ado, I reached out with my {Mist Warden} senses and initiated an infiltration. I didn't have Mist-hack anymore, but that ability was included in Mist Authority. So, if she had a system, I intended to infiltrate it.

At first, it looked like she didn't, and I was on the verge of giving up when I saw a dense cluster of Mist in her stomach, just behind where her navel would be. That was new, so I dove into it, and to my surprise, I found that it resembled a Nexus Implant's system. It wasn't a one-to-one comparison, but with Universal Language and my vast experience interpreting the building blocks of the system itself, I was more than capable of interpreting it.

But the equivalent of a Mistwall that surrounded it was absolutely daunting and virtually impenetrable. Virtually, though, was not completely, and I began my campaign to rip through her innate defenses. One after another, the nodes that held it all together fell. I hadn't been idle during the past few months, and I'd spent more than a little time conquering every level of my Mistrunning training program I could.

They were stubborn, but in the end, they were overcome, and just like that, her system was laid bare. So, without further ado, I used Assassinate.

Immediately, she went rigid, almost as if she was fighting the inevitable effects of my ability. She had no way of knowing that it was pointless. Once I used Assassinate, there was nothing in the world that could prevent her death. That was the whole point. The only limiter I'd ever found was that I had to be able to infiltrate someone's system before I could use the powerful ability. So long as I satisfied that requirement, I could kill anyone.

Once every few weeks, at least.

But there were so few occasions where I couldn't solve my problems via my other methods that the ability was often overlooked. Not so this time.

A moment after her body locked up, Freddie pierced her through with his spear. But I knew from experience that that was incapable of killing such a monster. And yet, only a few seconds later, a rush of Mist crashed into me before she fell, dead before she ever hit the ground.

Freddie turned to look at me, and for a second, he seemed as if he wanted to ask a question. However, he quickly thought better of it and instead said, "Come. We must prepare for the second wave."

CHAPTER THIRTY

A RIGID DEFENSE

There is so much more to this universe than I can ever under-
stand. Rings within rings, plots inside plots, and all of it built
out of people lying to one another. Nobody has the whole pic-
ture. Anyone who says they do is lying.

—Alistaris Kargat

"Are you okay?" I asked, my hand resting on the arm of Patrick's mech suit. It was warm to the touch, which was evidence of just how hard he'd been pushing.

"I'm alright," he said, his voice strained. "Just a little low on Mist is all. That guy was tough."

"That's understating it," I said in agreement. The mystics had far outstripped my expectations. From a physical standpoint, I was fairly sure that I was stronger and faster than them. However, with the way they could use Mist, it didn't really matter. It was like they had access to every skill, all at once. Meanwhile, I was stuck using the only tools I had available—which were good tools but, against the mystics, seemed inadequate.

Still, there was hope. We had put them down, albeit with Freddie's help. Yet, if I'd have been able to focus on just one of them, I felt certain I could have eventually won. Of course, that was assuming that they didn't have other abilities up their sleeves, which was quite the assumption, given what I had seen. Even so, I'd learned quite a lot from the encounter, and my chief takeaway was that the woman seemed far stronger than the man.

I took a few minutes to reload all my weapons, during which time Freddie simply stood facing the direction where the ship had crashed. His posture suggested that he didn't have a care in the world, but his bloody wounds said otherwise. He'd been pushed to his limits, as well, though he didn't seem the least bit troubled by that fact.

I could also see that his wounds were healing at a visible rate. It wasn't quite on the same level of the female mystic's regeneration, but it was faster than I could manage without using the healing associated with [Mist-Infused Body].

"How strong are you?" I asked, still reloading the HIRC's massive magazine. It was a process of minutes, but it felt like it was taking forever.

"Strong enough," Freddie said without looking back.

"Were you stronger than the woman?" I persisted.

"No," he admitted. "That was their coryphaeus. She was the most powerful combatant in this cohort. The male was her second, though a powerful one. There will be more, but they will be much weaker. They will make up for it in numbers."

"How many?" I asked, finishing with the HIRC and starting in on the Stinger.

"After what we have already killed?" he sighed, looking back at me. "At least ten more mystics. More than a thousand Adjudicators. Perhaps twice that in crew. Do not think to give them mercy. The presence of the Adjudicators and mystics suggests that the ship belonged to the Arbiters of Orion, a mercenary group known for their effectiveness and dedication. They will not surrender, and each member will fight to the death. They will give no quarter, nor expect any in return."

"That's pretty hard-core for mercenaries," I said. In my experience, the sorts of people that fought solely for money tended to have the weakest wills. The moment things got tough, or they saw a more advantageous situation, they broke. I said as much to Freddie, then added, "What makes these so different?"

"Commitment. They don't work for credits," he stated. "They work for progression. For access to Rifts. That gets them closer to the peak."

"The peak?" I asked, starting to reload my ADS.

"You are there," Freddie answered. "The moment you became capable of manipulating Mist directly, you were nearing the summit. You stand atop the tallest mountain, but the journey is not over. Now, you must learn to fly."

"Figuratively or literally?"

"There is no difference."

"Huh."

I didn't know if he was telling me that I could, perhaps, one day fly without the benefit of a ship, but if so, I was definitely on board with the idea. The notion of soaring through the air was enough to put a smile on my face. However, it faded only a second later when I realized that I had a long way to go before something like that was even possible. Still, one thread of thought was already going through the mechanics of how to manipulate the Mist to get to that point, and the initial results were that it was theoretically possible. After all, I knew how Double Jump had worked, which gave me some hints as to how to accomplish the feat Freddie had mentioned.

But I knew I couldn't afford even one thread of thought for that at the moment. I'd need everything I had for the coming battle. So, after one last acknowledgment of how cool the idea was, I pushed it aside and focused everything on the task at hand. Once I had my weapons fully reloaded and Patrick had recovered enough of his Mist to be effective, we let Freddie lead us away from the village.

As we went, I couldn't ignore the sheer destruction the battle had caused. Hundreds of people had died, and that was just from what I could see. The collapsed buildings surely concealed many more casualties.

"How many got to the Bulwark?" I asked via the Secure Connection I shared with Patrick.

"A little more than a hundred," he answered. "Not enough. Not nearly enough."

His statement mirrored my own thoughts, and as I beheld the destruction the Arbiters of Orion had caused, my fury began to mount. I had killed plenty of people in my life, many of them innocent. However, I'd never set out to slaughter a bunch of civilians. That was an important distinction. Sure, the results were similar, but the intention was what mattered.

Or perhaps I was simply trying to excuse my own actions, which were similar enough to the destruction all around me that the mere thought that there wasn't much separating me from the people I chose to fight made me a little nauseous.

Soon enough, we left the remnants of the terraced village behind and entered the wilderness. The forest had been pruned and cultivated, making it feel more like a walk in a park than a trek through the wilds, but I paid that no real mind. Instead, I was wholly focused on what we would find when we reached the crash site.

And sooner than I expected, we arrived at a new battlefield.

On the ground, the ship seemed so much larger than it had in the air. Part of that was perspective, but some of it was simply the incongruity inherent in seeing such a behemoth half-buried in a crater of its own making.

Churned earth stretched for half a mile in every direction, the result of the ship's unplanned and uncontrolled impact. Fallen trees and lush turf dotted the mounds of black dirt, and amid it all were hundreds, if not thousands, of people. Huge clumps had already congregated, where they were listening to their surviving leaders, but there were still some stragglers clambering free of the wreckage.

Most of those were obviously wounded and had been disoriented by the crash. But I didn't feel pity for any of them. Noncombatants or not, they'd come to Earth to conquer my people. To kill me. To slaughter the innocents who lived in the village behind us. Those thoughts, as well as many more like them, shoved aside any pity that might've been hiding in the depths of my heart.

They needed to die.

As Freddie had said, those aliens around the wreckage of their warship would offer no quarter, and they deserved none in return. I steeled my heart and sharpened my mind on the whetstone of that reality. It wasn't the first time I'd had to adopt such an attitude, and I knew that if Earth was going to win the coming war, it would not be the last. That was the sacrifice I would have to make so that my species—my home—could remain free.

With that in mind, I drew my BMAP from my arsenal implant. I'd already loaded it with a drum of the most destructive shells I could find. So, I said, "You two better stay back. I'm not sure how big this is going to be."

Freddie and Patrick both drew back into the trees. We still hadn't been seen, so I took a knee and used Stealth. Once I felt the ability envelop me, I used Explosive Shot, then Execute. I normally didn't bother with either when using the BMAP, but I wanted to make a statement. I knew others were watching. They had to be. And I wanted them to know what would happen to aliens who meant humanity harm.

Finally, I used Empowered Shot, waited a second, then fired. The weapon discharged with a thump, and even as it arced through the air, I used Vanish, then cycled my other abilities again. By the time the first shell began its descent, another was on its way.

Just before the first shell hit, one of the mystics who'd survived the crash raised her hands. A summoned Mist shield not dissimilar from the one used by the staff wielder bloomed into being. But she was not nearly as powerful as he was, and though the shield managed to protect the other aliens in the immediate vicinity, it shattered under the sheer weight of the explosion that enveloped the area.

It was a glorious thing, and the resultant fireball encompassed the entire crash site for almost a half-mile radius. Even from my position so far away, I could feel the heat, and the shock wave that arrived an instant later nearly knocked me from my feet.

And then the second shell hit. This time, there was no Mist shield to block it, and the result was an even more massive eruption of fire and force. The third followed soon after. And a fourth. A fifth, as well. I emptied all twelve shells from the BMAP's drum, bathing the crash site in utter destruction. I felt an influx of Mist that announced hundreds—if not thousands—of deaths, but I knew it was only the beginning.

Plenty had managed to shelter behind hastily raised Mist shields, and as a result, they'd managed to survive. Even as I exchanged the BMAP for the reloaded HIRC, I aimed to change that. By that point, Patrick and Freddie had joined me, and both had begun their advances.

Patrick used the Dragon, cutting a bloody swath through the survivors. The Adjudicators who'd survived fired back, and the crew members added their own efforts to the mix, but his armor proved up to the task of protecting him. Meanwhile, Freddie strode forward as if he hadn't a care in the world. When bullets came close to hitting him, they were redirected into the ground or off to the side by subtle manipulations of Mist that I could barely even see. At the same time, he thrust his hand out, sending darts of pure Mist to take out crew members. He didn't bother targeting the black-armored Adjudicators because he knew his Mist-manipulation attacks would do no good.

So, he had to be creative with how he attacked them, which was why, when he got close enough, he started picking up boulders with sheer Mist manipulation and tossing them at the armored Adjudicators. It was something I'd never even thought possible, but it seemed that the more I learned about mystics, the more I was coming to realize how much I didn't know.

However, watching Patrick and Freddie only took up two threads of my Split Mind. The others were all focused on the battle that had begun. The HIRC spat dozens of rounds with every passing second, and it was so powerful that even the Adjudicators' vaunted armor couldn't stand up to the steady stream of deadly rounds. However, the mystics among them were a different story altogether.

They managed to block the barrage of bullets coming their way, though I could see the power of their hastily summoned Mist shields weakening with every passing moment. Still, I wanted to do something to change things up and keep them on their back feet.

Which was why, when I got close, I started tossing grenades, as well.

They reacted, but they didn't have the benefit of something like [Multimind], so their split focus was enough to give me an opening. Even as the grenades exploded—high in the air, where the mystics had used Mist manipulation to throw them away—I used Teleport. Suddenly, I was among them.

I had exchanged the HIRC for the trusty ADS, and I fired with wanton abandon, peppering them with draining pellets of norcite. They tried to summon more shields, but they were already so drained by my previous efforts that the new manifestations were too weak to stop the point-blank shots. The norcite pellets passed through Mist shields like they weren't even there, burying themselves in the mystics' flesh.

Then, suddenly, I launched myself forward, dragging the interdiction blade free of the sheath at my back along the way. I attacked, moving far too quickly for them to react, and the results were predictably bloody. Body parts flew, and mystics screamed in pain as I showed them none of the mercy they would have denied us. In seconds, they were dead.

Yet, there were still more to kill. So, I set my sights on another clump of mystics who were only a few dozen yards away. They saw me coming, and yet, they had no new tactics to deal with my assault. They fell just like the others before them. By the time I moved to the third group, the fear began to set in among their ranks, and they tried to flee before I had a chance to throw myself into their slaughter.

That's when Freddie showed up, his spear flashing with brutal efficiency as he tore them apart with well-practiced ease. We pincered the group, attacking them from both directions. Panicked, they tried to scatter, but Patrick was there, as well, using his massive shield of Mist to block their path.

Just like that, the battle became a slaughter.

The crew members tried to escape, to flee into the wilderness, but by that point, I was more than capable of running them down. So, once the last of the mystics and Adjudicators fell, I followed them into the wilderness, using Mist Authority to both find and rip the energy from their bodies. I didn't even have to break stride as I reached out with tendrils of Mist, killing them before they even knew what had happened.

It wasn't painless, though. Not for me, and certainly not for them. I took more than a few hits, but my upgraded subdermal Sheath, combined with the passive effects of [Shielding] as well as my infiltration suit kept me from taking any serious wounds. It still hurt, but I was more than used to pushing through much worse.

The routed crew members were decidedly much worse off, and their screams of agony filled my ears. I didn't precisely revel in them, but I wouldn't let myself pity the invaders, either. After all, they had come to my planet to do much worse to the entire population, so I regarded it as just punishment for their intended sins.

So, even if I found it distasteful, I forced myself to hear every scream. I made myself focus on every cry of agony. Every contorted expression of anguish. Every ounce of panic. I knew they were pitiful. I knew I was killing people that a better person than me would have spared.

But I hadn't come to take prisoners.

I had come to exterminate the pests who wanted to infest my planet and bring it to its knees. I couldn't afford to shy away from the grim realities of that endeavor. So, I didn't fool myself into believing I was doing good. Those sorts of thoughts didn't belong in a war. Instead, I kept telling myself that what I did was necessary for victory.

And I killed them all.

Patrick and Freddie helped. They did what they had to do, as well, and with grim determination that I completely understood. But by virtue of my gifts, the bulk of the responsibility fell on my head. I embraced it because, at the end of the day, I was the only one capable of doing so.

When the dust settled, I'd once again committed a massacre. Thousands of alien invaders lay dead. I stood over the latest batch—maybe twenty or thirty who'd taken shelter in a cave—just staring at their corpses. Outwardly, they bore no signs of what had killed them, but with the senses I'd gained from the {Mist Warden} class, I could vividly see the damage I had wreaked. They were just empty husks. I'd torn every nanite from their bodies, leaving them completely devoid of energy.

It was brutal.

But it was also necessary.

Or that was what I told myself. Perhaps that was the only way I would ever be able to sleep at night.

"It's over," came the sound of Patrick's voice. I turned to see him standing behind me. He'd put his armor away, a signal that the last of the aliens were dead. Freddie remained behind him, an inscrutable expression on his face as he beheld my handiwork.

"No, it's not, Pick. It's just beginning," I said.

"Do you think they deserved it?" he asked.

I shook my head. "It doesn't matter. They came here intent on killing us," I stated. "Mercy is the prerogative of the powerful. That's not Earth right now. We can't afford to hold back."

Even as I said those words, I wondered how true they were. I knew I wasn't a hero. I'd never claimed to be, and I certainly hadn't lived up to that standard. But increasingly, I felt like I was the only thing standing between the aliens and Earth's unmitigated destruction.

Perhaps that was my fate.

Maybe that was why my uncle—or whoever was manipulating him—gave me the Tier 7 implant in the first place.

I sighed. Or maybe not. I had no idea what any of those people were thinking. Their intentions were a mystery. But I did know one thing—anyone who came to Earth thinking they were going to enslave or destroy humanity would have to go through me before they could ever hope to accomplish those goals.

Hopefully, that would be enough.

CHAPTER THIRTY-ONE

TOO FAR

It's not only about credits. It's not even about raw resources. It's about power. Ideology. It's about keeping your foot on the necks of the people you feel are inferior. That's what drives organizations like the Gomari Confederation. The money is just a means to an end.

—Alistaris Kargat

I sat on the hill overlooking the crash site, and in my mind, I could still see all the corpses I'd created. Some had been ripped apart so thoroughly that it took some degree of imagination to figure out what went where. Others showed no signs of trauma because I'd killed them with Mist Authority. Whatever the case, they'd all been heaped into piles by Alistaris's cleanup crew, then carted away somewhere where his technicians could retrieve anything useful from their bodies. It was grim, gory work, but some of the implants could prove valuable, and even if they weren't, the bits and pieces that had gone into constructing them would be.

I suppose nothing in the universe ever really went to waste. Desecration of the dead was a simple matter of resource management. Still, I struggled to wrap my mind around the necessity, and so, in the aftermath of the battle, I had found myself mired in something of a malaise. That pervasive miasma of melancholy had taken hold of my mind, and it refused to surrender its grip.

Even when I wanted nothing more than to move on to the next mission. The next target. The next group of invaders I was meant to murder.

The war had already begun, and the quarantine had yet to be lifted. Once it did, my kill count would be certain to increase significantly. And while I didn't particularly feel bad about killing aliens who, if given a chance, would enslave humanity and pillage its resources, I couldn't engage in mass murder without thinking twice about what it meant. About what it was doing to me. I might have been functionally immune to post-traumatic stress, but guilt—even the watered-down version I felt for aliens—had still made a home in my mind.

I wasn't haunted, but I couldn't ignore the ramifications of my actions.

After an hour or so, during which I pondered the psychological impact of what I had been forced to do, I saw Patrick trudging up the hill. He seemed happy, almost carefree. Perhaps that was understandable. He'd been sorting through the results of the gnomes' grim reclamation of cybernetics and other implants, and he'd probably come away with quite a few pieces that would facilitate further development. More, he'd proved himself worthy when he'd held his own against not only the mystic, but also in the ensuing battle. He'd come a long way since Mobile.

But then again, so had I.

I sometimes wondered if I could even still call myself human anymore. It felt inadequate to describe what I was turning into. For what I had already become. After all, humans couldn't manipulate the very Mist, could they? Or they weren't supposed to be capable of such a thing. Me, though? I could rip the nanites from a person's body so thoroughly that they couldn't survive the loss.

That was a terrifying level of power, and I knew I'd only scratched the surface. I still had a long way to go, which went well past terrifying and into some new realm of horror. And that was from my perspective. I could only guess what my enemies thought of me.

"Have fun?" I asked as Patrick approached. I tried to force a smile, but I fear it came off more as a pained grimace.

He grunted as he sat, his metallic fingers digging into the soft turf. Then, he sighed. "I don't know if that's how I'd put it. I did get some neat materials, though. That ship is a treasure trove. Not to mention the implants some of those people had. We could spend months sorting through it all."

"Oh? Is that how you plan to spend the beginning of the Integration?"

His smile faded. "No. I'm with you until the end, Mira. You know that. We're fighting this. We have to. I think I understand that better than ever now."

"Do you?" I asked. "What changed?"

He shrugged, then pushed his hair out of his eye. He could've just as easily covered it with faux skin—we had the money for top-notch stuff—but he'd so far refused. Part of that was pride—he didn't want to give in to what he considered vanity—but it was also because he didn't like the idea of having to remove and reattach the skin every time he wanted to tinker with something.

Whatever the case, I'd pointedly ignored his inner struggle. If he wanted to talk about it, he would. But from my experience, that day wouldn't come until he was on the verge of psychological collapse. I could empathize with that. I'd certainly never been the most open person, and I didn't think that was going to change anytime soon.

"This," he said. "What happened here. I mean, I knew the aliens were bad news, Mira. I saw it, same as you. I listened to your stories, and I thought I understood it. But these people, they attacked without reason. They—"

"They had a reason, Pick. What I've been doing for the past month or so, they look at it as an escalation. They think I'm a Templar. So, to deal with me, they sent the people who specialize in that kind of thing," I said. Freddie had explained it even better than Alistaris, which only exacerbated my guilt. It was my fault the Arbiters of Orion had been called in, and by proxy, I was to blame for all the deaths they had caused.

"They didn't have to do what they did," he said. "They specifically targeted the civilians. They tried to get past me just to murder the people in that bunker."

"I've done the same thing. I've killed people who couldn't defend themselves."

"You did it because they invaded our world. This is different."

"It doesn't always feel so different," I murmured.

He didn't have an easy answer for that, so he just put his arm around my shoulders and pulled me close. Thankfully, the bodies were all gone, so there was nothing but the downed ship to spoil our view of the setting sun. If it hadn't come in the wake of mass murder, perhaps it would have felt romantic. As it was, the moment was more melancholy than anything else. Still, I couldn't deny my gratitude that Patrick was there. He didn't have to say anything. Instead, his comforting presence was enough to stave off the worst of the psychological torment that came from my actions.

It couldn't last forever, though, and soon enough, a pair of Dengyts found us. Vaguely, I recognized their faces, but I'd never bothered learning their names. Even so, I knew them as part of Alistaris's inner circle.

The female, who had long purple hair and the largest eyes I'd ever seen, said, "Miss Braddock, Commander Kargat requests your presence."

"Miss Braddock," I muttered to myself as I shook my head. "Sounds official. Maybe I should get a rank in your little army. General, maybe. Admiral would sound good."

"I . . . I don't know if that's possible, ma'am."

"I'm joking," I said, reading her fear. She was terrified of me, and rightly so. She was likely more aware than most of what I could do. Her partner, a male with spiky green hair, looked positively nauseous just being in my presence. Still, they were prepared to do their duty, even if they were horrified by the monster before them. As I pushed myself to my feet, I said, "Fine. Let's get going."

After that, Patrick and I were led down the hill. However, we didn't head toward the downed ship, which was crawling with gnomes and scavenger bots.

Instead, we took a northerly turn and passed through a copse of trees on our way to Alistaris's ship. The Dengyts had already built a temporary fortification around the craft, complete with high walls and a relatively dense Mist shield. As always when I'd dealt with the Dengyts, there were plenty of bots and drones about. Some were meant for surveillance, but others were plainly intended for defense.

One thread of thought was occupied with ideas of how I might overcome those defenses. It was all academic, of course. I didn't think the Dengyts were my enemies, but it was always good to be prepared. And besides, it was good practice for the inevitable war on the horizon. After all, who knew what sorts of defenses my enemies might employ? There was a good chance they'd be similar to the Dengyts' measures.

Soon, we were led to a gate that was guarded by a half dozen gnomes. Each one was wearing an armored infiltration suit, and they all carried assault rifles that looked like they would pack quite a punch. When we reached that gate, the Mist shield retracted, and the gate itself slid into the wall, allowing for entry. We stepped inside, and as we crossed the grounds, passing a few temporary buildings along the way, the gates slid shut behind us. Eventually, we reached the ship, which we boarded and quickly found our way into the common area.

It looked quite different from *The Leviathan*, largely in that it was sleeker and far more sterile from a design perspective. Yet, it was similar enough that I recognized all the rooms for what they were, and we soon found our way to what would've been the common area. It had been converted into a command center, complete with a host of terminals and a large table in the center. A holographic model of Earth shimmered just above it.

At a glance, I could see that dozens of locations had been marked across the Earth's surface. Some of those, I knew to be alien strongholds, many of which I'd had a hand in dismantling. However, there were seventeen evenly spaced locations that I'd not seen in our previous strategy sessions. That did not bode well.

"What's up, Al?" I asked as we walked in.

Alistaris sighed and rubbed the bridge of his bulbous nose. "I have repeatedly asked you not to refer to me as Al."

"It's a term of endearment," I stated, plopping down in one of the chairs. It was gnome sized, so it was a bit of a tight fit. I threw my leg over one arm of the chair and pulled a ration bar from my arsenal implant. "Want one? They're not very good, but I've kind of gotten hooked on them. Something about that faux-banana flavor."

I ripped the package open and took a bite.

"If it makes you feel any better," Patrick said, "when she gives you a nickname, it means she likes you. Whether or not you like that nickname is irrelevant. I've learned that the hard way."

"You wound me, Pick. I care about your feelings."

"In your way, I'm sure you do," he said, grinning as he placed his hands on the back of one of the other chairs and leaned forward. "So, what's going on, commander?"

Alistaris just shook his head at our exchange, then said, "We have a problem."

"What's new?"

"I know you noticed the new additions to the map. Those seventeen locations represent Earth's doom."

"In what way?" I asked.

"The literal one."

"Uh . . ."

"Do you know how to destroy a planet, Miss Braddock?" he asked.

"Build a big enough bomb and anything can be destroyed."

"Certainly. But there are two problems. First, if you do that, it's incredibly difficult to harvest the valuable bits," he stated. "Second, a bomb big enough to completely destroy a planet like Earth would vaporize almost everything worth taking. Certainly, some of the most durable resources would survive, and they would be valuable. However, the real credits are in the more mundane resources. That's what makes the universe spin."

That made sense. Most people couldn't afford quality. Instead, they had to settle for something in the middle. Or worse, poor-grade goods. And they bought an awful lot of them.

"That's where these locations come in," he said. "They're drill sites. Over the next month, they will dig down to the planet's core, where they will plant an appropriate quantity of explosives. I don't need to explain to you how much more efficient that would be."

I nodded. "My uncle told me about a story from his time," I said. "There was an asteroid coming to Earth, and to stop it from causing mass extinction, they sent a team of drilling experts to land on the asteroid. They drilled down and blew it to pieces."

"That sounds ridiculous," Patrick said.

"He said it was one of the most famous stories from his time," I pointed out. "People wouldn't have latched on to it if it was ridiculous. Maybe there was something lost in translation."

He shrugged. "I guess."

"If you're done talking about fairy tales, this is a serious matter," Alistaris said impatiently.

"Oh, sure. Sorry, Al."

He let out a groan. "Those drill sites are the first part," Alistaris said. "The second issue is in the upper atmosphere."

With that, he gestured to the holographic globe. A web of smaller lights bloomed into being, encircling the representation of the planet. Alistaris went on: "Those are satellites. They form a web of Mist surrounding the planet. When activated, they will prevent any debris from drifting off into space. That way, once the planet is destroyed, the resources can be quickly, efficiently, and easily collected by the Gomari Confederation. This is what I've been warning you about all along."

"So, they want to destroy the planet. We'll stop them."

"We have less than a month," he stated. "We need to destroy seventeen drill sites, each one with enough defenses to repel an army. That's the minimum. Then, once that's done, we'll need to do something about those satellites. Because once they go up, there's no getting off the planet."

"Even with [Smuggler] skills?" asked Patrick.

"This isn't a soft quarantine," Alistaris pointed out. "It's a semipermeable Mist shield that will encircle the whole planet. The only people who can get in or out are the ones they allow. It's a military blockade combined with a—"

"We get it, Al. So, how do we do this? What's the plan of attack?"

"There is no we, Miss Braddock. I have been called back to the core to answer for my failures," he stated.

"Failure? We just downed a ship manned by the Arbiters of Orion! That's not a failure. I've accomplished every single mission you've sent me on, and—"

"That's the problem, Miss Braddock," he said softly.

"What?"

"You did the job. You accomplished the missions. But in the process, you scared them," he said. "You hit them too hard and too fast. They believe you're too much of a threat to allow to exist. As a result, those Gomari bastards have escalated this planet's situation. They don't care about the human resources they stand to gain. There are trillions of potential slaves out there, so the loss of a billion isn't going to make them blink. They would rather harvest this planet the easy way than fight you."

"But I thought—"

"I know what you thought. The reality is that we were always fighting a losing battle. I'm sorry, Mira, but you and your planet are doomed. Everyone who matters knows and has accepted that as fact," he said.

"Fuck you."

"What?"

"You heard me. Fuck you and your people who matter. You think this is going to stop me?" I growled, jabbing my finger at the holographic globe. "They've got a few strongholds? So what? I'll rip through them and murder every last alien who stands against me. I don't care. I'll probably kill the ones who surrender, too. And then I'll fly up into the goddamn atmosphere, and I'll disable those satellites, too. You think I can't? After what you've seen me do, do you really believe any of this is going to stop me? If so, then fuck you, Al. I don't accept that we're beaten. I won't. Because we're winning! Look out there at that ship. We won! And we'll keep winning until all those assholes are dead!"

"You can't kill everyone," Alistaris said quietly.

"Watch me."

That single sentence said more about my mindset than the entire rant that had preceded it. I didn't care if the entire universe was set against me. If that was the case, then they would just have to die.

"Are you with us, or are you against us?" asked Patrick, his voice as steely as mine was agitated.

"Neither," Alistaris stated. "I don't have a choice. If I don't go, I'm sentencing my people to death."

"Then go. But you've got time, right?" Patrick asked. "Almost a month before you can't get out. So, help us until then. Once the quarantine is about to lift, get out."

"We don't need him," I spat.

"We do need him, Mira. We need all the help we can get," Patrick persisted. Then, he turned back to Alistaris. "What do you say? I know you want to see this through, right? Well, this is your chance."

For a long few moments, Alistaris remained silent. It stretched long enough to where I expected him to refuse. But then, he finally said, "Okay. We'll stick around until three days before the quarantine lifts. That gives us three weeks. We've got our work cut out for us."

"Thanks," Patrick said. "You won't regret this."

Pointedly, I didn't say anything else. As far as I was concerned, we didn't need his help, and I intended to prove that by destroying every last alien on the planet.

CHAPTER THIRTY-TWO

THE FIRST DIG SITE

No planet can make it alone. There are too many forces out there that are hell-bent on exploitation and oppression. We need allies. The problem is that alliances rarely come cheap, and usually, they're just as exploitive as any occupation.

—Patrick Ward

We don't need him," I muttered, more to myself than to Patrick. "He can run off to whatever corner of the universe he came from. And he can take his ridiculous eyebrows with him."

"Mira, you said that out loud," Patrick said, cutting his eyes toward the pair of gnomes sitting in the cockpit's other two chairs. There were five more in the cargo hold, and each one was supposed to be a capable fighter.

"I'm aware," I stated. I didn't care if they heard me. I'd have said the same thing to Alistaris if he was there. As far as I was concerned, Earth didn't need anyone who didn't want to be there. Humanity was more than capable of defending our planet, and we could do without opportunistic gnomes who wanted to cut and run at the first sign of trouble.

Patrick disagreed.

And if I was willing to look past my anger, I probably would have changed my tune. The reality was that the planet was up against the wall, and the only way to fight our way free was to use any and all resources at our disposal. That included the Dengyts, as much as I wished it didn't.

He glanced back at the two passengers, saying, "She doesn't mean it, guys."

"I meant it," I stated without bothering to look back. I preferred to seethe instead. Besides, I wanted to focus on the mission in front of us. From the briefing, I knew that the dig sites would be heavily defended, and by more than just a few bots and a Mist shield. There would be Adjudicators and mystics there, too.

Patrick chose to change the subject. "It's encouraging that Freddie was able to mobilize Earth's Templars," he said, piloting *The Leviathan* through the clouds. We were moving at top speed, courtesy of a few crates of high-quality Rift Shards Alistaris had given us. At least he hadn't hesitated to commit his wealth to the cause. "Do you think they'll be successful?"

"I don't know. Maybe," I said. "There are a lot less of them than I expected."

Apparently, the process of creating a Templar was a brutal one, and as such, barely any had survived to achieve the rank. At present, there were only thirty or so true Templars on Earth. There were quite a few more acolytes and apprentices, but according to Freddie, they weren't much more capable than run-of-the-mill soldiers.

Still, if there were thirty people with Freddie's power out there, it was a huge boon for our prospects of defending Earth. I only had to remember the battle against the enemy mystics to recognize that much.

The plan to utilize those assets was simple. After gathering the Templars, he would lead them on an assault against one of the dig sites. Meanwhile, Patrick and I would do the same. When one fell, we'd move on to the next. And the next after that. We were up against the clock, and I knew that if we were going to achieve our goals, we couldn't waste any time. So, my personal strategy reflected that.

I could only hope that it would be effective enough to save Earth.

"Every journey starts with one step," said Patrick.

"Huh?"

"You had that look."

"What look?" I asked, cutting my eyes at him.

"Your anxious look. You're worried about whether or not we can do this thing, right?" he guessed. "Well, that's what I was talking about. Every journey starts with a single step. That's what Remy used to tell me, and I think it applies here."

I gave him a small smile. "My uncle used to say something similar," I replied. "I guess old men like to speak in clichés, huh?"

"Are you implying that I'm getting old?" he asked with mock affront.

I laughed. "Never that," I responded. "You're still young at heart."

"I'm not even thirty."

"Right. We've got long, full lives ahead of us," I said. "So long as the planet doesn't get exploded by greedy aliens."

"Or exploited."

"Ha. I see what you did there."

"I try," he said with a smirk as he guided *The Leviathan* into a banking turn. We descended from the clouds, and I saw the landscape stretched out below us. The desert was different than the one outside of New Cairo. Instead, it was all rocks and ravines, with oddly shaped formations throughout. It was only a few hundred miles away from what was left of Fortune to the north, though there was little reason to visit the ruins of another town. A few people remained in that city, but most had fled after the city had been destroyed by the detonating Pacificians.

"How far is it from here?" I asked as Patrick set the ship down in the shadow of a huge pillar of red rock.

"Seventeen miles," he answered. Then, he pointed to the east. "That way. What's the plan?"

"You and the gnomes take out the auxiliary shield generator. I'll hit the base hard and fast, explode whatever I can find, and kill any aliens who're there," I said.

"Mira, that's dumb. You don't have to do everything yourself."

"No. I don't have to. I get to. Seriously, Pick. I can't be in two places at once. That shield generator needs to come down. Otherwise, you know good and well that I can take this whole fortification out on my own."

"Our intelligence suggests that this dig site is protected by a mystic by the name of Kalar Syphos," said one of the gnomes.

"I read the report," I said. "Believe me—I can take care of that tentacled bastard."

Indeed, Kalar Syphos was estimated to have power on par with the male mystic I'd fought back in the tiered Templar village. That meant I was more than capable of defeating him. I just needed to take out the other defenders before he mustered a response, which meant that my plan involved quite a bit of stealth. If everything went well, I'd slip in, kill a bunch of defenders, then take out Kalar Syphos in a one-on-one battle.

"I think someone should go with you," Patrick insisted. "I can just—"

"I need you to go with the gnomes—"

"We are not gnomes," said one of the gnomes in the back. "We are Dengyts. Please refrain from using slurs to—"

"I need you to go with those mooks back there to keep them in line," I rephrased, glaring at the Dengyt who'd interrupted me. "They don't want to be here, remember? I wouldn't put it past them to take one look at the defenses and pass out from fear. Or run away screaming. I don't trust them, and I won't expect anything from them until they actually prove they're on our side.

"Besides, Pick, having a bunch of people with me is just going to slow me down," I said. "If I'm alone, I can get in, do what needs to be done, and then get out."

"Fine."

"That doesn't sound very enthusiastic," I said.

"Caught on to that, huh?"

"Don't be grumpy."

"I'm not grumpy, Mira. And don't make a joke out of this. It's serious business," he stated.

"I'm well aware of how serious this is," I pointed out icily. "Better than most, I know what's at stake."

He sighed, then ran his hand through his hair. "Look. I'm sorry. I don't mean to—"

"Not in front of the children," I said, giving an exaggerated nod at the Dengyts. Then, I said to them, "Don't worry. Mommy and Daddy aren't fighting. We still love each other very much."

"Stop teasing them. They're terrified of you, Mira. At this point, it's just bullying," Patrick pointed out.

"Fine. Everyone understand the plan?" I asked.

They did, so with that, we engaged in our final preparations. I went back to the quarters I shared with Patrick and donned an appropriate outfit for sneaking into an enemy base and murdering everyone there. Black was the prevailing theme, which I thought fit the situation very well. After that, I checked that all my weapons were loaded and ready, then made certain that I had enough provisions—including a couple of Mist boosters—to see me through whatever issues might arise. After all, I'd once accidentally ended up on the moon, so who knew where my latest adventure would take me?

In any case, I was as prepared as I could be, so I proceeded to leave *The Leviathan* behind. As usual, once everyone else was outside, I activated Bastion. "Alright, then. Keep 'em in line, Pick," I said, looking at the collection of Dengyts. They looked so small—like children—but I knew that each one of them was deadly in their own right. I could only hope that they would channel that into protecting Patrick and accomplishing the mission.

"Be careful. You're not invincible," he said.

"I'm very aware of that," I responded with a shake of my head. "I'll be fine, though. This is just another mission."

We shared an embrace, then parted ways. I didn't dare use the Cutter for fear that it would be detected, so I had no choice but to cover the ground on foot. Fortunately, with my high attributes and long training, running seventeen miles was simple enough, and I managed the feat in less than half an hour.

Soon, I saw my target.

Most of it was located within a deep ravine that extended for miles to the north and south. It was also hundreds of feet deep and at least half a mile wide. A river cut along the canyon's floor, the current moving swift and sure.

And stretching over that river was a facility unlike any other I'd ever seen before.

The main facility spanned the ravine, suspended high above the river on what looked like an elegant bridge. At the center of that bridge was an enormous cylinder from which descended a massive drill that was at least two hundred feet in diameter. The rest of the stronghold was built into the sides of the canyon, with each floor connected by a series of stairs. From the plans Alistaris had provided—and I had memorized—I knew there were also elevators and stairs inside.

More importantly, there was a ventilation tunnel nearby.

For most people, it would have been entirely invisible and completely undetectable. Not only was it camouflaged by a high-grade holographic display, but it was also protected by an incredibly durable Mist shield. The result was that it was well hidden and nigh impenetrable.

But not for me.

Because I could see the Mist, stealth abilities were almost useless against me. And the same could be said for holographic displays. So, to me, the ventilation tunnel stood out like a great, flashing light.

"Are you in position?" I asked through the Secure Connection I shared with Patrick, having embraced Stealth the moment I'd come into range of the facility.

"Not yet. You run too fast."

"It's the gnomes slowing you down, right?"

"No."

"Be honest."

"Fine. But it's not their fault. They have short little legs," he said. "You should cut them some slack. They're here for us, remember? They could have left already."

"They're here because of Al. Most don't care about Earth," I stated.

"But they're here. They're helping. That has to count for something," Patrick stated. "I'm just saying—accept that they stayed to help and quit trying to make them regret sticking around."

I sighed, then told him that I would try to follow his advice. After that, I settled in to wait for him and the Dengyts to get into position. After a few more minutes, Patrick announced that they had arrived. So, I said, "Hit it hard and fast. I'll take care of things here."

The plan wasn't complex. When they destroyed the auxiliary shield generator, it would create a vulnerability in the main facility's defenses. My job was to exploit that weakness and infiltrate the dig site before making my way to the drill. I would have preferred to simply assault it from afar with the BMAP, but with there were two things preventing that from being a viable possibility.

First, they had an active-defense system that would destroy any incoming projectiles. Or ships. Or people. And that included the shells from the BMAP or any grenades I might throw. So, that necessitated that I plant charges from the inside. The second issue was the nature of its shield, which, because of the auxiliary power source, was largely unassailable. Even Mist Authority was useless to take it down, largely because the nanites continuously replenished.

But once that system was cut, I would have a few moments to infiltrate the base and get on with the business of tearing the whole thing apart. So, I waited until Patrick announced, "Alright. Get ready for it. Three . . . Two . . . One . . . Go!"

I saw the flicker of Mist, then used Mist Authority to rip the much flimsier local shield apart. It fell quickly and easily, and I dove at the grate covering the ventilation shaft. Without skipping a beat, I drew my interdiction blade from the sheath on my back, injected some Mist through the weapon, and slashed.

Once.

Then again, my blade fell, severing the grate. I reached out with inhuman quickness, catching it before it dropped. By then, two seconds had passed, and I knew I was already on borrowed time. So, I leaped into the shaft, thrusting my hands and feet out to arrest my momentum. I managed to get inside just before the Mist shield flickered back into being as one of the alternative Mist sources came online.

But it was too late.

I was already inside. Now, I just needed to do what I'd come to do.

I waited for a few minutes, during which Patrick said that they were moving to the secondary location so that they would be in position if I needed help. I knew I wouldn't, but I chose not to point that out. The last thing I needed was for him to feel useless.

Once I was sure there would be no response, I slowly inched my way down the ventilation shaft until I reached another grate. Once there, I cast my senses out, using Observation and Mist Authority to search for any potential enemies. At first, I didn't sense anyone, but then, I felt something brush against that thin tendril of Mist I'd extended into the corridor below.

I reacted immediately, launching myself downward through the grate and raising my sword to block an oncoming attack. My blade clanged against another, and I was thrown backward almost ten feet. The plasti-steel on the nearby walls cracked as a shock wave tore down the hall, and I nearly dropped my interdiction blade as my hands went temporarily numb.

I didn't need to look at my attacker standing at the other end of the hall to know who it was. Still, I glared across the space between us, taking in the details I had only seen in a packet given to me by Alistaris.

"I assume you are the one who killed my colleagues," said Kalar Syphos. They were slim, with androgynous features that were apparently typical of their agender species. Sprouting from the mystic's head were a series of red tentacles that put me in mind of a sea anemone. Alistaris had told me that that was not normal, and that the mystic was known to manipulate Mist for the effect.

Vanity, I supposed, was not limited to humans.

"That's me," I said.

"But you are no Templar," they said, cocking their amphibious head to the side. It looked like it belonged to an axolotl, though without the inherent cuteness of the little salamanders. They were dressed in a pitch-black robe and carried a truly obnoxious weapon.

"Is that a scythe? Seriously? You couldn't have picked something more practical?"

"This is the traditional weapon of my people, you disrespectful child," Syphos snarled. "You would do well to tread lightly, lest you invoke my ire."

"Or what? You're already here to kill me, right? Are you going to kill me harder?" I asked. "Come on. You're better than that. I think. Honestly, I don't know. You might just be that stupid."

I saw Syphos's shoulders tense just before they attacked, so I was ready when they charged down the hall. What I wasn't ready for was the blade of Mist that came slashing my way well before they came within range. However, because of my long practice with Mist Authority—as well as Split Mind—I reacted quickly enough to rip that expression of Mist control apart before it sliced into me. The nanites that comprised the Mist fell apart in glittery motes, washing harmlessly past me.

I was just patting myself on the back when Syphos fell upon me, their scythe lashing out with inevitable force. I blocked with the interdiction blade, but the blow was so powerful that the impact drove me to one knee. Even as the plasti-steel floor cracked beneath me, I kicked out, slipping past the mystic and rolling to safety a second later. Then, I used Teleport to push me even farther down the hall.

I twisted to see Syphos standing precisely where I'd left them.

"How? You are no Templar!" they screamed.

"Oh, shucks. You got me. Was it the lack of a white robe that gave it away?" I asked flippantly.

"What are you?" they hissed.

"Just Mira," I answered.

Then, without further conversation, I ripped the ADS from my arsenal implant and fired. Even as the pellets flew across the hall, I launched myself in their wake, hoping to take the mystic by surprise.

CHAPTER THIRTY-THREE

SPECIAL

She is special. Even in the context of the wider universe, Mira can do things most people can't. Some of this is by design. We may never know who was behind her carefully planned development, but it set the stage for her to become the unique person she is. But there's far more to what she became than a one-of-a-kind Nexus Implant.

—Alistaris Kargat

The norcite pellets slammed into the tentacled mystic's hastily conjured shield, but the nature of the material meant that they were barely slowed. However, they lost just enough momentum that, when they hit Syphos, the alien's armor was enough to protect them from the draining projectiles. Still, the shield shattered, giving me the opening I needed to barrel into them.

I hit with a shock wave of force that cracked the walls and ripped the tiles from the floor, but the mystic managed to sweep their scythe out just in time to block my descending blade. I held nothing back, instead putting every point of my Constitution into the blow, and the result was like a bomb had gone off.

Even as the hall was torn asunder by the explosion of force, my blade pushed the haft of Syphos's scythe back just enough that I nicked their cheek. Their mouth fell open in shock as I let out a grunt of effort, but it didn't last long before they kicked out, taking me in the stomach. The impact pushed me back almost a dozen feet before I slid to a stop.

"Not bad," they said. "I—"

Ferdinand II's report interrupted whatever they were going to say, and I didn't stop firing until his drum went empty. None of the rounds made it to the mystic's body—they were far too weak to make it through the reconjured shield—but that wasn't the point. Instead, I only wanted to distract them from what I was doing with my other hand.

A trio of small globes rolled across the ruined floor, too inconspicuous for Syphos to notice amid the barrage of gunfire. But they definitely noticed when the three spheres erupted, bathing them in green gas. Meanwhile, I had yanked my respirator from my arsenal implant, slamming it into place over my mouth and nose before the poison could reach me.

That small distraction was almost enough to get me killed.

Syphos was done talking, it seemed, and they weren't just going to stand around and breathe the rapidly expanding cloud of poison. Instead, they'd launched themselves across the distance between us, sweeping their ridiculous weapon out with intimidating speed. Still, it was an impractical weapon, probably chosen for some cultural significance—or perhaps simply because they liked the aesthetic—so the attack didn't land nearly as quickly as it should have. Even so, I had to scramble to raise my sword in a one-handed block that was wholly inadequate to deal with the sheer force the mystic could bring to bear.

Fortunately, I was no novice, and I knew the weaknesses of my situation well enough to adapt my block accordingly. So, I angled the sword, slipping just enough to the side to avoid the worst of the impact. Even with that to mitigate the force, I felt the blow rattle the bones of my arms and shove me hard enough into the floor that what few tiles had survived the previous exchanges shattered like all the rest.

I lashed out with Ferdinand II, whipping the butt against Syphos's knee. It felt like hitting a brick wall, but it buckled ever so slightly, giving me an opportunity to dive away from the next attack. I rolled, then used Teleport a second before the blade of the scythe skewered me. Even as I reappeared a few dozen feet away, I dismissed Ferdinand II and my interdiction blade, replacing them with the Stinger. I completed my roll, coming up facing the oncoming mystic.

I fired, and the first few rounds were rendered ineffective by another shield. However, I couldn't help but notice that their movements had fractionally slowed, which was the whole point of the poison I'd deployed. It didn't kill people—or it wouldn't truly harm anyone on the level of the mystic. Instead, it attacked the nervous system as well as the Mist, slowing reactions and restricting the flow of nanites.

Hopefully, it would be enough.

I continued to fire, and each shot got a little deeper into the shield Syphos had raised. However, I could tell that I wouldn't get through before they reached me. So, I switched gears and, with one of my threads of thought, attacked the shield with Mist Authority. At first, it was like banging my fists against a mountain, ineffectual and frustrating.

Yet, a simple shift of my attitude made all the difference in the world.

Normally, I overcame my enemies with sheer application of overwhelming force. That wasn't always the answer, though, and even if I normally didn't use all the tools at my disposal, I'd been trained to attack my problems in a variety of ways. Still, those lessons were only a shift of thought away, and instead of imagining myself as a giant battering ram of strength, I thought of my efforts as a steady wind, eroding a mountain over millennia.

It didn't make it go any faster, but it certainly altered my strategy enough to make a difference. So, even as Syphos charged through the hail of gunfire, their scythe raised for an attack, I slowly tore the shield down.

Time felt like it slowed as I chipped away at the Mist shield, but in reality, the pace of the fight was so fast that an ordinary person couldn't track it. I continued to fire until Syphos reached me, then I once again summoned my interdiction blade to exchange a series of blows that left my arms feeling like jelly.

[Multimind] showed its worth as I devoted various threads to different tasks. One focused on the physical fight, while another was wholly trained on the slow erosion of the Mist shield. Still another monitored the environment, while the fourth cycled my abilities to best effect. As a result, I far outperformed what I'd once considered my peak efficiency, which allowed me to keep pace with the powerful mystic.

Still, I knew I couldn't keep it up.

Already, my own Mist reserves were starting to run low. I was using too many abilities, and far too quickly. On top of that, my mind felt like it was starting to overheat from the strain of keeping track of so many disparate threads of thought. Sometime, and soon, I would start to make mistakes. And when I did, Syphos wouldn't hesitate to take advantage.

If I wanted to win, I needed to change the paradigm.

I needed to take a risk.

So, I yanked one thread of thought away from monitoring the environment, instead dedicating it to manipulating the Mist. That sudden surge turned the gentle eroding wind into a hurricane of gusting destruction. Whole swaths of nanites were yanked away with every passing nanosecond, and yet, it wasn't enough to topple the shield.

It was a good thing, then, that I had another card to play.

As the mystic drew closer, I dodged their incoming attack, exchanging the Stinger for the ADS as I did. Then, I squeezed the trigger. We were so close that Syphos had no chance to react, and my previous efforts had weakened the shield just enough that the norcite pellets made it through with enough force to bury themselves in the mystic's body.

The reaction was immediate.

Syphos threw themselves backward in an effort to create as much distance as possible. However, now that I had them on the back foot, I wasn't going to let up. So, I kept up the pressure, following closely as I continued to pepper them with as many shots from the ADS as I could. I got seven shots off before Syphos lashed out with their scythe, knocking the weapon from my hands and sending it flying down the hall.

Then, they quickly reversed course and, before I could even react, buried the blade in my chest. It sliced through my shield and armor as well as the sub-dermal Sheath like none of it was even there, and it cut my lung into two pieces. It would have destroyed my heart if I hadn't shifted an inch or two to the side at the last possible second. Still, it was a debilitating injury that Syphos clearly thought was enough to win the battle.

They grabbed my hair and pulled me close. I screamed as they twisted the blade, further destroying my lung. I gasped, coughing up blood as I grabbed the haft. But my actions were panicked and unproductive.

"Such a shame," they said, their voice a mixture of high- and low-pitched sounds, with a slight quiver to indicate just how close I'd come to killing them outright. "You could have been special."

I rammed the blade of my hastily summoned nano-bladed dagger into their side. The attack lacked strength, but my efforts to breach their shield had never stopped. And it had finally borne fruit.

I twisted the dagger, spitting blood as I responded, "I am special."

Then, I finally completed my infiltration of their core. It wasn't the same as a Nexus Implant—or the system that came with it—but it was close enough that, with my long experience, it amounted to the same thing. In seconds, I had uploaded a Ghost that sent the Mist inside their body into rebellion. Immediately, the nanites attacked one another and everything around them.

Syphos screamed in pain as the *Virus* Ghost I'd spent months perfecting did its job. Their body seized, and I ripped myself free of the scythe's blade. A few chunks of my lung and ribs went with it, but I quarantined the pain in its own thread of thought as I put some distance between myself and the mystic.

Meanwhile, they struggled to get their Mist under control, and for the most part, it was an effective strategy that depended on their incredible ability to regulate the nanites in their own body. Yet, the Ghost I'd uploaded was perfectly suited to interrupt that control, and it was clearly giving Syphos quite a bit of trouble.

Or perhaps that was the obvious agony.

Perhaps they hadn't been subjected to the same training that had helped me develop my own pain tolerance. Whatever the case, it gave them just enough trouble that when I summoned the HIRC, they were caught by complete surprise.

The huge weapon barked, filling the hall with a hail of gunfire that cut through their unprotected body with ease.

Miraculously, Syphos whirled their staff, blocking the initial stream of rounds. Yet, the sheer volume of the HIRC's output was overwhelming, and without the benefit of their shield, the outcome seemed preordained. My prediction proved accurate a second later when the first rounds snuck through their guard and sent a spray of blood arcing behind them. Then another. And another. They stumbled, and I adjusted my aim.

I knew it was over.

Presumably, somewhere beneath all their pain, they did, too.

But even so, it wasn't until I'd literally ripped them limb from limb that they finally perished. I continued to fire for a couple more seconds, splattering what was left of them against the wall. Finally, I released the HIRC's lever, and its barrels spun down. In the absence of gunfire, the hall was incredibly quiet. I could hear my own heavy, raspy breathing, and my heartbeat was like a bass drum.

But I had won.

That was all that mattered. I turned my attention to the silhouette that indicated my health, and I was unsurprised to find that my lung had been almost completely destroyed by the mystic's scythe. That normally wouldn't have been possible, but Syphos had somehow sent a pulse of condensed Mist along the blade, facilitating my injury.

Whatever the case, it was a problem that needed tending. So, I focused on [Mist-Infused Body] and activated the rapid-healing portion of the skill. I gritted my teeth as the nanites that comprised the Mist went into a flurry of activity, rebuilding my lung in seconds. When they were finished with their task, they went inert, and I let out a gasp of relief as the constricting bands around my chest released their grip.

My shoulder sagged.

Every time I fought one of the mystics, it felt like I was balanced on the edge of a knife. Sure, I'd been in difficult battles before, but ever since my class had evolved, it had, at times, felt like I was on an entirely different level than my enemies. The best example was when I'd massacred the irradiated wildlings that had long ago nearly killed me. But the mystics—they were different. They pushed me in a way nothing else could.

And I knew that unless I grew significantly more powerful, one of them would end up killing me.

It was a sobering thought, but one that I chose to use as fuel for my progression rather than a source of fatalism. For now, though, I needed to finish my mission. So, after gathering the scythe—which still felt like it was pulsing with Mist—I contacted Patrick via the Secure Connection and said, "The mystic is down. Proceeding with the rest of the mission."

"Are you okay?"

"Had to use my wild card," I said, referencing the healing ability associated with [Mist-Infused Body]. "But I'm fine."

"Do you need backup?"

"No," I said. "I'm fine."

"Are you sure?"

"I'm fine, Pick," I repeated.

That got my point across, and he went silent. That lack of response made me feel a little guilty, and I resolved to make it up to him at some point in the future. In the meantime, I needed to finish my mission. So, once I'd slipped the scythe into my arsenal implant, I exchanged the HIRC for the more compact Stinger. Thus armed, I set off through the facility, and when I turned the corner, I came face-to-face with twenty guards of varied alien species. They had clearly been waiting for the dust to settle on our battle—the last thing anyone wanted was to get in the middle of something like that—so my sudden presence elicited some degree of shock.

I used that to my advantage, cutting them down with extreme prejudice. After all, I wasn't there to take prisoners, and as far as I was concerned, the fact that they were there at all established that they were my enemies. So, killing them—even when they couldn't really fight back—was never going to cause any guilt on my part. Still, it meant that my journey to my real target—the drill—took a few extra minutes.

I likely could have used Stealth to sneak through, but after the struggle against the mystic, I wanted to take my frustrations out on someone. The aliens in the digging facility were unlucky enough to be given that role.

Over the next few minutes, I swept through the area, killing everyone who got in my way. So, by the time I reached the bridge leading to the digging apparatus, I had racked up quite the body count. Pointedly, even that much killing had barely moved the needle of progression, so I knew it would likely take a mass genocide on the level of what I'd done to the Pacificians for me to gain any appreciable number of levels.

Still, that had never been my focus, so I pushed those thoughts away as I crossed the bridge.

A few combat bots tried to stop me, but I quickly dispatched them with a judicious application of Mist Authority. I didn't even bother wasting my ammunition on them. After all, it was expensive.

Without breaking stride, I marched across the bridge. Vaguely, I was aware of some aliens on the floors below. I didn't care about them, though. They were entirely inconsequential, and besides—they would die soon, anyway. So long as they didn't attempt to bar my way, I was content to leave them be.

And they were far too frightened to challenge me.

Soon enough, I arrived at the central pillar and got my first look at the drill. I knew from the packet I'd read that the drills were designed to leave behind a series of powerful Mist-infused explosives on their way to the core. I wasn't certain how it was all supposed to work—that level of explosives knowledge was far beyond me—but the intended result wasn't difficult to understand.

Nor was my plan overly complicated. So, I planted my own explosives along the drill's outer fuselage. I used more than was probably necessary, but I figured it was better to overdo it than fall short.

Once I'd finished, I called Patrick via Secure Connection. "Alright. I'm ready for a pickup."

"Ugh. Pickup? Really? How long have you had that one in the bank?"

I giggled at the play on words. "Longer than I want to admit."

"Fine. Hold tight for . . . two minutes."

"Gotcha. I'll be on the top of the giant drill."

With that, I got to climbing. I didn't even have to flare Balance on my way up, and after only a minute or two, I reached the top. Then, I settled in to wait. In the distance, I saw a few aliens who were too afraid to approach. I waved at them, muttering to myself, "Hope you all don't get out of range before everything goes boom."

They pointedly did not wave back, which I thought was rude. Just when I was considering pulling out my rifle to take a few pot shots, I saw *The Leviathan* on the horizon. So, I stood and waited for my pickup.

CHAPTER THIRTY-FOUR

A CAMPAIGN OF DESTRUCTION

I think about death a lot. About everything just ending. I know there are people out there who believe something comes next. Something better as a reward for a life well lived. But I don't know. That's always felt a little too convenient to me. In my experience, good deeds are punished, not rewarded. So, why should life and death be any different?

—Patrick Ward

I watched from the ship as the explosion enveloped the entire canyon. We were far enough away that I felt certain that we wouldn't be affected, and yet, Patrick had raised *The Leviathan*'s Mist shields, anyway. He'd even used one of his abilities to augment their power, which I thought was overkill.

It wasn't.

The shock wave rocked the ship, knocking it backward a few hundred yards before Patrick managed to stabilize it. The gnomes in the cockpit were fine because they'd been strapped into their seats, but the ones in the back probably hadn't enjoyed the ship's bucking.

I glanced over to see Patrick smirking at me.

"What?" I asked innocently.

"Told you so."

"It wasn't that bad!"

"Do you want to see the numbers? By my calculations, that explosion was—"

"Not listening!"

It wasn't my fault that my bombs were often far more powerful than they really should have been. The problem was that they were affected by so many of my modifiers that trying to predict the payload of any given charge was little better than a vague estimate. I could do the math well enough, but there were far too many variables for my calculations to be completely accurate. As a result, I often underestimated just how much of a punch I could pack into a single explosion.

Still, I wasn't going to admit that to Patrick, especially when he was wearing that smug expression. I refused to give him the satisfaction.

"I think it's safe to say that site is out of commission," he said.

"Any word from the other teams?"

He shook his head. "Not yet. But they should be trickling in soon," he stated. "I just hope the Templars can take care of any mystics that might be present."

I nodded. Kalar Syphos had been far more powerful than I had expected. They weren't as strong as the coryphaeus we'd fought back in the Templar stronghold, yet they weren't that far off. And I'd had to fight them alone. If the other dig sites had a similar presence, I suspected that the Templars would experience some losses.

But I couldn't worry about the overall strategy. I had my role to play, and that was enough to occupy my minds. I needed to trust that Alistaris, now that he was completely committed, would take care of the overarching plan.

Still, I was aware of how quickly things could go wrong.

It had happened often enough to me, after all.

So, I was on pins and needles as I saw the giant fireball of the explosion I had caused engulf the dig site as well as the canyon. It spread much farther in the ravine than it did on the surface, but it still managed to impact the environment for miles around. As a result, I couldn't help but wonder what I could do with something like the bomb that had created the irradiated crater where I'd once almost been killed by a horde of mutated wildlings.

That kind of bomb had been devastating even before the incorporation of Mist. With my modifiers and perhaps some modern materials, it wasn't implausible that such a weapon could destroy a whole planet.

"At least it wasn't the moon this time," Patrick said, making me feel like he was reading my mind. "We can call that progress."

"I hate you."

"No, you don't. You love me."

"God knows why . . ."

"It's my rugged good looks and manliness," he said, tapping the metallic side of his face.

I couldn't help but laugh. The two Dengyts behind us just looked at us like we'd gone a little crazy, and perhaps they were at least partially right. By all accounts, I should have been thinking about all the people I'd just killed. The facility hadn't been teeming with personnel, but it wasn't empty, either. As a result, the bomb I'd just set off had taken at least a few hundred—maybe as many as a thousand—people with it.

But the reality was that, even if they were mostly innocent, I couldn't bring myself to regret killing them. The aliens were invaders, one and all, and the moment they'd chosen to set foot on my planet, they'd established themselves as my enemies. On top of that, the ones in the dig site were actively working toward the destruction of Earth, so in my mind, they deserved what they'd gotten.

Pointedly, I ignored the possibility that those workers might not have had a choice in their fate. There was every chance that, like humanity, they had been manipulated and forced into their current circumstances. Looking at it like that, they could have been classified as victims as much as the people from Earth.

Yet, I didn't give credence to that, largely because such philosophical questions weren't designed for answers. It was easy to get wrapped up in morality when your people weren't being killed and enslaved. Peace gave that luxury. But I was at war, and that meant discarding notions of right and wrong for the realities of pragmatism. If we wanted to survive, we had to do terrible things. That was the simple truth of it, and no amount of pearl clutching or navel-gazing would change that.

In the war I was fighting, there was no such thing as innocents.

Those thoughts occupied my mind as Patrick regained control of the ship and, once the devastation had settled, piloted the ship close to the dig site to ensure that everything had been destroyed. To my relief, there was nothing but wreckage, and even that had been twisted all out of shape. Most of the structure had been scattered across the desert, and according to our scans, no one had survived.

"Should we salvage what we can?" I asked, glancing at Patrick.

One of the Dengyts said, "A team has already been dispatched. We will add whatever we find to the war effort."

"Which means we'll never see any of it," I reasoned. "So? You want to pick it over, Pick?"

"Only you could make that terrible of a joke after what just happened," he muttered, shaking his head. "But no. Anything worthwhile will take days to find. We have other things to occupy our time."

That much was true. We still had another dig site to hit before we returned to our base, and that was if everything else went well. I knew it wouldn't, though. Time was not on our side, and I could recognize that some of Alistaris's teams were less capable than others. Because of that, I expected a few failures.

And we couldn't afford to leave even one dig site intact, either. While getting most of them would undoubtedly save the planet, the result of one site's survival could still be catastrophic for life on Earth. No—if we wanted to save the planet, we needed to get them all. Then, we needed to take out the satellites that would facilitate the aliens' blockade. Only then would the planet be safe.

After confirming that the job was done, Patrick guided *The Leviathan* away. However, we didn't return to the base Alistaris had established. Instead, we zipped across the landscape until we reached another target. Not for the first time, I wished we could just drop a series of bombs and be done with it, but I knew that wasn't possible. Any fortification worth anything would be equipped with a durable Mist shield, but in addition to that, they were built with Mist-infused materials that were incredibly durable. Because of that, the only way to reliably destroy them—without using ordnance so powerful that it would leave the surface of the planet in ruins—was to attack them from the inside.

And that wasn't even considering the passive defenses that would destroy any projectiles before they even reached the structure.

So, with that in mind, our options were limited. Fortunately, the second target wasn't nearly as well defended. That fortune, however, was mitigated by the fact that they were ready for us. After all, the destruction of the previous site hadn't happened in a vacuum, so the occupants of the second fortification were on high alert.

Too bad for them that they were ill-equipped to deal with me.

After landing, Patrick and the Dengyts headed off to disrupt the auxiliary energy source of the Mist shield while I, once again, prepared to infiltrate the facility. And unlike before, it went off without a hitch. I wasn't immediately attacked by any mystics, and soon enough, I'd set off an equally enormous explosion, which I watched with some degree of satisfaction as we flew away.

That's when we started getting reports from the other teams. To my surprise, most of them had met resounding success. However, there were more than a few that had failed their tasks. Someone would have to pick up that slack, and I suspected it would be me. After all, I was the best person for the job.

Yet, I was more concerned with one particular report.

"Do you want to save him?" Patrick asked.

"Huh?"

"You saw the same thing I did," he said. "Rex and his team are pinned down and trapped. Someone needs to go in and get them."

"He already set the charges. The mission is all but accomplished," I argued.

"But you like him. Or at least you'll tolerate him. I know you want to swoop in and rescue him and his team," Patrick stated.

"I mean . . ."

"I knew it! You like him, don't you? Should I get a cowboy hat, too?"

"This."

"What?"

"This is why I didn't want to say anything," I stated.

"You would let him die just so I wouldn't tease you?"

I shrugged. "Maybe."

It was a lie, of course. The moment I had seen that Rex and his team had been cornered and needed rescuing, I had decided to go. However, I wasn't going to tell Patrick that. So, I said, "Let's just go. We can be there in thirty minutes, right?"

"A lot sooner. I've made some upgrades to *The Leviathan*," he stated.

"Upgrades? What kind?"

"The kind that make her a lot faster," he answered. "I added a condensed Mist intake and a—"

"Never mind," I said. "Just knowing that it'll go faster is enough."

"But I really wanted to talk about the Mist ratios and burn rates."

"Fine," I said, rolling my eyes.

Then, for the next ten minutes, I had to endure what felt like a lecture on the inner workings of *The Leviathan*'s Mist reactor. It was a little adorable how excited he got about those sorts of things, but that didn't make what he was saying any more interesting. But I suppose that wasn't any different than when I subjected him to long explanations on all the different grenade types I'd constructed over the past few months.

Except that explosions were inherently more interesting than engines. That he couldn't understand that was probably Patrick's greatest flaw.

The moment we flew over the site, I saw the issue. There were four mystics down there, identifiable by their tightly controlled auras. In addition, I saw almost a hundred other aliens, all surrounding a giant cylinder. The facility was a little different than the other two we'd attacked in that it was comprised of a perfectly circular outer ring that surrounded a pillar that, in turn, housed the drill that was intended to make its way to the Earth's core, depositing devastating charges along the way.

However, according to Rex's messages, the pillar was locked up tight, preventing the aliens from reclaiming it. He'd already planted his charges when the alarm had been raised, eliciting a reaction from the aliens. So, his completion of the mission was assured; the only question was whether or not he would make it out alive. Alone, he stood no chance, but fortunately for him, he was no longer alone.

As I unbuckled my safety harness, I said, "Get us within a mile, then hover in place. Over that lake will do, I think."

"What are you going to do?" Patrick asked, already following my orders. He had learned not to question them when someone's life was on the line. I wasn't always right, and he knew that better than most, but even the wrong course of action was better than getting caught up in an argument.

"Going to find the biggest, baddest alien down there and pick a fight. Just keep it steady."

With that, he left the cockpit and headed through the ship and into the cargo bay. Once there, I got a few curious looks from the squad of Dengyts, but thankfully, they were content to leave me to my business. Or maybe they were already aware of what was going on. Either way, I gave the leader—a blue-haired gnome who was a bit stockier than the rest—a nod before planting myself at the opening cargo doors.

Then, I summoned the Emperor.

As much as I enjoyed explosions and hand-to-hand fighting, there would always be a special place in my heart for long-range sniping. It was how my uncle had carved out his place in the world, and I'd always felt the urge to live up to the standard he'd set. Of course, I was nearly certain that I'd long since surpassed his abilities, but raw power had never been the point. Instead, it was about doing justice to all the training he'd put me through.

So, with that in mind, I dropped to one knee and took aim. As I did, I embraced Stealth, then used Explosive Shot, Execute, then Empowered Shot before finally squeezing the trigger. My target was the mystic with the most tightly controlled aura. Even with Observation, I couldn't really make out more than an ill-defined smudge, but I still trusted my aim.

The resultant shot took them center mass, sending them sprawling forward. It wasn't enough to kill them. I'd known that from the very beginning. However, that was what the other six shots in the Emperor's magazine were for.

And two of them were already on the way by the time the first hit. The mystic never even had a chance to react before they hit them, and I saw bits of something fly away upon impact. I thought it was an arm, but I couldn't be sure. So, I continued to fire, shouldering the strain of using the Emperor as best I could. By the fifth shot, the surrounding aliens were affected, with many of them being thrown away by the sheer force of the shock wave.

The sixth shot slammed into the alien mystic, and I saw their aura fluctuate as they tried to activate whatever their version of skills was. Still, they weren't prepared for the seventh shot, which hit with the force of an exploding bomb— and not a small one, either—obliterating them completely. I felt the influx of energy that confirmed the kill, and I shifted my sights to the next target, but the Emperor wouldn't be ready for a repeat performance for some time yet, so I put it away after I'd surveyed the scene of the attack.

"Get me within a few hundred yards," I told Patrick through Secure Connection. "Wait ten seconds, then put me right on top of them."

Patrick confirmed my instructions, then swooped in. Once we were close enough, I took out the BMAP, loading it with a special cannister before letting loose. I probably could have blown everyone up, but then, the pillar would have been destroyed—with Rex and his team inside—so I used something different.

The gas cannisters exploded upon impact, bathing the entire area in thick green smoke. Then, I slapped my respirator on, switched to my Stinger, and readied myself to leap into action the moment Patrick guided *The Leviathan* close enough. On cue, he did just that, and I jumped from the cargo bay, spraying the aliens with a steady barrage of concentrated gunfire.

Most of them couldn't see through the smoke, and even if they could, it was designed to incapacitate anyone who breathed it. So, I cut through them with ease, right up until I had to face off against the enemy mystics.

They hadn't escaped my previous attacks unscathed, and because of that, they were far weaker than they probably should have been. As a result, I only had to pepper them with a few norcite pellets from the ADS, and the fight was basically won.

Of course, that was understating it. The battle was tense, and there were a couple of close calls. However, that was true of any battle against those sorts of opponents. Fortunately, I held them at bay long enough for the Dengyts to arrive and turn the tide. In the end, we won without incurring any losses.

"Open up, idiot," I said, standing before the barricaded door. The Mist shield was thick and active, and the pillar had been built like a bunker. I could have ripped through it but probably not without killing everyone inside. "We're here to rescue you."

"Rescue? We don't need rescuin'," he insisted. "But I guess since you're already here . . . may as well open up, I s'pose."

With that, he opened the door. When I saw him, I was a little alarmed to see that his cybernetic arm had been ripped clean off, and he'd lost a good portion of his hat at some point. But he was alive, which I found strangely comforting.

"I 'preciate it," he said, tipping what was left of his hat. "Them mystics is somethin' else. Course, I don't need to tell you that, huh?"

"I think I've got a good handle on them," I stated. "Now, let's get going so you can blow this thing up."

"Now you're speakin' my language," he said with a grin. I couldn't help but return it with one of my own.

CHAPTER THIRTY-FIVE

AN INTENTIONAL EXPLOSION

I've seen versions of war that most people can't even contemplate. True destruction that boggles the mind and strikes palpable fear into anyone who really understands how close we are to utter annihilation. That is what awaits anyone when they reach the peak.

—Alistaris Kargat

I need a new hat," Rex grumbled as he sat on the bench, staring down at what was left of his headwear. Bits of it decorated the floor, evidence of just how tenuously it clung to its form. To me, it looked like a stiff breeze would send the rest of it scattering to the wind.

But I wasn't terribly concerned with his hat. Instead, I asked, "What went wrong?"

"Mystics," he said, setting the hat aside with a sigh. I felt *The Leviathan* lifting off the ground. "They were waitin' on us, like they knew we was comin'. Took out the ship, then surrounded us as soon as we were inside. Only thing that kept us from bein' overwhelmed was one of the gnomes hackin' into the system and raisin' the shields. Otherwise . . ."

"Damn," I muttered with a shake of my head. Most of the attacks had gone off without a hitch, but a few teams had met with unexpected resistance. Rex's group were the only ones who'd survived. But at least they'd accomplished their missions before they went down. Small comfort.

"You think they knew?" he asked.

"I don't know," I admitted. To me, it looked like the aliens were aware that something was coming, though they'd had no idea of the details. Likely, they had been surprised that we were capable of mustering enough of a force to attack everything all at once. That, I expected, was the only reason we had been successful so far.

I left Rex and the other survivors in the cargo bay and headed to the cockpit, where Patrick was piloting the ship back to the temporary base. I settled into my seat and asked, "Do you think it worked?"

"All reports point to yes," he answered without taking his eyes from his instruments. "But I can't believe it's over."

"It's not. We still have the satellites to destroy," I stated. "On top of that, who's to say the aliens won't try again? I mean, they want to blow up the planet, right? So long as those satellites exist, they can always give it another shot."

"That's a depressing thought," he acknowledged.

"Story of our lives," I mumbled with a resigned shake of my head. Despite experiencing a victory, our situation was just as depressing as ever. I didn't think the aliens were going to stop just because we'd set them back. No—they were going to try again. I had no idea how long it took to get those dig sites up and running—or how many credits it had cost—but I had to believe that the Gomari Confederation had invested enough that they wouldn't quickly abandon those plans. "I sometimes feel like we're wasting our time."

"We're not."

I sighed. "I don't know, Pick. I'm starting to wrap my head around why Al wanted to abandon Earth," I stated. "They're just going to keep coming back, aren't they? So far, all we've done is react to them. We're just treating the symptoms here. We're not actually curing the disease."

"I know. I just don't have any ideas on how to do that last part."

"Me, neither," I admitted. "On the plus side, I got an upgrade."

As I said it, I glanced at my [Warfare] tree with some satisfaction. For months, I'd only seen a trickle of improvement in the Command branch. However, during the most recent mission, I had seen its progress skyrocket into the first tier and nearly reach the second. I could only think that was due to the fact that I was working with so many other people.

"I got a new ability," I stated. "It's called Planetary Defense."

I looked at it:

Planetary Defense (A)—Create a protective Mistwall around an entire planet.

The description was not very helpful, but after examining the ability, I discovered that it was far more complex than any ability I'd ever seen. As the description suggested, using the ability would allow me to create a web of Mist around a planet. That, in turn, would act as a permeable Mist shield that I could control in a variety of ways. However, utilizing the ability would require me to spend months—or perhaps even years—putting it together. It was like the most complex Ghost combined with a supremely powerful Mistwall, which also incorporated the principles of cybernetics.

On top of that, utilizing the ability would require more power than I wanted to think about. A thousand Mist reactors like *The Leviathan*'s wouldn't even cut it, and I suspected my estimates, which were based on pure feel rather than advanced mathematics, were inadequate to describe the sheer volume of power the ability would require.

Suddenly, I understood why the Pacificians were willing to use people as batteries.

Using Secure Connection so the gnomes in the back seats of the cockpit wouldn't hear, I explained the ability to Patrick, ending with, "It seems powerful. It's A-grade. I just don't know how I'm supposed to implement it. I can't even practice it because of the scope."

"You could build models, though, right?" he guessed.

"I don't know. I could structure it like a Ghost, maybe."

"I could dive into your training apparatus," he suggested. "Alter it for the new parameters. It would lose its previous functionality, but I think . . . I think I could make it work. If you want to go down this road, I mean."

"Maybe," I repeated. I hated the ambiguity of the new ability. It felt so imprecise. Normally, I preferred simple and straightforward paths of advancement. This was markedly different, and it made me uncomfortable.

Still, my uncle had once told me that comfort was the enemy of progress. In order to make any sort of gains, a person had to get out of their comfort zone. Otherwise, they would stagnate.

So, perhaps the new ability would push me forward in ways nothing else could.

Those thoughts occupied my mind as Patrick guided *The Leviathan* back to the temporary base. Because of that, I wasn't the first one to notice that something was wrong.

"You see that?" Patrick asked, pointing out the window. I followed the gesture, seeing a huge plume of smoke twisting its way into the sky.

"Is that . . ."

"I think so," he answered. "I'm going to circle."

He did just that, and what we saw was not good. The Dengyt base had been entirely destroyed, and nothing but a crater remained where it had once been.

I tried to contact Alistaris via Secure Connection, but I got no response. However, using my {Mist Warden} senses, I did see that there were hundreds of individuals in the area. They were all cloaked in some sort of stealth ability, and there were three auras that I suspected were mystics.

"They're still down there," I said aloud.

"Is it a trap?" Patrick asked.

"I don't know. Maybe. There's a chance they just haven't left the area yet," I stated.

"What do you want to do?" he asked.

"Kill them all," I stated. "There's no shield. No fancy defense systems. They're vulnerable."

"Are you thinking what I think you're thinking?" he asked.

"They're not the only ones who can make craters," I said by way of answer. Then, I turned to the Dengyts and asked, "Are any of your people still in contact?"

They both shook their heads and said that they couldn't hail their companions. One added, "They could be blocking communications."

"They're not," I said. "I can see that kind of thing."

That was an assumption that had yet to be verified, but I felt certain that it was true. In addition, I was reasonably sure that, if there were any gnomes down there, I would've been able to recognize their auras. No—I was almost positive that only enemies remained in the area.

And that meant that I could get busy with a counterattack.

After only a little more discussion, during which Patrick continued to scan for surviving Dengyts, I left the cockpit behind. When I reached the cargo bay, I had to field a few questions from the rest of the squad, including Rex's people. I answered as well as I could without sending them all into a panic, ending with, "It'll all be explained later. For now, I have something I need to do."

With that, I headed to one of the crates in the corner. It was about four feet tall and heavy enough that it wasn't easy for me to move. Fortunately, there was a hand truck nearby for just that purpose. So, I wheeled the crate next to the bay doors, then set it down.

"What is that?" asked Rex, who'd joined me, clearly hoping to help.

"A special little gift for the people who think we can't bite back."

"That doesn't answer the question," he stated.

I shrugged. "You'll get the answer you want in a few minutes," I said. Then, I popped open the lid of the plasti-steel crate before unfolding the sides to reveal the contents. It was a large drum, not dissimilar from the ones I'd seen in the Pacifician moon base. It was an apt comparison because it contained the same Mist-infused fuel that had made the explosion I'd caused so very destructive.

"Is that what I think it is?" Rex asked, kneeling down next to the barrel and inspecting the intricate wiring on the outside.

"If you think it's a bomb, then yes."

"What's in the barrel?"

"A mixture of ground Rift Shards, liquified Mist, and a few other odds and ends to make it go boom," I answered. That explanation was an understatement for what I knew was far and away the most powerful bomb I'd ever created. That was including the ones I'd detonated on the moon.

Of course, I expected the resulting payload to be much lower, considering that I wasn't blowing up a base containing hundreds, if not thousands, of barrels full of potential reactants. Still, the explosive was far more powerful, and it would be even stronger due to my increased modifiers.

In short, I was about to see just how much of the general area I could blow up.

According to everything I knew, there wouldn't be any long-lasting ramifications, but even I had to admit that I didn't know everything. So, there was still a bit of mystery involved, considering my lack of overall experience with bomb making. Sure, I dabbled, but my knowledge couldn't even begin to rival the experimentation the rest of the universe had done on the subject.

But a homemade bomb could be just as destructive as something made by an arms manufacturer who'd been doing it for centuries. The only difference was that mine was a lot more unpredictable.

In theory.

I was about to figure out how accurate that prediction really was.

"That's a lot of . . . Uh . . . That's going to be a big explosion," Rex said.

"That's the point," I stated, looking up at him from where I was kneeling beside my bomb. "I'm tired of holding back. I'm tired of playing by rules while these assholes invade our planet with impunity. They're down there right now, thinking they won some great victory. They're practically dancing on our people's graves. I won't stand for it. They want to hit us? Okay, it's war. But they better understand that I'm going to hit them back, and harder."

"Fair enough," he said. "You need any help?"

"No. I need to do everything associated with this so that I know my modifiers apply," I answered.

He looked a bit offended at that, but from what I'd seen, his abilities with explosives couldn't hold a candle to mine. He was an expert, but I didn't need expertise. I needed raw power, and I had that in spades.

So, I went back to priming the various charges attached to the bomb. They were only meant to apply a spark, which would in turn create a chain reaction that would detonate the much larger explosive. Hopefully, I'd packed enough fuel.

In any event, I was about to find out.

"Pick," I said via the Secure Connection. "I need you to get a few miles away, then accelerate at *The Leviathan*'s top speed."

"Top atmospheric speed? Or top top speed?"

"The fastest you can go without igniting the atmosphere," I said, knowing that *The Leviathan*, being designed for space travel, was capable of far greater speeds than Earth's atmosphere could accommodate. "Also, get as high as you can."

"Gotcha. High and fast. That's speaking my language," he responded. Then, I felt the ship gaining altitude. The temperature of the air coming in through the open bay doors dropped, and I could see the gnomes huddling together. Fortunately, there was a thin Mist shield that preserved the air inside the cabin and prevented the worst of the cold air from getting in. Still, it was anything but comfortable. Finally, after a few more minutes, Patrick said, "We're on approach."

The Leviathan was no bomber, but we had practiced our makeshift technique enough that I was fairly sure of the timing. As such, Patrick started his countdown, and I repositioned myself to push the bomb overboard. "Ten seconds," he said.

"Nine."

He continued the countdown until, at last, saying, "One. Go!"

I shoved the bomb overboard.

I knew it wouldn't be a direct hit, but with the size of the explosion I expected, I didn't think it would matter much. Holding on to a nearby strap, I leaned forward so I could get a good view of the detonation. The seconds passed as we raced away, covering enough distance that I expected we would be safe from any impact.

I was wrong.

A pillar of fire, miles high and crackling with blue Mist, bloomed into being as it erupted into the atmosphere. Then, the shock wave tore across the landscape, obliterating trees and wildlife in an instant.

And it kept going, moving far faster than *The Leviathan* could.

"Hang on!" I shouted just before the wave of force hit the ship. It bucked, nearly flipping end over end, and everything that wasn't strapped down flew across the cargo bay. Fortunately, everyone else had already buckled their harnesses the moment they'd felt *The Leviathan* accelerate.

Everyone but me.

I held on to the strap, but it snapped after only a moment, and I was sent tumbling through the still-open cargo bay. Fortunately, I was no stranger to dangerous situations, and I used Teleport before I got out of range. A moment later, I was back inside and clutching one of the bulkheads with the Hand of God. A few seconds later, the ship righted itself.

For a few more seconds, I watched as the cloud of fire, smoke, and Mist shrank into the distance. Then, over the Secure Connection, Patrick said, "I need to set the ship down for a minute to run diagnostics. That was a lot rougher than I expected."

"Alright."

I was still a little stunned by the sheer size of the explosion I had caused. It wasn't as large as the one I'd set off on the moon, but it wasn't a lot smaller, either. I could only imagine the damage I'd wreaked on the landscape.

The Dengyts and Rex's people were still recovering when Patrick guided the ship to a landing in an open prairie a few minutes later. We were dozens of miles from the blast site, but the dust cloud had darkened the atmosphere as far as I could see.

As everyone found their equilibrium, I headed to the cockpit to find Patrick running diagnostics on the ship. As he did, he said, "I had the Mist shields up, but that bomb was . . . It cut through the shield."

"That was probably the norcite powder I mixed in," I said. "I didn't want to miss the mystics."

"Damn, Mira. You should've told me that."

"You think it'll be an issue?" I asked.

"How should I know? I'm no bomb expert. That's you, remember?"

"Just because I have some skills doesn't mean I'm an expert," I stated. In fact, the only thing I felt qualified to call myself an expert in was Mistrunning. Everything else, I was still learning.

And I needed to change that in a hurry.

"We're going to have to check it out," I said. "Will the ship be okay?"

"Of course it'll be okay," he said. "Just give me a minute to make sure there won't be any lasting damage. Then, we can go see if anything survived."

"Okay," I said, hoping that I hadn't done any irreparable damage to the ship.

As it turned out, *The Leviathan* was fine, though Patrick said that was more due to some of the modifications he'd made than anything else. So, with that established, we set off back toward the blast site. However, when we got within a couple of miles, Patrick said, "This is . . . not great. This is as far as the ship can go. The Mist is acting weird."

"Weird how?"

"Well, less weird and more nonexistent. It's like the opposite of a Dead Zone out there," he stated.

"Is it safe?" I asked.

"Sure. Probably. I have no idea."

"That's . . . not a helpful response."

He shrugged and looked back. "I'm aware. Best I can do, though."

"Fine," I said, sighing. "I'll check it out. Everyone else needs to stay here."

CHAPTER THIRTY-SIX

DEPRIVATION

I once dreamed about exploring other worlds, thinking it would be some grand adventure. But now that I know what's waiting out there, I just want to be left alone on Earth.

—Patrick Ward

What's going on?" asked Rex as I once again reloaded my weapons. He and the rest of his team definitely looked a little worse for wear, and the Dengyts that had been tasked with helping me on my mission were clearly anxious. They only knew a little of what had happened, but what they did know wasn't good.

"The enemy attacked the base," I answered. "None of our people were alive, but there were a ton of bad guys there. So I blew them up."

"I picked up on that last part."

"Now, I'm going to check things out," I said. "Make sure there are no survivors."

"If there are?"

"I'm going to kill them" was my simple answer. "I'll interrogate them first, of course. But I don't think they'll be in any condition to talk. Things are going to be weird down there."

That was certainly the truth. The addition of norcite powder into the bomb was technically considered a war crime in the wider universe. However, I figured that since Earth had yet to be Integrated—that didn't come until after the quarantine was lifted—I didn't have to follow their rules. And besides, when the destruction of my planet was at stake, abiding by rules and laws seemed a lot less important.

Useless, even.

Besides, what did I care about the laws of a civilization that was willing to let my planet be destroyed? After all, clinging to some code of morality would serve no one but the would-be conquerors.

Regardless, there was a reason using norcite in bombs was forbidden. Even using it in the ADS was heavily restricted, and technically, I shouldn't have even had access to the ammunition. Gala had broken quite a few laws by selling it to me, and for that, I was incredibly grateful.

In any case, the reason it was such a heavily restricted substance was because of its ability to depower the nanites that comprised the Mist, rendering them inert. If there was enough of it concentrated in one area, that shift would be permanent. So, the norcite-laced bomb I'd detonated had almost certainly left the blast zone and its surrounding area in a Mist-deprived state. How long that would persist was anyone's guess, but I suspected it wouldn't be a short amount of time.

With that in mind, I finished reloading my weapons and left *The Leviathan* behind. Patrick had landed the ship quite some distance from the blast zone, but even so far away, I could feel the effects. The Mist was thinner than I'd ever felt it, and I could practically taste the toxic norcite in the air.

I pushed my discomfort aside and started toward my destination. With every step, I felt like I was suffocating. Not physically but, rather, from a perspective of Mist. There just wasn't enough of it, and as I went, I could feel the restrictions weighing down on me. It was as if my attributes experienced a precipitous fall with every few hundred yards I traveled. I counteracted it by retracting and compacting my aura, but with every passing minute, I could feel the increasingly desolate atmosphere chipping away at it.

And every mile I traveled meant that those chips grew larger. If I stayed in the area for much longer, I knew it would have negative—and possibly permanent—effects. Perhaps that was why norcite bombs were banned.

Still, I had a job to do, so I kept going. I tried using the Cutter, but it wouldn't even summon. The error message I received told me that Mist fluctuations had triggered the fail-safe, and it would be locked until the atmosphere stabilized. So, I had no choice but to proceed on foot.

Gradually, I made my way through the wilderness, and just like the integrity of the Mist in the area, the landscape steadily grew more desolate. At first, that desolation presented itself in the trees' loss of leaves, but soon enough, the limbs followed suit. And eventually, the trees themselves had been knocked down by the shock wave. After that, the trees turned into burned-out husks, and when I drew close to the bomb's blast radius, they'd been disintegrated altogether, leaving nothing but a barren landscape behind.

I tried to keep a running commentary with Patrick via Secure Connection, but the decreasing Mist levels rendered that impossible. So, I was entirely alone in the silent and desolate world I had created.

I kept going until I finally reached the primary blast zone, as characterized by mounds of overturned earth and an atmosphere almost entirely lacking in Mist. I had to use two threads of my Split Mind to keep my cocoon of personal Mist intact, and even that wouldn't last forever. More, I felt weaker than I had since my first stint in Mobile, which was saying something considering how far I had come since that town had been destroyed.

I crested a hill of charred soil and gasped as the results of my actions were laid bare.

A huge crater, maybe a mile wide and maybe a quarter as deep, stretched out before me. And there was nothing inside—just bare earth, scorched and blackened by the bomb I had set off. Yet, I could see a few hot spots of Mist, like oases in a desert.

Or beacons in space.

I needed to inspect them, though I was undeniably terrified of what I might find. Visions of mutated aliens danced in my mind as I descended the slope toward the first concentration of Mist. It was only a few hundred yards away, so it didn't take me long to arrive at my destination. The weak Mist signal was buried beneath a few feet of burnt soil, so I retrieved a shovel from my arsenal implant and got to digging.

It was only a few moments before the spade hit something solid.

But after a little prodding, I recognized that it was soft, as well. I'd found a body, I was certain. So, I carefully continued digging, keeping one thread of thought on my surroundings; I wasn't sure if the alien below me was alive, but I wasn't going to take any chances.

As it turned out, my caution was unnecessary. The alien was indeed alive, but their body was so desiccated and charred that it was hardly distinguishable from the surrounding soil. Still, they were alive—an issue I ended with a few quick strikes with the sharp blade of my shovel. As their head fell free, the Mist dissipated into the atmosphere. On instinct, I reached out, snatching at the rapidly degenerating cloud of nanites and dragged it to me. It took a subtle shift in my mind to absorb it, but as deprived of the Mist as I was, I quickly figured it out.

That helped to allay some of the effects of remaining in such a barren environment. More importantly, it felt like it caused something to click inside my mind. Until that moment, I'd never really considered directly absorbing the Mist I ripped away from various people. Yet, in retrospect, it seemed like such a natural progression that I was incredibly surprised I had yet to make it.

But now, I could see all sorts of uses. I didn't typically run low on Mist, but there were a few of my abilities that really drained me. Most notably, using the Emperor was incredibly taxing, and the healing associated with [Mist-Infused Body] took every ounce of Mist I had at my disposal. But if I could somehow form a bridge between the ambient Mist and the ability, I could . . .

Could I become immortal?

I already suspected that I could live for quite some time without my organs. I'd once seen a video of my uncle persisting as nothing but a severed head and a bit of spine, and I was certain I could replicate that feat. Yet, with the ability to take ambient Mist via Mist Authority and funnel that into the ability that could rebuild my body in seconds, the limits I'd once thought were hard and fast suddenly seemed like they were little more than gentle suggestions.

However, the tiny bit of Mist I received confirmed that I would need a much more powerful source if I was going to do anything worthwhile. Still, it was a significant breakthrough that I hoped would help me unlock untapped potential I'd never even considered might exist.

But for the time being, I needed to continue my inspection. That first alien's survival suggested that all the beacons of Mist shining throughout the crater were living creatures. And I intended to put an end to that.

So, I continued forward, growing ever more uncomfortable by the second. Part of it was the lack of Mist, which left me feeling like I was drowning in nothing. But related to that was the pervasive weakness that came with it.

I persisted, though, and I quickly found my next foe. This alien was even more desiccated than the last, and I ended them with a single blow from my shovel. That gave me another chance to absorb their Mist, which went far more easily than the first time, almost as if my body knew precisely what to do with such a situation. Perhaps it did.

In any case, once that creature was dead and the minuscule amount of Mist absorbed, I kept going. However, after only a short few steps, I heard something that made me whip around in alarm. Yet, when I did, I saw nothing but the expanse of charred earth. Still, I could have sworn I heard something that sounded like whispers.

"Definitely just the wind," I muttered to myself as visions of desiccated corpses rising from the ground haunted my thoughts. "Or my imagination."

After taking a couple more looks around and finding nothing, I continued on my task. It mostly went as I'd expected, though there were a couple of instances when the nearly dead aliens attempted to attack me. Their flailing was weak and ultimately useless, but it was still more than a little disconcerting.

The whispers of the wind continued, as well, though it thankfully didn't grow any louder, which was only moderately comforting.

Eventually, I reached the center of the crater, where I found my first real surprise. One of the aliens had dragged itself out of its earthen grave and was propped against a mound of dirt. The creature was incredibly long-limbed with a sinuous form that was clearly very inhuman. Its skin had the texture of charcoal, but I wasn't sure if that was due to injuries or if it was a natural state.

Regardless, that rugged black skin coupled with their orange eyes to give a distinctly demonic appearance.

Or maybe that was the horns jutting from either side of its head.

I put my shovel away and drew the interdiction blade as I approached. It watched me, and when I finally drew near, it let out a cough, saying, "You won't need that, monster. I can't even move, much less fight back."

Judging by the grooves in the burnt soil, it looked as if it had dragged itself as far as it could, then given up.

"You came here to kill everybody on the planet," I said. "From where I'm standing, that makes you the monster."

"Naive fool."

"Maybe," I acknowledged. Then, I cocked my head to the side and amended, "No. That's not accurate. I'm definitely naive. But I can't really be blamed for that, can I? Information isn't exactly flowing from the tap around here."

"Do you hear the whispers?" it asked. "We all do."

"Nope. No whispers at all," I maintained.

"Liar," it spat, coughing up a wad of black phlegm. "You think yourself special because you survived without an implant? A quirk of genetics, nothing more. That doesn't make you strong."

"Oh, you think I'm a Templar, huh? Do my clothes look white?"

"I am blind."

"Ah. Right. Well, I'm not a Templar. I'm not a mystic at all. Just a good old-fashioned human with a big, beefy implant."

"But that doesn't . . . Wait . . . You are a Seeker."

"No clue what that is," I admitted, though I got the gist from context.

"A normal person who seeks the power of the mystic," they said. "One who has reached the summit through murder and training."

"Oh. Then yep. That's me. Love some good ol' murder," I said. "Though that's probably obvious from the bomb I dropped on you and yours."

"I know of you."

"Do you?"

"The genocidal terrorist who slaughtered millions of peaceful beings," they said, coughing once again. I was keeping a close eye on their Mist, which was tightly controlled but almost entirely inert. "You are why we came. Through your actions, you have sentenced billions to death. And you believe you have won? It is laughable."

"I'm not laughing," I said. "And I've won every battle so far."

"Battle? We are nothing more than a scouting expedition. The most expedient way to accomplish the goal. Now, your planet will be subjected to an invasion you can scarcely imagine. And—"

"Oh, you're going to kill us all even harder than before? Is that supposed to scare me? Leave your two-bit evil-villain monologue in the trash where it belongs. You came here with the express purpose of killing everyone on Earth and harvesting its resources. There's nothing past that. No escalation that makes a difference. So, I'll just save you the trouble and say that it doesn't matter what the next steps are. I'll meet them head-on, and I'll kill every last one of you who sets foot on my planet."

"Bold claim for someone so powerless," the long-limbed alien spat.

"It's worked out so far," I stated. "Millions dead, remember?"

"How long can you keep it up, though? You will die. Everyone does. The universe functions on a timeline of eons. When you're gone, we will be back. And we will get what we want. Your little backwater of a planet cannot resist. You can't fight back. You will all be conquered, enslaved, or killed. It is only a matter of time. It is inevitable."

"Maybe," I said, my mind roiling with anger and frustration. The alien wasn't wrong. I wasn't going to live forever. And even if I managed a victory, the aliens would just wait until I was dead and gone to come back. "But you won't be there to see it."

With that, I lunged forward, but not with my sword. Instead, I did so with Mist Authority, slamming my will into the alien's with as much force as I could muster. For a moment, they resisted, and we remained at a stalemate. But then, I flexed the entirety of my mind and shattered their resistance. Mist erupted out of them, gushing like a geyser, and with multiple tendrils of thought, I snatched at the various leaks, drinking deep of that Mist.

The alien screamed. Whether those screams were of pain or horror, I had no idea. Nor did I care. Instead, I absorbed their Mist greedily, ignoring their pleas.

As I did, they shrank, physically and in terms of their suddenly exposed aura. When I'd finished, the alien was no more substantial than the desiccated husks I'd encountered throughout my exploration of the crater. I watched them die as the last of their Mist winked out.

Then, I let my shoulders sag.

I knew that, though spiteful, their words hadn't been a lie. Earth was not in a great situation, and things weren't going to get any easier with Alistaris presumably gone. I hadn't recognized his Mist aura before I'd dropped the bomb, and he certainly wasn't capable of surviving the destruction I'd left in my wake. Without his leadership—or information network—I questioned how successful any resistance could be.

We had accomplished the mission, and Earth probably wasn't going to be exploded the second the quarantine lifted. However, I knew they would be back. I knew they would try again. And next time, I wasn't sure that we'd be in a position to stop them.

I sighed, then looked around. I had all the destructive power in the world, and yet, if I didn't know where to aim it, it was useless. And now that Alistaris was gone, I felt rudderless in a way I hadn't for quite some time.

So, it was with a somber attitude that I trekked across the crater and completed my grisly task. Dozens more had survived, but even then, I knew most of them wouldn't have lived through the night. There were only a few that might have made it past a few more hours, and I expected that they were all mystics. None were as strong as the long-limbed alien I'd killed in the center of the crater, though.

Finally, once I'd finished, I headed back to *The Leviathan*. Along the way, the Mist levels slowly rose until they had reached an acceptable density. I felt a little better after that, but even when I reached the ship, the reality of Earth's situation still weighed heavily on my shoulders.

CHAPTER THIRTY-SEVEN

IN THE AFTERMATH OF DISASTER AND SUCCESS

Lots of people love the idea of being a warrior, but the reality of it is one of horrifying loss and crippling sadness. I've lost so much. So many people I'll never see again. I know we were justified. I know we didn't have any choice. But I still struggle with the cost of resistance.

—Patrick Ward

I sat on top of *The Leviathan*, staring out at the unsettled sea as slate gray clouds rolled in from the south. It was fitting weather for my mood, which was just as dark as the coming storm. As I sat there, I held a small Rift Shard in one hand while one thread of my [Multimind] dragged Mist away from the thumb-sized crystal. It took quite a lot of effort, but over the past two weeks, I'd managed to develop that facet of Mist Authority well enough to manage a small trickle of absorption.

It wasn't enough to do anything worthwhile. As it turned out, Rift Shards were incredibly stable—more so the larger they were—and taking anything from them without running them through some sort of conversion apparatus was almost impossible. Yet, I had persisted, largely out of stubbornness, and managed some small success.

Taking Mist from living things was far easier, as I'd established back in that crater, though without the deprivation spurring me on, my progress with the unstructured technique was decidedly slow. I had chosen to look at it as a challenge.

However, that particular facet of progress was not the point. Instead, I'd discovered that constantly flexing Mist Authority resulted in significant movement regarding my [Shielding] skill. It wasn't perfect for progressing that particular skill, but it was something I could do constantly and without any outside input. As a result, I found myself quickly pushing toward the higher tiers.

I wasn't there yet, but by my calculations, it wouldn't take more than a month of solid training to complete the skill and merge it with Mist Authority. After that, I could absorb the skill crystal for [Recovery] and start working on that, as well. Within a year, I hoped to reach the end of that line, which would result in an evolution of that string of abilities.

I just wasn't sure if I had that much time.

Over the past two weeks, Patrick and I had been in touch with the various teams tasked with destroying the dig sites, and to my surprise, every single one had been successful. However, that hadn't come without significant cost. Some teams had been obliterated down to a single member, and a few had even sacrificed themselves to accomplish their missions. On top of that, the entire command structure had been destroyed in the attack on the temporary head-quarters. And finally, Alistaris, who was the lynchpin of the entire operation, was missing and presumed dead.

Without him, we had very limited knowledge-gathering capabilities, and because of that lack, combined with a severely diminished number of capable warriors, our chances of overcoming the blockade had become extremely slim.

So, we had been in limbo ever since, directionless and a little hopeless.

I glanced to my left, where a series of abandoned ships rested. The last time I had seen them, they'd been quite magnificent, but Biloxi had clearly fallen on hard times after Nova City's destruction. I wasn't certain why the city had been abandoned rather than making a deal with some other city, but I knew it was probably my fault. Behind me, the city was a ghost town of crumbling buildings without a resident in sight.

I could see the flicker of a Mist aura offshore, which told me that the kelp was still thriving on the seafloor. Yet, there was no one there to harvest it.

"We need to figure out our next move," came Patrick's voice from behind me. I didn't need to glance back to know that he'd just climbed up from the hatch. "We're only a week away from the end of the quarantine."

"I know," I said softly, continuing to drain what I could from the Shard.

Patrick settled in beside me. With our shoulders touching, we both just watched the oncoming storm. When the first raindrops started to fall, Patrick broke the silence by saying, "He might still be alive. The Dengyts think so."

"It doesn't matter, Pick. Alive or dead, we have no idea where to even look. And besides, what are we going to do even if he's alive? Rescue him? Wherever they would keep him is bound to have top-notch security. We can't just walk in and pick him up. It'll be another battle, and one where we'll have to face the best they have to offer," I reasoned. Then, I let out a sigh. "Besides, we don't have enough information. For all we know, they're holding him at the bottom of the ocean."

"That doesn't sound like you."

"Yeah, well, I'm tired, Pick. Why does it always have to be us? Where's everyone else? There are powerful people across the planet. We know some of them. But the fate of the world rests on my shoulders? How is that fair?" I asked.

Indeed, that had been on my mind ever since the crater. At every turn, I'd made so many mistakes, most of which ended with unintended consequences. And with the power I had at my disposal, that usually meant death on a scale most people couldn't imagine. Yet, I knew it wasn't all my fault. Sure, I wasn't perfect, but what person my age—of any age, really—could say any different? When I'd destroyed Nova City, I wasn't even twenty. And I wasn't that much more mature when I took down the Pacificians.

People my age weren't supposed to decide the fate of a world.

"It's not fair," he said.

"But?"

"But nothing. It's not fair. You shouldn't be in this position. None of us should. Doesn't change the fact that you're different, Mira. You know that. You're special. And you're probably the only person on the planet right now who can stop what's coming," he said. "I know you like to make light of your abilities, but the things you can do . . . You're just different. Alistaris knew it, and that's why he got you on board."

"And now he's probably dead. Or imprisoned somewhere we can't get to him."

"Yep. But the fight doesn't end until it's over."

I let out a long, deep breath. Then, I gave him a half smile. "That sounded terrible."

"Something Remy used to tell me," he said by way of an excuse. "Still, it's appropriate. This is just a pause. Not an end. It's a setback, nothing more."

"The blockade's coming up in a week."

"Then we'll figure out a way to get through it, Mira. I mean, you just drained a Rift Shard without any machinery. I think you'll figure the rest out."

I glanced at the Shard. It had gone dark and gray, just like when we used the Shards as fuel for *The Leviathan*. "I didn't even notice," I said.

Then, I heard something that cut through the smattering of rain. Something I'd heard a few other times since the crater. At times, it was easy to mistake it for the wind, but it was too clear for that. And I felt like I could almost hear a voice riding alongside the sound. In the beginning, I'd asked if Patrick could hear it, too, but he couldn't. It was just me.

"You heard it again, didn't you?"

"It's nothing," I lied. I knew there was something to it, though I really had no idea what it meant. However, my mind kept drifting back to the whispers the mystic who'd briefly survived my norcite bomb had mentioned. "So, what do you think we should do?"

"I don't know."

I sighed. "Good pep talk," I said, pushing myself to my feet. "Really helpful."

"It's not my fault, Mira, and I'd appreciate it if you didn't take your frustration out on me."

"Yeah. I'm bad about that. Look, Pick—I don't know what—"

Just then, I heard something that definitely was not a disembodied whisper on the wind. A sonic boom erupted overhead. I whipped my gaze upward to see a ball of fire ripping through the clouds. A few seconds later, it crashed down into the sea about a quarter of a mile from shore. The impact sent a ten-foot wave of water ashore, but it dissipated only a few feet from *The Leviathan* before retreating back into the ocean.

"What the hell was that?" demanded Patrick.

"I don't know," I admitted, already grabbing my Stinger from my arsenal implant. I slammed my respirator over my mouth and said, "Stay here. I'm going to go check it out. I'll keep an open line with Secure Connection, and if I call for help, I expect you to come running. Got it?"

"Wait for me. I can . . ."

But by that point, I'd already leaped from *The Leviathan*'s roof and was sprinting into the surf. I heard Patrick finish, "And she's gone."

I dove into the crashing waves, then kicked forward with an efficient swimming stroke that propelled me into deeper water. As I did, I cast my {Mist Warden} senses out, keeping an eye on any predators in the area. There were a couple of small sharks and a handful of other dangerous fish, but none of them were interested in me. So, I kept going, swimming toward the glowing beacon of Mist in the distance.

I had no idea what it was, but the Mist aura it gave off was powerful, which suggested that it was an attack of some kind. I was ready for it, though. The Stinger was more than capable of firing underwater, and though it would lose a bit of its kick, my modifiers were sufficient to mitigate that detriment and then some.

I swam forward, covering the distance in only a minute or so, and by the time I reached the crash site, the disturbed cloud of silt from the seabed still hadn't dissipated. So, visibility was very limited. Fortunately, I still had Observation to pick up the slack, and my {Mist Warden} senses helped, as well.

I waited, treading water as the area cleared to reveal something large and egg shaped. Using Observation, I could tell that it was metallic, and I could see that there were some glyphs on the side. However, even with Universal

Language, I couldn't decipher them. When nothing changed about the egg for another few minutes, I swam forward to inspect.

As I drew closer, I saw that there were some glass ports on one side. So, I approached and peered inside.

"Get medical supplies ready!" I shouted to Patrick through Secure Connection.

"What happened? Are you hurt?"

"Not me! It's Gala!"

Indeed, the minotaur was inside the egg, which I belatedly realized was some sort of spacecraft. It only took one look to tell that she was injured, though. Her fur was matted with bright-red blood, and one of her horns had been broken off at the tip. More importantly, she was entirely unconscious. Even when I banged on the window, she didn't flinch, and I feared the worst.

I inspected the egg-shaped craft, swimming around it in a frantic search for a way to open it, and I found a hatch a few seconds later. It was locked, though, so I had to reach out with Mist Authority and hack into the system. It was equipped with a stout Mistwall, but by that point, I could rip through all but the most powerful defenses in seconds. So, in only a moment, the Mistwall fell, and the system was laid out before me.

It was incredibly simple—much simpler than something like *The Leviathan*—which lent credence to the budding notion that it was only meant for short trips. That led to the idea that it was an escape pod not dissimilar from the ones we had on our ship. And given Gala's condition, that seemed very likely to be true.

In any case, it only took me a moment to direct the hatch to open, which it did with a hiss and an expulsion of Mist. Water flooded in, and yet, Gala still didn't awaken. So, I wasted no more time before grabbing one of her massive wrists and dragging her free. She was huge, and even though I had plenty of strength at my disposal, the giant minotaur made for an awkward burden. Fortunately, I had some experience with water rescue—the training my uncle had subjected me to had been incredibly thorough, after all—so I managed to bring her to the surface with only minor difficulty. After that, it was a simple task to drag her to shore.

There, Patrick met us with one of the Dengyts.

"He's got a medical skill," Patrick said by way of explanation as I pulled her fully onto the sand. The Dengyt immediately went to work, jabbing a syringe into Gala's chest. I saw Mist swirl, and she took a shuddering breath, but she remained unconscious. With Observation flared, I could tell that her heartbeat was weak and her lungs were full of liquid. I was about to say as much when the Dengyt continued his task, addressing those concerns via various lifesaving methods.

I recognized some, but without my old medical skills that I'd lost upon gaining the {Mist Warden} class, I could only observe.

Which admittedly was not my strong suit.

So, I practically held my breath as the Dengyt saved Gala's life, and after a few more minutes that felt like hours, the minotaur's huge bovine eyes fluttered open. The moment she focused, she sprang to her feet with far more agility than I would have expected. In the blink of an eye, she had Ferdinand out and pointed at the gnome.

A second later, her mind caught up to her reactions, and she focused on me. Then, she saw Patrick, and her shoulders slumped.

"Good," she breathed, her voice sounding a little stranger than normal. It was deeper, though still feminine. "You're here. We don't have any time to waste."

"What's going on?" I asked. "Why are you here? What happened to you?"

"I made the stupidest decision of my life," she said. "Your little friend is up there in the Bazaar, and he's about to be executed. I tried to spring him, but they were a little more than I could handle. Would've been a different story if I had all my equipment, but . . . I left that behind. The point is that we need to go up there, rescue your friend, then get back here before the quarantine drops."

"Alistaris is up there?" I asked.

"Yep. Pumped full of chemicals and interrogated for the past two weeks. They got everything they could out of him," she said. "He's stronger than I expected. Barely gave them anything. But now that they've pumped him for all the information they can get, it's time to remove him from the equation. I figured you might want to stop the execution."

"Please don't blow up the Bazaar," Patrick said suddenly.

"What?" I asked.

"The Bazaar. Don't blow it up."

"I wasn't planning on it!" I insisted.

"But things don't always work out like you plan, right?"

"Anyway," I said, turning away from him and focusing on Gala. "How do we get up there?"

She nodded toward Patrick, saying, "He's a smuggler, right? And that ship of yours is built for this kind of thing. I'm sure you can figure out how to break quarantine. I'll show you how to get onto the space station without raising the alarm."

"Why?" I asked.

"What do you mean?"

"I'm asking why you're willing to do this. I mean, selling me a few weapons is one thing. Being friends, sure. I can buy that. But if I understand what's going on properly, what you've just done is going to have wide-reaching ramifications on the rest of your life," I guessed. Indeed, I didn't know much about the rules of the Bazaar, but from what I knew, she'd just made a huge mistake.

"First of all, a little fight up there isn't enough to get any real attention. There have been whole wars fought in the past hundred years," she stated. "None of you knew a thing about it. And second, I'm helping because Jeremiah was my friend."

"Is that it?" I asked. "Nothing to do with the implant?"

"I wouldn't say nothing."

"Is that it?"

"For now," Gala stated.

I only had hints of how powerful she really was, but from what I had seen, there was no way I was ever going to bully her. She would tell me what was going on when she got good and ready, and not a second sooner. Still, I said, "I expect an explanation about all of that when we get back. Or on the way, if you're willing."

She shook her head. "Not much to it. You're an experiment. People have a vested interest in keeping you breathing. That's it."

I sighed. It wasn't much more than I already knew about the Tier 7 Nexus Implant, but it felt like there should be more to it. Or maybe that was driven by my desire to be truly special. Whatever the case, Gala was right. We didn't have time to get into it at the moment—not if we were going to rescue Alistaris.

"Alright. Then let's get going," I said.

After that, the four of us headed into the ship. Rex and his team, as well as the remaining Dengyts, had all taken shelter in one of the nearby buildings, but I let them know what was going via Secure Connection. They offered to come along, but I refused. I knew it was going to get dangerous up there, and I didn't think bringing everyone along for the ride was the best course of action. For what it was worth, Gala agreed, cementing my supposition that it was the right path.

Soon enough, we were all inside the ship, and Patrick was lifting off. Hopefully, we wouldn't be too late to save the Dengyt commander.

CHAPTER THIRTY-EIGHT

RESCUE MISSION

Earth doesn't even qualify as a backwater. It's on the edge of the frontier, and the only people who care about it are the desperate or unscrupulous. I'm one of the former.

—Galatira Iamaxis

You're really not going to tell me the whole story, are you?" I asked, glancing back at Gala. She'd crammed herself into one of the back seats of *The Leviathan's* cockpit, and it was clear that she found it extremely uncomfortable. But then again, I was pretty sure that the ship hadn't been built with enormous minotaurs in mind, so I didn't exactly feel bad about it. "Just going to keep it all to yourself."

"There's nothing to tell, Mira."

"You keep saying that, but it feels like me being an experiment kind of opposes that statement," I stated.

Gala sighed. "It wasn't complicated. More of a coincidence, really. There was nothing special about you, except that Jeremiah had the right combination of obsessiveness and resources to get the most out of the implant," she said. "Even then, he was supposed to have given it to his daughter. The fact that he didn't was one of the reasons he ended up the way he did."

"She wouldn't take it," I said. I knew the story. Jeremiah had intended to give the Tier 7 Nexus Implant to my mother, but she'd turned it down in favor of living a normal life. And that normal life had ended up with her dead at the hands of some no-name mugger.

"I know that. And I understood it. The people who gave your uncle that implant didn't care, though. So, the moment they realized what was going on, they pressed the right buttons, bribed the right people, and called in all the right favors. The results were that he ended up dead, and you ended up on your own," she said. "It was a calculated risk meant to force you to either step up to the challenge or die. Either result would have been valuable for their research."

Failure, it seemed, was still valuable.

"Who is it?" I asked.

"It doesn't matter, Mira."

"It matters to me."

"Fine. It was the Ark Alliance, okay?" she answered. "Alistaris is your handler. Or he was until they called him back home. When he chose to stay on Earth, they withdrew their protection. The Gomari Confederation found out, so they sent the Arbiters of Orion to capture him."

"Why not kill him?"

"They intend to. They just wanted to get as much information as they could out of him before the execution," she explained. "They're also waiting to see if his family will pay a ransom."

"Will they?"

"Alistaris cut ties with the Dengyt home world a long time ago," she replied. "Until your little stunt kidnapping the princess, he hadn't spoken to anyone in the core for years."

"So, let me get this straight—the Ark Alliance gave my uncle this implant so he could shove it into my mother," I recounted. "They wanted to see what would happen, right? But then she refused, and it ended up in me instead. Ever since then, they've been . . . What? Manipulating events to try to force me to develop the way they want me to? That's why my uncle's dead? That's why Al came after me in the first place? Was the whole heist a setup?"

"Calm down, Mira," Gala said.

"Don't tell me to calm down," I growled. "You just told me that the people I've been working with are the reason my uncle died. Under those circumstances, I think I'm pretty damn calm."

My eyes flicked to the single gnome in the cockpit. She was trying to keep a straight face, but I could tell that she was on the verge of losing it. With Observation flared, I could hear her rapid heartbeat. And with my {Mist Warden} senses, I could see the fluctuations of her aura. Not only was she terrified, but she was also on the edge of activating some sort of ability.

"Don't," I spat in her direction.

"She's not at fault, Mira."

"Gala, I don't need you to—"

"This isn't helping anyone!" Patrick shouted. "All that matters is whether or not you want to rescue Alistaris. The rest of this interrogation can wait until then, okay? So, do you want to go get him?"

"Of course I do."

I owed him, after all. He'd helped save Patrick's life, and on top of that, he had chosen to stay on Earth when he had every reason to leave. If that hadn't established him as my ally, then nothing would. As Patrick had said, everything else could wait until he was safe. However, if I found out that he was complicit in my uncle's death, then nothing could save him from me.

"Then we should probably get ready because it won't be long before we're there," Patrick stated.

I nodded, though if I was honest with myself, I resented him a little for being the adult in the room. Or the cockpit, as it were. Still, I remained silent as he guided the ship into the upper atmosphere. Once we were there, I felt him activate some sort of ability before a swirl of Mist swept through the ship, enveloping it. As it did, he pressed a button on the command console, and another wave of Mist—this one originating from the Mist reactor—spread through *The Leviathan*.

However, my attention rested squarely on the bubble of diffuse nanites just ahead. Or above, I suppose. It was the system's enforcement of the quarantine, and I knew that if Patrick's measures were somehow inefficient, things would go very badly for us. I knew that his [Smuggler] skill was supposedly up to the task, but that meant very little when system censure was on the table. So, I couldn't help but clench up as we passed through.

And other than a slight tingle, I felt nothing.

"That was anticlimactic," I muttered. I looked back to Gala and asked, "So, if we wanted to, we could just leave, right? Take off through the galaxy and try to forget Earth ever existed?"

"You could."

"But?"

"Nothing. I would advise you to do just that if I thought you would even give it a second thought" was her response. "I know you won't, though."

"You think you know me?" I asked. Sure, I'd spoken to Gala on enough occasions that I thought of her as a friend. But I didn't think she really knew me. Not like Patrick.

"I know you well enough to predict what you'll do. But I've been wrong often enough that I can't say I'm sure of anything," she answered. "If you did choose to leave, I can tell you where to go so that you might survive, though. I even have some contacts who might consent to hide you."

I shook my head. "I can't do that."

"Even if this is your last chance?" she asked.

"Especially because it might be my last chance," I answered. Indeed, the idea that the rest of Earth's population would soon be trapped on the planet while a bunch of aliens plotted how to strip its resources was precisely the reason I needed to get back to the surface as soon as possible.

If I had more time—and a lot more people—we could have gone ahead with Alistaris's original plan to destroy the satellites that would create the blockade once the system quarantine was lifted. However, I knew that we'd never even get close without a significant fleet of ships to cover us, so that plan was out of the question.

We had prevented the planet's destruction, but we were a long way from solving the next problem on the list. Yet, even living cut off from the rest of the galaxy was better than having the planet exploded while we were on it, so I didn't want to dismiss the progress we had already made.

Part of me just wanted to try dismantling the system of satellites anyway, but I knew that was a suicide mission. But they were protected by a fleet of ships—the extraordinarily advanced *Infinite Conquest* among them—and each satellite housed thousands of combat bots and soldiers, as well as dozens of mystics. If I went in without a plan—or help—I was doomed to failure.

And even if I had accepted my own mortality, I wasn't eager to fight a losing battle that would end with me dead and forgotten.

But Alistaris—he knew the system, and he'd already conceived a plan. So, we needed him if we were going to continue fighting for Earth's freedom.

All those thoughts and more swept through the various threads of my mind as Patrick guided *The Leviathan* through the quarantine and toward the giant space station that we knew as the Bazaar. From the outside, it was a curious structure composed of various interlocking circles, each one more than a mile wide. However, I knew that the inside was far larger than the exterior suggested.

It also had the densest Mist aura I'd ever seen.

"It's impressive, isn't it?" said Gala, leaning forward. "I can't see auras like you, but I've heard from a few Templars that the system stations are true masterpieces."

"System stations?"

"Made in the core and connected to the system on a much more fundamental level than most technology," she said. "They're incredibly advanced, and in ways that few truly understand. Even the shipwrights who make them don't fully comprehend how everything fits together. They just follow the plans implanted in their minds alongside the [System Engineer] skill. I've heard that there are a few near the peak who know how it all works, but they're not telling anyone. It's almost a religion to them."

The system was an intriguing subject, but I knew that it was a dead end. Nobody really knew where it had originated, even if they claimed otherwise. Some said it was just a part of the Mist, but others believed that it had originated with the eldest races who'd had to adapt to the Mist the hard way. Whatever the case, the system was almost universally regarded as a sentient thing, which meant that tricking it was possible.

And on the frontier, it was almost encouraged.

"How are we getting in?" I asked.

"Gala sent me some coordinates already," Patrick said.

"Oh."

I watched as Patrick approached the Bazaar—or system station, as Gala had called it. And after a few more minutes, I saw him use another ability. I still wasn't sure what all his [Smuggler] abilities were called, but as far as I could tell, this new one was meant to mask our approach. Soon enough, we came into sight of a large open entrance that was guarded by a semipermeable Mist shield.

There were a few other ships coming and going, and Patrick released his ability before joining the queue. Before long, we were passing through the Mist shield and landing in an open spot.

"That seemed a lot easier than it should have been," I remarked.

"Thousands of ships come and go from system stations every day," Gala stated. "There's no reason for them to suspect we're anything but another merchant ship. Besides, it's not like security is particularly tight this close to the quarantine dropping. Add the Gomaris to the equation, and nobody's going to care about one extra ship."

"What about people like Ana?" I asked. "She came here with the expectation of taking advantage of the world opening up after quarantine."

"She just has to accept it. It's part of the risk we all take when we come to the frontier."

"This is a terrible system," I pointed out.

"Can't argue with that, but you have to understand that most of the universe couldn't care less about what happens to a world like this. They have their own problems, so they can't afford to worry about a planet that's halfway across the universe."

That certainly fit with my understanding of how people worked. At one point, I would have called it human nature, but everything I had seen suggested that it was a pervasive attitude across all species. It was difficult to care about others when you were worried about your own fate, after all.

Regardless, once we'd landed, everyone made certain that they were ready. For my part, I used Mimic to take on the appearance of a red-skinned alien I'd killed a couple of years before. She was mostly human looking, except for the hue of her skin and a pair of tiny horns jutting from her forehead. At the look I got from Patrick, I said, "I'm public enemy number one for the Gomaris. I don't think it's a great idea to walk around with my normal face."

"Do I need a disguise, too?"

"No offense, but I don't think anyone's looking for you," I said. I glanced at Gala. "But her, on the other hand . . ."

"I can move around without notice if I like," she said. "But the Dengyts should stay in the ship unless we need backup."

That garnered some resistance from the gnomes, and I understand why. It was their leader we intended on rescuing, so they had a personal interest in the mission. However, Gala only had to point out that the enemies would expect a troop of Dengyts to come to the rescue of their commander, and they let it go.

After that, Gala, Patrick, and I left the ship behind.

Trekking through the Bazaar was both a familiar and novel experience. I recognized the corridors, but the people inside were plainly projections. Visually, that was obviously due to their transparent nature. However, it was even more obvious to my {Mist Warden} senses because none of them had the slightest aura about them. Yet, I knew that I could disperse them with the slightest nudge with Mist Authority.

But the worst part was that the whispers that had dogged me since the crater were even louder than back on Earth. I couldn't quite make out what they were saying, but I was closer than ever before. It was almost enough to keep me there. Almost, but not quite.

Still, I kept one thread of thought continuously trained on those whispers as we traversed the miles of corridors. Eventually, after passing through a few less-than-prosperous sections, we reached an intersection. There, Gala held up one of her giant hands and said, "Stealth from here on in."

With that, she disappeared. I could still feel her, but her aura was so subdued that, from a distance, I might've mistaken it for a slight ripple in the ambient Mist. For his part, Patrick activated some sort of device on his belt, and when I asked what it was, he responded via Secure Connection that it didn't actually have a name. Then, he added, "I'm calling it the Stealth Generator, though. I finished the design a couple of weeks ago, but this is the first time I'm using it. I built something similar into the mech suit, though. This is just smaller and way more efficient."

"Neat," I said.

"Neat? Who says neat?"

"I think it's neat. Very impressive."

He groaned silently, and I embraced Stealth. After that, we took the right-hand turn, and a few hundred yards later, Gala informed me that we had arrived at our destination. It was another large chamber, much like the one that held Gala's shop. However, instead of hundreds of cube-like rooms, it housed a single facility that was placed right in the center. Outside, there were dozens of enemies representing all sorts of alien species. I didn't bother noting their characteristics because none of them seemed particularly dangerous.

"How much do you want me to hold back?" I asked.

"Don't blow anything up," Gala said.

"Can I use Ghosts?"

"If you can get them to stick, but I'm fairly certain you can't," she said. "These aren't—"

Even as she spoke, I'd been infiltrating the nearest alien's system. It fell in seconds, and as I'd uploaded my *Kill Switch* Ghost, the other threads of my [Multimind] were hard at work doing the same to three other aliens. In the couple of seconds it took Gala to express her doubts, the enemies had already begun to drop.

"Oh," she said.

"Would be easier if I could use something like Plague, but I don't want to infect Alistaris, too," I said through Secure Connection as I strode forward. "I won't get them all, but—"

At that moment, a surge of Mist exploded in the center of the compound, then swept through me. Immediately, I felt my system go haywire, and I collapsed only an instant later.

Behind me, Patrick and Gala were even more affected than I was, and both hit the ground as soon as the wave of Mist tore through them. More distressingly, all our various stealth measures fell away, exposing us for all to see.

"Target down!" came a voice out of nowhere. Then, a dozen figures suddenly appeared all around me. They were wearing the black armor of Adjudicators, and each one had an assault rifle pointed in my direction.

A thirteenth enemy flickered into view. He was tall, four-armed, and wore a tight-fitting yellow jumpsuit that showed just how alien his anatomy was. His torso bulged in all the wrong places, and his legs had multiple joints where only one should've been. However, his face was mostly human, save for a pair of compound eyes and a trio of antenna emerging from a mop of white hair.

He held a pair of slender swords and, more importantly, had the aura of a mystic.

"Mirabelle Braddock. I've wanted to meet you for quite some time," he said with a wide smile that revealed a set of pointed shark's teeth. "I do so look forward to becoming intimately acquainted with everything you have to offer."

CHAPTER THIRTY-NINE

CORNERED PREY

Everyone else is always one step ahead. I understand the reasons behind it. Mira and I, as well as the rest of humanity, are playing catch-up. The rest of the universe already knows how to win the game, but we're just starting to learn the rules. I just hope we can figure it out before we end up losing everything.

—Patrick Ward

I felt weak.

Useless.

As if everything I had done since leaving Nova City had been for nothing.

And I wasn't going to stand for it. So, kneeling there, with the Mist inside my body swirling out of my control, I wrestled my shock and fear into submission. As I did so, one thread of thought remained trained on my surroundings. The smug alien stepped closer, a smile spreading across his face. With each passing instant, I felt the Mist normalizing.

But I wasn't going to wait for my skills and abilities to be available. The moment he came within range, I sprang at him, yanking the interdiction blade out of its sheath on my back. With my other hand, I pulled Ferdinand II from his holster at my waist. Yet, I didn't bother shooting the mystic. Instead, I fired on his lackeys.

The first shot smashed through the nearest alien's head, exploding it like an overfilled balloon. But I didn't pause to appreciate the way its blood and brains misted into the air because I was too busy aiming a lethal strike at the mystic. My sword came in low, but it never reached the smug creature. Instead, my blade bounced off of an impromptu Mist shield, rebounding so violently that it sent me stumbling to the side.

Then, shackles of Mist latched on to my wrists and ankles, lifting me high into the air. Another tendril of Mist grabbed my forehead, preventing me from moving even a muscle.

Then, I heard a ringing laugh.

I seethed as I saw the alien grip his slender belly, cock his head back, and let out a good-natured chuckle. It sent a shiver up my spine.

"Impressive," he said. "You're almost on the level of a real mystic. But—"

One of his followers dropped dead.

"What?"

Then another.

He whipped his head in that direction, clearly unsure of what was going on. Another fell a second later. Then, his Mist shackles dissolved, and I fell to the floor, landing lightly. Even as I did, more of his followers dropped.

"I've figured you guys out," I said, bending down to pick up my sword. "You talk a big game. You act like you're these mysterious experts."

He lashed out with his aura, but I batted it aside. Now that I knew he was there, I could do so easily. He wasn't nearly on the level of the female mystic I'd fought back in the Templar town, so it wasn't even that difficult to block his strikes. The only reason they'd landed in the first place was because I wasn't expecting them.

Which was stupid.

But it wasn't the first time I'd let my own hubris get me into trouble. Fortunately, I was powerful enough to push past my mistakes and take control of the situation. And I wasn't going to give my enemy that kind of opportunity. So, I grabbed my Stinger from my arsenal implant as I continued: "But you're just a different kind of mediocre. I'm not."

Then, after infusing the magazine with Explosive Shot, I fired. He blocked the first few rounds with his swords—he could move incredibly quickly—but once I flipped to fully automatic, he didn't stand a chance against the powerful assault rifle. In seconds, I'd filled his body full of gaping holes.

The moment he went down, something huge rushed past me, and it wasn't until I saw her stomping on the mystic that I realized that Gala had recovered. That shouldn't have been surprising, given that I could feel that the oppressive Mist had dissipated. That didn't last long before one of the Adjudicators responded to my sudden freedom.

Wearing that same all-black armor, they threw a grenade in my direction. I dove to the side, but it didn't explode. Not the way I expected, at least. Instead, I felt another wave of Mist tear through the area. However, this time, I managed to shield myself with Mist Authority. The explosion ate away at the corona of Mist I'd raised around myself, but that attack dissipated before it made it all the way through.

I fired on the nearest Adjudicator, and the kinetic force of each shot knocked them backward. Their armor remained intact. However, Gala had once again been stunned, and Patrick had never recovered from the first surge. So, I knew I was on my own.

I also realized that I was in a terrible position.

Surrounded by Adjudicators who couldn't be touched by Mist Authority, I knew it was only a matter of time before they overcame my defenses. So, without further hesitation, I rocketed toward Gala. As I did, bullets flew in my direction, clanging off the plasti-steel tiles of the floor. After sliding to a stop next to her, I dragged her to her feet. She grunted, saying something unintelligible, but I wasn't interested in hearing it. Instead, I pulled her to safety behind a low wall, where we took cover from the still firing Adjudicators.

"I need you to get Patrick out of here," I shouted over the sound of gunfire. "Can you do that?"

"If they don't throw any more disruption grenades out," she said. "What are you going to do?"

"Distract them. Kill as many as I can."

"Those are Adjudicators . . ."

"I know. I've fought them before," I said. I reached into my arsenal implant and retrieved a smoke grenade, which I tossed out into the open area. It hissed and spat a wall of billowing smoke along the way, and I shouted, "Go!"

Gala sprang into action, racing across the chamber and scooping the unconscious Patrick up in her huge arms. A couple of Adjudicators tried to follow, but I took aim and fired upon them, sending one sprawling and the other diving for cover. That told me that those suits of armor weren't quite as impervious as I suspected. Did I have enough power to get through them?

Maybe.

I would have to find out.

The moment I saw that Gala had left the huge chamber, I went on the offensive. Dragging the HIRC from my arsenal implant, I leaped from cover and let loose, bathing them in a barrage of gunfire. The results were predictable, and even though most of those rounds didn't get through the Adjudicators' armor, they could do nothing about the enormous momentum of those shots.

It was only the first salvo, though. I continued to fire, even as I reached out with Mist Authority and snatched the Mist away from anyone who wasn't protected by that Mist-insulating armor. The Adjudicators were incapable of responding because I kept them off-balance with the HIRC's prodigious rate of fire, and soon enough, I was among them. My interdiction blade fell upon the spots where I knew the armor was the thinnest. Necks and joints were my favorite weak spots, but there were a few others that I wouldn't turn down.

In the end, I tore through them without mercy but with a significant degree of difficulty. The Adjudicators were no mystics, but they were highly trained and high-level, which meant that they were equipped with skills and attributes that were potent enough to give me quite a bit of trouble.

But I persisted, pouncing on every weakness I could find, and one by one, they fell before me. Eventually, the room went silent, and I was all alone. The Mist still felt extremely unstable, but it was enough that I could still activate Secure Connection.

To my distress, Patrick didn't answer, so I contacted Gala instead. "Is Patrick safe?" I demanded.

"He's fine," she answered. "We retreated to my shop. I can't protect him any-where else."

"Won't they be looking for you there?"

"If they come looking for me there, they're going to regret it" was her response. "I needed to go there, anyway. All my equipment is stored there."

"I'm going to keep going. I finished the Adjudicators and the mystic. The regular guards on the outside of the facility, too," I said, eyeing the squarish building across the massive chamber. It was a hundred yards across, and it looked like it was at least that deep, as well. That meant it was large enough to house hundreds, if not thousands, of enemies. "Do you know where they'll be keeping him?"

"Sending you a packet," Gala said. "It's a map. I'm not sure how accurate it is, but it should be close enough to get you in the general vicinity. But I'll file my horns if there's not another mystic or two inside."

"Then I'll kill them, too."

"Mira, you can't—"

"Don't pretend this isn't what you wanted," I spat. "You knew we were going to have to fight through the facility if we wanted to rescue Alistaris. Probably wanted to see how your little experiment performed, huh? Well, I'm about to show you and everyone else that I'm not going to just dance to your tune. You wanted a weapon, didn't you? That's what this was all about? That's what you got. So, don't even try to act like you're concerned for my welfare all of a sudden. We both know that's a lie, except as a means of protecting your investment."

"That's not fair, Mira."

"Well, that's life, ain't it? If I don't come back, make sure Pick gets out. You owe me that, at least."

"I . . . do. I will," Gala said. "When you get him, meet me back at my shop. If you have anyone on your tail, I'll take care of them."

"Affirmative," I said, then severed the Secure Connection.

After that, I took stock of my ammunition situation. I still had plenty of grenades and more than half a magazine of Stinger ammunition. However, the

HIRC was down to ten percent. I reloaded Ferdinand II, which took care of that, and the ADS hadn't even seen any use during the previous fight. Neither had the BMAP, so it was full, as well.

Of course, the interdiction blade was ready to go as always.

With that, I took a few extra moments to let my Mist regenerate before finally using Vanish and slipping into Stealth. I would have used the latter straightaway, but I was being watched. Regardless, once I used the former, I was invisible to anyone who might be looking for me.

And I knew that my little battle with the mystic and the Adjudicators hadn't gone unnoticed. They were going to be ready for me, so I needed to be at the top of my game if I was going to avoid getting caught. That in mind, I took a deep breath, then trotted toward the building. I spared a brief thought for how odd it was that people had built structures inside the space station, but it seemed to be a common custom, so I supposed I was missing something. Or people just didn't like having open space above their heads.

Whatever the case, I quickly covered the ground, but instead of entering through the front door, I took a leap, kicked off the wall, and propelled myself to the lip of the roof. With my attributes being what they were, it was simple enough. When I got there, I knelt in place as I observed the trio of guards who were watching the location where I'd just used Vanish. They weren't Adjudicators, so I didn't even have to leave Stealth to reach out with Mist Authority and infiltrate their systems. I uploaded a new Ghost called *Brain Death*, the purpose of which was just what the name suggested—it severed all neurological connections, rendering the victim permanently comatose.

It didn't kill them, but it was almost instantaneous, so by the time I finished uploading the Ghost to all three systems, the first was already falling. The others followed a moment later.

It was so easy, killing regular people. If someone wasn't a mystic or didn't have access to the Mist-blocking armor that the Adjudicators used, I could tear through them in seconds. The only limit was my perception.

Which was a scary thing, and it came with a significant degree of responsibility that I certainly wasn't qualified to shoulder. Regardless, I had the power, so I needed to get used to wielding it, especially if Earth was going to stand any chance of survival. So, without further contemplation, I set off across the roof until I found a door leading inside. The room on the other side of the door was a typical office, with various security terminals that I was sure were meant for surveillance. I took a moment to jack into one, then spent the next couple of minutes verifying Gala's map.

It wasn't that I didn't trust her. Sure, she'd kept a lot of information from me, but she'd never actively lied. On top of that, I felt certain that she wouldn't do anything to hurt me. Still, I had long since adopted a trust-but-verify attitude, and as much as I wanted to believe Gala was on my side, I wasn't willing to exempt her from that policy.

As it turned out, her map was accurate, save for a few small details that I noted. In addition, I spent the next few minutes noting the locations of all the occupants. Along the way, I left behind a few Ghosts that were meant to eat away at their systems well after I was gone. Because I knew the Gomaris would replace anyone I killed. Bodies were cheap, after all. However, the more I could interfere with their equipment, the better.

Besides, it didn't take long.

It also sparked an idea that had been bouncing around in the back of my mind for a little while. I wasn't prepared to implement it just yet, but I did give it the full attention of one thread of thought. Hopefully, by the time I needed the plan, it would be ready.

Pushing that aside, I headed deeper into the building. I maintained Stealth the entire way, so even though the people inside were clearly looking for me, I passed them by without incident. I also started planting seeds for my eventual escape. I knew that Alistaris wasn't in any state to sneak around, so I reasoned that I would need a distraction if I was going to get out without getting into another firefight.

I knew I would probably win, but I was less certain that I could do so while keeping a Dengyt of unknown condition alive. I intended to be prepared for the worst, and if it didn't come down to that, then so be it.

Soon enough, I reached a stairwell that I knew would lead me down to the level where Alistaris was being held. So, with a mixture of anticipation and caution, I descended. Yet, I encountered no significant issues until, at last, I found myself staring at a mystic flanked by three Adjudicators.

None of them had detected me, but they were placed at the end of the hall, behind which was Alistaris's cage.

And it was a literal cage that looked fit for some sort of animal. I could feel the Mist flowing through the bars, too, and I saw the restrictive bindings that would block access to his skills. He had also been beaten to a bloody pulp, which made him nearly unrecognizable. Without his aura to identify him, there was no way I would've known if I was looking at Alistaris or some other similar-sized Dengyt.

The mystic was short and broad, with a heavy beard and thick muscles, which led me to believe that Patrick would have labeled him a dwarf, like in some of the ancient books he liked to read. But there were a couple of key differences, most notably that the mystic's skin looked like it had the consistency of rough bark, and his eyes glowed with green light. The three Adjudicators with him seemed of similar stature, suggesting that they were the same species. However, with the black armor on, it was difficult to tell.

Whatever the case, I figured it wouldn't be that difficult to take them out.

Especially because I intended to kill the mystic first.

I wasn't certain if I could do it, but this was my first chance to attack one without them knowing I was there. That meant there was a good chance that I could employ the lessons I'd already learned and infiltrate the mystic's system-like core. If I could do that, I could take them out without a fight.

But I knew it would take every ounce of concentration I possessed, so I withdrew the various threads of my mind from their current tasks, then applied them all to the new objective. Like that, I extended a thin tendril of my Mist Authority, inching closer with every passing second.

I didn't rush.

I refused to let my impatience affect me.

Instead, I crept ever closer, thrusting the sliver of Mist Authority forward with glacial speed. Soon, I hit my first obstacle, which took the form of a thin Mist shield that I would never have even noticed if I wasn't looking for it. The thing was only a nanite thick, which told me that it was never intended to keep me out. Instead, it was an alarm. After coming to that realization, it was easy to find the emitter, which was a nearly microscopic device built into the wall.

Using Mist Authority, I infiltrated its system, and rather than shut it down, I merely changed its parameters to ignore my presence. Then, I moved on, soon encountering another. And another after that. In all, I was forced to overcome seven Mist alarms before I finally reached the mystic.

Then, after taking a deep, steadying breath, I pushed forward, hoping that I truly was capable of taking him out without a fight.

CHAPTER FORTY

BANE OF MYSTICS

There are many mystics in the universe, and like any other population, some are good, others are bad, and a scant few are exceptional in either direction. But the vast majority are, by definition, average, and there is a wide gulf between each extreme.

—Galatira Iamaxis

I narrowed my eyes as I leveraged every thread of thought at my disposal toward accomplishing my chosen task. And to my ultimate surprise, I tore through the alien mystic's natural defenses in mere seconds. It was like ripping through so much paper, which was such a far cry from what I'd experienced while trying to infiltrate mystic cores in the past that I almost lost my concentration.

Still, despite that brief stumble, I managed to maintain my focus until his core was laid out before me. It was a small, pitiful thing that elicited a pang of sadness. I knew that the process to become a mystic was a terrible thing that usually resulted in those would-be mystics becoming untethered wildlings. So, I'd assumed that they were all just as committed as I was to training and progression.

Clearly, that was not the case, considering what I saw of my latest victim's core. It wasn't just anemic, though that was a good description. In addition to being small, it was diffuse, and when I trained my senses on it, I got the feeling that it was even weaker than its loose structure would suggest. Obviously, I'd stumbled upon someone who'd become a mystic, then thought they'd made it. Given that, they probably didn't think they ever had to work again.

A silly idea, and one I intended to underline.

So, I reached out, and following instincts whose origin I didn't really recognize, I squeezed.

The only sign that the mystic felt it was a slight widening of his glowing green eyes before, suddenly, they went entirely limp. They were dead before they hit the floor.

For normal people, being cut off from the Mist was painful and exhausting, but they could live through it. For a mystic, though, attacking their supply of Mist was tantamount to cutting a human being off from oxygen, but even more dramatic in its effect. The result was that when I squeezed that core of Mist, the dwarf mystic lost the motivating force that kept them alive.

Usually, that wouldn't have been possible. However, they were so weak, and their core was so small that I had no trouble wrapping my awareness around it and squeezing the life out of it. In more literal terms, I cut those nanites off from everything else, isolating them and draining the energy from the cloud of microscopic robots we referred to as Mist.

Any other time, and I might have wondered how I'd learned that particular technique. Yet, I had other issues on my mind because the Adjudicators certainly noticed the sudden death of their resident mystic, and they were intelligent enough to recognize that there was an enemy among them. So, they leveled their assault rifles in my direction and fired.

Fortunately, I'd never left Stealth, so they didn't know precisely where I was. However, they did a fine job of covering most of the area, which meant that I was forced to use Teleport to avoid being peppered with bullets.

Mist drained out of me, but because I had a handle on the mystic's core, I had no issues yanking their Mist free and adding it to my own store. It wasn't as dense as my own, but it was enough to replace what I'd just used. Which didn't really seem fair, but I wasn't going to argue with something that benefited me.

Teleport took me right behind one of the Adjudicators, and the second I appeared, I ripped the interdiction blade from the holster on my back and hacked at his more lightly protected neck. But even though the armor was thinner there, that didn't mean it was nonexistent, and I couldn't thrust any Mist into the blade to make it more powerful. Still, I had quite a lot of strength from my inflated Constitution attribute, and I didn't let it go to waste. The blade didn't cut through the Adjudicator's armor, but the sheer momentum of my attack broke his neck.

He flopped to the ground, just like the mystic, already dead when he hit the tiles.

By that point, though, the other Adjudicators had reacted to my presence. They swung their weapons around and fired. I dodged, but not quickly enough; thankfully, that's where [Shielding] proved its worth. It didn't stop the powerful gunfire, but it did slow the bullets down enough that, when they hit the armored portions of my infiltration suit, they stopped cold before they even got to my subdermal armor.

Even so, it threw me off just enough that I missed my next attack, which should have gone the same as the first and ended with another Adjudicator going down. Instead, my blade glanced off the Adjudicator's helmet, sending out sparks as metal ground against metal. Then, another burst of gunfire thudded into me. Each bullet ate a little of my Mist aura, ruining the integrity of my shield.

It was still effective enough to keep the rounds from getting past my infiltration suit, though I knew it wouldn't be long before they got through. After that, my subdermal armor would be put to the test.

And I knew it would eventually fail, too. It wasn't heavy armor, and though I'd upgraded it almost a dozen times since acquiring the cybernetic Sheath of subdermal armor, it still couldn't compete with more obtrusive gear. What it did have on its side was that it did nothing to affect my speed or flexibility, so when I moved, I did so with all my hard-won agility.

I bounded off the nearby wall, kicking into a leap that took me all the way to the other side. Behind me, Adjudicators continued to fire, but they couldn't move their weapons quickly enough to keep up. So, when I finally went in for another attack, I was blessedly free of hampering gunfire.

I couldn't bring my weapon around in time, so I aimed a flying kick at the Adjudicator's neck. It landed with all my momentum and weight behind it, and he went skidding backward into the wall. Or he would have if I hadn't grabbed his weapon and, as soon as my feet hit the ground, yanked it toward me. He maintained his grip, which meant that he was suddenly jerking in the opposite direction.

Which took him straight into my outstretched arm, sending him into a flip that took him to the ground. That's when I took my interdiction blade in both hands and brought it down in a hacking attack that dented the armor in his throat. He tried to scream, but the blow must have crushed whatever passed for a voice box because the sound came out in a choking cough.

Unfortunately, I couldn't spare the time to finish him off because his partner—the last remaining Adjudicator—hit me with a shoulder tackle that sent me thudding against the wall. I felt a couple of ribs break, but more distressingly, he maintained his grip, pinning me into place as he pummeled me with what felt like a dozen body shots a second.

Clearly, he was using some sort of ability.

Which wasn't fair, considering he was entirely insulated from my Mist attacks. But I wasn't really in any position to consider the fairness of the world because, with every passing moment, Constitution was being put to the test. If I let him keep going, I was going to end up with more than just a couple of broken ribs. So, with that in mind, I reached out, grabbed his helmet, and twisted with every ounce of strength I could muster.

At first, nothing happened. The Adjudicator had clearly worked quite a bit on his own Constitution, and as a result, he resisted my attempt to break his neck with impressive vigor. Yet, even though I didn't typically train for muscle mass, instead focusing on agility and endurance, I still had a Constitution approaching five hundred. And against that, there was nothing he could really do.

I let out a roar as I finally overcame his strength, and his neck snapped to the side. It didn't break, though. I could tell that because I hadn't heard the sound of breaking bones, which, with Observation, I certainly would have. Still, I knew I'd at least torn a couple of muscles, and he stumbled backward, flailing as his head flopped side to side.

That was the opening I needed, and I brought my sword around in a brutal strike that hit the side of his head with enough force to send him stumbling away and into the opposite wall. I was on him in an instant, hitting him again.

And again after that.

All in all, it took seven more attacks before he fell to the ground. I still didn't knock him out, though. He was hardheaded like that, apparently. But he was defenseless when I finally managed to land an attack to his neck. It didn't cut through his armor, but it did crease the sturdy material. The next cracked it a little, and the one after that finally cut through. At last, I was rewarded with the sight of orange blood.

After that, it was just a few more good hacks before his head rolled free.

"That armor is no joke," I muttered to myself, wiping the sweat from my forehead. Then, I looked back at the lone remaining Adjudicator. He'd stumbled down the hall a bit, obviously trying to get away. Yet, I knew he wouldn't make it. Perhaps the crushed throat wouldn't kill him. But I intended to hasten him along. So, I pulled the Emperor from my arsenal implant, took aim, and used Empowered Shot before firing. The first shot took him in the back, sending him sprawling to the floor where he skidded to a stop fifteen feet later. But the armor kept the round from destroying his torso.

The second shot was far more effective, tearing through that armor and obliterating his insides. He died unceremoniously.

I took a deep breath, then let it out in a sigh.

The Adjudicators had been more difficult to kill than the mystic, which just seemed wrong to me. Obviously, the dwarf—which was how I'd chosen to think of them—had not been very powerful, which was both disappointing and reassuring. Just because someone was a mystic didn't mean they would be all-powerful. Indeed, they seemed to be just as subject to the laws of averages as anyone else.

I took solace in that.

But I also wondered where the ones I'd already killed fit onto the spectrum. Was the woman I'd fought back in the Templar village strong for a mystic? Or was she just the best of the rejects? I didn't know, and I wasn't certain if I would find out anytime soon.

As I turned my attention to the door, the tenor of the ever-present wind-like whispers reached a fever pitch, yet I still couldn't understand what they were saying. After only a few seconds, they faded away, but I couldn't escape the feeling that I was missing something extremely important. Perhaps I could ask Freddie about it, assuming that he hadn't gotten himself killed already.

That was a very real possibility, considering that we had lost touch with most of Earth's other defenders when Alistaris had been abducted. Hopefully, rescuing him would give us some much-needed direction.

So, I approached the door with some degree of optimism, and I reached out with Mist Authority. However, I was surprised to find that the door wasn't locked. That put my guard up, but I reasoned that even if I was walking into a trap, that fact couldn't dissuade me from my mission. Trap or not, I had to rescue Alistaris. If it was one, though, I was confident that I could tear through whatever measures my enemies had taken to contain me.

I commanded the door to slide open, then I stepped inside the room.

That's when I saw more of Alistaris than I ever wanted to.

He hung from the ceiling, naked as the day he'd been born. His arms were extended above his head, and around his wrists were shackles that were, in turn, attached to a pair of Mist-infused chains that stretched to either side of the room. His legs were similarly bound, which made for something of a unique sight.

But even more distressing was his condition. His face was completely purple and so misshapen that I wondered if the integrity of his skull had been breached. Moreover, his body wasn't in much better condition, and I could see bones bulging from his torso as well as his arms in all the wrong places.

I wasn't even sure if he was breathing, he was so still.

Which was why I flinched a bit when he opened one eye and said, "You shouldn't have come here."

Before I could respond, a pair of autoturrets descended from the ceiling and opened fire. I tried to leap out of the way, but something whipped out and wrapped around my right leg. Then my left received similar treatment. I ripped it free, but by that point, the bullets were tearing into me.

I dropped to the ground, curling up in the fetal position as I depended on my aura to protect me. It didn't.

The bullets shattered it in a second or two, thudding into my back. The infiltration suit blocked the first few, but it had never been built to stop that kind of damage. So, it wasn't long before it failed, too, leaving me with only my subdermal armor for protection.

And I couldn't deny that that elicited a bit of panic because, when I'd tried to extend a tendril of Mist Authority in the direction of one of the autoturrets, I'd slammed against a dense Mistwall. Frantically, I worked to dismantle it, but it was at least as high-grade as anything I'd ever encountered. I knew I could get through it, but just as surely, I knew it would take time, as well.

And that was one thing I didn't have.

So, I shifted my entire mind—every single thread—to the task as I tried to pummel my way through. At first, it felt like I was banging my fists against a brick wall, but I was nothing if not persistent, so it was only a matter of seconds before I shattered the first layer. The second came soon after that. And the third. Each node I took down further destabilized the shield, which made my job all the easier.

Even so, I was trying to do it while a powerful gun was busy filling me full of holes. Each shot threatened to topple my focus, but through an exercise of willpower, I maintained concentration long enough to finally batter my way through the Mistwall and take command of the weapon. As soon as I did, I turned the barrels toward its twin and let loose.

At the same time, I sent another thread of Mist Authority at the second gun. As I attacked it from that angle, the other autoturret assailed it from the other direction. And before long, I finished it off.

But by that point, I was more than a little injured, with multiple gaping gunshot wounds in my back and torso. According to the readout on my HUD, both my lungs were punctured, my liver had been all but destroyed, and I had more broken bones than I could count. Yet, it could have been worse. Machines didn't get modifiers like people did, so they could only depend on their not-insignificant designs, as well as the skill of their makers, to deal damage. These two autoturrets had been powerful, and against anyone else, they probably would have had no issues bringing any intruder down.

But I wasn't anyone else.

And I had barely survived.

Now, I just needed to fix the damage. So, I gathered my Mist, then used the healing associated with [Mist-Infused Body], instantly recovering. I hated that I'd had to use it; normally, I wanted to keep it in reserve for emergencies. But I reasoned that if ever there was a crisis, this was it.

The ability took hold, and my body mended. Bones snapped back into place, and my organs rebuilt themselves. At the same time, my flesh knitted itself back together as slugs were ejected from my body. It was an odd feeling, and it was anything but painless, but I endured the few seconds of discomfort before finally rising to my feet.

"Wish I could do that," Alistaris muttered. "Would you mind freeing me? Because I feel a bit exposed."

I reached out with Mist Authority and, after a few moments, found the system that controlled his chains. A second later, I'd burst through the Mistwall and deactivated them. He fell to the floor in a boneless heap. I rushed to his side, already retrieving a med-hypo from my arsenal implant. Then, I jabbed into his naked hip, dispersing it a moment later.

"Can you walk?" I asked, pulling a spare shirt from my storage. I draped it over his shoulders.

"I'm fine," he grunted, pushing himself upright. "You have another one of those hypos?"

I did, so I gave him another shot. Then another after that. Normally, I would have been a little worried about overdoing it, but Alistaris claimed he could take it. So, I chose to trust his judgment. Soon enough, he'd donned my shirt, which hung down past his knees like a dress. I looked him up and down, but I didn't say anything.

Still, he asked, "What?"

"Nothing."

"You smirked."

"I did not," I insisted, though I could feel the corners of my mouth turning upward. "Must be a trick of the light or a cultural misunderstanding. I would never smirk at you, regardless of how ridiculous you look."

He sighed. "Very well," the Dengyt said. "May I have a weapon? I have been disarmed."

"Sure," I said, dragging my old R-14 from my arsenal implant. I handed it over. "It's not the best weapon in the universe, but it'll work."

"It will do just fine," he said, ejecting the magazine. He checked it, then jammed it back into the well. "Let's go. I presume you have a plan for your escape."

"Sure. Fly away."

"That's not a plan."

"Close enough. C'mon. Let's get out of here."

And with that, I headed toward the exit. All the enemies were already dead, so I didn't even bother with Stealth.

CHAPTER FORTY-ONE

ESCAPE

Consequences. It's a concept that most of the universe does not fully understand. On the surface, that doesn't seem to be the case, and yet, they consistently push people past their breaking points. Eventually, they snap. And one day, one of those people is going to set everything ablaze.

—Alistaris Kargat

It smells weird in here," I remarked as we strode down the wide corridor. "Like a mixture of ozone and antiseptic, with a little gunpowder mixed in. I can't say it's a pleasant aroma."

"Please take this seriously," Alistaris said, limping along.

"I could carry you."

"No," he growled.

"Hear me out. If I did carry you, would you prefer to ride on my shoulders? I think I could rig up a harness with a couple of my belts," I said. "Or are you one of those princess-carry kind of guys? I bet I could even strap you across my chest so you could—"

"Miss Braddock."

"What?"

"Please stop talking."

"What?" I asked innocently. We'd recently passed into the more populated part of the Bazaar, and we were definitely getting some odd looks. I didn't blame those people, really. A gnome walking through a space station wearing nothing but an oversize—to him—Leviathan tee-shirt wasn't such a common sight that people wouldn't take notice. Making it even more attention-grabbing was the fact that he was carrying an assault rifle almost as big as he was.

He sighed. "Nothing. Where are we going?"

"Meeting a friend, then heading to the hangar where we parked *The Leviathan*," I answered.

"And this friend is?"

"Gala."

"Gala who? It's not that uncommon a name."

I shrugged. "You know what? I never got her last name," I admitted. "Does that make me a bad friend? Or just self-absorbed?"

"The latter," he said without hesitation.

"Ouch."

"This cannot come as a surprise to you," Alistaris pointed out.

Indeed, it didn't. I was well aware that I acted like the world revolved around me and my misadventures. Yet, in my defense, it often did. However, I knew it was an issue, and it was one I'd resolved to try to fix. I had not been successful.

"Anyway. Gala's a giant minotaur lady," I said. "She's—"

"Are you talking about Galatira Iamaxis?" he asked, stopping in his tracks.

"I just told you I don't know her last name," I stated. "Why? Is she a big deal?"

"I didn't think she had gotten involved," he said. "I knew she was in the system station, but . . ."

"I'm going to need an explanation," I said when he trailed off.

"Galatira Iamaxis is a former Erdikar Dreadnought commander," he said. "A war hero who was forced to resign after her sister disgraced their family. Normally, that would have been a death sentence—people don't just leave the Erdikar Dreadnoughts—but she was too popular. She could have led a revolt, if that had been her goal. Most people expected it. And yet, she did precisely what she said she was going to do and headed out to the frontier to peddle weapons. I suppose I should have made the connection . . ."

"You're not doing so great on the all-knowing-mastermind front," I stated. "I thought you knew every step I took."

"I did. In the beginning, but lately . . . You've become difficult to track," he admitted. "Is Commander Iamaxis going to join us?"

"She's the reason I'm here. I think they came for her first, then she tried to rescue you. It failed, and she escaped in some sort of tiny ship. Ended up coming to me for help. By the way, you're welcome for the rescue," I said. "Most people say thank you when somebody risks their life for them. But hey—I suppose manners have never been your forte."

He sighed. "Apologies. I will thank you properly once we're safe," he responded.

"I was joking. Sort of. But let's get moving. Gala's waiting for us."

After that, we set off through the so-called system station I'd always referred to as the Bazaar. For me—and all the other residents of Earth—it was a special and miraculous thing. However, for everyone else in the universe, it was nothing unique. I had to keep reminding myself that my little corner of the frontier was a backwater, and Earth was so far behind that we weren't even in the race.

Not in any way that mattered.

That meant I couldn't afford to hold back. Instead, I needed to seize on any advantage I could find, the realization of which solidified the plan that had been brewing in the back of my mind since I'd first arrived in the Bazaar. It was crossing all sorts of lines, but I was no longer holding back.

I let out a slight chuckle at that, which brought a curious glance from Alistaris. I said, "Sorry. I just had a silly thought."

The reality was that I'd stopped holding back a long time ago. Yet, there was a difference between not restraining myself and actively seeking to do as much damage as possible, regardless of the consequences. The system was so stacked against Earth that I was only a hair's breadth from throwing all morality aside and embracing the burn-it-all-down mentality. After all, if society had no intention of stopping a technologically superior group from coming in and literally destroying my planet, then I reasoned that I owed nothing to that society.

Aside from my ire, of course.

Regardless, I was rapidly approaching the point where I had nothing to lose. So, the idea that I would hold back anything was kind of laughable, especially considering that I'd already killed millions of people.

What were a few million more, right?

In any event, Alistaris and I got plenty of odd looks on our way through the Bazaar's corridors. Once or twice, people looked like they were going to try to stop us and demand to know what was going on. In those situations, all it took was a glare from me to bring them up short. If they'd come any closer, I would have ripped the Mist from their bodies, and without significant hesitation.

Perhaps that said something about my current mentality. Or how addictive power could become.

Not that I was eager to learn any lessons, of course.

Eventually, we found our way to the massive chamber that held Gala's shop, and to my surprise, there was no one there. Certainly, the stacked cubicle-like shops were probably occupied, but I'd half expected to find a squad of Gomari warriors as well as a few enemy mystics barring our way. There was no one, though, which put my hackles up.

"It's quiet," I said. "A little too quiet."

"What?"

I sighed. "Nothing," I said. Then, I added in a mutter, "Patrick would have gotten it."

It was only a few more minutes until we found our way to Gala's shop, and when we arrived, I saw that there were quite a few scorch marks on her door.

In fact, her cubicle looked like someone had beaten it with a large hammer, though the door slid open the moment we came in range.

Gala poked her massive head out and said, "You weren't followed, were you?"

I'd been keeping my senses—the normal ones as well as the one associated with my class—so I would have detected if anyone had been trailing us. So, I said, "No. Not sure how long that's going to last, though. I left a mess back there."

"Better come in, then. I've got some medical supplies for your friend," she said.

I let Alistaris go first, then I followed. As I did, I asked, "How is Patrick?"

"Fine," came his voice. "A little embarrassed is all."

I saw him sitting on top of the counter, his back to the wall. He looked fine, but I knew that having his Mist disrupted like that had to have been both disconcerting and painful. On top of that, it tended to make people feel extremely vulnerable. Patrick showed no signs of that, but then again, he probably would have kept that kind of thing to himself around Gala and Alistaris.

Regardless, when the door slid shut, Gala unceremoniously picked Alistaris up and set him on the counter. He objected weakly, but she ignored him. Instead, she immediately started to treat his wounds via a series of injections. I couldn't help but notice the Mist swirling as she worked, suggesting that a skill was in play.

Once she'd finished, Gala said, "That's the best I can do. It'll take time or someone more skilled than me to do any more."

"Thank you," said Alistaris. "Do you by chance have any other clothes? I fear this . . . shirt looks ridiculous on me."

"I think it suits you," I remarked.

He ignored it. Gala said, "I think I've got some clothes that autosize. Come with me."

After that, the Dengyt hopped down from the counter and followed Gala through a door that had just appeared. At one point, I'd seen that same spot turn into a closet containing a multitude of weapons, so I knew there were shenanigans about. More importantly, I could see the subtle flow of Mist that suggested that the entire cubicle was far more than it seemed.

"I think this whole place is some sort of spatial anomaly. Bigger on the inside than it looks from the outside, I mean," I said.

"Probably," Patrick agreed. "It's not uncommon technology in the wider universe. I've seen it mentioned quite a few times during my research, but it requires a bunch of materials that aren't available on Earth. Although, the theory isn't that dissimilar from your Cutter."

"Or your armor."

"That's tied to my skill. Completely different thing."

"Oh," I said. Then, I asked, "How are you?"

He ran his hand through his hair and, with a sigh, answered, "Embarrassed, like I said. I feel like I should have done more. After all the work I've put in . . . I don't know. It's just disappointing."

"Have you gotten any further studying the Adjudicator armor?" I asked, knowing that he'd begun to investigate methods of incorporating the norcite-based material into his own mech suit.

He shook his head. "Getting that to play with my abilities is like trying to light water on fire," he said. "It just feels like I'm missing something important."

"You'll figure it out. In the meantime, I got a present for you," I said. Then, I retrieved an item I'd picked up after the battle. I tossed it to Patrick, and he caught it. "I thought you might want to study to see how that sort of thing works."

"Is this . . ."

"One of the grenades they used to disrupt the Mist. Yeah," I answered. "Maybe it can give you some insight into how to block it next time."

The item in question didn't look like one of my grenades. Instead, it was a ten-inch-long cylinder with tiny spikes jutting out all over. Inert, it didn't seem all that dangerous, but I remembered well how it had disrupted the Mist, rendering Patrick and Gala insensate. For my part, I'd quickly overcome it, but it wasn't difficult to imagine a situation where someone used something like that to better effect. So, I'd taken an extra couple of minutes to search one out so that Patrick could hopefully figure out how it worked.

From there, it wouldn't be long before he could counter it.

Before either of us could continue the conversation, the thunderous sound of gunshots filled the air. I could tell they were coming from outside, but to my surprise, my {Mist Warden} senses couldn't penetrate the cubicle's walls. As I sprang to my feet, drawing the Stinger from my arsenal implant, Patrick slipped off the counter and pulled his pistol from the holster at his waist. Then, his cybernetic arm opened, revealing a cannon I'd never seen before. But there was something about it that seemed familiar.

"Is that what's left of my old scattergun?"

He nodded. "Sort of. I used it as a base design. New, enhanced, and improved. No more pretending to be nonlethal for this bad boy," he said, looking at the thing appreciatively. "Mist-infused electronet of pure destruction."

"You just made all those words up."

He shrugged and grinned in my direction. Just then, Gala and Alistaris returned, but both had clearly found some equipment. For his part, the Dengyt wore an infiltration suit not unlike mine, though his featured a host of holsters filled with various weapons that seemed to fit his size. In his hands was my R-14.

Gala, though, wore a full suit of real armor that, in a way, reminded me of the black gear of the Adjudicators. However, it differed in a couple of key ways, the most notable of which was the color. It was bloodred with gold accents. Second, it was absolutely flooded with Mist.

For her weapon, she didn't bother with a firearm—aside from Ferdinand at her waist. Instead, she'd armed herself with a giant sword with a blade wider than my shoulders. It reminded me of the weapon wielded by the red-suited android I'd fought back in Olympus, and whose name I couldn't be bothered to remember.

"What's going on?" I asked.

"Defenses activated," she said. "I knew they wouldn't stand for this."

"It was a trap," Alistaris said. "They expected her to come. Now, they'll throw everything they have at us."

"How many?" I asked, my words punctuated by the muffled gunfire of Gala's defense system.

"At least a hundred. More than one mystic, I'm certain," he answered. "If I'd have known they had this kind of presence . . ."

"The Gomaris are like avastian burrow roaches," Gala said. "There's always more of them than you think."

"What's an avastian burrow roach?"

"Context," Alistaris said.

"No, I get they're probably some sort of pest. It's just a very evocative name, and I think a little curiosity is perfectly—"

"Mira," Patrick cut me off. "Not now. This is serious."

I sighed and rolled my eyes. "Yeah. Fine. Putting on my serious face."

I scrunched up my face, which brought a bit of a snicker from him.

Gala sighed and said, "Children."

"This is what I have been dealing with all this time," Alistaris said.

"You have my sympathies."

"Hey, we're not that bad!" I insisted.

Gala just shook her head. "In any case, they think they have us pinned. Mira, you're our flanker. Patrick, I need you in your suit. Commander, you will circle around behind and assassinate any officers."

"Uh, how are we getting out?" I asked. "Only one exit, as far as I can see."

She fixed me with an unreadable glare, then gestured at the back wall. Suddenly, it slid open to reveal a pair of doors. "That leads out back."

"Oh. Secret door. Nice."

"Please take this seriously."

"I am. Totally," I said, using Vanish. It was unnecessary, but I liked the effect. The moment I'd disappeared from sight, I used Stealth. Then, without skipping a beat, I reached out with Mist Authority and commanded the door to open. It did, and I slipped outside. I heard Gala say something back inside the cubicle, but I ignored it. Instead, I focused every thread of my mind on the coming battle.

Vaguely, I was aware of Alistaris exiting behind me, but he went in the opposite direction. For my part, I slid along the back side of the cubicle wall, holding my Stinger. As I did, I kept my overall plan in mind; it wasn't time to put it into motion, but that wasn't the point. It required quite a bit of preparation if I was going to pull it off.

So, I moved a bit more slowly than was absolutely necessary, but eventually, I reached the end of the cubicle wall. When I did, I circled it and took a look at the force arrayed against us.

There were more than two hundred Adjudicators, each one in gleaming black armor. In addition, I saw dozens of mundane soldiers as well as a multitude of mechs and drones. It was an army, and not a weak one, either. It made the forces I'd fought back on Earth look like ragtag militias.

In the back, I sensed a pair of tightly controlled auras, and it didn't take long after that for me to lock in on their owners. One was a tall and slim alien with four arms, while the other was a short, green goblinoid creature that was so wrinkled that I suspected they were absolutely ancient. The tall one was obviously much weaker than the goblin, but neither were nearly as powerless as the one I'd dispatched so easily back in the compound where Alistaris had been held captive.

"I'm going to take care of the mystics," I said through Secure Connection. "It's not—"

The goblinoid whipped his head in my direction, and a moment later, I saw a giant hand of concentrated Mist racing toward me. I hammered Mist Authority against it, scattering the would-be attack.

But another came directly after that, slamming into me and knocking me across the huge chamber. I didn't stop until I hit a line of cubicles, denting the exterior upon impact. It hurt, but I didn't take any serious injuries. However, there was already another attack coming my way. My mind going a thousand miles an hour, I used Teleport to avoid it, then reached out with Mist Authority to take control of one of the bots.

The latest version of my *Rage* Ghost took hold in an instant, and it immediately spun around, burying its allies under a barrage of bullets. They didn't do much damage—the enemy was entrenched behind a series of Mist shields—but that was never the point. Instead, I'd only intended for the thing to cause a distraction, which it did remarkably well.

I took aim and fired upon the mass of soldiers, and my rounds were certainly not as inconsequential as the bot's. They tore through the warriors with undeniable fervor, while another thread of thought sent a different tendril of Mist Authority to hammer into the goblinoid mystic.

He easily slapped it aside.

But by that point, yet another thread slammed into his partner, who wasn't nearly as quick on the draw. In an instant, I'd infiltrated their system-like core and torn it to pieces. They dropped without ever having affected the battle.

Meanwhile, Patrick and Gala came thundering out of her cubicle. He wore his mech suit, with his sword extending from his arm and the shield held out before him. Gala didn't bother with any of that, instead leaping into battle like a berserker. Her giant sword swept out, cleaving four soldiers in half with a single attack. Their fellows attempted a counterattack, but their shots clanged off her armor ineffectively. And then, she was among them.

Not to be outdone, Patrick stomped into battle right behind her. Even as I parried another giant hand of Mist, I saw Patrick slam his shield of blue Mist into an Adjudicator, sending them sprawling backward. Then, he brought his sword down in a vicious overhand attack. Like Gala's, his armor was impenetrable to the small arms fire. However, neither of them was impervious to the likes of the Adjudicators.

Still, they held their own, which allowed me to focus on the fight at hand.

It was not going well.

Even as I fired upon the goblinoid mystic, I used multiple threads of thought to slam into him with Mist Authority. But without even moving, he blocked each one, even going so far as to send multiple attacks my way.

I held my ground for a few more seconds, but it quickly became increasingly clear that I was entirely outmatched. I brought the full weight of my [Multimind] to bear on the fight, but I made no headway. In fact, his attacks were getting closer and closer by the second. I needed to do something.

Anything.

Just when I was getting ready to take drastic measures, one of the Adjudicators barreled into me. I recovered quickly, hammering the Hand of God into their throat, but that small distraction proved to be my undoing.

The goblin mystic's own expression of Mist slammed into me, wrapping around me like a constrictor snake. But it didn't just exert physical pressure. Instead, it was mental, as well. And finally, it felt like it was squeezing the Mist right out of my body.

At last, the goblinoid moved. Just a single step, and then a cocky smirk. Even from fifty feet away, I could feel the arrogance radiating from him.

And then, a deep gong-like sound swept through the area, and the goblinoid exploded. The stranglehold of Mist faded, and I fell to the floor, gasping for air. When I looked up, I saw Alistaris standing where the mystic had been. He had a long, wicked knife in his hand, and he was absolutely covered in green flesh, blood, and a few other unidentifiable bits.

I gave him a nod.

He returned it with one of his own.

Then, we both turned our attention back to the battle at hand.

CHAPTER FORTY-TWO

BEHIND THE CURTAIN

Mystics can die just like anyone else. You just have to know how to get to them.

—Alistaris Kargat

I tossed a handful of grenades, one after the other, into the amassed army of Adjudicators and other combatants. A second later, they exploded, sending huge clumps of the enemy flying into the air. Few died, but that wasn't the point. My intention was to disrupt, and in that arena, the grenades were very effective.

As the explosions erupted all around, Alistaris once again disappeared, though now that I knew what to look for, I could just barely sense his presence. But with the two mystics dead, no one else on the field could. So, he was free to wreak as much havoc as he wanted to. That took the form of Adjudicators simply exploding from the same attack he'd used on the goblinoid mystic.

Vaguely, I could tell that the ability functioned off of an injection of Mist, but beyond that, it was a mystery. However, it did support one thought—I was extremely glad he was on my side. I wasn't sure if I could have survived such an attack—after all, I was far more durable than a typical mystic, from what I'd seen—but I didn't want to find out. At best, I'd walk away injured, and at worst, I would explode like everyone else did.

As I sprinted sideways, bathing the army in gunfire, I reached out with Mist Authority, latching on to anyone who wasn't protected by Adjudicator armor. Because of [Multimind], I could take out three or four at a time, but there were enough that that was only good as a supplementary attack. Moreover, even the nonarmored soldiers were a step above any I'd seen on Earth, so they were more than capable of injuring me.

Because of that, I couldn't stand still for more than a second. Still, I managed to down quite a few of them during that opening salvo.

The real star was Gala, though. Now that she was armed and armored appropriately, she was a terror who cleaved our enemies with frightening ease. I'd always known she was powerful. Jeremiah had suggested enough on more than one occasion, and finding out that she was an Erdikar Dreadnought had seemed to support that notion. I only had secondhand information as to what any of that meant, but now that I was getting an up-close-and-personal look, I understood precisely why everyone spoke of that group with such fear and reverence.

Finally, Patrick held up his end of the fight, as well. He didn't leap into battle like Gala. Instead, he favored a more conservative and measured approach. Yet, he was nearly as effective in his chosen style, and the alien threat fell before him. I did recognize that his armor didn't hold up quite like Gala's, though; however, he used his shield to great effect, blocking the worst of the damage before it even got to him.

At the same time, he attacked with the rebuilt scattergun or his sword, depending on the situation. For the former, the result was a web of arcing lightning that tore through the mundane soldiers with ease. The Adjudicators were less affected due to their norcite armor, but for them, he had his sword. I was proud to see that he held his own.

I had my own issues to worry about, though.

So, as seemed to be my response to most of my problems, I chose to solve them by pulling out a bigger gun. In this case, I exchanged the Stinger for the HIRC and let loose. Gala and Patrick had killed a few of the enemy, but I mowed them down with ruthless efficiency. Even the Adjudicators couldn't stand up to such a barrage, and though they survived, the sheer momentum of the HIRC's issue was enough to send them sprawling to the ground. That, in turn, gave my allies the openings they needed to finish them off.

I was just busy patting myself on the back when I felt something stir in the Mist around me. On instinct, I used Teleport, disappearing and reappearing thirty feet away just as a trio of black-clad Adjudicators flashed into sight and attacked the spot I'd recently vacated. Clearly, they hadn't expected me to suddenly disappear, so they were caught briefly off guard. I answered that by swinging the HIRC around and burying them under a bombardment of powerful gunfire.

Yet, when the weapon ran dry of ammunition, they were still alive. In fact, I could see that the powerful weapon hadn't even scuffed their armor. Sure, it had sent them to the ground, but that was it.

I needed more power.

So, I pulled the Emperor from my arsenal implant and was about to bring it to bear when all three disappeared once again. Only a second later, I felt another shift in the ambient Mist, which allowed me to dodge just in time. However, another attack came only a second later, slicing into my back. It was only a flesh wound, but I was more concerned about what it represented.

These newcomers could attack with almost no warning, which meant that if I wanted to beat them, I needed to sink deeper into my {Mist Warden} senses. Those were capable of detecting the assassins, if only barely. So, without any other options, I did just that, even going so far as to close my eyes.

As I did so, I dismissed the Emperor, exchanging it for the interdiction blade. Then, when I felt a stirring of the Mist, I reacted. The clang of metal against metal echoed above the other sounds of battle, but I didn't hear it. Instead, I was already moving to intercept the next attack. Then, another after that.

I moved faster than I ever had before, the blade becoming an extension of my body. I shut off Observation so I could focus entirely on the shifting of the Mist. And when I did, I felt everything so clearly. The subtle currents of nanites in the air. The swirl before my enemies used an ability. The surge when they activated it.

And the whispers.

This time, it wasn't just a wind. Instead, the words were crisp and clear, though I still couldn't understand them. It was another language, but it was also much more than that. It was like the whispers were on an entirely different wavelength that I had yet to truly perceive. It was maddening, and I wanted nothing more than to delve even deeper than ever before. Yet, I couldn't spare the time nor effort to do so. Because even as I struggled to interpret those whispers, my blade was moving at previously unattainable speeds, intercepting the assassins' attacks almost as soon as they manifested.

And then, I went on the attack.

A block became a Riposte, and a head flew free from a neck. Then, another. And another after that.

But I wasn't content with killing the assassins. I wanted more. I needed to sink deeper into that odd, nearly meditative state. So, I flickered forward, using Teleport without even trying, and when I reappeared, I was already attacking. I didn't stop there, either. Every second brought another Teleport, and each instance of the ability came with another severed head.

I felt more in tune with the Mist than I ever had before, but it still wasn't enough. I craved more. I needed to hear the whispers more clearly. So, with my eyes still shut, I continued as I had. In any other situation, I would have run out of energy after the third or fourth usage of Teleport. However, I had sunk so deeply into the Mist that I freely took from the atmosphere what I needed, and I never even had to touch my own reserves.

Or perhaps there was no difference between one and the other. With every passing second, the delineation between me and the Mist became blurrier. And with that, I became stronger, funneling that Mist into various abilities and into my attributes so I grew exponentially faster and stronger. For the briefest of instances, I felt like I could understand the whispers. They weren't words. More like feelings. But it went deeper than that, too. It was as if those whispers represented the ideals that reality only barely glimpsed.

I didn't stop until they were all dead, and even then, it took Patrick shouting my name through Secure Connection to pull me out of that miasma of Mist. When it finally happened, I stumbled to the floor and skidded across the ground until I hit a pile of dead and dismembered bodies.

I tried to stand, but my legs wouldn't support me. I felt drunk and exhausted, elated and like I'd lost something incredibly precious all at the same time, and for the first time in a long while, I was entirely incapable of making sense of the various feelings flitting through my mind. I said something, though it came out in a slurred, incomprehensible mess.

That was nothing compared to what was going on in my head. I felt grounded, yet ephemeral, but neither of those descriptors were adequate. More than anything, though, it was like I was being ripped in two different directions. One side was anchored to how I perceived reality, but the other was desperate to explore something else. Something I was not equipped to understand or describe.

Or survive.

I knew it. But that knowledge did nothing to dissuade me. Instead, I yearned for the release it represented. The only reason I didn't go was because I literally couldn't. Otherwise, I would have thrown everything away.

Slowly, the feeling faded until, at last, my eyes fluttered open. When they did, I saw nothing but a plasti-steel ceiling flowing past. For a moment, I was confused until I recognized that I was bouncing up and down on someone's massive shoulder. That was when I realized that Gala was carrying me as she sprinted down the corridor. My head flopped to the side, and I saw Patrick running beside her in his armor.

Alistaris was nowhere to be seen, but that wasn't surprising, considering that I couldn't even move. He was probably just on the other side. Or perhaps he'd run ahead. Whatever the case, I didn't think he'd been left behind.

Gradually, feeling came back. As it did, I thought to check my condition on my HUD, but to my shock, no menu presented itself.

"What?" I croaked.

"Shh. Be still," Gala huffed. "We're almost there."

I barely heard her because of the panic rushing through my mind. I tried to access my interface, but I found no response. That, coupled with a rapidly intensifying pain at the base of my skull, suggested the worst. But I could still feel my abilities. The same with my skills. Aside from my terrible condition, I didn't feel any weaker. And I knew I would recognize it if I did because I routinely used suppression manacles and collars during training. Those took me down to human baseline, and even with half my body still limp, I knew I was a long way from that.

In fact, I almost felt stronger, and with every passing second, my {Mist Warden} senses grew sharper. I couldn't just see the Mist. I could feel it, right down to the tiniest nanite. And with a flick of my mind, I felt that I could control it, too.

I didn't get a chance to further investigate before Gala thundered to a stop, and I saw *The Leviathan* looming over us. Patrick shouted, "Were we followed?"

"There was no one left to follow," Alistaris said. I'd regained enough motor function that I could turn my head, and I saw him suddenly appear behind us. "She killed them all. Even the ones who were trying to surrender."

"I didn't . . ."

The words didn't come out any more intelligibly than my last attempt to talk, which was far more frustrating than I would have expected. In any case, I think I got my point across with a vicious glare aimed in the Dengyt's direction. Or that was how I imagined it; in reality, I might've blinked a couple of times.

Regardless, we quickly boarded *The Leviathan*, and Gala laid me down on my bed. "What happened?" I finally managed to say. My words were still slurred, but they were clear enough that Gala could understand.

"Something I never thought I would see with my own two yes," she said as I felt the ship lift off. "What was it like? How did it feel?"

"I don't . . . Explain . . ."

"Right. Frontier. You reached the peak, Mira."

"What . . . mean?"

"It means that you can now control the Mist directly, like a mystic," she said. "I've only met two other people who've done what you just did, and they didn't manage it until they were centuries old."

"I can't feel . . . interface."

"Of course not. You don't have a Nexus Implant anymore."

My heart beat a lot faster after that. "W-what?"

"You absorbed it. It's a pseudocore now. Look—you've seen what passes for an interface with mystics, right? It's a collection of Mist just below their chest."

I nodded.

"Good. That's called a core. It takes them years to form one, but when they do, it functions a lot like a Nexus Implant," she said. "You won't have an interface, so no statuses flashing before your eyes anymore. But you will get a sense of things. You're also stronger now."

"H-how?"

"The nanites," she said. "Not the ones you use for your skills. Those get cycled fairly regularly. The ones in your body are different. They stay with you, growing more efficient. That's part of how the training works. Potential refers to the number of nanites in your body. I don't remember the formula, but it boils down to the higher your number, the more you have. Training teaches them how to work more efficiently. That's why you get stronger."

"But . . . How . . . Stronger?"

"They're no longer constrained by the Nexus Implant," Gala explained. "They can function at maximum capacity. But even more importantly, that core of yours is bound to be special. I'd be surprised if you're not the strongest person in this entire sector now."

"Don't feel so strong . . ."

"You will. In the meantime, just rest. We'll talk more later."

With that, she turned to leave. By that point, the ship was already in the air and, presumably, descending into the atmosphere. Which meant it was the perfect time to enact my plan.

"Gala. How far away from the Bazaar are we?"

"We're a few hundred miles now. Patrick is circling so we use less fuel on the descent. Why?"

I didn't answer the question, instead asking another one of my own. "Do you have any friends left in the station?"

"No. Almost everyone left when the Gomaris showed up. It's best to assume that anybody left in that system station is an enemy. Or enemy adjacent, at least," she answered. Then, her eyes narrowed. "Why are you asking these questions?"

"So, there's nobody on board that station that you want to live?"

"Mira . . ."

I pushed myself upright. It was far more difficult than I expected. Then, I forced my way into my arsenal implant. Without the interface, it was like groping around in the dark. However, I'd done it often enough that I easily managed it. Then, I found the device I'd left inside and pulled it out.

"Is that what I think it is?"

"If you think it's a detonator, then yes. Yes, it is. So, I'm not going to get in trouble for this, am I? Like, no weird penalties from the system, right?"

She shook her head. "No. This close to the Integration, the rules get a little fuzzy," she said. Indeed, we were only a few days away from quarantine being lifted, which meant that we were on the verge of joining the rest of the universe without restrictions or protections. "Are you sure you want to do this? There are a lot of people on board."

"Enemies."

"Enemy adjacent."

"Same difference," I said. Then, without further discussion, I pressed the button. I felt the Mist agitate, then watched a tiny thread race across the bedroom and through the wall. That was the signal I'd sent to the hundreds of bombs I'd left throughout the station. Unless something went incredibly wrong, that meant that it should be exploding in . . .

"Mira!" Patrick shouted.

"Guess it worked, huh?" I asked. "Tell Patrick it was all part of the plan, will you? He needs to focus on landing the ship. And I need my rest, right?"

"Right," Gala answered, shaking her great bovine head. "You really don't hold back, do you?"

"Not much point in that anymore. It's kill or be killed, isn't it? I intend to do the former."

"You would have made a passable Dreadnought," she stated.

"I have no context for what that means, but thanks," I said. "Assuming it's a compliment."

"Coming from me? Yes. From others, probably not. Anyway, rest. The real test is coming."

A PATTERN OF BEHAVIOR

Contrary to popular belief, the system was not built to encourage violence. It is molded by our nature, and as such, it has become a tool of death, oppression, and destruction.

—Galatira Iamaxis

I can't believe you did that," said Patrick, looking up at the sky. "There have to be some sort of repercussions for it, right? It's part of the system."

I didn't bother following his gaze. There was nothing to see up there, after all. I'd seen to that myself when I'd planted more than a hundred bombs throughout the Bazaar and detonated them during our escape. I had no idea how many people I had killed, and if I was entirely honest, I wasn't truly concerned with that, either. Still, I didn't like not being rewarded with at least a couple of levels.

According to Gala, my potential had still grown, but because my Nexus Implant had been absorbed into a pseudocore, I no longer had an interface. I had to monitor things by feel, which meant that I was a bit lost. Certainly, since we'd gotten back, I had regained feeling throughout my body, and the few tests I'd run told me that I was roughly half again stronger than I'd been before going to the Bazaar, but I still wasn't entirely certain what it all meant.

Hopefully, Freddie could advise me.

I'd gotten in contact with him upon landing, and he'd told me that he was on his way. Yet, I had no idea how quickly he could cover ground, so I wasn't sure when he would make good on his promise to discuss the changes I'd undergone.

Gala was some help, but beyond our initial conversation, she'd had frustratingly little to offer. So, even as we marched ever closer to the end of the quarantine—it would fall in less than two more days—I felt like I was stuck in limbo.

Fortunately, I still had access to my abilities, though some of the lesser-used ones were a little clunky to activate. The ones I relied most on, though, were just as smooth as ever. I reasoned that was due to simple habit. I'd gone through those motions so often that my body and mind remembered them like instincts.

But I felt sure that those were limiting my potential somehow. As Gala had told me, the Nexus Implant was meant to constrain the usage of Mist. Because of that, I was almost positive that I was hamstringing my own abilities. Sure, Empowered Shot said it could only increase my damage by a couple hundred percent, but who was to say that was a hard limit? I felt like if I focused hard enough—or knew how—I could augment that damage even more.

The same went for all my other abilities. Modifiers, too.

The loss of my Nexus Implant had been jarring, but I was almost certain that it would be a good thing. With it, I had the benefit of exact numbers telling me my limits. But without it? There didn't appear to be any.

I was probably wrong. Something constrained the power of the mystics I'd fought. I just didn't know what, precisely, that was. Hopefully, Freddie could shed some light on the subject. But in the meantime, I needed to come to terms with my new parameters.

"I don't think it matters that much," I said. "It's not really part of the system. I mean, it's connected, but there's no rule saying you can't blow it up. It's just that most people wouldn't dream of doing that because then they'd be cut off from a lot of things that make people's lives easier. I mean, can you imagine if people had to survive without Mist shields? They'd have died out a couple of years after the Mist enveloped Earth."

"That's still mostly true," he remarked.

"People are better equipped to fend for themselves now. Plus, we're at war. Things were always going to go this way," I said.

"I still can't believe you went through with it," he mumbled.

I could understand that sentiment, but from my perspective, it would have been stupid not to. Clearly, the enemy had infiltrated the Bazaar to the point that it was functionally useless to us. More, it provided an easy platform from which they could persuade people to betray their kind. I had simply removed that from the equation.

Sure, it was a drastic step. I understood that. But our situation was desperate, and I had never been good at half measures, anyway. Even so, I could see why Patrick struggled with it. The Bazaar had always been there, to the point it was just one of those unassailable facts of life. Yet, the reality of it was that it was just one more mechanism by which the aliens controlled us. That he couldn't see that was disappointing, but it was anything but surprising. For better or worse, Patrick was stuck in a pattern of thinking that refused to adapt to the changing times. I couldn't afford to let myself do the same.

"What do you think is the next step?" he asked.

"I don't know," I said, leaning forward with my hands on my knees as I looked out at the horizon. Before me spread a sea of grass as far as I could see. Behind me, I could feel *The Leviathan* as well as the temporary base the Dengyts had erected. The moment we'd landed, Alistaris had gone to work reestablishing communications with his varied assets. The gnome had an admirable work ethic, and what's more, I'd gotten a glimpse of his power. To say I was impressed with the way he killed that mystic was an understatement.

But the same could be said for all my allies. Both Patrick and Gala had proved their worth in the brief battle. Without everyone's help, I likely wouldn't have survived. That was the benefit of friends, I supposed.

I leaned back in my chair and grabbed a drink from the nearby chest, and as I opened it, I let out a sigh. I knew everything was about to change. There was no stopping it. We had done what we could to avoid Earth's destruction, but there was still a possibility that we'd missed something vital. On top of that, the blockade was still in play. That meant that, while we'd avoided the short-term devastation of the planet, the threat was still just as pervasive as it had ever been.

"I think the first step is going to be to get into those satellites," I said. The problem was that they were well protected, and even if we managed to take out one or two, the system wouldn't fall until every single one of them had been destroyed. The reality was that we had a long way to go before we could say that Earth was safe.

And even if we did manage to break the blockade, there remained the persistent threat that they would just come back and do it again. Alistaris kept saying that we'd eventually push it past the threshold where cost would exceed benefit, but I wasn't so sure. From my perspective, it had probably already gone well past that point. Now, it felt like a personal vendetta on the part of the Gomari Confederation.

After a few minutes, Alistaris approached. When he arrived, though, he didn't say anything. Instead, he just stood there for a few minutes that felt like much longer. Finally, he said, "This certainly is a beautiful planet."

I glanced back at him and said, "I'm sure your planet was beautiful, too."

"We like to think so. But where I was born, the entire planet had long since been settled," he explained. "The only danger came from what we volunteered for. Or from one another, though that was kept mostly in check."

"Sounds nice," Patrick remarked.

"It does, doesn't it? But it was a soulless place of towering palaces and decrepit slums," he described. "Equality had long since been abandoned, and the rich believed themselves to be fundamentally better than everyone else. I know this because that was how I was raised. For a long time, I believed that those on the bottom echelons of society deserved their miserable lives."

He sighed, looking away. "We could have fixed it. The inequality was self-imposed. We liked it that way. The stratification of our society by power and wealth was a part of the design. It made those people desperate, but with how strong we were, they couldn't do anything but try to climb their way out of the muck. To their credit, some made it. A few were strong enough and lucky enough to survive to the summit. Yet, millions more failed. They spent their lives toiling at our behest, doing jobs that no one in their right mind would choose. And I just watched it from on high, judging them for their inability to win a broken game."

"What changed?" I asked, assuming that something had to have altered his perception of the world in which he'd lived. After all, he'd since dedicated his life to helping the populations of frontier planets like Earth. That didn't sound like something a spoiled rich scion of a powerful family would do.

"Everything. I met a girl," he admitted with a wisp of a smile. "She wasn't rich. Nor was she powerful. But she was good, and in a way I'd never seen before. All she wanted to do was help people."

He sighed, running a hand through his wild white hair. "They killed her," he stated. "My own family had her taken from her clinic. She was tried and convicted of treason before I even knew she'd been arrested. They sent her to a penal colony, where she spent the next two weeks mining norcite on an asteroid at the edge of our territory."

I could see the tears glistening in his eyes and hear the frustration in his voice as he said, "That's how long she lasted. Two weeks before she gave out. Most last a little longer. That's what mining norcite does to people. There are suits that prevent the effects, that shield people from having their Mist depowered. But they're expensive, and we always had plenty of prisoners to choose from."

"What did you do when you found out?" asked Patrick.

Alistaris shrugged. "What could I do? Even in my grief, I saw the rotten society for what it was. I knew I couldn't change anything," he answered with more than a little bitterness. "So, I did what I thought Beka would have done in my situation. I left home, enlisted with the Ark Alliance, and dedicated my life to helping people who couldn't help themselves.

"I'm a laughingstock, you know," he went on after a second. "My parents have all but disowned me. My old friends—people I've known for most of my life—won't even speak to me anymore. I'm a pariah. The Dengyt who threw everything away to roll in the mud with his inferiors. That's why I helped the princess in the first place. Stupid. They didn't even acknowledge my efforts. But I'm grateful because it brought you to my attention."

"I thought you had been watching me all along," I said.

"That's true. But knowing who you were and what you represented was one thing. Seeing what you could do was something else altogether," he stated. "In any case, I came out here to express my gratitude for what you did. You risked everything to save me, and that's not something I will soon forget."

I turned to him and grinned broadly. "Aww, Al. You're making me blush."

"Please don't call me that," he said, but I could tell his heart wasn't really in the objection. I suspected that, deep down, he liked the nickname I had given him. After all, it had come from me. That probably counted for a lot.

"Sure thing, Al."

He sighed. "Leave it to you to ruin a poignant moment," he said, shaking his head. But I saw a slight smirk turn up the corners of his mouth, so I counted it as a win. "Regardless, we need to talk about what comes next."

"Patrick and I were just discussing that."

"And?"

"We're kind of lost," Patrick stated. "Mira thinks we need to hit the satellites, but I don't know how we're supposed to do that."

"I have some ideas," Alistaris said. "But none of them will work right now."

"Why not?" I asked.

"They'll be ready for whatever we do," he answered. "I think it's best to lie low. Only respond to threats to the planet's safety. Once they let their guard down, we hit hard and fast."

"What then?" asked Patrick.

"What do you mean?"

"I mean, after we destroy the satellites and take down the blockade," Patrick elaborated. "What's to stop them from just doing it again? Or invading with ground troops? I'm not saying we shouldn't do it. I'm just asking what we're supposed to do with the ongoing threat because I'm not sure they're going to just leave us alone now."

"It's a good question," I agreed. "Is this resistance ongoing? What's our win condition?"

"Living another day."

"What?"

"That's what we have to focus on," Alistaris stated. "We keep resisting. We keep costing them resources and credits. And eventually, they'll give up. They'll move on to easier targets. We do that on enough frontier planets, and we can slowly chip away at their influence until they have to cede ground. Make no mistake, this isn't the sort of war that can be won by a single decisive strike. It's a battle of attrition. A fight to see who can keep going. This is about endurance."

"And you and yours are in it for the long haul?"

"Long enough," he said. "They made a mistake when they tried to kidnap me. Now, I've got every reason to make this as difficult as it can be for them."

After that, we all went silent, and as I stared out at the swaying grass, I wondered if Alistaris was really seeing the bigger picture. To me, it felt like we were missing something vitally important.

I just wasn't smart enough to see it.

Eventually, Alistaris headed back to the compound. Patrick wasn't far behind, though he ended up in *The Leviathan*. For my part, I remained in place, pondering the problem I couldn't see a way to solve.

Infinite Conquest was still up there, and it was probably the source of the soldiers we'd met so far. However, I didn't think a frontal assault on the ship would do much good. We didn't have enough people. Nor did we have enough ships. Challenging it was suicidal.

The satellites were far more vulnerable, and I expected that we could at least take out a few of them, but there were so many of them that I could see why Alistaris didn't consider attacking them to be a viable option.

As I sat there, I realized the irony of the fact that I was more powerful than ever, and my limits were even more ephemeral than I could understand. And yet, I was still too weak to do what needed to be done. I couldn't be everywhere at once, and even if I could, I was incapable of fighting everything arrayed against us. The reality was that I needed allies, and those were in short supply.

And that should not have been the case. We had an entire planet of people with a vested interest in keeping it from being destroyed. However, human nature meant that even if we could get in contact with everyone, the chances that they'd consent to work together were nil. It was a depressing comment on our species that even when we were facing a disaster of global proportions, the chances that we could meet the challenge with a unified front were so small that it wasn't even worth trying.

With that on my mind, the idea of leaving was even more attractive than it had ever been before. I could understand why Alistaris wanted to leave. He was as committed to the cause as anyone could be, but he could also see the writing on the wall. He knew what was coming, and the moment he'd chosen to stay, he'd almost assuredly made peace with the fact that he'd chosen to go down with the proverbial ship.

Was I doing the same?

No. I wanted to believe we had a chance.

I wasn't sure which was worse: the Dengyt who knew it was hopeless but chose to stay anyway or the girl who thought she had a chance in an unwinnable fight.

In the end, though, it didn't really matter. If things kept going the way they were, we'd all end up just as dead as everyone else.

It was a depressing thought, especially after we'd experienced nothing but victory in the war against the Gomaris. I knew it was because we were balanced on the edge of a knife. One slip, and we'd come crashing down to a reality that was hell-bent on keeping us oppressed and in line. It had almost happened in the system station when that goblinoid mystic had latched on to me. Then, it had nearly happened again when my body was driven out of commission by the absorption of my Nexus Implant.

The only reason I'd survived was due to my allies' quick intervention. But what would happen next time? What if they weren't there? I would die, and whatever resistance we'd managed so far would die with me.

It was a lot of pressure, and there was only one way I knew how to deal with that kind of situation. I needed to train. I needed to grow stronger and to get a handle on whatever new abilities I had at my disposal. Because I knew there was more power on the horizon. I just needed to forge ahead and grab it.

That seemed as good a strategy as any other.

THE DAWN OF A NEW AGE

The quarantine system was supposed to be foolproof. Or that was what history tells us. When it was implemented, it was intended to give frontier planets a chance to adjust to the Mist without undue interference. However, where there are rules and regulations, there are always those who will endeavor to bypass them. So, it was always inevitable that people would find a way around it. As a result, the fall of the quarantine rarely affects the fate of a world. Earth will almost assuredly be different.

—Alistaris Kargat

When the last day of quarantine dawned, I found myself lying abed and wishing for all the world that I didn't have to confront what was coming. I knew it was a silly thought that more befitted a child than a grown woman, but it was still a persistent one. So, I lay in bed, staring at the plasti-steel ceiling as I pondered the changes on the horizon.

I knew the cessation of the quarantine was a big deal, but for the most part, Earth had been open to the aliens for quite some time. Perhaps even from the very beginning. That wasn't how it was supposed to go, but the rules had never seemed to apply to them. The next phase was called the Integration, and it was intended to establish a planet as a part of the wider universe. Yet, I'd learned that most worlds never got past that point. Indeed, most were stripped bare of all resources or entirely destroyed.

Only a lucky few managed anything more.

But even that characterization presupposed that incorporation into the universe was a desirable thing. It wasn't. Not from my perspective, at least. Why would anyone want to join a bunch of worlds who thought it was justifiable to harvest a planet's resources, leaving absolutely nothing of value behind? They enslaved and oppressed, consuming everything they could see. As far as I was concerned, they could stay on their side of the universe, and Earth could occupy its tiny corner of reality.

That was not a viable option, though.

Because Earth had value. Perhaps not enough to garner the attention of the truly powerful. We were on the frontier, after all. But the level of attention we'd already received suggested that our planet would never be left alone. No—as long as we were weak, we'd be under constant assault. The only answer was to beat them back, making every step they took as costly as possible. Maybe that would dissuade them.

It was all about money, after all, and the moment the situation on Earth became too costly to turn a profit, it would be abandoned. And only then would humanity be free to make its own way.

That felt like a pipe dream to me, though. The Gomaris had already proved their commitment to taking the planet, and I suspected it would take more than a few minor setbacks to force them to rethink their position.

As I lay there, my mind spiraling into increasingly pessimistic scenarios, I kept coming back to the last ability I had unlocked. Planetary Defense sounded like it was precisely what we needed, though I'd never had the opportunity to truly explore its capabilities.

Now, with my Nexus Implant—and all my skills—having been absorbed, things were a little different. In some ways, I had more access than ever before. However, it felt like, in order to see the shapes of my skills and abilities, I had to squint and cross my metaphorical eyes. Still, with my training, especially with my old {Mistrunner} skills, I was well-versed in mental exercises.

So, with a flex of my mind, I managed to see the shape of my core. It was more diffuse than my Nexus Implant had been, and in fact, it reminded me of some of the more complex systems I'd bypassed during my adventures. Yet, it was different enough that it only took a single glance to recognize that it was a wholly unique thing.

To a degree, it resembled the cores I'd encountered in the mystics I'd defeated, though a little more structured—like someone had built a model meant to represent the cores I'd seen in the mystics.

Regardless, I pushed my awareness among the cloud of nanites, and after only a few minutes, I started to recognize the structures of my skills. The first I noticed was, predictably, [Mist-Infused Body], which was characterized by tendrils that extended past my pseudocore and into the rest of my body. I even found the cluster of nanites that governed the rapid-healing ability that had come with it.

Then, I saw [Warfare], which was easily the largest structure apparent. It was also tightly wound and extraordinarily dense, likely due to the fact that so much had been packed into it. The same could be said for [Espionage] and [Combat Maneuvers], though they both had a different feel to them. By comparison, the structures for [Navigation], [Shielding], and [Multimind] were anemic and tiny. Yet, I could feel the potential power in all three.

It took a little while—I barely paid attention to the passing time—but eventually, I started to identify the individual abilities. Some, like Planetary Defense, were obvious. Others were intertwined with different abilities, probably because they were related to one another, but eventually, I found them all.

And then there were the inert nanites that, for a little while, confused me until, at last, I realized that they were abilities I'd yet to unlock. For a while, I poked and prodded them, but to no effect until, at last, I just shoved my awareness into the cloud of inactive nanites. They lit up, weakly at first but growing stronger with every passing second. I leveraged my mind toward the task, and loose nanites swooped in, attaching to the inert ones. They fed off of one another until, at last, one of the abilities lit up with the same energy as all the rest.

I let out a breath I hadn't realized I'd been holding as a wave of exhaustion washed over me.

"Did I just unlock an ability?" I muttered to myself.

"What?" asked Patrick, sticking his head through the door.

"Were you just waiting out there?"

"No. I was walking by. Are you feeling better? I didn't want to push you . . ."

"I'm fine," I said, struggling to sit up. "But I think I just unlocked an ability. And not by training, either. It's . . . Mist Cloak, I think. It lets me surround myself with a dense layer of Mist that acts as a shield. Huh. So, it's kind of like [Shielding] but available in the other tree. Neat."

"I really don't know what you're saying," Patrick stated, stepping into the room and sitting on the edge of the bed. "Are you sure you're okay?"

"I'm fine. Tired, but fine."

Then, I went on to tell him exactly what I'd just discovered, which elicited the shock I would have expected. After all, in the space of a few hours, I'd just accomplished what would have otherwise taken months of training. Maybe more, considering that it had been the last ability available in that branch of the [Espionage] tree.

"What does this mean?" asked Patrick.

"I have no clue," I admitted. "But it feels like I just learned how to cheat or something. But it's so weird. I don't know how people dealt with training and growth before the Mist because not having a status to look at is extremely disconcerting, you know?"

"You can feel the difference, though, can't you?"

"Mostly. I think I picked up the modifiers in that branch, too."

"So, is that how you're supposed to advance now? You just think about it really hard?"

I fixed him with a level stare.

"What?" he asked innocently.

"It is way more than just thinking about it really hard."

"Oh, is it? That's what it sounded like when you described it . . ."

"It's like solving a puzzle while meditating on something entirely different," I said. "Without [Multimind], there's zero chance I could have done it. It would have taken years."

"You think that's what the mystics do, then?"

I shrugged. "No idea. Probably something similar. Freddie did talk about meditating a lot," I said. "Plus, you saw those Templar acolytes, right?"

"I think they were apprentices."

"Whatever. They were just meditating," I said. "That's probably what they were doing—trying to unlock abilities. Or something. I do know they can't absorb skill shards, though. So, I don't know how they do abilities."

"Maybe they have to build them," he suggested.

"Maybe."

The idea of building any of my skills myself seemed incredibly difficult, and the abilities wouldn't work without that framework. However, on second thought, I was dealing with extremely advanced skills. [Warfare] alone had incorporated five other skills during its two evolutions. Of course it would look like a complicated and beautiful mess of Mist structures. The same could be said for most of my other skills, and even the ones that were, for lack of a better term, first-generation skills were high-grade. So, it stood to reason that they would be complex. If someone were to start small, then with enough time and effort, they could build their own abilities.

After all, that's what Ana did.

A pang of regret wafted through my mind. The skillsmith had fled the Bazaar well before Alistaris had been taken, so I knew she was still alive. However, I expected that I'd never see her again. After all, there was little reason for her to come to Earth when, by all accounts, the Gomaris planned to completely destroy it.

Whatever the case, I couldn't help but wonder if my suppositions concerning mystic skill construction were accurate. Fortunately, I didn't have to worry about that kind of thing because I already had the maximum . . .

"Wait . . ."

"What?" asked Patrick.

"A person's Nexus Implant is the limiting factor to how many skills they can have, right?" I asked.

"Yeah. Obviously. Why?"

"I don't have a Nexus Implant anymore, Pick."

"I know," he said, furrowing his brows. "We talked about this before. Are you having memory issues? Gala said you might—"

I threw a pillow at him. "Idiot. I don't have an implant anymore. That means that, theoretically, there's no limit to the number of skills I can have," I explained. "I mean, I'd have to build them myself, but . . . I mean, I think I can . . . Whoa."

"Whoa?"

"The possibilities are endless," I stated.

"They are," came Gala's familiar voice as she stepped into the doorway. "But they're also not."

"Were you eavesdropping?" I asked.

"I was."

"What? I mean . . . Thanks for being honest?"

"Don't turn statements into questions. It makes you seem ditzy," she said.

"Ouch?"

"Mira, stop," Patrick said. "She's trying to help." Then, he turned to Gala and asked, "You are, right?"

"I am," the minotaur woman stated. "What I was trying to say is that, yes, the possibilities are endless. Yet, there are limitations. Chiefly, time is a consideration. To build a proper skill without the benefit of the appropriate class will take years. And that's looking at it optimistically. Realistically, you're looking at decades. And that's just the first one. Now, you can get around that with the right guidance. Perhaps your Templar friend can help you with that once he arrives, but you still don't have time to build something from scratch.

"The second issue is that your core can only hold so much. I'm sure you've seen that," she explained, stepping into the room.

"It does look a bit crowded in there."

"Most mystics will spend their time trying to expand their cores," she said. "They start with only a few nanites, but the oldest and most powerful will have a core whose size exceeds even your own, and by no small margin. Those lofty existences are not your concern."

"Why not?"

"Because they would not venture out into the frontier," Gala stated. She shook her great head, her horns sweeping from side to side. "They don't think like us. They exist on a different level than anyone else. Even speaking to them is a chore. There is zero chance that one of them will ever visit Earth."

"Huh. What do they do, then?"

"Whatever they want," Gala answered. "No one can stop them. They can't be killed. They simply exist as part of the Mist."

"Not really what I was asking. Like, are these ultrapowerful people like us? Do they sleep? Eat? Go to the toilet?"

"No. Get your mind out of the gutter."

"Then what do they do? And don't say something cryptic like 'whatever they want.' That's bullshit, and you know it."

She sighed, then scratched the point where her horn met her skull and said, "That's a hard question to answer, Mira. They are enigmatic figures who avoid public scrutiny. I know one of them protects an entire planet, carefully guiding the development of everything from the flora to the monsters to the people. Another is off exploring the galaxy and looking for the origin of the Mist. A few just wander around, experiencing everything they can. Most that reach that level just disappear, never to be heard from again."

"What? Why?"

"You're asking me, but who am I supposed to ask? Once, I was not an unimportant figure, at least in my sector of the universe," Gala said. "But those people are myths. They may as well be gods. No one knows what they do, and anyone who claims otherwise is lying. The point I'm trying to make is that there are limitations to what you can do. They're not hard-and-fast walls, but they're there all the same. It takes time to overcome those obstacles."

"Which we don't have."

"Precisely," Gala said. "It's better to simply work with the tools you have. Right now, you're more powerful than any mystic they'll throw at us. You don't need more power. We need a plan."

"Which we don't have," I said again.

Gala shook her head again. "True enough, but we're working on it," she said. "Case in point, we're meeting in a few hours, then we're going to watch the quarantine fall. Just wanted to let you know in case you wanted to join."

With that, she left the room. Patrick soon followed, saying that he had work to do. Once again, I was all alone, and in that solitude, I couldn't quite buck the notion that Gala was wrong. The tools I had weren't enough to solve our problem. Sure, we could probably delay the inevitable for a while, but if the Gomaris proved to be a little more stubborn than we hoped, we'd never be rid of them.

On top of that, there was the issue that if we made one little mistake, everything would come crashing down on us. I couldn't stomach that. So, I once again turned my attention to my pseudocore. Or maybe it was just a core like any other. The differences between me and a mystic seemed so minute that I wasn't sure they were even real, rather than simply a result of my skewed perception.

Either way, once I looked at that core, my attention kept going back to Planetary Defense. In the past, I'd dismissed it as unworkable due to the requirements involved. Yet, now there were other possibilities. Maybe I didn't have time to build a new ability or skill, but who was to say I couldn't alter an existing one?

I dove into it, familiarizing myself with its dizzyingly complex structure. However, the moment I did, I came to realize that I was in over my head. Even with all my advantages working my favor, simply understanding what I was looking at was a massive chore. I saw each piece, but putting them together into a cohesive whole was beyond my capabilities.

But that was fine. I'd never met a challenge I couldn't overcome. So, over the next few hours, I persisted, and to my dismay, I made almost no progress. However, *almost* was an important distinction because I did make a minute amount of headway. It was barely noticeable, and it only represented a fraction of a percentage of the entire ability. It was enough to buoy my spirits, though.

So, it was with some degree of optimism that I finally pushed myself out of bed, got dressed, and headed over to the compound so I could participate in the meeting. As it turned out, it was not very productive. Certainly, we came to a consensus about how we would move forward, responding to any incursions as soon as we learned of them, but that was insufficient to encourage me that we could win.

It was the best we could do at the moment, though. Hopefully, that would change, but in the meantime, the end of quarantine loomed ahead of us.

When the time came, we all headed outside, where Patrick had taken the liberty of setting up a series of camp chairs. I settled into one and looked up at the night sky. On the prairie where we'd set up camp, the sky always seemed so much more expansive than anywhere else I'd been.

So it gave a great view of the quarantine falling.

I didn't think anyone else could see the surge of energy that sped across the sky, but they did see something I didn't.

"Did you get a notification?" asked Patrick.

I shook my head. "No. What did it say?"

"The Initialization is complete. Let the Integration begin. Quarantine is now lifted. Now, you may embark on a new life as a fully Integrated citizen of the universe," he read. "Then it said a bunch of stuff about being able to travel off-planet now."

As soon as he said that, another flash of Mist shot across the sky, signaling the beginning of the blockade. I watched as a blue shield formed across the entire atmosphere.

"One quarantine ends, and another begins," I muttered to myself. "I guess it's time to get to work."

CHAPTER FORTY-FIVE

BAILING WATER

I don't know why I stayed. It was hopeless, and just like I'd seen happen a hundred times before, the planet was doomed. Still, I stayed. I wanted to help, and I still don't know why I didn't just pick up and leave the moment I knew we were going to be blockaded.

—Alistaris Kargat

don't know if I can keep doing this," I said, looking up at Patrick, who was pulling on a tee-shirt in our bedroom. "It's too much."

And it was.

The past few months had devolved into a blur of death and destruction where I spent most of my time whipping back and forth across the planet and trying to put out proverbial fires. Sometimes, I was called in to keep a group of aliens from establishing a foothold from which they would inevitably enslave or oppress the local population of humans. That was normal enough. But other times, I was forced to respond to yet more attempts to destroy the planet.

"I know it's hard, but—"

"It's not, though," I insisted. "That's the problem, Pick. I don't know how many people I've killed in the past week, much less overall. I thought I was strong enough to take it. I really did. But this is so much harder than anything I've done before. I think it would be easier if they could put up a fight. But they can't. It's just extermination at this point, except instead of killing a bunch of roaches or rats, I'm murdering people."

"Mira, they—"

I interrupted him again, saying, "I know, Pick. I know. They're invaders. Aliens. They want to kill us all. I recognize that it needs to be done, and I'm as committed as ever." I shook my head. "But it weighs down on me like you couldn't believe. I hate it. I hate remembering the people I killed today. I hate knowing that tomorrow I'm going to get up and go somewhere else and kill a bunch of people who can't really fight back."

It was all true, and the feeling had been building since that first week after the quarantine had lifted. I felt like an overused weapon on the verge of collapse. Before, it had been so easy to get wrapped up in the struggle of it all. The challenge. But now? With everything that had changed, they couldn't even hurt me, much less kill me. Even the mystics were like putty in my hands, and I routinely slapped their pitiful attacks aside without skipping a beat.

And then there were the whispers.

They were getting worse by the day, and they rose to a crescendo every time I went in to attack one target or another. In a way, it felt like the souls of my victims were screaming at me. I knew that wasn't the case. The origin of those whispers was the Mist itself. Yet, it was easy for superstitions to survive a clash with logic, and I couldn't help but feel more than a little discomforted by what I heard.

"I don't know what to tell you, Mira."

I sighed. "You don't have to tell me anything. There's nothing to say, really. This has to be done, and I'm the only one who can do it," I stated with more conviction than I really felt. However, I was well aware that it was the truth. Even a thousand fighters couldn't accomplish the things I had done. They just didn't have the power. "Where are we on the ammunition manufacturing?"

"It's slow," he answered, sighing as he sat on the bed next to me. "We took the Bazaar for granted."

"Even if I hadn't blown it up, the blockade would have kept us from resupplying."

"I know."

"I did what I thought I had to do, Pick. I don't see anybody else taking the world on their shoulders."

"I'm not—"

"Save it," I said, sliding off the bed. He reached out to grab my arm, but I dodged it easily. "I'm going for a walk. I need to clear my head before the next mission comes in."

Before he could say anything else, I teleported out of the room. Out of *The Leviathan*, in fact. I appeared outside, grabbing at the ambient Mist to regenerate what I'd just spent. It came easily, flooding into my core to fill the gap. Meanwhile, I strode off into the forest, using one thread of thought to keep an eye on my surroundings.

There was nothing, and I quickly found my way to a nearby stream. It was a beautiful sight that suggested a tranquility that I could feel was a facade. Everything was. The few victories we'd managed, the fights I'd won, the progress I'd made—it was all a surface-level disguise for the disgustingly unwinnable war I'd started.

In the past, I might have lashed out at something. Perhaps I would have kicked one of the rocks lining the bank of the stream. Or maybe I would have punched one of the trees. But after living a life of so much violence, I just couldn't muster the energy to perpetuate more destruction. So, with a huff, I settled down on a fallen tree and buried my head in my hands.

It was like that, almost an hour later, that Freddie found me.

I felt him long before he knew I was there, so I wasn't surprised when he settled down on the trunk beside me. He didn't say anything, though. Instead, he just sat there. So, I reached out in an attempt to get a sense of his Mist aura. But when I did, I found that it was entirely controlled, to the point that I could glean nothing.

"How do you do that?" I asked.

"Practice" was his answer. "This is a beautiful spot. Sometimes, we get so caught up in fighting and all the horrible things in this world that we don't see how lucky we are to live on such a planet."

"I don't need a pep talk, Freddie."

"I do," he countered. "I've found that it often helps to remind myself what's truly important."

"And what's that?" I asked.

"For me? Or for you?"

"Pick one," I answered.

"For me, what's important is that I pass on what I know," he said. "That's my calling. I've never been particularly powerful. In fact, I'm dead average. Perhaps my control is a bit better than most, but that's just repetition. But what I'm good at is teaching. I think that's what I would have done in the old world. There's just something about seeing a student finally understand the lessons I'm trying to teach."

"Is that why you're here? To teach me?" I asked.

"Oh, no. You're far past where I can teach you anything about the Mist. It's an interesting thing. We have been at this for decades. Nearly a century, in fact. We have the benefit of knowledge most people on Earth can only dream about," he explained. "And yet, in only ten years, you have exceeded even our most talented Templars. By no small degree, either. I suspect that, in this sector, you are the single strongest individual. Perhaps in many sectors. I know you have no context for the power you wield, but—"

"What's the point?"

"What do you mean?" he asked.

I stood, then stepped forward. Reaching out with a tendril of Mist, I lifted a rock and tossed it into the river. Then, with forty-two identical tendrils, I did the same, picking up a rock with each one. Then, I started to juggle them. It wasn't even close to the limit of my abilities—I wasn't even sure if limits existed—but it made my point well enough.

I turned to face Freddie and said, "This. I know I'm strong, Freddie. But what the hell am I supposed to do with it? I can't be everywhere at once! Every day, people die before I can get to them. The other teams, they're trying to pick up the slack, and on some days, they manage it. But all it takes is one mistake. One little slipup. And they all die."

I sighed, then tossed all the rocks into the woods. "But do you know what the worst part is? It's not even the deaths. People die all the time, and I barely know any of them," I said. "No—it's the fact that when they're gone, I'm the only one who can fill in. Most days, I race from one crisis to another, just murdering people left and right. And I don't know how long I can keep it up, okay? I don't know how long I can stay sane!"

As I shouted, some of my aura leaked out, sweeping through the forest and kicking up dust as well as stripping the bark from nearby trees. For his part, Freddie remained unfazed. My shoulders sagged, and I sat next to him, burying my face in my hands as I muttered, "I don't know if I can do what's necessary. I don't know if I can be what Earth needs me to be."

"You can't be."

"What?" I asked, looking up. I hated that my eyes were moist with tears.

"I said you can't be what Earth needs you to be. No one can. Not alone," he answered. "Everyone has limits, Mira. You've just found yours."

"I can't believe that."

"Why not?" he asked earnestly.

"Because if I can't do this, if I can't save everyone, Earth is . . . It's all going to end," I said. "Do you know what that feels like? Does anyone?"

I had the weight of the whole world on my shoulders, and as strong as I was, I could only take so much. With every passing day, I drew closer to the point of collapse. And after that happened, Earth would fall. I knew it. So did Patrick. Alistaris. Gala. That was why they'd all been pushing me so hard. And what's worse is that I couldn't blame them, either. They needed me to be the hope that nobody else could be.

Because if I wasn't, everyone was going to die.

"Have I ever told you the story of how the Templars were founded?" Freddie asked.

"What? What does that have to do with anything?"

"It happened so long ago that the only people who remember are the Templars," he said. "And we don't even remember his name. We just know the story. His planet was doomed, too. The coming of a world serpent, not aliens, but the stakes were similar to your own. He started the Templars, hoping to help his people escape what was coming. They didn't have the system. Nor were they capable of space travel. The Mist was mired in mysticism and religion. Yet, they accomplished amazing feats.

"He failed, though. The budding organization of Templars were not strong enough, and the world serpent came," Freddie went on. "Do you know what happened next?"

"They all died?" I asked. I had some experience with a world serpent. I'd seen a facsimile of one in a Rift, and I'd never quite gotten over the sheer scale of the thing.

"They did not. The Founder sacrificed himself," Freddie said. "He defeated the serpent and shielded the world, providing a thousand years of salvation. They used that to advance, to grow, and when they were once again exposed to the world, they were prepared to do whatever was necessary to survive. And they did, due to his sacrifice."

"Are you saying that I need to sacrifice myself?" I asked.

Freddie shook his head. "No. Of course not," he said. "I'm telling you not to."

"What?"

"My organization is a shadow of what it once was," Freddie went on. "We see evil, and we stand aside. We are not worthy of the Founder's sacrifice. Nor is Earth worthy of yours."

"What do you suggest?"

"Escape."

"There's a blockade."

"That won't stop you."

"But all those people . . ."

"Are not your responsibility," Freddie said. "You are—"

"You're no better than the rest of them, are you?" I accused. "If you could leave, would you?"

"I think you misunderstand. I don't want to escape. I want to be punished," Freddie stated. "Do you know how many children I've seen become wildlings? Teenagers with their whole lives ahead of them. I told them pretty lies to get them to eschew Nexus Implants. And for what? So I could grow the numbers of Templars? To spread an ideology that I don't believe in? Hundreds of lives ended so I could meet my quotas."

"W-what?"

"Originally, I was told that they were special. The ones I was sent to target were supposed to have better chances of becoming Templars. They didn't. It was all random because nobody knows why some survive and some don't. I killed them," he said. "Your friend Alistaris is right to hate us. We're not worth saving."

At that moment, I realized that Freddie hadn't come there to comfort me. In fact, I wasn't sure why he was there at all, except to unburden his soul. Now that Earth seemed doomed, that sort of thing was probably going around.

I looked at him for a long moment, and all I saw was a broken man with a million regrets weighing down on him. And I found it so disgusting that it made me want to vomit.

I didn't begrudge him for breaking. That was out of his control. But in his eyes, I saw something I couldn't stomach.

Surrender.

Freddie had given up, and he wanted me to do the same. That brought a well of anger bubbling up inside me, and I shoved myself to my feet. Once I did, I said, "I intend to keep fighting until the last cell of my body is destroyed. Maybe you're willing to just lie down and die, but I'm not. I won't. I refuse!"

As I spoke, Mist swirled around me, kicking up dirt and pebbles and stripping whatever bark was left from the nearby tree trunks. With a deep breath, I settled my aura and continued, "Thank you, Frederick. You put everything into perspective."

Then, without another word, I strode back toward the camp, ready to continue the war we'd been fighting since the beginning.

It didn't take long to cover the ground, and soon enough, I arrived back at *The Leviathan* to find Patrick in the cargo bay where he was tinkering with his armor. He didn't even look up as he asked, "Get it out of your system?"

"Look, I'm sorry," I said. "I didn't . . ."

He sighed and turned to face me. Then he stepped forward and wrapped his arms around me in a tight hug. He didn't say anything. Instead, he just let me sink into his embrace, and in that moment, I felt like the whole world melted away.

"Thank you," I mumbled into his chest.

"You don't have to thank me, Mira. I'm here for you. You can talk to me. You don't have to keep it all bottled up," he said, cradling my head with his cybernetic hand. "We're in this together. Remember that."

Then, I told him what Freddie had revealed, ending with, "I don't think we can depend on him."

"What an asshole."

"He's not an asshole, Pick. He's just . . . broken."

"No, he's definitely an asshole. Giving up just because he feels guilty. If he was really sorry, he'd be working to save as many people as he could to make up for the people he lost," Patrick stated. "And he tried to rope you into it, too? In your moment of weakness, he just twisted the knife. That makes him an asshole."

I pulled away and shook my head. "Maybe."

But I wasn't so sure. Freddie was probably more damaged than even I wanted to acknowledge, and I felt like I had no right to judge him. None of us did because we hadn't felt what he'd felt. We hadn't been through what he had been through. As such, we couldn't really understand the grief staining his heart.

I sensed Alistaris heading in the direction of *The Leviathan*, so I dried my eyes and told Patrick about the Dengyt's impending arrival. So, we were both ready when he stepped through the ship's hatch.

"Are you ready for another mission?" he asked without preamble. In the past couple of months since the quarantine had lifted, he'd lost weight. More, he looked like he hadn't slept in a week. Not surprising, considering he was the organizational lynchpin for the entire resistance.

"What's going on?" I asked.

"One of our teams got ambushed," Alistaris answered. "Initial reports are that there are nearly thirty mystics and more than five hundred Adjudicators."

"Do you want me to just blow it up?" I asked. I certainly had that capability. I could drop another bomb from *The Leviathan* and wipe out an entire city if I wanted to.

"Not possible. They've already deployed antiprojectile cannons," he answered. "We can't afford to lose any more people."

"What was the team's target?" I asked.

"What else? Another dig site. They're bound and determined to blow this planet up," Alistaris said. "The team managed to take out the machine, but they were taken soon after."

"Seems simple enough. We go in, kill the bad guys, and rescue our people," I said. "Sound about right?"

"Ensure that the machine is completely destroyed and gather any intelligence you can," he added. "But other than that, yes. That's it."

"So, same as always," I reasoned. "Alright. Let's get this thing going, then."

After that, Patrick and I went to the cockpit, and Alistaris transferred the coordinates to Patrick. Then, we were on our way. The trip was supposed to take a little more than an hour, so I settled into the navigator's seat and focused on my aura control.

That's how I passed the time until Patrick said, "We're here."

I opened my eyes to see a massive set of ruins the likes of which I'd never beheld.

CHAPTER FORTY-SIX

BAD TO WORSE

I wish I could take some of the burden from Mira's shoulders, but I know I couldn't bear the weight. In most ways, she represents our only hope, and if she fails, Earth falls. That is a lot to take on, but the harsh reality is that she can do things nobody else can. I just hope she can endure the crippling expectations she's put on herself.

—Patrick Ward

A vast cityscape stretched out before us, looking like a jungle of concrete, glass, and steel. Huge and hollow skyscrapers stretched toward the gray sky, monuments to a distant and more prosperous past. Or perhaps they were memorials of a culture long lost to the Mist and human neglect. Some of those skyscrapers ended in jagged peaks, but a few remained intact. A couple had collapsed altogether, and the only remnants of those once-great structures were huge piles of rubble.

I saw quite a lot of green scattered throughout the city, but it wasn't as much as it should have been.

"What is this place called again?" I asked.

"New York," Patrick answered. "Or that's what it used to be. Remy talked about it before. Apparently, it was the greatest city in the world before . . . Well, you know. He said that it was one of the first to fall, too. With everything having changed, people went crazy. Suddenly, the worst of the worst had the power to do whatever they wanted. They overwhelmed the city's government and took over. Different groups took over different territories, but Remy said none of them were good guys."

"I can imagine," I said. If there was one thing I'd learned about human nature, it was that people would eagerly take advantage of the weak and powerless. "What happened after that? I don't see any signs of habitation."

Indeed, from our position high above the city, I couldn't see a single glowing light. That made me wonder where the aliens had set up shop, but I was more interested in the place's history at the moment. I would worry about the aliens soon enough.

"War," Patrick said. "They fought among one another. Eventually, they weakened themselves enough that when a surge of wildlings swept through the area, they couldn't adequately defend their territories. Most of them died, but some got out. By the time they tried to come back, the area had gone wild."

"So, you're saying there are a bunch of wildlings down there?" I asked. I didn't see any, but their Mist auras were much harder to detect than normal humans. It was similar with the beasts who tended to blend into the environment. By contrast, humans—especially ones with Nexus Implants—blazed in my awareness like fiery beacons of blue Mist.

"Underground," Patrick stated. "You should have read the packet on the way over here."

"Why? You'll give me the highlights, right?" I said with a slight smirk. "Otherwise, why do I keep you around?"

He returned my smirk with a smile of his own, saying, "I don't think I need to defend myself in that area."

"You're not that good at—"

"I mean, clearly, you keep me around for my cooking and brewing skills. You liked that last beer, right? It added more hops."

"It was . . . uh . . . great. Good. I could really taste the extra . . . um . . . hops."

"Ouch."

"I liked it!"

"No. It's okay. I'm an unappreciated genius, and I've long since resigned myself to suffering for my art," he said.

I rolled my eyes. "You are so dramatic," I said. Then, I added, "We should probably find somewhere to land. You sure they didn't detect the ship?"

"I'm just as positive as I always am."

"Fair enough" was my response. It still felt a little odd, knowing how competent Patrick had become. I still remembered a time when he was a liability, like when he'd nearly gotten killed by a group of backwoods bandits. That was just after we'd left Mobile, and back then, he could barely even protect himself. Now, he was flying a ship within a few miles of an enemy position, and he could confidently say that they had no idea he was there.

As I gave that some thought—through the lens of nostalgia—Patrick guided *The Leviathan* to an open space just outside of town. Once he'd set the ship down, I asked, "Do you want to come with me?"

"I'll stay back," he said. His armor gave him some degree of stealth, but it was easily bypassed by anyone with appropriate skills. And that was saying nothing of the enemy mystics we knew were down there. "I'll keep the ship running so that when you need a pickup or some cover, I'll be in good position."

He knew that it was the right choice—we both did—but he didn't like being left behind. Likely, it would prompt another furious bout of enhancements for his armor. He'd already improved it a hundred times since he'd first created it, and I knew he'd barely scratched the surface of what was possible. Due to his abilities, he could seamlessly integrate new materials as well as advanced weapon designs.

Even Gala had been impressed, and she'd already lent her expertise in firearms to his efforts. When the two of them got going about one gun or the other, they lost track of everything else. It would have been annoying if it wasn't so endearing.

Well, as endearing as talk about deadly weapons could be.

In any case, once we'd established our protocol for what to expect, I headed to the back, where I donned my gear. Often, the infiltration suit had proved useless. Anything that could get through my natural defenses wasn't getting stopped by the flimsy armor. Yet, I wore it anyway. Probably out of habit, but there was a healthy dose of that same nostalgia involved, as well. Either way, I quickly dressed, adding a set of no-nonsense black fatigues on top of the skintight suit. Then, after saying goodbye to Patrick, I left *The Leviathan* and set off toward the city where I hoped to rescue the captured team and destroy the dig site the aliens had established within the ruins.

I didn't bother summoning the Cutter. The hover bike was still useful, and with it, I could travel incredibly quickly. However, it was also limited in a couple of ways. First, with all my progress, I could reach incredible speeds on foot. I hadn't tested it recently, but I estimated that I could exceed a hundred miles an hour on a straightaway. The big difference, though, was that I could corner much better than the hover bike. That meant that in a ruined city like New York, traveling on foot gave me a lot more options without losing too much speed.

The second major problem with the Cutter was that its Mist signature was absolutely overwhelming. I wasn't sure how sensitive the enemy mystics were, but for my part, I could sense the powerful Mist engine from miles away. I thought it was best to assume that they could, as well.

So, I'd chosen to go on foot.

As I made my way into the city, I couldn't help but marvel at the skyscrapers. Certainly, they couldn't compete with modern structures like the megabuildings back in Nova City, but what they lacked in size, they made up for in presence. And variety. Some looked like they'd been constructed primarily from steel and glass, but others featured stone or cement facades that I found extremely interesting.

But more, I couldn't help but imagine what life might've been like in the city during its prime. I saw plenty of rusted-out vehicles, most of which had vegetation growing in and around them, and I recognized a host of openings leading to the tunnels Patrick had mentioned. The Mist was thicker down there, suggesting that that was where I'd likely find the wildlings who'd taken over the city.

Gradually, I progressed through the city, eventually crossing a bridge that had miraculously survived, passing onto an island where the team was suspected to have been captured. That was where I encountered the first pack of wildlings. They looked little different than all the others I'd seen during my travels, yet their auras were markedly stronger. If they were any weaker than the alpha that had nearly killed me outside of Biloxi years before, I would have been surprised. And there were a few that had even denser auras, giving me the impression that they would have rivaled the clown wildling for sheer might.

Fortunately, I had impeccable control of my own aura, so cloaking myself in concealing Mist—in my new version of my old Stealth ability—I could easily remain undetected. Still, I suspected that the more powerful of the wildlings could sense that something was amiss, judging by the way they looked around in confusion, so I didn't linger.

Even so, I found it fascinating, looking at them with my Mist senses. I'd never seen it before, but now that I had moved past my reliance on the Nexus Implant, I saw tiny tendrils of Mist extending from each wildling. It seemed that the length of those Mist flows depended on the strength of the wildling. Most only went three or four feet, but others were dozens of feet long. It was a poignant reminder that humanity didn't really understand wildlings at all. Even with the insight I'd gleaned, all I could say for certain was that they were much more than the beasts most people considered them.

Not that they weren't wild, dangerous, and bestial. They were. But knowing that, if left to their own devices, they would eventually evolve and regain some semblance of humanity—many generations hence—I found myself wondering precisely what they might become. If they were so strong now, it didn't seem unreasonable to expect that they would become a mighty force.

I moved on, exploring the island as I searched for the captured team or some signs of where the aliens had set up shop. But I found nothing, leading me to believe that they'd gone underground.

So, once I'd exhausted the possibilities aboveground, I found one of the entrances to the tunnel system, then descended into the darkness. Fortunately,

I was more than capable of seeing in the darkness, so I had no trouble finding my way. As I did, I discovered three things.

First, the purpose of the tunnels soon became apparent when I stumbled upon an abandoned train. It was a design I wasn't familiar with, and it clearly didn't use Mist for propulsion. But the general shape was right, making the purpose of the tunnels obvious.

Second, large portions of the tunnels had been at least partially flooded, making traversal a pain. With my training, I managed, but it wasn't pleasant. And it slowed me down quite a bit. Still, I made decent time.

The final discovery was one I'd already suspected. The city above was home to a large population of wildlings, but the tunnels were absolutely lousy with them. It felt like I couldn't go more than a hundred yards without coming upon a pack of them. Most of those groups were composed of only ten or so members, but there were a few with numbers climbing into the hundreds.

Thankfully, the vast majority were asleep.

Otherwise, it would have been an even bigger pain to avoid bumping into them. Still, I managed to do just that as I traversed those tunnels. As I did, the density of the ambient Mist continued to rise until, after a few hours, I finally came upon my destination. The tunnel just ended in a giant, gaping hole at least a quarter mile across. I leaned over the edge, and somewhere down below, I could see a powerful Mist signature.

It took a few moments for me to make sense of it, but when I did, I let out an involuntary sigh. It was a drill, but not like the ones we'd already destroyed. No—this one was much larger and freestanding, which meant that it was more like a vehicle that could bore through the earth than anything else.

And it had already gone nearly a mile.

"Pick, this is bad," I said.

"What's going on?" he asked over the Secure Connection I'd just established. It had taken a little practice, but I'd managed to get the hang of using the ability without the benefit of the framework provided by an interface.

"They're drilling," I answered. "Straight down."

"We've been destroying drills for a while," he said. "What's different about this one?"

"The bombs on board the drill are strong. Maybe stronger than anything I've seen before," I said. "If I were the one to set them, I'm pretty sure it would result in a bigger explosion than one we saw on the moon."

Indeed, that had created a crater that was visible from Earth with the naked eye. If I were to detonate a bomb like that in the Earth's core, the planet would almost assuredly rupture. And this looked much more powerful, judging by the Mist signatures I saw. If it was detonated by someone with even a moderate skill in demolitions, Earth wouldn't survive.

"What do we do?" he asked.

"I have to go down," I said. Then, I muttered, "God, this is going to suck."

Indeed, not only was climbing down going to be a pain, but there was every chance that I was going to encounter a small army of mystics and Adjudicators. After all, the drill was half a mile wide. That was as big as a lot of bases we'd assaulted.

Standing there, I truly considered just dropping a few bombs on the thing and hoping it would all detonate. It would be incredibly damaging, but it wouldn't destroy the Earth like it would if it got close to the core.

But I chose not to for two reasons.

First, that wasn't my mission, and I still hoped to rescue the team that had been taken captive. I didn't know any of them, but they were still human. And more importantly, they were part of the resistance. We needed as many people as we could get, and if I was honest, I couldn't stomach the idea of sacrificing them. That felt like letting the aliens win.

Second, I could see that the drill was protected by a Mist shield. I suspected that was to protect it from the heat and pressure once it proceeded closer to the core, but if it could stand up to those forces, then it could probably protect the drill from my bombs. And I wasn't willing to take the chance of revealing myself for something that may not work.

So, that left me with one option—I needed to climb down a sheer wall, bypass the shield by manipulating the Mist, and rescue the people on board. At the same time, I needed to destroy the drill. Oh, and I needed to figure out how to escape with a dozen people tagging along for the ride.

"Sounds easy when I put it like that," I whispered to myself.

"Be careful," Patrick cautioned.

"Will do. Cutting the connection," I said. "I'll let you know when I'm on my way up."

I'd made the mistake of using Secure Connection around mystics before, which was what had nearly gotten me killed in the system station after rescuing Alistaris. At the time, I couldn't even see the thread-thin tendril of Mist connecting me to whomever I was talking to, but mystics of a certain caliber certainly could. I didn't know if there were any down in the drill who could claim that level of power, but I wasn't going to take any chances.

So, I cut the Secure Connection, checked that I had everything I would need, then started the climb down. As I did, I cloaked myself in a thick layer of Mist that would hide me from any observation. Then, I retracted it to within a nanite's width of my body, hiding the signature I knew the ability would emit.

At first, the climb was easy enough, largely because the rock was pitted with easy handholds. However, it quickly became much more difficult, and my progress slowed to an interminable crawl. That's when I started to experiment with Mist. Until that point, I'd only used it for minor telekinesis and within the framework of my old skills. Yet, based on everything I had seen, the only real limit to what I could accomplish with Mist was my imagination and willpower.

I had plenty of the latter, but my imagination had always been lacking. So, I endeavored to change that, starting with my climb down the cliff left behind by the drill. To that end, I extended tiny tendrils of Mist—hundreds of them that were only an inch or so long—and forced them to grip the wall. Or rather, to adhere to the collection of Mist that infused the wall.

And to my surprise, it worked.

I could have hung there for days, if I so desired. However, when I tried to pull free, I got a bit of a surprise when the Mist resisted my effort. After a brief shock, I realized that the problem wasn't with the Mist but, rather, with the fact that I needed to manipulate it to let me go.

Shaking my head at my own stupidity, I took that extra step. It made things a little awkward, but I managed it. Right up until I reached a little past the halfway mark, when a powerful surge of Mist erupted from below and washed over me. It ripped my Mist tendrils free of the wall, and suddenly, I was falling. I knew I could survive a fall from that distance. From any distance, actually. But doing so would definitely leave me injured, not to mention that hitting the Mist shield would almost certainly expose me to the aliens.

My mind whirled with potential solutions, but as I fell, I could think of nothing. So, I braced myself for the inevitable.

CHAPTER FORTY-SEVEN

THE RULES OF WAR

Templars are just people. We have hopes and dreams, flaws and fears just like everyone else. The only difference is that we somehow managed to peek behind the curtain. For many of us, that is the source of those fears.

—Frederick Eagin

For a brief moment, I panicked.

There's something primal about the feeling of falling. It didn't matter if, by all accounts, I could survive a fall from basically any height. No—the most primitive part of my brain was convinced, if only for a second, that I was about to die. But then, reason reasserted itself, and I came upon a different problem. Sure, I didn't think I was going to break my neck upon impact, but I had every reason to believe that it would still be disastrous. Even if I didn't injure myself, falling into that Mist shield would certainly alert anyone who was paying attention. And that would cause almost as many problems as falling to my death.

But I had been in so many lethal situations that the panic quickly became survival instinct, and in that moment, I grabbed hold of all the Mist in my immediate vicinity and shoved against it. And just like that, my fall came to a sudden halt. I hovered in midair for the briefest of seconds before I lost hold of the Mist and resumed the fall.

I tried to recapture whatever magic I'd managed to bottle with that first attempt, but without the panic coursing through my mind, I was frustratingly unsuccessful. So, I quickly shifted gears and manipulated the Mist to use Teleport, which took me back to the wall, where I used my previous tactic to adhere to the surface.

For a while, I just hung there, my heart beating out of my chest as I tried to calm myself. Then, another explosion of Mist swept over me. This time, I was ready for it, though, and as soon as it passed me by, I slapped my hands and feet against the wall, steadying myself before I could fall more than a couple of feet.

Like that, I descended. It wasn't comfortable, and each wave of Mist sent panic to flood my mind. But I soon discovered that I could inoculate myself against it with a hastily built cocoon of my own Mist. It wasn't perfect. Indeed, the pulse of hostile Mist ripped huge chunks from my makeshift armor. However, so long as I kept my focus intact, I could repair the damage before it caused any problems.

Still, it was extremely uncomfortable, and it required every ounce of attention to keep myself from falling. Without the effects of [Multimind], I wouldn't have managed it at all. Even with it, the strategy required constant focus.

Fortunately, I was well used to that sort of thing.

For the next few minutes, I continued my descent, one tedious inch at a time, until I finally found myself within a few feet of the Mist shield. And only a couple of feet beyond that was the surface of the drill, which was more like a giant ship than anything else. Regardless, I knew I had to time things perfectly, or I would, at the very least, be detected. Considering I was on a stealth mission, I wanted to avoid that.

So, after I settled myself in the wake of the most recent pulse of Mist, I manipulated the shield to allow for passage, then dropped to the surface of the drill. Once there, I pressed myself flat, letting the shield close.

But even that was difficult. The shield was a powerful one, and holding back the Mist had felt like trying to hold back a tsunami. I'd managed, but only just, and even that much had left me a little rattled. Clearly, they'd upgraded their technology. That told me they were serious about protecting the drill, as if I didn't already know that.

In any case, I started slithering across the surface as I searched for a way inside. And after a few more minutes, I found just such an entrance, which presented as a small hatch that was obviously meant for emergency access. That was perfect for my needs, so after spending a few seconds infiltrating the system, I commanded it to slide open. Once it did just that, I slipped inside, climbing down a ladder and, after casting my senses around to ensure I was alone, dropped down to a corridor.

And just like that, I was inside.

Now, I just needed to search for the captive team, then figure out how to disable the enormous drill. After that, it was just a question of doing what needed to be done. Hopefully, I could accomplish that while avoiding any unnecessary fights. After all, with how many people were supposed to be on board—Adjudicators and mystics alike—I didn't want to bring any undue attention to myself. I was powerful, but against that many, I didn't think I would fare very well.

So, with that in mind, I wrapped myself in as much Stealth as I could muster, tamping my aura down along the way, and crept forward. The corridor itself was the expected plasti-steel, but there were hundreds of rooms along the way. A quick look inside told me that I'd stumbled upon the largest collection of Rift Shards I'd ever seen. They were all low-quality Shards, no bigger than my thumb, but there were so many of them—literally hundreds of tons—that I didn't think their relative weakness was such a problem.

I shuddered to think how many credits the Gomaris had invested into the drill. It wasn't long before I discovered what all those Shards were for when I stumbled upon a Mist engine that was a hundred times bigger than the one that motivated *The Leviathan*. And there were dozens of them, too, with a bunch of alien workers of all sorts of races shoveling Rift Shards inside.

The Mist engines were connected to giant cables, which I followed through the ship and to their eventual destination, which was the actual drill mechanism. When I'd first heard that the aliens were drilling through the Earth's crust, I'd expected an actual drill. But in retrospect, that was silly and probably more based on cartoons than I wanted to admit.

The reality was far more terrifying.

It was actually composed of hundreds of Mist-powered lasers, all spinning and capable of focusing on a single point. The Mist cost was absolutely staggering, and the sheer runoff from the operation was responsible for the pulses of Mist that had nearly sent me plummeting down a mile-long shaft.

After finding that, I knew that it wouldn't be long before the aliens reached the core. When they did, it wouldn't take long before they got precisely what they wanted from the operation.

Eventually, I discovered their cache of explosives, as well, and I was impressed with the sheer volume of material. The charges themselves weren't terribly sophisticated, but then again, I didn't expect them to be. Bombs, at their core, aren't all that complicated, and there was no reason to veer away from the simple designs that worked. The only real difference was the fuel, and these bombs were made of some Mist-dense substance I'd never encountered. I stole a few dozen—more for academic purposes than anything else—but the rest I left alone.

But just after I turned away from the first cache, something occurred to me. It was just an idea, but I ran with it, closing the door and extending a few tendrils of Mist. Once I felt what I'd expected, I grinned.

Personally, when I created explosives, I tended to avoid using Mist as a trigger. Instead, I liked to use mundane detonators. Aliens approached it differently, probably because they were far more accustomed to using Mist for everything.

In practice, the difference wasn't huge. It didn't make the bombs any better or worse. Just a different approach, but one I'd just realized I could exploit.

Extending as many Mist tendrils as I could handle, I started to drain the power from the nanites that composed the Mist triggers. The first one took about twenty seconds, but each subsequent instance went a little faster. By the time I got to the tenth set, I accomplished my goal in less than a second.

So I went for the next few minutes, disarming dozens of bombs at a time until, at last, the explosives were rendered completely inert. Then, I realized that I could do the same to all those Rift Shards, so I returned to the first room and got to work.

It took a slightly different approach, and it took a little longer at first, but once I got the hang of it, I swept through the facility with a vengeance, draining their fuel and removing the lethality from their explosives. Along the way, I also uploaded a version of *Extermination*, which was the Ghost I'd used back in Olympus. There were some subtle differences, largely because I'd been working on refining it when I'd absorbed my Nexus Implant into my core, but also because of the changing nature of my power. The result was that it was far more powerful, and as a bonus, it was easier for me to hide.

So, it was easy to expect it to be quite a bit more lethal.

The other advantage was that the Adjudicators on board didn't always wear their armor. As such, they were incredibly vulnerable, and I was more than willing to take advantage of their lowered defenses. They received their own version of *Extermination*, which was timed rather than reliant on my signal for activation. My reasoning was simple: if the Adjudicators were wearing their armor, any signal I sent would have been blocked. So, as much as I didn't want to rely on a timer, it was a necessary adjustment.

It did put a time limit on my efforts, though.

One day. That was all I had to complete my mission before the Adjudicators started dropping dead. With that in mind, I continued to work, infecting as many alien personnel as I could while slowly undermining their entire operation. It was grueling work, but I was more than willing to endure.

On the eighteenth hour, I hit my first obstacle when the drill came to a screeching halt. It only took a moment for me to realize that the drill's workers had probably loaded the Mist engines with inert Shards, and to predictable results.

At first, nothing really changed. But then, the mystics made an appearance.

Most of them weren't very powerful. No stronger than the first one I'd killed on the system station we'd always referred to as the Bazaar. But there were a few that seemed a notch above that. In any event, they couldn't detect me, but I knew it was only a matter of time before they discovered the issues. When that happened, there was a good chance that they would start looking for a saboteur.

So, my timer accelerated.

I hurried to get as much as possible, but I knew it was only a temporary measure. I wanted nothing more than to simply blow it all up. However, I had no idea how detonating my explosives would react to the bombs already on board. For all I knew, the result would be an even larger explosion than the one I had created on the moon. Because despite my efforts, I knew I couldn't disarm every bomb in the drill facility.

And if I was honest, I also knew that I had a tendency to overdo things. On top of that, we'd already gotten deep enough beneath the Earth's surface that a large enough explosion would do irreparable damage to the planet.

No—I couldn't risk that.

But what I could do was work to disable the thing. So, with that in mind, I continued my sweep through the facility, uploading my Ghosts, draining Rift Shards, and disarming bombs. And when I'd finally exhausted those possibilities, I turned my attention to the laser mechanisms themselves.

Fortunately, they worked off their own self-contained systems, so I spent the next couple of hours uploading a Ghost that would, when the time came, completely disable them while destroying their operating systems.

By the time I'd finished that, though, my time was up. So, I set myself up in one of the rooms containing the inert Rift Shards and waited the last few minutes until, at last, the time came. When it did, I signaled the activation of *Extermination*, and only a second later, I felt an influx of Mist that told me I'd just killed more than a thousand people. A moment after that, I received another wave of Mist that meant I'd killed a host of Adjudicators.

I hadn't gotten them all, though. And there were quite a few mystics still running around, as well. So, I knew that the next part of my plan would still be quite tricky.

With that in mind, I waited until, at last, I felt a deep shudder as the drill came to a complete halt. The lasers had been disabled, most of the Rift Shards in the facility had been drained, and the bombs had been disarmed. On top of that, most of the normal personnel had been killed, and a good portion of the Adjudicators were dead, as well. I'd already done irreparable damage to the operation, but I still had one part of my mission left.

I needed to find and rescue the captured team.

So, I took a deep breath, then left the room behind and began my search. There were a few possibilities for where they were being held—seven rooms that I'd been unable to access for different reasons—so those were my first targets. The first three just featured locks I couldn't bypass without setting off alarms, but now that I'd accomplished my primary goals, I could afford to be a little less circumspect. So, I tore through them, setting off the alarms along the way. Unfortunately, those rooms contained nothing but expensive-looking equipment that I quickly and efficiently disabled before moving on.

The next two had been filled with mystics, though with the alarm going off, they'd flooded out of what I suspected were their quarters and were currently searching for me. Or whatever they assumed was the cause of the alarms. Either way, I found nothing but empty rooms.

However, the sixth door, which had been guarded by a half dozen Adjudicators that were now dead, was the jackpot. After forcing the doors to open, I stepped through to see what looked like a holding facility. A dozen cells lined either side of the hall, each one guarded by a Mist shield. I walked inside to see that each cell held a handful of humans and a couple of Dengyts.

I'd found the prisoners.

Now, I just needed to free them and find some manner of escape.

First, though, I took care of the first part and sent a dozen Mist tendrils out to deactivate the shields barring entry into the cells. They winked out a second later, and the moment they did, the stench of death hit my nose. I didn't even need to look to recognize that each and every one of the prisoners was already dead.

Which meant that . . .

"You are far too easy to manipulate, Miss Braddock," came a voice from the entrance. I whipped around to see a tall figure wearing all black. A helmet hid his face, but his proportions suggested that he was human. Or at least human-like. That didn't mean he wasn't an alien; humans existed on other planets, after all. But after seeing so many oddly shaped aliens over the past months, it was a little surprising. What wasn't surprising was the huge surge of Mist that quickly enveloped me.

I let it.

I even pretended to struggle, gasping, "Why? What's going on?"

"Isn't it obvious?" he asked, stepping forward, his voice carrying with it a reverberation that made it sound far deeper than normal. He flicked his hand, and the Mist encasing my body contracted. My bones creaked under the pressure, and I let out a cry of pain that wasn't altogether feigned. "They said you were too smart to fall for this all-too-obvious trick. But I knew you would come running to save your allies. That's what you do, isn't it? The noble warrior. The hero."

I snorted at that.

"What?" he asked.

"A hero? Me? You need to check your sources."

He cocked his helmeted head to the side. "I don't understand."

"I've killed as many humans as you have. Innocent ones, too. Do you know what they used to call people who fight like me? War criminals."

"War . . . criminal. A curious term," he said, obviously unconcerned. He was completely confident in the viability of his trap, and I could see why. There were a handful of other mystics standing at the door, and his control of Mist was second only to the goblinoid mystic that had nearly killed me back in the Bazaar.

"I know. Always seemed like an oxymoron to me," I admitted. "As if wars can have rules. That's a bunch of bullshit meant to keep the weak from having a chance. The only people who can afford to fight according to some rules or laws are the strong. Everyone else does everything they can to avoid annihilation."

"Interesting, I—"

At that moment, I flexed my own control of the Mist, tearing through his grip. As I did so, I ripped the interdiction blade from the scabbard on my back and sent the sword screaming in his direction in an overhand cut. He reacted quickly, raising his hand and conjuring a shield of Mist that absorbed the blow. However, he couldn't stop the momentum, which slammed him into the ground. I followed it up with a kick that harnessed every bit of strength I could muster, and when it connected, I felt bones crack before he went flying down the hall to hit his cadre of mystic companions.

I tossed a grenade after him, then summoned my Stinger. Now that I'd established that the people I had come to rescue were dead, I wasn't nearly as concerned with remaining quiet. I let loose with a barrage of gunfire as the battle truly began.

CHAPTER FORTY-EIGHT

RUNNING BATTLE

I've seen so many planets die. Some were outright destroyed, much as the Gomaris want to do to Earth. Yet others experienced a much slower death as the wider universe exploited and oppressed until there was nothing left. Then, they were abandoned, and their people left to wither and die. I wish I could stop the cycle, but I'm only one person.

—Galatira Iamaxis

I fired, but the storm of bullets never reached their target. Instead, the enemy mystic blocked each shot with a deft manipulation of Mist. Though I'd expected it, it was still an impressive display of control. I couldn't help but wonder if I could mimic his technique.

However, my grenade was far more effective as it rolled past the mystic leader and exploded in the midst of his subordinates. I'd made the grenade myself, incorporating a few pellets of norcite, so it tore through them with ease. They died in less than a second, leaving only the leader, whose armor and Mist-manipulation abilities had kept him safe from the explosion.

After the shock of enduring the initial barrage—and, presumably, my escape from the grip of his Mist—he recovered quickly, sending another stream of nanites screaming toward me. I dodged, but the collection moved like a snake, adjusting to strike me on the shoulder. It spun me around, but I kicked off one of the walls, flipping sideways before landing on my feet. I continued running toward him, burying him beneath a stream of Stinger fire along the way. He blocked each shot, but it was never meant as anything but a distraction.

The real attack was the tendril of Mist I'd extended along the floor.

It erupted from the ground, latching on to his core as I battered his defenses into nothing. There were hundreds of pseudonodes, but with [Multimind] augmenting my thoughts, the mystic's defenses fell in seconds. He tried to martial his Mist to create a shield against my intrusion, but I tore through the nascent barrier before it could truly form. Then, I plunged deep within his core.

At first, I marveled at the organization of nanites. He had skills, of a sort. Five of them. Yet, they were more nebulous than what might be present in a Nexus Implant. It was as if they were intended to be more malleable. Or like they had yet to fully form. The mystic, for all his power, was nothing more than a work in progress.

I was almost sad to have to tear it all down.

Of course, that wasn't going to prevent me from doing just that. Not only did I have a job to do, but he would either capture or kill me unless I ruthlessly destroyed him. So, with those options before me, I knew precisely which one I'd pick. And when I aimed for destruction, the results were inevitable.

I ripped through his core with reckless power, tearing those delicate constellations of nanites to pieces. At the same time, I used the same strategy I'd used with all the Rift Shards I'd rendered inert and drained his personal pool of Mist of all its power. I couldn't absorb so much energy, so I just let it dissipate into a nebulous cloud all around him. So, it looked like his aura had suddenly entered the visible spectrum.

It was an illusion, though. Those nanites were powerless.

Predictably, the mystic panicked, and I used that to my advantage, continuing with that barrage of gunfire. As his Mist drained out of him, he couldn't muster the power to block those rounds, and so, in only seconds, he'd gone from completely unassailable to being riddled with powerful balls of superheated Mist.

It was beautiful, watching his blood splatter all over the wall. He was strong, though, and even if I'd drained most of his core, his body was still incredibly durable and powerful. So, while the blood spatter was satisfying, the true effect was little more than an annoyance for the mystic.

Still, the shock was still there, robbing him of reason. That effect wasn't surprising, either. I suspected that he'd never endured anything like what I had just forced upon him. So, it was likely terrifying, having the very Mist upon which he'd always depended so heavily sucked out of him.

I fed on his terror.

I reveled in his shock.

And I intended to extend it.

So, without even bothering to dismiss my Stinger, I summoned the ADS and unleashed a barrage of norcite pellets in his direction. He never recognized the danger they represented until the spread overtook him, embedding those little balls of Mist-nullifying metal in his body. Normally, they would feed off the Mist in his core, but considering I'd already drained that, it went to work on the more stable nanites that had fused with his body. The results were horrific.

He immediately dropped to the ground, seizing as his muscles protested the sudden intrusion. Vomit spewed from his mouth, and judging by the smell, there were plenty of other fluids expelled from more private orifices. After that, I approached with an unhurried gait. I wanted him to feel the fear of what was about to happen. With what he'd done, killing the team of my allies, it was the least I could make him endure.

Soon enough, I stood over him.

I reached down to his twitching body and removed his helmet to reveal an unremarkable human face. I asked, "Are you from Earth? Or some other human planet?"

Through gritted teeth, he growled, "Earth . . ."

"Why?"

"Only chance . . . of . . . survival . . ."

"That didn't work out so well for you, then," I said, dismissing my firearms. "You should've been better."

I drew my interdiction blade, and then, without further hesitation, I aimed a chopping attack at his neck. As I did, I infused it with a steady stream of Mist, increasing the cutting power. It sliced through the mystic's neck, sending his head rolling free.

For a long second, I just stared at his corpse. It was still twitching, though without a head, I knew the mystic was dead. In that moment, I wondered how anyone could abandon their planet so callously. Yet, I knew the answer to that question. People were, at their core, programmed for survival. In a battle with the good of the entire world and a chance to ensure their own continued life, many would choose the latter, even at the expense of the former. That was just human nature.

Indeed, it seemed to be the driving force of every species I had encountered.

Which was a sad thing. People were meant to work together. To support one another so that we could build our way to a better collective life. That was how things were supposed to work.

But that was a useless ideal. People weren't built like that. Instead, we were all selfish and self-interested, with little nuance aside from extending that attitude to protecting our own friends and family. It was a depressing reality, and one I didn't think would change anytime soon. Especially not with Earth's doom hanging over everyone's head. Perhaps if he had more time—like a few more centuries—we'd be better off.

Probably not, though. With only a hundred years of Initialization, we'd already made a mess of things. So, there was little chance of us making productive use of even more time. At best, some tyrant would emerge to rule the planet and usher in an era of strength. At worst, we'd all kill one another off. And there wasn't much in between those two extremes.

In any case, I kicked the mystic over and knelt beside his corpse to see if he had anything I wanted to take. His clothing—or armor, I suppose—appeared to have merged with his body, so unless I wanted to hack him to pieces, there was nothing to loot. So, I turned my attention to the slain prisoners. Predictably, they had nothing worthwhile on them, either. The aliens had stripped them down to nothing but their clothing, and that was nothing special.

So, that left me with little else to do but leave.

I knew that would be complicated, though. Doubtless, the rest of the mystics in the facility, as well as the Adjudicators I'd yet to kill, would try to stop me. And now that the alarm had been raised, I had to expect them to be far more attentive than they had been on my ingress. Anything else would be surprising, which would make getting out far more difficult than getting in.

And then, even after escaping, I needed to climb out. I considered calling Patrick in, but I wasn't going to risk him and *The Leviathan* for something that I could very well do myself. With all that in mind, I embraced Stealth and commanded the door at the end of the hall to open.

I was immediately assaulted by seven twin streams of Mist that rammed into me. I went flying backward under the impact as a group of mystics rushed into the corridor. When I hit the ground, I did so in a roll before quickly coming to my feet and fending off another bombardment of Mist streams. They didn't lack strength, but they felt unsophisticated, especially when compared to what I'd seen from the last mystic I'd killed. Of course, that didn't mean they weren't deadly.

So, I leveraged every thread of thought to defending against the snaking tendrils of Mist that continued to assail me. It wasn't easy, and it took all my focus, but I managed it well enough to buy myself a little time. When I did, I took a grenade from my arsenal implant and sent it sailing in their direction. These mystics reacted much more quickly than the last group, and someone latched on to it with a thread of Mist, slamming it into the floor. At the same time, another one manifested a dome of Mist around it. When it exploded, it did so to little effect, save for whatever Mist it had cost to create that shield.

Frustrated, I dove into one of the cells, taking cover as I went over my options. They were too far away for the ADS, which was only effective up to a range of fifteen feet or so. After that, the norcite pellets spread too far apart to disrupt any but the weakest enemies. And due to their close proximity—as well as the confined nature of the corridor—I didn't dare use the BMAP. The Emperor was really only good against a single powerful target.

That left me with either the Stinger or the HIRC.

I chose the latter, largely because I'd never met a problem a generous barrage of bullets couldn't handle. So, I summoned the massive weapon, then swung out to bring it bear against my enemies. I was firing even before I was fully set, though my powerful body handled the awkward positioning easily.

The mystics at the other end of the corridor were not prepared for the bombardment of thousands of rounds per minute. With my massive modifiers, as well as the sheer power of the weapon, each bullet was stronger than my old Pulsar sniper rifle, and I'd added extra damage by using Explosive Shot.

The results were, in a word, impressive.

Deadly, too, though that was a given.

The mystics made a good show of defending against the barrage, summoning a series of strong Mist shields. Yet, they were not prepared for the sheer power I could bring to bear, and as a result, their shields were shattered. Their bodies fell soon after. So did the wall on the other side of the adjoining corridor. And the next one after that. My gunfire tore through three different walls before finally stopping. When I finally ceased my fire, every mystic was dead or dying.

Still, I knew they were dangerous.

So, I stowed the massive hip-held gun, then drew my interdiction blade. I would be lying if I called what followed mercy killings. I ended their lives, but it had nothing to do with bringing their suffering to a halt. Instead, I dispatched them with the brutal efficiency of an extermination.

Others might have felt some sense of satisfaction from it. But by that point, I'd killed so many people that I'd begun to dissociate from the realities of what that truly meant. Part of me mourned what I'd begun to consider a loss of humanity, but mostly, I just knew it was necessary. They'd brought a war of extermination to our table. I was just adjusting to their rules.

Or lack thereof.

Once I'd finished the gruesome yet necessary task, I once again took stock of my options. I knew there were plenty of other mystics out there. Initial reports were that almost a hundred were involved. On top of that, I could feel them. They were only faint whispers on the nonexistent wind, but they were there, nonetheless. If only those signatures had been slightly stronger, I could have simply killed them without having to move a muscle.

I hadn't reached that point, though. Not yet, at least. So, once I'd reloaded the HIRC as well as the Stinger, I set off through the facility. Everywhere I went, I saw bodies—the results of my Ghost—and with that, I did feel a sense of grim satisfaction. Not at the killing. But, rather, that the strategy had worked.

Of late, I'd begun to let myself get caught up in my mystic-esque powers, and while they were powerful, there was still a place for old tactics. My firearms were still very effective—more so than at any other point—and my

{Mistrunner} abilities were just as deadly as ever. I would do well to remember that.

I stalked through the corridors, keeping my Stinger out. It was a good thing, too, because I quickly encountered an intersection of corridors full of Adjudicators. There were at least a hundred of them, all seemingly wary behind metal bulwarks as well as Mist shields facing in every direction.

I could practically feel their fear, too.

Which was appropriate, considering how easily I breached their shields to send a half dozen grenades into their midst. The little balls of destruction went in each direction, and when they exploded, they did so with a carpet of fire that was hot enough to instantaneously melt their norcite armor. I knew this because I'd sacrificed more than a few crates of my ADS ammunition testing it. And considering I had no way to replace it now that the Bazaar had been destroyed, it was even more valuable than ever before.

The trick was to infuse just the right amount of Mist into the accelerant. I wanted it to fuel the impending inferno, but the resulting flames had to be completely natural, or the norcite would nullify them. So, I'd spent quite a lot of time and valuable materials perfecting it. However, the results were more than worth it, at least from my perspective. The dozens of Adjudicators being melted alive were probably less appreciative of my efforts.

In any case, the moment the fires petered out, I sprang into action. Even the ones who hadn't actually succumbed to the flames had been affected, and the integrity of their armor had been breached. As a result, the gunfire that followed was more effective than ever. The Stinger barked, sending one burst after another into the stunned warriors until, at last, they all died, confused, injured, and without any knowledge of what had actually happened.

A fitting fate for people hell-bent on destroying my planet.

After that first intersection, I encountered a handful more. Using the same strategy to dispatch those enemies, I lost count of how many I'd killed. Hundreds, at the least. Maybe the entirety of the thousand-strong force my information said the facility boasted.

In addition to the Adjudicators, I killed quite a few mystics. Compared to the ones I'd already slain, these were weak and ineffectual, and they had little chance of standing up to me. Even when they responded in force, it was a simple thing to ram through their weak Mist shields and drain them the same way I'd sapped the motivating energy from the Rift Shards.

It was almost boring. Or perhaps *repetitive* was the right word. Maybe *unremarkable*. Regardless, the process was necessary, and I at least took satisfaction in the fact that I'd rid the world of a few more alien invaders.

Along the way, I accessed a terminal and deactivated the shield as well as the drilling apparatus. It had already stalled due to my previous efforts, but I wanted to make it permanent—or at least as much as I could, which meant that they would have to replace the entire system if they wanted it to work again. So, with that done, I found my way to the hatch that had provided for my entry, then climbed through.

The whole time I'd been inside, I'd considered ways to escape the mile-long shaft, but I'd only found a few options. The first would be to go with my initial instinct and call Patrick in for a pickup. However, I expected that would come with a few issues, largely that he would have to blow a hole in the surface to gain entry to the shaft. That, in turn, would rain debris down on me. And while I had every reason to suspect that I could endure that kind of thing, I didn't want to push my luck.

Or maybe I just didn't like asking for help.

The second option was to climb my way to the top using much the same technique I'd employed on my way down. The only issue with that was that it would be slow. Very, very slow. Safe, though, which was definitely in its favor.

The third option was one that had been dancing in my thoughts for some time. Theoretically, it should be possible. I'd done similar things in the past, and on my way down, I'd come close to grasping the basics. Still, the idea that I could fly my way to the top was a daunting proposition.

Which was probably why I preferred it.

Or maybe that was just the possibility that I could fly, which I had to admit was incredibly attractive. Even as I tried to force myself to go over the pros and cons of the three options, I knew which one I would inevitably choose.

Once I acknowledged that, I braced myself for what I hoped would be a smooth flight.

CHAPTER FORTY-NINE

THINK HAPPY THOUGHTS

We don't really know where the Mist came from. Even those of us who claim to understand it are really just repeating something someone else told us. It has always been there, and it always will be.

—Frederick Eagin

I leaped high into the air and shoved against the Mist behind me. And I shot upward, but for only twenty feet, and then I started to fall. I repeated the action, throwing as much power as I could behind it, but it only threw me up a few extra feet. Frustrated, I scrambled for an answer, and I settled on the nanite cluster in my core that had once included Double Jump. With a couple of threads of my [Multimind], I examined the inert ability, and I quickly found a structure that I thought would work. So, I embraced it, quickly manipulating the Mist to create a tiny platform from which I could leap.

Like that, I progressed for a few hundred more feet until one thread of my mind found a different method that would more accurately meet my expectations. After all, I wanted to fly, not jump from one platform to the next. For that, I found the echo of my oft-forgotten and recently discarded Disengage ability. Because it was no longer an actual skill, it wasn't easy to see how it had functioned, but after a moment's inspection, I realized that it worked by manipulating the Mist of my aura to drag me in a specific direction. It took me a few moments to figure out how to reverse the polarity, but when I did, I felt things click together.

Suddenly, I was soaring upward.

For a few seconds, at least. And then, my Mist ran dry, and I started to fall again. Slightly panicked, I grabbed at the ambient Mist, shoving it into the adjusted ability until I stabilized. Like that, I hovered in midair, transferring the ambient Mist into flight.

Closing my eyes, I focused on the manipulation of the nanites, and slowly, I figured out how to move left and right, backward and forward. Up and down. Without [Multimind], there was no way I could have managed it, but with that skill, which I'd completely unlocked weeks before, I had enough mental power to make quick work of any calculations associated with flight.

Still, it took me a few minutes before I was comfortable with it.

That's when it hit me. I was flying. Certainly, I knew about the existence of jet packs, but they were both clunky and difficult to use. Never mind that they used even more Rift Shards than *The Leviathan*. For so long, I'd thought of personal flight as a distant dream. Yet, here I was, soaring through the air.

Despite everything that had happened—or maybe because of it—I couldn't stop myself from giggling in pure happiness. As I flew through the air, building speed all the while, I let out an excited whoop.

But it was over far before I had my fill, and I sailed over the lip of the shaft before landing with a splash. That's when, far below, the facility exploded, sending a column of dense fire to erupt from the hole and flood the area where I had just landed. At the last moment, I solidified the aura around my body, but I could do nothing to mitigate the shock wave of force that swept me from my feet and sent me flying down the tunnel.

I couldn't stop myself, but I could certainly harness the momentum for my own use. So, using the ability I had just learned, I subtly adjusted my trajectory, controlling my flight even as I soared to ever greater speeds. Without my many advantages, I would have splattered against one of a hundred different walls or obstacles, but with my new abilities in flight, I managed to narrowly avoid that fate.

And when I finally erupted from one of the entrances, trailing a stream of fire, I was going hundreds of miles an hour. I sailed high into the air, gasping for breath as I tried to take stock of the situation.

The drill wasn't my fault. I'd tried to keep it from exploding. Yet, it had, suggesting that the trap had been multitiered. They'd known I would come, and when their ambush failed, they had decided to sacrifice the entire operation in the hopes I'd be caught in the blast. It was a callous use of their equipment and people, but I had to admire their dedication.

Humans would probably never make that sort of sacrifice. Not willingly, at least.

Perhaps that was the difference between victory and defeat.

In any case, as I slowed to a stop, I wasn't surprised to see a dozen ships in the area. I was surprised to see *The Leviathan* dancing between them, peppering them with curiously effective cannon fire. It was much smaller than any of the other ships, to the point where it looked like a bug attacking a flock of birds, and yet, it was holding its own.

"Patrick!" I screamed through Secure Connection.

"Kind of busy here!" he yelled back, obviously strained. "I thought you weren't planning to blow anything up this time!"

"It wasn't me!"

"Are you sure?"

"Of course I'm sure! I'd know if I blew something up," I spat.

"Because you sometimes blow things up by accident."

"The explosions are never the accident. It's the size of the explosions that sometimes surprises me," I muttered.

"Sure. Where are you?" he asked. "I'll swing by and pick you up. I can't . . . Wait . . . Are you flying?"

"Uh . . . Maybe?"

"How are you flying?" he demanded. "And can you teach me? Hold on."

After that, I saw *The Leviathan* swoop around one of the large ships, narrowly avoiding returning cannon fire as he sprayed it with the ship's cannons.

"It's a . . . mystic thing? I mean, I'm not a mystic. But . . ."

"So, that's a no."

"That's a no," I agreed apologetically. "But you're doing great."

"I can't get through their shields or armor," he said, annoyed. He let out a grunt as *The Leviathan* made a hairpin turn, then added, "This ship isn't built for this kind of thing."

"Do you want help?" I asked.

"What are you going to do?"

"Yes or no?"

"Go ahead. But where's the other team?" he asked.

"Didn't make it," I said. "I'll explain it later. I'm going in."

"Going in?"

I didn't answer. Instead, I shot forward, pushing myself as quickly as possible. The wind whipped against my face, making me wish I had worn some goggles. But in my defense, I'd never expected to learn to fly, so it was an understandable oversight. In any event, I quickly accelerated to the sort of speeds usually reserved for my Cutter, only slowing when I approached the closest ship.

It was enormous, at least two hundred yards long and half as wide. But when I got close, I quickly surmised that its Mist shield was nothing special. So, using a tendril of Mist, I ripped through it and infiltrated its system.

But instead of simply deactivating it, I found the controls, overrode them, then aimed the thing at the ground. As I did, I forced it to accelerate to top speed, where it quickly crashed. Then, I yanked my BMAP from my arsenal implant, took aim, and buried the thing beneath a barrage of explosive shells. The first few did very little damage, but the ship had been built to rely on its Mist shield, which I'd just deactivated, so it wasn't long before the thing erupted into a truly impressive explosion.

Then, I shot off toward the next ship. This one was a little more difficult to infiltrate, and when I did, I found that I was locked out of the controls. Obviously, they knew I was there, and they weren't messing around. Whatever the case, they seemed to have missed the system meant to operate the cannons, which I took hold of, aimed at the next closest ship, and let loose.

After the first shot landed, the targeted ship attempted a maneuver that was probably supposed to mitigate some of the damage, but its pilots clearly hadn't expected to be subjected to friendly fire. As a result, the ship's shields were soon overwhelmed, and it went down just like the first.

That was when a hatch opened nearby, and a dozen Adjudicators as well as a few mystics came flooding out. I wasted no time in responding to their presence, swooping in with my interdiction blade out. With flight on my side, I could move incredibly quickly, though I still didn't quite have the control I would have preferred. So, I confined my maneuvers to simply charges.

But I was fast.

And fast meant deadly, especially when it came with an incredibly sharp blade aimed at an Adjudicator's neck. The first few soldiers had no chance to respond before their heads rolled free, but even when their comrades knew what to expect, they were almost powerless to combat my efforts. I was moving too quickly for them to adequately track, much less stop.

The mystics were a different story, but they were relatively weak in comparison to the others I'd fought. So, it wasn't difficult for me to slam tendrils of Mist into their cores and destabilize their abilities. After that, they went down even easier than the Adjudicators. Soon enough, they were all dead.

And they'd conveniently left the hatch open.

That led me to think that Earth's forces could certainly use a nice combat ship. I said as much to Patrick before turning the ship's cannons on the other ships in the area, and to great effect. They fired back, and my thoughts of hijacking a ship for our use were squandered by the damage it picked up.

So, to make sure that the crew didn't survive, I tossed a couple of my strongest charges into the open hatch, then flew away. It exploded a moment later, and the resulting shock wave sent me tumbling through the air until I crashed through the window of an ancient building. I quickly recovered my wits and took stock of the situation.

"I'm guessing you meant to do that," Patrick said.

"I wanted to blow it up, yes."

"That was a large explosion."

"I meant it to be," I lied. Indeed, the resulting explosion had been at least five times the size I'd expected. But Patrick didn't need to know that.

So, I gathered the Mist and pushed myself back the way I had come. It wasn't long before I'd infiltrated the next ship, though the response was much the same. I ended up having to kill a dozen more Adjudicators when I tried to hijack the cannons, and by the time I finished, they'd locked me out. I wasn't sure precisely how they'd managed that, but no matter what I did, I couldn't get in.

Not via the Mist, at least.

Physically, I had no trouble ripping the hatch open and descending into the depths of the ship. After that, I swept through the ship like a deadly wind. I didn't bother doing anything fancy. The Adjudicators proved to be the toughest to kill, largely because I couldn't reach them inside their armor. However, even that couldn't hold up to my interdiction blade. The mystics, oddly enough, were much easier to slaughter.

As I killed them, I couldn't help but wonder if all the rejects had been sent to Earth. Given how easily I could kill most of them, that was the only thing that made any sense. But in the back of my mind, I had to acknowledge that it probably had something to do with my growing power. It hadn't been that long since I'd absorbed my Nexus Implant, and even in that short amount of time, my abilities had grown significantly.

I didn't know why, either. On the surface, it was easy to assume that it had something to do with the Tier 7 Nexus Implant. It was special, and I knew that mattered. Yet, I felt that there was something else there, too. Maybe the strange alchemy of my specific skills, combined with the Tier 7 Nexus Implant, and with a little bit of talent thrown in was responsible. Or perhaps it was the rigorous training I'd undergone.

I had no idea.

But the results spoke for themselves as I tore through the ship's crew and defenders before reaching the bridge. A four-armed reptilian alien I took to be the captain tried to plead for their life, but I ignored them. Instead, I slaughtered everyone inside, then found the controls.

"Uh . . . Patrick? Do you know how to pilot a ship like this?" I asked.

"Sure. Let me—wait a second—damn it. Just find the control console and jack in," he said.

"I can fly it normal."

"No. You can't. Just trust me. Jack in and use your Mist powers to fly it. Otherwise, you're going to—"

At that moment, the ship hit one of the many skyscraper ruins in the area, tearing through the structure. The building didn't immediately fall, which was a testament to its architecture, but that didn't last more than a few more moments before it started to collapse.

"Try not to run into any more buildings!" Patrick scolded.

"I didn't do that! I hadn't even taken control yet!"

"Then maybe you should do that."

"Whatever," I muttered as I retrieved my personal link from the Hand of God. It wasn't strictly necessary, but I'd found that using a hard connection made it easier to concentrate on something specific. Once I made the connection, I quickly took control of the ship and guided it to the ground. I did a little more damage to the surrounding buildings, but that was inevitable, given the size of the ship. Still, I made it more or less intact. "There. Told you I could pilot the ship."

"First of all, you really shouldn't point to this as a success," he stated. "Second, you did it the way I told you to."

"You don't know that. Plus, what was wrong with how I landed?" I demanded, already running to the nearest hatch. After all, there were still quite a few ships out there. As I did, I reengaged the Mist shield, just in case the others tried to attack my new prize.

Before Patrick could answer—he was still flying around as a distraction, which required quite a lot of his attention—I stepped outside and saw the corridor of damage I'd left behind. "Oh," I said. Obviously, my passage hadn't been quite as clean as I'd thought, considering that two of the skyscrapers had already fallen, leaving the entire area clouded with thick dust. I wouldn't have been able to see at all without a combination of Observation and my Mist senses.

Coughing, I mounted the Mist and shot into the sky, partially for clear air but mostly so I could continue the battle.

Annoyed, I didn't bother with anything special with the next ship. Instead, I simply threw myself at it like a bullet, leading the way with my indestructible Hand of God. When I hit, I felt it in my bones, but due to the sheer durability of my body, it didn't do any real damage. The ship certainly couldn't say the same—if inanimate objects could speak—because I tore through the Mist shield and the fuselage like they were made of paper. And just like that, I was on the bridge and killing aliens.

Before I finished, Patrick's voice came over the Secure Connection, saying, "They're retreating."

"To where?" I asked. "They can't get through the blockade, can they?"

"I don't know. Do you want to chase them?" he asked.

I sighed. "No. We won't catch them," I answered, finishing the last alien off. I continued, "This whole mission has been one long screwup. It was a trap."

As I spoke, I took control of the ship, using whatever piloting skills I possessed—which weren't very well-developed—to guide it down to the ground. After I landed, I continued, "They set us up, Pick. When I got down there, the prisoners were already dead, and there were a bunch of mystics waiting on me."

"So it wasn't a real dig?"

"No—it was real," I answered. "That just wasn't its main purpose. If we had ignored it, I'm sure it would have been disastrous. But the real goal was to corner me."

"They know who you are?"

"They'd have to," I stated. "I've killed a lot of aliens recently. I'm sure that made waves."

"What do you want to do?" he asked.

Despite the fact that he couldn't see me, I shrugged as I responded, "I don't know. I think the first step is to get Alistaris involved. He needs to send some people this way because I don't think we want to rely on my piloting skills to get these back home. Plus, I'm sure there are a hundred ways ships like these can be tracked. And—"

"Mira! Watch out!" Patrick yelled.

Then, everything went white, and I felt like my entire body was being ripped apart, cell by cell.

CHAPTER FIFTY

UNLIMITED

Theoretically, there is no limit to what a powerful mystic can do. Despite studying it for centuries, we still don't know everything about how Mist interacts with people. We can see the mechanics of that interaction easily enough, but there are so many things we can't explain. In a way, that's reassuring, but it's also terrifying.

—Galatira Iamaxis

Pain unlike anything I'd ever felt before tore through my body. I couldn't think. I couldn't feel anything other than agony. And for a brief moment, I knew I was going to die. Then, some part of me simply refused to let that happen. I don't know if it was my core, my mind, or something more ephemeral, but in that moment—a split second before my body succumbed to whatever force had begun to rip it to pieces—something inside of me looked death in the eye and spat in its face.

It spat back.

More, it enveloped me in a way nothing else ever had, and it redoubled its efforts. It was almost as if death saw my refusal to succumb as an insult to the very building blocks of reality, and it wanted to punish me for that affront. And the means of that penance was pain. Lots and lots of pain, and to a degree that left the vast majority of my mind blank.

But there was one thread that focused on what was actually happening—or rather, on how to combat it. Something had torn me apart. Likely an explosion, based on how violently it had happened. All around me, there was Mist-laced fire, and bits and pieces of my body had flown in every direction.

That explained the pain I was trying to ignore even as it gripped nearly every thought in my [Multimind]. I ran from it, putting mental walls all around me as I tried to endure. As I tried to fix what was happening. In doing so, I focused almost entirely on the Mist all around me, on dragging as much to my core as I could.

And without my body to constrain it, I found that the connection I felt to the ambient ether was incredibly strong. Infinitely so. It felt like I was staring into a vast abyss, and all I needed to do was simply take the leap and fall into infinity.

That's what the whispers begged of me, at least. They were so clear. So powerful. Since I'd absorbed my Nexus Implant, barely a day had gone by that I hadn't heard those tantalizing whispers. Now, though, they had become screams. Not of terror or torment, though. Instead, they were pleading. Begging. They wanted me to join them.

And every facet of my being desperately wanted to give them what they wanted.

I couldn't, though. Not with Earth's fate hanging over me. I needed to save everyone. So, as enticing as those whispers were, I pulled away from the edge of that proverbial cliff and focused on survival. With control I'd never acknowledged, I latched on to the Mist all around me, and I flooded the cluster of nanites that governed the ability associated with my [Mist-Infused Body], forcing it to rebuild the damage that had been done.

And for the first time ever, it was found wanting.

There wasn't enough left to reform. My body had been so thoroughly destroyed that I couldn't simply build on whatever remnant remained. And that ability—as powerful as it was—was entirely incapable of doing what was necessary. So, I discarded it. If it couldn't do what had to be done, then I'd have to do it myself.

But I did keep one thing.

The template. Buried somewhere in that ability was a map of my body, a snapshot of the physical manifestation of who I was. And though the ability itself was incapable of putting me back together, that template gave me the guidance to do what my limited ability could not.

Still, I didn't really know what I was doing. Instead, I simply dragged more Mist into my core, shoving it toward that map with only the simplest of instructions: rebuild me. As simple as that command was, the desire behind it was so powerful that the nanites couldn't refuse. And so, they responded to the desperate plea in my mind and, slowly, layer by layer, recreated my body.

For some parts, it grabbed the material all around me. The meat and bones and everything else that had once been me. Where that failed, it used metal and plastic and whatever else was available, converting them on the fly. The results weren't entirely organic. Nor were they completely artificial. Instead, it was somehow both but neither.

I didn't have any choice, though.

Nor could I truly appreciate what was happening. Pain still raged within and without, and in the single thread of thought I'd kept quarantined from the agony, I knew my time was limited. Even as I built a husk of a body, it was just that—a lifeless shell. I needed to connect it. To suffuse it with my essence. Otherwise, the moment I ran out of Mist—and that was coming sooner than I wanted to acknowledge—whatever constituted me would dissipate into the atmosphere, and the body I'd built would fall, dead and lifeless.

For a while—which was subjective—I despaired, uncertain how I was meant to solve the problem. Yet, a spark of instinct or inspiration showed me the way, and I forced a branch of Mist from my core, sending it down my new leg. When I did, I felt something. It was barely more than a tremor of life, but it was enough to confirm that I was on the right track. A single branch wasn't enough, though. I needed more. I needed to suffuse the body with my personal Mist until my body's every last cell was touched by at least one nanite.

So, that's what I endeavored to do. It started out by sending tiny tendrils of Mist from that main branch, but soon enough, it became something else. Something on a far smaller scale. I don't know how long it took. As I sank into that task, an eternity might have passed. But slowly—ever so slowly—I accomplished my goal, infusing my body with power and life and whatever else constituted my identity.

Suddenly, I let out a gasp as my eyes opened.

And all I saw was blue-tinged fire. All I felt was some indefinable force tugging at me, trying to rip me to pieces. A roar of an explosion told me that only a fraction of a second had passed since everything had gone white, but I felt like a thousand years—or more—had passed. I was a different person, body, mind, and if such a thing existed, soul.

I raised my hand, and with a flex of Mist, the world went quiet. The roiling flames ceased to move, and the shock wave that had already torn my body to pieces simply ended. Then, the pieces of the ship fell to the ground, having been robbed of all momentum. The fires winked out, and only silence reigned.

That's when Secure Connection reestablished itself.

"Mira! Mira!" shouted Patrick.

"I'm fine," I responded, the echoes of that indescribable pain still coursing through me. Even those remnants made a mockery of my Pain Tolerance, though with every passing moment, it became easier to keep the torment quarantined. I was more concerned with the fact that, suddenly, I saw everything so much more clearly.

And the Mist was everywhere.

In the air. In the bits and pieces of the ship that had just exploded. In the bodies of the people I'd killed. And it was all alive, swirling around with what felt like obvious intent. It wasn't, though. The nanites weren't alive. They were just . . . something else that I didn't quite understand. That I couldn't. Not until I joined them.

But I knew that walking down that road—or plunging over the edge of that cliff—would require the cessation of whatever made me who, or rather what, I was. If I did that, I would join the whispers that had once again faded into the background. They were louder than they had been before the explosion, but not nearly so insistent as they had been when I'd been without a body.

"How?" he muttered. "You're strong, but . . ."

"Not now," I said, stepping past the still-smoking rubble. The fires had faded, but the heat remained. However, it didn't touch me—not in any way that mattered. "What happened? Where did that come from?"

"The upper atmosphere," Patrick said. "The shock wave knocked *The Leviathan* almost ten miles away . . ."

That's when I really got a view of my surroundings. There wasn't much left of the buildings that had once characterized the area. Instead, they'd been reduced to rubble. A couple had made a show of persistence, but only skeletons of what they'd once been remained. A few metal frames, but even those looked like they were only a stiff breeze away from joining the rest of the area.

Otherwise, I found myself in the middle of a massive crater that reminded me of the one inhabited by the irradiated wildlings.

"It was like a beam of pure white light. I thought . . . Mira, are you sure you're okay?" he asked. "The ship isn't up to flight right now, but—"

"I said I'm fine," I reiterated, though I didn't know how true that was. Barely anything of who I was remained. Even the Hand of God had been destroyed. So too had my arsenal implant. My Sheath. And my clothes. There was nothing left but whatever I'd used to cobble together a body.

I looked down at my naked form, and I saw nothing out of the ordinary—not at first. But then I realized what was missing. There wasn't a single scar on my body. The moment I recognized that, a wave of nausea swept through me. I fell to my knees and vomited. But even that was performative. I didn't need to vomit. The feeling was driven entirely by the memory of how my body should have reacted.

Because what I was had transcended anything so mundane as nausea.

In fact, I already felt disconnected from my humanity, and in a way I couldn't adequately explain. Nor could I fully wrap my mind around what it meant. Was I no better than those androids I'd so disdainfully dismissed as artificial? No. I was still a human being. It was no different than if I'd had a few cybernetics installed.

But I knew that was untrue.

Even the most extensive cybernetics kept the brain intact. Mine wasn't like that, though. In fact, I wasn't even sure I needed a brain anymore. Or anything else. During that explosion, I'd been nothing but a cloud of Mist, and yet, I'd still been capable of thought. Of pain. Of enacting a plan to meet my goal of survival.

I had no idea what any of it meant.

But I couldn't stop asking myself what seemed a very pertinent question: Was I immortal now? No. I distinctly felt that much, at least. If I'd taken too long, I would have dissipated into the Mist.

Probably.

Everything was a little muddled, at least in terms of what had happened during that brief instant.

Whatever the case, I had survived, albeit in an unconventional way, so any questions as to what precisely had happened could wait for later. In the meantime, I needed to escape ground zero and regroup back at the camp. Once there, we could figure out how to proceed.

So, without further ado, I set off across the crater. It was actually much larger than anything my first impressions suggested, and it took me almost an hour of walking to reach the edge. When I did, I was confronted with a steep slope that extended nearly three hundred feet above me. That's when I remembered that I could fly.

"Stupid," I muttered to myself as I gathered the Mist around me and leaped into the air. To my surprise, the process of flight came far easier than ever before. I only had to think it, and the Mist responded to my every whim. And when I really pushed, I could move incredibly fast. Like, top-speed-of-my-Cutter level of fast.

It was at that point that I realized how much I'd lost. My arsenal implant was gone, and so was the hover bike my uncle had posthumously gifted me. My weapons, too. The only thing I had left was my body.

And the Mist that seemed desperate to respond to my every command.

For a moment, I considered going back to the center of the crater to see if I could recover anything, but I knew how useless that would have been. Without the anchoring cybernetic, the arsenal implant would have become untethered and disappeared into whatever quantum space it existed in. The same was true of the Cutter.

No—my equipment, some of which had been with me since the very beginning, was gone. And that realization came with a sudden loneliness I couldn't explain. I had never been the sort of girl who became attached to her weapons. The only reason I'd named my pistol was because Gala had insisted. But I'd have been lying if I claimed that I didn't keenly feel the loss.

Hovering in midair, naked as the day I was born, I sighed.

My world had just irrevocably changed, and I wasn't certain how to deal with that new reality. I hung there for a long moment, then I spun around to behold the aftermath of the explosion I had somehow managed to survive.

What I had done was not normal. I knew that. Even in the wider universe or among mystics, it couldn't have been common. Perhaps it was even entirely unheard-of. For all I knew, what I had done was completely unique.

And that was terrifying.

But walking a new path always was. I'd felt similarly adrift after losing Jeremiah, and again when I'd thought Patrick was gone. I had persevered, though, and even if I'd done some terrible things in the aftermath of both of those incidents, I had survived, and I had grown stronger. I intended to do so again.

So, after I collected my thoughts, I pushed against the Mist and took off. It took me a moment to recognize that I'd done so without thought for which direction I was going. However, after only a moment, I realized that I was following the tendril of Mist that constituted Secure Connection. Before, I'd had to concentrate to see it, but now, it was plain as day. If I hadn't recognized that I had changed, that would have driven it home.

I didn't travel at my top speed. Instead, I barely exerted myself as I flew away from the blast zone. Eventually, I left the island behind, crossing a short span of water before flying over the rest of the ancient and abandoned city. While the crater had been contained to an area only a couple of miles across, the effects of the explosion were evident even ten miles away from the epicenter. Buildings had been destroyed, and the wildlings who'd been just outside the area had begun a stampede in an effort to escape the explosion they were ill-equipped to understand.

Each one glowed with so much potential that, all gathered together, they were nearly blinding to my Mist senses. It was just further evidence of how they differed from the people who'd received Nexus Implants, and I couldn't help but wonder if the world wouldn't have been better off if we'd never had those foisted upon us. Sure, they helped us adjust, but they also clearly hindered people in a way that, in retrospect, felt entirely unnatural.

Would Earth have been better off without the system or its Nexus Implants? Maybe not immediately. But as the wildlings evolved, they would certainly be much stronger than if they'd been fitted with those implants. That line of thought made me wonder if those Nexus Implants were just another means of control. Sure, everyone had told me they were there to help people adapt to the Mist, and that made sense.

Except nothing in the universe was meant to help people. Indeed, everything I had seen since, well, forever suggested the opposite. So, what was more believable? That some altruistic group of aliens had instituted a system whereby people would be saved? Or that they'd done so in the hopes of containing any threat of new races outstripping their power?

I knew the answer to that question.

But just because it was more likely didn't mean that it was true.

So, with those thoughts dancing in my mind, I flew across the landscape, outpacing the fleeing wildlings until I eventually found where Patrick had landed. Or crashed, really, given the state of *The Leviathan*. It was tilted on its side, with only part of its landing gear having extended, and there were great dents in the fuselage, suggesting that he'd guided it to a rough landing.

I hit the ground at a light jog, then entered the open cargo bay. It didn't take me long to find Patrick in the engine room, where he was busy working on the propulsion system. I could see the Mist leaking from the fuel box, which couldn't have been good.

"What did you do to my ship?" I demanded, trying to keep my tone good-natured.

Patrick turned, and his jaw dropped. "Where are your clothes?"

"Shit."

I knew I'd forgotten something, but I wasn't going to let my embarrassment show. So, I put my hands on my hips and said, "Don't try to change the subject. Why did you crash my ship?"

"It's my ship, too!"

"And you crashed it."

"I saved it! Do you have any idea how big that blast was?"

"Kind of. I was only at the center of it," I said dismissively. That's when his face fell, and without another word, he stood up, crossed the room, and threw his arms around me.

"I thought I lost you," he muttered.

"You almost did," I said. "But . . . Things have kind of changed."

Then, I told him as much as I could about what had happened. It wasn't a short explanation, and in the end, it didn't really reveal much.

"I think we need to ask an expert about this," he stated.

"We only know one expert, and he's an asshole."

"Freddie is the best we have."

"But—"

"Mira, you can't figure this out on your own. You know that. So, swallow your pride or your anger or whatever it is that you're feeling and let's go have a talk with him," he said, gesturing with a wrench. "You know I'm right."

"Fine. But I still think he's an asshole," I muttered. Then, I turned and marched back to our quarters where I hoped to find some clothes.

CHAPTER FIFTY-ONE

GUIDANCE

I hate the things I've had to do. The lives I've ruined. The lies I have told. And for what? So when the time came, we would be abandoned to a fate none of us earned? The Templars were supposed to save us. And yet, we find ourselves in the same boat as everyone else on Earth.

—Frederick Eagin

The trip back to our temporary base was characterized by a subdued attitude. We'd set out to save a team of like-minded defenders of Earth, and we'd come away empty-handed. What's more, the aliens had destroyed any information or equipment we might have taken from the situation. But even then, I was more focused on the things I had lost.

My arsenal implant was gone, and my guns had been destroyed right along with it. All the bombs I'd made, my hover bike, and even my clothes had been disintegrated by the bomb that should have taken my life. I had survived, and in doing so, I'd crept closer to a revelation that I felt was always just over the horizon, but knowing that didn't help me in the short term. I still had no weapons, no armor, and no hover bike.

But at least I'd proved much harder to kill than even I would have suspected.

Once, I'd seen a video of my uncle where he'd survived for some time after being decapitated. And despite that gruesome image—and all the implications that followed—I couldn't stop myself from hoping that I would be capable of repeating that feat. Of course, I didn't want to be decapitated. The last thing I desired was to be put into that kind of a situation. But at the same time, I hoped that if I did find myself beset by those circumstances, I could endure.

Now, I knew I'd shot well past that mark. I didn't even need a body to survive—at least for a little while. And I could rebuild my body during whatever time I had. It was a disturbing level of power that I still couldn't quite wrap my mind around.

Still, it had saved my life, and I'd gained power as a result. I didn't have a status to tell me I'd gotten stronger, and there were no pretty skill trees to consult. Yet, I knew that I'd made some serious gains. Without testing, if I'd had to guess, I would liken it to a similar power jump to what I'd experienced after killing the Pacificians and evolving my class.

Which was terrifying.

Because I was already far and away the most powerful individual on the planet. I'd come to grips with that reality when I started taking down mystics left and right. They'd thrown the best they had against me, and they'd continuously come up short. That was all the evidence I needed to recognize that I'd reached an uncommon—perhaps even unique—level of power.

It wasn't enough, though.

I knew that right down to my roiling core of Mist. For all my might, the aliens still had all the advantages. Sure, I could escape, and more easily than ever before. I could probably even take a few people with me. But Earth seemed no closer to being saved than when we'd first begun. That was a depressing, yet persistent, thought.

"Are you really okay?" asked Patrick, glancing over as I sat in the copilot's seat. He'd finally gotten *The Leviathan* running, though it was clearly not in great shape. Hopefully, he was right when he'd claimed that he could get it back to perfect condition once he had time and access to all his tools, the largest and most expensive of which were back in the temporary base.

"I don't know, Pick," I admitted with a shake of my head. Then, I looked down at my hand and said, "I rebuilt everything, cell by cell. Maybe atom by atom. A few hours ago, this was the Hand of God. Now, it feels like flesh and blood. No—that's what it is. It's not artificial. It's real."

"Can you do it for me?" he asked.

"Do you want that?"

As he piloted *The Leviathan*, he shrugged. "Maybe. Sometimes. The cybernetics are useful, and most of the time, they're way better than my old limbs."

"But?"

"But it's not the same. You know that as well as anybody, right?" he said. He wiggled his artificial fingers. "I can feel with these, but there's something missing. It's not like using a real hand. Real fingers. No matter how good the cybernetics, it's just different. Not worse. In a lot of ways, it's better. But it's . . ."

"Different. Yeah."

I didn't feel that from my new hand. Or the rest of my body. In fact, everything felt better than it ever had before. Though it did come with the added caveat that my every sense was heightened, and I could feel the saturation of Mist like never before.

"I can try it if you'd like," I offered. "I don't mind."

"Maybe" was his noncommittal response. I understood his hesitation. After all, there were infinite ways it could all go wrong. But I vowed to help him if I could.

"What do you think caused that explosion?" I asked.

He shrugged, clearly relieved at the change of subject. "I don't know. Like I said, it was just a beam of light from the upper atmosphere," he answered. "A satellite, probably."

"Or a ship," I suggested.

"Yeah. Or that."

And considering that there was a massive ship up there with all sorts of advanced weaponry, I didn't have to think long before I came to the inevitable conclusion. "It's *Infinite Conquest*. I'm sure of it," I said.

"If that's the case, we've got problems. That thing . . . Alistaris said that it was advanced even in the core systems," Patrick explained. "That means that for us, it's . . . It's insane."

"It would have to be something big," I stated. "That blast radius was miles wide. It could destroy an entire city. I guess I'm not the only one that likes to blow stuff up."

"Be serious."

"I am," I lied. As troubling as what had happened was, it didn't really change anything about what we had to do. We'd always known that the aliens possessed far superior firepower. Seeing it in action was terrifying, but it didn't give us any new information.

The next couple of hours were punctuated by idle conversation and Patrick's questions about how I had survived. It clearly scared him, what had happened, but I think that knowing what I could do frightened him even more. Or maybe it just reminded him of how much of a freak I really was.

Finally, Patrick guided the ship to its customary spot, where he set it down only a few dozen yards from the compound Alistaris and the Dengyts had built. Once there, we went through the postflight checklist.

"I'll go let Al know what happened," I said. "You want to come?"

He shook his head. "I'm going to start working on the ship," he said. "It's going to take a while to get her back to normal, and I want to get a jump on it. Let me know if anything important happens."

"Will do."

Then, I headed to the nearby hatch and let myself outside. Night had long since fallen, and the sky was filled with a carpet of stars. I took a moment to admire it, wondering which ones of those stars hosted other planets that, presumably, had similar problems to Earth. Of course, I also saw the moon, and my eyes found the crater I'd left behind after my lone trip to the lunar surface.

Hopefully, I wouldn't have similar control issues as I continued to fight the Gomaris and the mercenaries they'd hired. If I repeated the actions I'd so flippantly taken on the moon, Earth wouldn't survive. That was the level of power I was dealing with now. Control was paramount because anything less would destroy the planet. I was certain of that.

Sighing, I pulled my attention away from the night sky and headed toward the facility. However, when I arrived, I was a little surprised to find that the gate didn't automatically open. More, the gnomes who were acting as guards kept their weapons trained on me as they demanded to know who I was.

"Are you serious? I'm Mira. You all know me."

"Mist signature's off," said one of the Dengyts, her weapon still pointed at me. I could have disabled her—and anyone else in the facility—if I so desired, but I knew that would cause more problems than it solved. I chose to wait for cooler heads to prevail, and soon enough, Alistaris arrived.

"You going to call off your dogs, Al?" I asked.

"Who are you?" he demanded.

"Mira."

"No, you're not. We've had Mira's Mist signature stored for months. You don't fit."

"Yeah, because I got blown up. That kind of thing tends to change a girl, if you know what I mean," I said. "I don't—"

At that moment, something hit me in the side, sending me sprawling across the ground. However, I arrested my momentum with a quick pulse of Mist, then shot into the sky. That's when they started shooting.

The first few bullets thudded into my rebuilt body, but they didn't penetrate more than a quarter of an inch. They still hurt, though, so I raised my hand and, with a deft surge of Mist, sent the gnomes flying backward. At the same time, I looked down to see a furious Freddie leaping in my direction.

And he meant business, too, because he glowed with a blue corona of Mist that roiled like fire. Before he reached me, I shot to the side, sending another tendril of Mist at him. Before he could react, I squeezed it tight and yanked him back to the ground. He hit with enough momentum to break a normal person's bones, sending a cloud of dust billowing from the point of impact.

But I knew he wasn't really hurt.

None of them were because I knew that if I took that step, things would progress well past the point of no return. If I really injured someone, I'd probably have to kill some of them. And considering that I didn't want that, I showed restraint.

For once.

"Enough!" I shouted, seeing a shimmer in the Mist that told me where Alistaris was. I slapped him aside with another tendril of Mist, deactivating his ability. He skidded across the ground, hitting the nearby wall. "I don't want to hurt anyone!"

Freddie roared, "Abomination! What did you do to her?!"

That's when I lost my patience and let the full extent of my new power loose. It exploded from me in an eruption of Mist that knocked all but the strongest unconscious. I didn't even know what I was doing—not consciously, at least—but that didn't make it any weaker.

Of course, Freddie and Alistaris remained aware. Neither of those two would succumb so easily. However, it did stun them, which allowed me to send thick tendrils of Mist out to wrap around them. Then, I pulled, yanking them in my direction. When they got close enough, I stopped their momentum and left them hanging in midair.

"Stop!" I yelled. "Just stop!"

"Impostor!" growled Freddie. "What did you do to her? Who are you? What are you?!"

"Oh, for God's sake, it's me!" I insisted. "I met you in the woods after you lost one of your apprentices to the Mist. He'd just turned into a wildling, and you were following him." Then, I turned to Alistaris. "You cornered me in New Cairo, sneaking up on me and trying to blackmail me into working for you. It worked, but we kind of moved on from that after I slaughtered a bunch of android assholes. Since then, we've been working together. Plus, every time I let you into my ship, you leave a bunch of trackers behind."

"That doesn't prove anything," Alistaris said. But Freddie at least looked mildly convinced. In any case, I had to spend the next few minutes recounting everything about meeting the both of them before they finally accepted that I was who I claimed to be. Even then, I could tell that neither of them was entirely convinced. But at least they weren't going to attack me anymore. If that persisted, I was going to have to make some tough decisions.

Finally, I set them both down and floated to the ground.

"When did you learn to fly?" asked Alistaris.

"You aren't you," Freddie insisted. "Far too much Mist. And your body . . ."

"Please stop looking at my body, you old pervert," I said, trying to lighten the mood. It didn't work, so I said, "Fine. Okay, so here's what happened . . ."

I explained how the mission went down, going into as much detail as I could. I even described how I'd learned how to fly, taking some degree of pride in Freddie's disbelieving reactions. More than once, he muttered, "Impossible."

Which just made it feel that much better. Or it would have if he wasn't staring at me with undisguised suspicion.

At last, I got to the part about the bomb, and I described how I'd pulled myself back together. It wasn't entirely accurate, largely because words failed to properly convey most of the experience. Yet, I did the best I could, ending with, "But it's not all sunshine and daisies. I lost my whole arsenal, my Cutter, and my clothes. So, I'm stronger now. A lot stronger. But I don't have any weapons."

"That . . . is quite a story," Alistaris said. Then, he turned to Freddie and asked, "Does that make sense to you?"

That's when I realized that Freddie was almost assuredly drunk. The pungent smell of alcohol combined with body odor hung off him like a cloak, and he looked like he hadn't bothered with basic grooming for weeks. And finally, he was more than a little unsteady, with his Mist aura undulating out of control. Which wasn't like him.

Or it hadn't been before he'd obviously given up on life.

But there was some life in his eyes now. Something that hadn't been there at any point since I'd first met him. That highlighted a simple fact: Freddie's decline had been ongoing for longer than I'd known him. Probably longer than I had been alive, given that Templars were known to live quite a long time. It was a grim reminder that, even if I was more powerful than most—maybe more than everyone—they all had their own lives, their own struggles. The world did not revolve around me.

Except that, in some ways, it did, which was a difficult thing to accept.

"She's on the verge."

"The verge of what?"

"Of Supremacy."

"So soon?" asked Alistaris.

"A body forged of Mist. An untethered mind. Control. It's all there," Freddie stated. "She need only take the final step."

"How?"

"Guys—what are we talking about?" I asked.

"Supremacy," said Freddie, his eyes shining with something manic, with something I didn't like.

"Okay—but what is that?"

"I have spoken of those people who have reached the peak," he said. "The ones so powerful that they're as gods to the rest of us."

"Yeah," I said, recalling the conversation.

"You are close to becoming one."

"A god?"

"Indeed. But it is a long step. A difficult one that most are never prepared to take," Freddie explained. "I didn't think I would ever see it with my own eyes, but there you are, glowing like the sun. It is beautiful and terrifying in equal measure."

"Can we use this?" asked Alistaris.

Freddie shook his head. "No. She won't soon take that final step, and forcing it would be unwise."

"In what way?" asked the Dengyt.

"She would not survive, and her body, mind, and soul would be absorbed into the Mist," said Freddie without hesitation. "She is more powerful now. Far more than either of us can comprehend. Even she doesn't know her limits. Yet . . ."

"Yet limits still exist," finished Alistaris.

"Indeed."

"So, nothing changes?" I asked, annoyed at the cryptic nature of the exchange. They made it sound like I was nothing more than a weapon. Certainly, I was that. I had accepted that role. But at the same time, I was a person, too.

"Everything has changed. But our situation is still dire," Freddie stated, some of his mania fading. "We are still doomed."

Then, without any other warning, he turned and walked away. I was tempted to reach out with a Mist tendril and bring him back so he could answer my questions, but I stopped myself. Freddie was broken, and though that brief exchange had tapped into the person he'd once been, it hadn't changed who he was now.

So, I turned to Alistaris and asked, "What's the plan? I know we lost a team, but . . ."

"I don't know," he admitted. "We thought you were dead until you arrived. I'm still not sure that you're not an impostor."

"I'm not."

"That sounds like something an impostor would say. For now, just head back to your ship. We need to figure out where, exactly, that blast came from. Once we're sure of that, we'll need to take care of it. I have some ideas on how to take down the blockade, but they're not certain," he explained. "The issue is that it's not just protected by a single defense. Norcite-plated satellites. Mist shields. Drones. It's all built to guard against Templars, so it's meant to defend against anything we can do."

"We'll figure it out," I said. "I have faith."

"That makes one of us," Alistaris admitted with a sigh. "Now go. Rest. I'm sure some new crisis will present itself tomorrow."

CHAPTER FIFTY-TWO

SCREAMS

I didn't know how to react when I thought I'd lost her forever. I knew nothing could have survived that explosion. It was too powerful. But then I heard her voice, and I saw her face. I was too shocked to wonder if she was still the girl I loved.

—Patrick Ward

I sat on a cushion of Mist, hovering a hundred feet above the ground, my eyes closed and my mind—every thread of it—focused on my surroundings. I could feel everything, and in a way that defied all my previous expectations. Every atom was laid bare to me, and through it all, I saw the Mist. Each individual nanite. Most were identical, but there were enough differences from one group to the next that I couldn't help but wonder if there were any limitations.

I could see them replicating, too. One became two, and two became four, and so on. For each one that was born, another went inactive, only to be consumed by the others for its materials. And so, the cycle continued, on and on into infinity.

There was something else there, though. Some connective tissue I couldn't really perceive. But I could hear it. Those whispers had haunted me for months, but I still wasn't sure what they meant or how I was supposed to deal with whatever that might turn out to be. I wanted to, though. In a way, I felt like I needed it. Understanding those whispers was the key to everything.

And yet, meaning remained elusive.

So, I shifted my focus to the object in my hand. It burned between my fingers, deactivating any nanites that came into contact with it. And considering that much of my body was composed of solid Mist, the pain should have been agonizing.

It wasn't, though, and I had no idea why.

Handling the norcite pellet—one of the few remaining pieces of my old arsenal—was uncomfortable, but it wasn't debilitating like it had been for many of the mystics I'd fought. In fact, I almost felt a kinship to it. Like in another world, it might've been a part of me.

Or like it was a reflection.

The moment that idea crossed my mind, I let out a gasp of understanding. Suddenly, what I was seeing—what I felt—made sense. Norcite was like a reflection of the Mist. Or an inversion.

And with that in mind, I adjusted my perception, twisting it around until I could feel the norcite more properly. And suddenly, the whispers became screams.

I recoiled, dropping the pellet.

My cushion of Mist disappeared, as well, and I fell right alongside it. For an instant, I plummeted toward the ground until I steadied my mind and reestablished the Mist. My heart continued to pound, though, and I opened my eyes to a brilliant sunset that was in such fervent opposition to the chaos in my mind.

I steadied my breathing and slowly pushed my mind into placidity.

Then, I closed my eyes and repeated the exercise. The moment I shifted my perception, the screams returned. Yet, they weren't really screams at all. It was more like I could hear into a different frequency. And buried in that was a story that I could almost perceive.

I pushed.

But it felt like I was up against a wall, beyond which was something I wasn't supposed to be able to see. I didn't like that one bit, so I kept shoving against it with my mind. The whole time, the screams persisted, screeching their way through my soul. I ignored them, and with no small expenditure of willpower.

Then, suddenly, I burst through.

And I saw everything.

The system itself was laid bare before me, all numbers and symbols I could never hope to understand. It was so complex that I briefly recoiled, and in that moment, the curtain hiding it all from me—from everyone—fell back into place.

Not one to let myself be locked out of anything, I returned to my toil with more fervor than ever before, breaking through the wall without difficulty. And then, I let myself bask in what I saw.

Upon second observation, those numbers were not so incomprehensible. Instead, they reminded me of all the equations and puzzles I'd learned to solve. But they were built into a recognizable structure that was connected to everything. I didn't know what any of it really meant—not yet—but I was more determined than ever to figure it out.

More importantly, I could pinpoint the tiny pebble of norcite that had fallen to the ground. It lay there like a solid chunk of nothing. An abyssal rock that represented a void amid the chaos of everything else. I yearned to understand it. To see what it truly was.

For the next few hours, I studied the numbers, and I began to understand what I saw. The numbers weren't really numbers. Rather, they represented the system that governed the Mist that, in turn, suffused every part of my reality. An interconnected web of controls and commands and predetermined algorithms that far exceeded even my mathematic prowess. It was as if I was looking at the inner workings of the Mist, at everything that made those nanites function the way they did.

By extension, it was as if I was looking at the underpinnings of reality itself. Did I understand it?

Not at all. I wasn't even certain that it was what I thought it was. But one thing was for certain—it was more complex than anything I had ever seen. Indeed, it was more complicated than anything I could have imagined. And looking into layer upon layer of impossibly intricate numbers and symbols, I felt smaller and less consequential than I'd ever felt before.

The norcite, though, was easy enough to understand.

It was like a black hole. Or a tiny eldritch creature whose tentacles sapped the life—or the Mist—from everything around it. Or that was just how it felt. In reality, it was more like anti-Mist, deactivating every nanite it came into contact with. But it went further. Nanites going inert was just part of the cycle. Instead, norcite infected them to such a degree that they could no longer be consumed by the other nanites. Thus, it ended the cycle.

What would the world look like if it was more pervasive?

Certainly, I couldn't survive such a thing. Nor could most people on Earth. The Mist was too ubiquitous. We were too dependent on it.

That was one thing I learned very quickly. The Mist was life. Norcite was death. Or nonexistence. It was difficult to truly pin it down, but I felt like understanding the relationship between the two was important.

So, I drifted down to the ground and once again retrieved the norcite pellet so I could resume my study. Like that, I occupied myself for the next few hours until I felt someone approach from nearby.

"I don't want to hear it," I said without opening my eyes. I was still hovering in midair, but only a few feet from the ground.

"I'm sorry," Freddie said.

"About what?" I asked, opening my eyes and looking in his direction. My perception was still shifted, so I could see the inner workings of the nanites inside him. It was a strange thing, seeing someone broken down to a series of numbers and symbols. His flesh was still there. But it was so suffused with the

Mist that it was practically invisible beneath the blanket of symbols. "Attacking me? Or what you said before?"

"Both," he admitted with a sigh. He looked at me for a long moment before shaking his head. "I still don't know if you're you."

"I still feel like me, so that's how I'm approaching it. What do you want?"

"To guide you."

"Guide me to what?" I asked.

"Templars are not without knowledge," he stated. "And I've been cleared to share some of the system's history with you."

"I thought that was a mystery."

"Not to us," he admitted. I couldn't recall if he'd ever claimed otherwise, but that seemed likely. Everyone else had said as much.

"And why would you share this with me now?"

"Because you're on the verge of transcendence," he said. "You'll learn it all eventually. You've probably already gotten a few peeks behind the curtain, right? Well, I requested permission to tell you what we know. Or what information is available to me, at least."

"So, you're in contact with the other Templars, huh? Did you tell them what's going on here?"

"I have."

"And?"

"And nothing. They won't get involved, except to free us to act," he said. "What few Templars remain on Earth have given themselves to Alistaris's command."

"Too little, too late," I muttered. If they'd have done that sooner, there was a chance that Earth might not have been facing annihilation. Or better yet, if the larger organization of Templars had acted, they might have wiped out the Gomari Confederation altogether. Yet, they remained in the corner of the universe, their hands clean.

All the while, we bled and died.

"Please control yourself," Freddie pleaded, his words breaking me out of my spiral. He'd fallen to his knees, obviously in pain—not surprising, given the way the Mist was swirling all around me.

I pulled it back, and with no small degree of effort. "Sorry."

He let out a shuddering breath. "It's . . . I understand. You shouldn't have so much power. Not yet. You can't control it properly."

"I'm aware. What do you think I've been doing out there?"

"Floating."

I sighed and rolled my eyes. "Just tell me what you want to tell me so I can get back to what I was doing."

"Very well," he said. He looked a lot less disheveled than the last time I'd seen him, which reminded me of his appearance the first time we'd met. Back then, he'd been on the heels of watching his apprentice become a wildling. "Do you know the origin of the system?"

I shrugged. "It was built to help people control the Mist," I said. "Like training wheels for evolution. Without Nexus Implants, people tend to devolve. Kind of like people have to break down before the Mist can rebuild them."

"Yes. But do you know who built it?"

"Not a clue. Aliens, I'm guessing."

"The Originators—the first mystics—millions of years ago. An entire planet of them who'd evolved the hard way. They were incredibly powerful, and they understood the Mist in ways we can't fathom. They built the system. Not to help people, but to control them. To keep them from evolving properly. But then, a group that would eventually form the Templars broke away."

He shook his head. "They went to war. Whole galaxies were destroyed. Then, they created norcite."

"How?"

"Sacrifice. Millions of them, all led by the most powerful among them. They gave themselves over to the Mist, creating a black hole the size of a galaxy, and with the purpose of subverting the Mist. When it reached a crescendo, the Originators were destroyed. But before they succumbed, they used their power to ensure that the system continued to evolve and spread. Meanwhile, the black hole reversed polarity and exploded—we don't know why—sending shards of the drained matter throughout the universe. We know it now as norcite."

"What does this have to do with me?" I asked. It was an interesting history lesson, but I had two major problems with it. First, the distant past didn't seem all that relevant to Earth's fate, except to provide context. So, it felt like a pointless lecture. Second, I didn't know how much I could trust it. The Templars had established that they had their own goals, and honesty didn't seem like a big part of their guiding philosophy. In fact, the only thing I'd seen from them was selfishness.

"Everything," he said. "Mira, you're playing with forces you cannot begin to understand. No one on Earth does. And if you don't stop, you're going to—"

"Die. That's the word you're looking for. We're all going to die unless I find a way to save Earth. Do you want to die?"

"No, but—"

"That is what's at stake here," I said. "Our backs are against the wall, and I feel like I'm the only person that can do what needs to be done. The enemy is stronger than us. They have more people that matter. They know more. They are better equipped. They have all the advantages. Except me. They don't have anyone that can do what I can do. And you want me to . . . What? Just step back and let them destroy Earth?"

"Do you have an alternative?" he asked. "The way you're going, there's every chance that things go out of control, that they continue to escalate until there's nothing left. That story wasn't meant to be aspirational. It was a cautionary tale of people going too far. That war killed quadrillions of people. And it has killed exponentially more since then. And here you are playing with norcite and planning who knows what. A billion people live on Earth. If we die, that's a tragedy. But if you keep going the way you're going, the death toll will be catastrophic for the entire galaxy. For the universe, perhaps."

"How?"

"You are on the verge of transcending. When you reach that point, you will gain unprecedented control over the Mist. In all the universe, only a handful of people have done that. And they only did so after centuries of training and study. You've only been alive for thirty years. That is nothing. You'll be like a baby with a grenade."

"What's the alternative? Give up?"

"Leave. The Templars are prepared to help you escape Earth. They will even take you in. Train you. Teach you how to properly use your power."

"And what happens to Earth?" I asked, already knowing the answer.

"Earth's fate has already been sealed. The planet will be destroyed. Perhaps not today. Maybe not for a decade. But it will happen. You know this," he answered.

I started to respond, but I held back. He was right. If we kept going the way we were, Earth was doomed. So far, we had held our collective head above water, but I knew just how thin our margins were. One slipup, and the enemy would get what they wanted. They would destroy the planet, harvest whatever resources they required, and then move on to the next world.

"So, I should run away."

"From a burning building, yes," he responded without a hint of shame.

"And what happens if we win?" I asked. "What if I stay, and somehow, we turn the Gomari Confederation and their mercenaries away? What if I refuse the Templars' oh-so-generous offer?"

I was almost certain that I already knew the answer, but I wanted him to say it.

"They are prepared to limit your impact," he said. "With everything they have."

"No pretty words, Freddie. Tell me what they will do."

"They'll join the Gomari Confederation in ensuring that this planet is destroyed."

"To kill me."

"To prevent you from endangering the entire galaxy," he countered. "The Gomaris won't let you win, though. They will bring everyone they have."

"That doesn't make sense," I said. "Al said that they'd give up once the costs outweighed the benefits. That was our entire strategy. Make it so difficult enough for them to continue that whatever resources they could harvest from Earth's destruction would be outweighed by the cost necessary to defeat us."

"The paradigm has shifted."

"Why?"

"Because of you!" he shouted. "Because of the threat you represent! The Templars have put a bounty out on you and would subsidize the Gomari Confederation's entire operation. More, they would contribute. You think the mystics you've fought so far were dangerous? They are nothing compared to Templar masters. Nothing. Take the deal, Mira. Earth is going to die. It will be destroyed. You don't have to go with it. It's the only move that makes—"

I reached out with a thousand tendrils of Mist, wrapping them around him in the space of a second. He tried to react. He attempted to counter. But his efforts were laughably weak. Or maybe I was just that much stronger than him. Whatever the case, he stood no chance against me.

I squeezed.

I could have sucked the Mist right out of him, but I chose not to. That would have brought death far too quickly. Instead, I wanted to look into his eyes as he realized that he couldn't stop what was coming. That was what he wanted me to feel, after all. So, as far as I was concerned, I was giving him a taste of his own medicine.

Vaguely, I was aware of someone shouting at me. Instead of dealing with that, I pushed against the Mist at my feet and soared high into the air, and I dragged Freddie with me. As I did, I never broke eye contact. Even as his bones were crushed to jelly, I stared into his very soul. And just before he died, I said, "I refuse your offer."

Then, I ripped him to pieces, sending a cascade of body parts and gore raining down on the ground below.

I remained aloft, just staring up at the atmosphere. With my eyes, I could see the faint blue tint of the blockade. However, with my other senses, I could see the flows of Mist that enabled it.

Somewhere out there, the entire universe was arrayed against Earth.

I refused to give in to defeatism, though. Instead, I let myself drift toward the ground only to see that Patrick was staring at me with a confused look on his face. "Why?" he asked.

When I touched down, I recounted what Freddie had told me. Once I'd finished, I said, "His offer wasn't real. The Templars have no intention of teaching me anything. They just want me off the board. I'm sure that if I took them up on their offer, I'd end up dead or enslaved. Our only chance is to win this war, and so decisively that no one else would dare mess with us again."

"And how are we supposed to do that?"

I shook my head. "I don't know," I answered. Then, I looked at the gore-covered ground and the strips of white cloth that had been Freddie's Templar uniform. "But at least we have one less enemy to deal with now."

CHAPTER FIFTY-THREE

ABANDONING SHIP

Hope is a strange thing. We cling to it, often when, by all rights, we have no reason to. Yet, even though we know it isn't real, it remains a comfort. A light amid the darkness, and one that we hope will lead the way to salvation. It will not. Only death and destruction can save us.

—Alistaris Kargat

Do you really think this will work?" I asked, staring at the holographic display meant to represent Earth. The sphere was familiar, but many of the lights surrounding it were new. They were meant to represent the forces arrayed against us. Some marked the satellites that controlled the blockade, each one as large as a space station and guarded by forces specifically created and equipped to kill mystics. The ships represented by the other lights were a little more vulnerable, but with the blockade in place, they were just as out of reach.

From where I was standing, our situation looked entirely hopeless, and not just because of the enemies represented by those lights. Instead, I was also worried about the Templars that were going to join the battle. Freddie had given me a choice—let them take me into custody or they would join forces with the Gomari Confederation and the Arbiters of Orion they'd hired to enact their will.

I had made my decision plain when I'd ripped him apart.

In a lot of ways, I hated myself for doing that. Until that point, Freddie had been an ally. Not quite a friend, but certainly not an enemy. Clearly, he'd expected that to soften the blow of his threat. It had only made it worse, and I had reacted impulsively.

But as much as I loathed my actions, I didn't regret them. As far as I was concerned, Freddie had established himself as a traitor to humanity. He was the enemy. And I knew precisely how to deal with enemies.

Alistaris shook his head, "I don't know, Mira. We're undermanned, underpowered, and outnumbered. But we also don't have much of a choice. We go now, or we resign ourselves to a long, slow descent into oblivion."

"Wow. You're a ray of sunshine," I said.

"Optimism would be a misplaced emotion in this scenario."

"There it is. That's the positivity I was looking for."

"Do you want me to spell it out for you?" he asked.

"That's just how she is," Patrick said.

"You, too? I'm disappointed, Pick."

In reality, I knew precisely how desperate our circumstances were. With Earth surrounded and blockaded, it was only a matter of time before we were too late in responding to one incursion or another. Our planet was doomed unless we did something about the people hoping to destroy it.

Of course, what nobody was willing to point out was the fact that even if everything went perfectly, there was nothing to say that the Gomaris or Templars wouldn't send another fleet to attack us. Or another after that.

They would keep coming until Earth had been reduced to a cloud of space rock waiting to be mined.

And even without that knowledge, Freddie's warning rang true. So long as I remained on Earth, everyone else was in danger. Yet, if I fled, the planet would be all but defenseless. After all, if I hadn't been around since the quarantine had ended, the planet would have already been destroyed.

Which was why Alistaris had spent the past two weeks pleading with the Ark Alliance to provide for the evacuation of Earth.

"These world ships. How big are they?" I asked.

"The largest is about half the size of your moon," Alistaris answered. "It can house nearly half a billion people. The other three are much smaller. And the fourth is a carrier for all the transports it will take to evacuate everyone."

"What about the conditions?" was my next question.

"Livable."

"That doesn't sound good," I pointed out.

"It isn't," he said. "These world ships are old. They're barely spaceworthy. Yet, they are the only chance humanity has of survival. We can house more than half the world's total population. The fifth ship is for farming and husbandry. This is the best I could do to ensure your people's survival."

I sighed and glanced away. It had been a while since I'd thought of Askar, the elf I'd killed back before the Pacifician incident, but when Alistaris had suggested evacuating Earth via a series of world ships, I'd remembered his story.

His people had been exploited, and his planet had been destroyed, too. The population had only survived aboard what I now knew were world ships. He'd described it as hellish.

And I took that to heart.

But between that and the population's annihilation, what choice did we have? Earth was going to be destroyed. Freddie had assured me of that. So, knowing that—and I believed it—the fact was that the world ships offered us the best chance of survival.

Or them.

For my part, I would have to go in a different direction. And I knew the Templars wouldn't stop hunting me. I was too big of a threat to them. To everyone, apparently.

There was a part of me that wanted to simply take the Templars up on their offer of training. Even if it turned out to be imprisonment, perhaps that was for the best. After all, if I was as dangerous as they seemed to believe, then maybe I needed to be held captive.

But I couldn't let myself go down that road. Even if I thought it was for the best, I wouldn't give myself over to their custody. I didn't have that in me.

So, the plan was for Patrick and me—and Gala, too—to head in the opposite direction. Gala said she had friends who might be able to hide me, at least until my powers developed enough that I wouldn't need further protection.

Not that I was certain I needed it now. I'd ripped Freddie apart without difficulty, and I expected I could do the same to any other mystics who came after me. But according to everything I'd learned, they wouldn't just send one person. Nor would they limit it to a few. They'd send whole battalions of mystics and Adjudicators after me. Eventually, they would wear me down.

I only had a vague idea of what sort of threat I posed, but Freddie had been insistent that it was enough to bring the weight of the Templars down on me. And something told me that if they couldn't possess me, they would ally with other mystics like those associated with the Arbiters of Orion. With that as context, it was only a matter of time before they killed me.

Unless I had allies and time to realize the potential they seemed so sure I would one day reach.

Thus, fleeing was my only option.

Before we could get to that part, though, there were a few steps we needed to take. First, we had to do something about the blockade. That entailed attacking and destroying the satellites. Second, we would have to destroy the fleet of ships. Looking at the holographic display, every single light represented a target we had to destroy.

And there were hundreds of them.

And in the interim, we had to contact Earth's population and convince them to flee the planet. Some were already in the know, but many had no clue that Earth was even behind a blockade. Certainly, the unavailability of the Bazaar—which I had destroyed—would have clued them in to something being wrong, but I did not envy whoever was tasked with wrangling a bunch of people with different agendas.

Hopefully, self-preservation would win out, and people would get in line. Otherwise, the casualties would be massive.

"I don't like the idea of jumping ship," I admitted.

"Neither do I," Patrick agreed. "But it's the only way humanity is going to survive. It's only temporary."

"It's the best we can do for them," I said. The bottom line was that, while I wanted to ensure humanity's survival, I wasn't one of them. I would be fine, one way or the other. So would Patrick and everyone else I cared about. As a result, I felt secure that I was doing everything I could. My issues were more rooted in the fact that I was admitting defeat. That did not sit well with me. "Whatever the case, this is how it has to be. Now, we need to get down to the business of figuring out the details."

After that, Alistaris took over. The plan of attack was threefold. First, I was tasked with infiltrating *Infinite Conquest*, which, based on all the intel Alistaris had gathered, was at the center of everything. Because of that, once I managed to get into their systems, I would have unfettered access to the satellites that governed the blockade. And that meant I could shut them down.

Then, whatever forces humanity could muster would attack the fleet of ships poised around the planet. It would be a brutal and bloody battle, but Alistaris thought we had a decent chance of breaking them—especially if I kept the flagship out of the fight. Our chances would go up if I could take control as I had with other ships.

Once we'd defeated them, the third and final phase—which we'd dubbed the Exodus—would begin. Hopefully, humanity could board the world ships and escape before the Gomaris recovered and sent more ships to block them.

It was simultaneously complex and incredibly simple, but one thing was certain: It all hinged on me. If I failed, then Earth was doomed. That was more than a little pressure, but if I was honest, it really wasn't any different from the life I'd been living for the past few months.

Or that's what I told myself, at least.

In any case, after we'd established the basic structure of the plan, everyone went to work. And for the next month, I engaged in damage control as I bounced from one attempt to destroy the Earth to the next. In the meantime, Alistaris and his people established a routine of convincing humanity to abandon their home.

And he came up with an ingenious lie to ease the process.

"I can't believe all those people think they've won a lottery," I muttered as I sat next to Patrick in the cockpit of *The Leviathan*. It had been entirely repaired, and in many ways, it was better than it had ever been before. "Are they stupid?"

"They just want to believe they have a chance at a better life," he said.

Indeed, the lie was just as simple as any other part of the plan. The leaders of humanity—or at least the ones Alistaris had chosen to contact—had told their people that a selection of the population would be given the opportunity to start anew on a paradisical planet on the other side of the universe. The way everything was described, it was the opportunity of a lifetime, and everyone should have known it was too good to be true—especially in our world—but they ate it up.

And they'd signed up in droves. There were more applicants than the world ships could accommodate, which meant that the lie of the lottery had become something approaching a truth. However, instead of simple chance, the applicants were subjected to grueling selection criteria with an emphasis on bringing people with valuable skills.

In the meantime, Patrick and I had prepared our ship, which was how we were getting to *Infinite Conquest*. He and Alistaris's people had given it every stealth measure they could, and I'd been practicing enhancing those with my abilities in Mist control. But more importantly, I spent most of my time training to overcome the blockade.

The first stage would require me to open a passage so that we could escape the atmosphere and assault *Infinite Conquest*. I was reasonably confident in that. But the second part meant that I needed to find the control terminal—Alistaris assured me there was one—in *Infinite Conquest*, infiltrate it, then either destroy or shut down the framework of satellites that enabled the blockade.

Then, the battle would begin.

And hopefully, we would win. After that, half of Earth's population would escape. The other half . . .

I didn't want to think about them.

Because no matter how it went, I had to focus on the ones I could help. The ones I could save. Otherwise, I'd never get off the ground.

In any case, when the time came, Patrick and I—along with a dozen of Alistaris's best fighters as well as Gala—had loaded into *The Leviathan*. We had our mission, and all of humanity depended on it.

Or at least half.

Which was more than enough to spur me along. So, once everyone was ready, I turned to Patrick and said, "Let's go."

He took a deep breath, then nodded before igniting the ship's Mist engine. It fired instantly. As it did, I initiated a Secure Connection with Alistaris and told him we were going ahead.

He said, "We're ready when you are. The moment the blockade goes down, ten thousand of Earth's best ships will be in the air."

"Will it be enough?"

"Theoretically?" he answered. "Yes. But it will be close."

"So, the same as the rest of the plan."

"Indeed," he stated. "But it's—"

"The only way. I know," I responded. "But it doesn't feel like the right way."

He didn't have anything to say to that, so I cut the Secure Connection as Patrick guided the ship into the air. We accelerated, whipping across the world with all the speed *The Leviathan* could muster. As we did, a bout of melancholy washed over my mind. If everything went right, I would never see Earth's surface again. No more trees. No more swamps. No wildlings.

I would never revisit Mobile. Nor would I ever spend another night on any of our favorite beaches. I could never return to New Cairo and see their pyramids. Or any of the hundreds of other places I'd visited.

"What are you thinking?" Patrick asked, glancing at me out of the corner of his eye.

"Wishing I had done a lot of things differently," I admitted. "I know that without me and what I can do, Earth would have already been destroyed. But at the same time, I also know that the Templar fleet that's on its way is after me."

They had yet to arrive, which was why we'd timed our attack the way we had. Once they joined the other ships already surrounding Earth, our fate would be sealed.

That seemed like a theme. Humanity's back was against the wall, and it felt like we had no choice but to throw ourselves at our opponents and hope we came out on top.

"I don't know how they can so callously destroy an entire planet," Patrick remarked. "Just for a few resources."

"Because they don't see us as people, Pick," I said. "The universe is infinite, right? There are thousands—maybe even millions—of other populated planets out there. What does the loss of one mean to these people? Nothing. They could strip a thousand of them, and nobody would bat an eyelash. Because we're not unique. Not to them, at least. So, destroying Earth isn't any different to them than cutting down a tree. Or digging a mine. Or whatever."

He just shook his head.

For my part, I continued to watch the passing landscape as I lamented what was coming. Eventually, though, we reached our designated location, and Patrick set *The Leviathan* down. Once he did, he started activating the various countermeasures meant to keep us hidden. For my part, I focused my senses outward, wrapping the ship in my own Mist. Then, I inverted it all.

The whispers once again became screams, but I'd practiced the technique often enough that I could easily ignore them. Instead, I concentrated wholly on the task at hand. The idea was to use my powers to create a Mist mirror that would reflect our surroundings back on any sensors that might detect us.

It was the same way my Stealth ability had always worked, though I hadn't realized it until recently. Once I had discovered that fact, I'd endeavored to extend it to the ship. And it worked, though it was incredibly difficult to keep it in place over something so large.

I managed, though.

Barely.

Gritting my teeth, I said, "I'm ready."

And just like that, Patrick lifted off, guiding the ship toward the upper atmosphere where the blockade loomed. Soon enough, we reached the shimmering wall of Mist. Reaching out with a hundred Mist tendrils, I deactivated the nanites in the immediate area. At the same time, I kept the flow of other nanites out of the resulting hole just long enough for *The Leviathan* to escape into space.

Without my [Multimind], I never would have managed so many threads of thought at once. But with it, I accomplished the task at hand.

And just like that, we had broken through the blockade.

Briefly, I considered telling Patrick to leave Earth behind. We had enough supplies to last for a few weeks, and we had access to all of Alistaris's star maps. We could escape and find a life somewhere else.

But those thoughts only lasted a split second before I discarded them. I didn't think I owed Earth much. They'd never really given me anything but grief. But there were individual people down there I wanted to save. And besides, I didn't want to lose. I didn't want to run away in defeat.

So, I said, "Well, that's one obstacle clear. Now, we just have to get through that without alerting anyone."

The *that* in question was a fleet of a thousand norcite-coated drones between *The Leviathan* and the looming form of *Infinite Conquest*.

I turned to Patrick and said, "You're up."

CHAPTER FIFTY-FOUR

INFINITE CONQUEST

Fighting an invasion is difficult, especially when the forces are uneven. Because of that, desperate measures are often necessary. Moral sacrifices have to be made. Boundaries must be crossed. That is the only way we can hope to win.

—Galatira Iamaxis

Space spread out before us, blocked only by a giant monstrosity of a ship called *Infinite Conquest*. I had seen plenty of holographic models of the vessel, so its appearance wasn't a surprise. Its hull was dark blue, with gold filigree decorating its sharp nose. Four symmetrical wings extended from the center of the ship, ending in circular modules that I'd once marked as crew housing. Now, though, I knew those were where the Mist engines were housed.

As prepared as I was for the sight of the thing, what truly put me off was its sheer size. I knew it likely didn't have the spatial distortion that made the interior of the Bazaar so enormous, but even then, the sleek fuselage was more than a mile long and half as wide. The wings extended much farther, and they too bore artful embellishments of gold filigree.

"It's as much a work of art as it is a piece of technology, isn't it?" I sighed. The herculean ship made *The Leviathan* look small and shabby by comparison. I found that irritating for some reason. "Such a shame we have to destroy it."

"Could always steal it," Patrick suggested. "Kill everyone on board and just take it off into the galaxy. We really don't have to do this."

"You know we do," I said. "If we don't, Earth is going to be destroyed. Like, not just taken over by some shady characters. They don't want to enslave anyone. They want to just break it to pieces, take the valuable bits, and move on to the next world. So, either we do this, or everyone dies."

"I know," he said. "I just wish it didn't have to be us."

"Who else is there?"

Lately, I had thought a lot about power and responsibility, and I'd come to the conclusion that, because of my strength, I had an obligation to do the things no one else could. In this case, that meant assaulting a legendary warship and bringing down the blockade around Earth so that at least part of the population could escape what was coming. I didn't like the notion of leaving even one person behind, but I'd come to terms with it.

I had to do what I could.

There would be plenty of time afterward to lament my inability to do more.

"Would your uncle do this?" Patrick asked.

I shrugged. "I don't know. I guess it depends on which version of him you asked," I answered. "Jeremiah was a complicated person, and over the course of his life, he showed a lot of hypocrisy. I think that if you asked him right after the Initialization, then he wouldn't have hesitated to commit to whatever it took to save as many people as possible. But later, things got muddled. He lost too much. He became jaded. Self-interested. He stopped caring about anything."

"He cared about you."

"Maybe."

I wasn't so sure that was the case, though. I think he liked the concepts I represented. To him, I was a fresh start. A chance to be everything he couldn't. But by the end, I'm not sure if he had the capacity to love anyone.

I didn't want to go down that path. I wanted to care. I wanted to help. I wanted to be a guiding light, even if that meant causing a huge explosion bright enough for everyone to see. In fact, that was precisely what I preferred.

"Are you sure about this? Once we get started . . ."

I knew what he meant. Once we were committed, there wouldn't be much of a chance to deviate. If we did, thousands of our allies would end up dead, which was to say nothing of the rest of Earth's population. On top of that, there was every opportunity we wouldn't get another chance to pull out.

But my answer was the same as it had been every other time I'd been asked the question.

"I'm sure. Do your thing."

Patrick nodded, then narrowed his eye as he guided the ship forward. He didn't go quickly, but that was because the thousands of drones between us and *Infinite Conquest* were each equipped with potent sensors. So, even with his skills combined with my own Mist manipulation, he didn't dare go too fast.

For my part, I focused on everything around us, gently nudging the tiny Mist tendrils that represented their senses away from *The Leviathan*. It was difficult and tedious work, but I knew that one little slipup was all it would take before we were detected and subjected to the copious weapons systems on board *Infinite Conquest.*

Gradually, with Patrick at the helm, *The Leviathan* threaded a thousand needles as it wove between the norcite-plated drones. I knew from experience that, even if someone beheld the ship with their own two eyes, they would see nothing but empty space. Patrick's skill was just that potent.

Because that was the whole point of having a [Smuggler] skill. It wouldn't be much use if the bad guys—or a customs officer—could simply look out the porthole of their ship and see *The Leviathan* trying to transport goods under their noses.

Fortunately, Patrick's potent skill combined perfectly with my own abilities, and before long, we made it through the densest collection of drones. Still, it took more than two hours, a process that was complicated by constant movement—both from the drones and our geosynchronous orbit. Regardless, Patrick accomplished the task with aplomb, putting the ship only a few feet from *Infinite Conquest*'s hull.

"Last chance to turn back," he said as I pushed myself out of the copilot's seat.

I leaned in and kissed him on the cheek. "I'll be right back," I said. "Don't worry so much. We got this."

"Yeah."

"I love you," I told him. With what was at stake, I didn't want to leave that sort of thing unsaid.

He turned, looking me in the eye, and said, "I love you, too. Be safe. Kill some aliens. And come home."

"Don't I always?" I said with a grin.

Then, I headed to the cargo hold, where I found Gala and a dozen stealthy gnomes. They were the best Alistaris had, and despite their tiny size, each one looked intimidating in their red-enameled armor and with firearms that looked almost as large as they were. By comparison, Gala was wearing a set of armor that looked a lot like the infiltration suit I'd lost. Except hers had a plethora of rigid plates that would doubtless offer a lot more protection. She also wore Ferdinand at her hip and carried an assault rifle in her hands. Over her shoulder was the hilt of a blade that, through my Mist senses, I could tell was infused with quite a lot of Mist.

"You ready for this?" I asked.

"Not my first ship assault," she stated.

Given her past, I supposed it wasn't. So, I retrieved a disc from the set near the back hatch. Then, I slapped it onto my chest. A second later, a thin layer of Mist spread across my body. It was meant to insulate a person from the vacuum of space while also providing oxygen. It was not very sturdy, though, and if it received even a little damage, the bubble of Mist would almost assuredly rupture. However, it was the best we had available. For all the equipment people on Earth had developed, space-exploration gear was not on that list. So, we didn't have any real space suits and were instead forced to rely on the discs, which were called temporary protective gear—or TPGs for short.

After everyone else had donned their TPGs, I checked to make sure that everyone was ready. They were, so I wasted no more time before opening the hatch. Fortunately, *The Leviathan* had been designed for space travel, so there was a thin semipermeable Mist shield that kept the atmosphere of the ship from rushing out.

I led the way, stepping out. As I did, pushed against the Mist behind me— the same way I flew—until my feet hit the fuselage. At the same time, I cloaked myself in a thick blanket of Mist, concealing myself from casual observation.

The others followed, though they were forced to use controlled bursts of air for movement until they hit the surface of the ship. Once they touched down, they engaged some sort of magnetic connection that kept them linked to the fuselage of *Infinite Conquest*.

We all knew where we were going, so there was no need for communication. Instead, I led the way to the nearby hatch before I extended my Mist tendrils to the terminal on the other side. Once I'd connected to it, it was only a matter of seconds before I'd overcome all its defenses. A few moments later, I'd disengaged the security alarm. Finally, I commanded it to open.

It did so with a hiss of air, but it was protected by a similarly permeable shield as what kept the air inside *The Leviathan*'s cargo hold. After glancing back at the thirteen other members of the strike team—I could see them despite their various skills and stealthy equipment—I slipped into *Infinite Conquest*.

I landed with no more than a whisper, then vacated the spot directly beneath the hatch. The transition from zero gravity to the simulated gravity of the ship was a little jarring, but I pushed past it. Instead, I focused on the team as they slid inside, one by one, until they were all present.

The interior of the ship was even more lavish than the exterior would suggest. For some reason, I'd expected it to resemble the Bazaar, but instead of unadorned plasti-steel walls, the corridors looked more like they belonged in a palace. Decorative molding, all in gold, lined the halls, with subtle patterns etched into the dark blue walls. With all of that, it should have looked so buy as to be claustrophobic, but the hall was spacious enough to prevent that.

Yet, that was only what I saw with my eyes. My Mist senses saw so much more. Every surface was densely infused with nanites, suggesting that the materials used in the construction of *Infinite Conquest* were incredibly expensive. More, they formed patterns that mimicked the ones on the physical material, enhancing the visual effect for anyone who could see it.

I stood in awe of the sheer opulence.

On Earth, we were scratching and clawing for everything we could get, and here the enemy was living in a space palace. More, if they'd put that much effort into a mundane corridor, what would I see in the captain's quarters? How much had they spent on the ship's weapons systems?

It was just further evidence that we were all out of our league. Our enemy wasn't just powerful. And the word *rich* didn't quite cover their affluence. They were so far above us that even looking at their ship made me feel shabby and undeserving.

And the most frustrating part was that I knew I was wrong. I had more raw power than anyone on that ship. In fact, I could rip it apart from the inside in a matter of hours, scattering all that wealth into space. Yet, despite the knowledge that it was invalid, that feeling of inadequacy persisted.

Following that came frustration.

Then anger.

Suddenly, I felt Gala's huge hand on my shoulder. I looked up to see her great bovine eyes staring down at me. She shook her head.

That's when I realized that the Dengyts all around me were struggling to stay on their feet. Even Gala was trembling as Mist swirled all around me. It wasn't benign, either. It was aggressive. Hungry. It was a reflection of my mood. With some conscious effort, I took control of it, bringing the cloud of nanites closer to my body. It still roiled, but I kept it under my thumb.

"Sorry," I mouthed as I saw Gala's shoulders slump. She took a deep breath, and the Dengyts reclaimed their feet.

I needed to be better than that. I'd grown more adept at controlling the Mist, but that little outburst had proved that I still had some ways to go. I wasn't ready for what was coming. I knew that. In a perfect world, I would have taken a few years to grow acclimated to my new level of power.

But I didn't have that.

Annihilation was knocking on Earth's door, and if I didn't meet it on my terms, everything would be destroyed. That was the problem with evil. It didn't ask you if you were ready to confront it. It simply showed up, and you had to react with whatever means you had at your disposal.

Hopefully, the powers I'd recently uncovered would be enough.

With that in mind, I harnessed my emotions and took control of the Mist all around me. Then, cloaked in various forms of stealth, we started down the hall. It wasn't long before we found the first enemy.

He was a curiously human-looking alien in a deep-blue uniform that was trimmed in gold, just like the ship itself. His clothing suggested that he was one of the crew. Or an off-duty Adjudicator. Regardless, I wasted no time before pouncing, ramming my hand into his chest. As I did, I yanked on his Mist, preventing him from activating any skills or abilities.

His sternum collapsed under the blow, and he fell to the ground, gasping for air. He tried to scream, but I stomped on his throat—having to go through his hastily raised hands at the same time—destroying his voice box. He died seconds later.

I suppose I could have just killed him with Mist. In fact, given the pool of green blood—the only thing to mark the crew member as an alien and not a human—from where his broken sternum had come through his skin, I probably should have done just that. However, I was still growing accustomed to having that ridiculous power at my beck and call.

Suddenly, I regretted my decision not to bring a couple of weapons with me. There were two major problems with that, though. The availability of suitably potent weapons was nil, which meant that I'd have had to take a gun from someone else, leaving them unarmed. And considering that I had my Mist powers to pick up the slack, it seemed better to avoid that. The second issue was one of storage. Until I'd lost it, I hadn't quite realized how much I'd depended on my high-quality arsenal implant. Even if I'd had my old weapons, without the ammunition storage of the implant, they'd have quickly become useless.

So, I'd made my choice.

And even if I had just experienced a bit of regret, I reassured myself that it was the right decision.

Regardless, it was the choice I'd made, and I had no other option but to stick with it. So, with that in mind, I dragged the crew member's body into a nearby room—it was empty—and we continued on our way. I had memorized the suspected layout of the ship, but that was based on the class of vessel rather than actual plans of *Infinite Conquest*, which had been heavily modified. Still, after only a few minor setbacks and a couple of hours, we made it to the control pavilion at the center of the ship.

It was actually a little disappointing in scope, with only a few dozen terminals manned by various aliens in blue uniforms. Yet, I knew it was the lynchpin of the whole operation. Through those terminals, I could disengage the blockade.

But there was only one problem.

Well, there were about a hundred problems standing between us and the terminals, which were shielded by an extremely powerful wall of Mist. In front of them and blocking the entrance was a checkpoint manned by over a hundred mystics as well as at least twice that many Adjudicators.

My eyes were drawn to a single enemy, though.

He was tall—probably six and a half feet—and clad all in black, which made him stand out from all the other blue-clad aliens. The other thing that marked him as different was the fact that his skin looked like melted wax, white, pasty, and scarred. And finally, the largest reason he drew my attention so completely was the sheer volume of Mist contained in his body.

Of course, he saw right through my attempts at stealth.

For someone like me—or him, I suppose—abilities, skills, and technology were minimally effective. Perhaps if I'd had better control, he might not have noticed me, but the same couldn't be said for Gala and the dozen Dengyts flanking her.

"Ah—as expected," said the alien in black. His voice was deep and raspy. He drew a gleaming sword from the scabbard at his waist. It glimmered with potential, containing more Mist than I'd seen in any other weapon. "I have so wanted to meet you, Mirabelle Braddock. Come with me and your allies will live. Resist and they will be captured, tortured, then killed."

For a moment, I didn't know how to respond.

Then, I realized that there was no reason to maintain my attempt at stealth. So, I let the cloak of Mist fall away as I said, "You know who I am. Seems only fair that you should introduce yourself."

"Of course," he said with an elegant bow. "I am accustomed to being known everywhere I go, but I suppose ignorance should be expected in this frontier backwater. I am Dal Kanik, and this is my ship. One of many in my fleet, but even after all these years, it remains my favorite."

Dal Kanik.

It was a name I'd heard in passing during Alistaris's briefings. He was the leader of the Arbiters of Orion—a mystic of untold power. Some even suspected that he was on the verge of achieving Supremacy.

Which meant that there was a good chance that I'd finally met my match.

"The man in charge, huh?"

"Just so."

"Do you honestly expect me to surrender?" I asked.

"I do not."

"Then why offer?"

"Curiosity. You could join us. I would even spare your allies," he said. "No one needs to die."

"Except for everyone on Earth," I pointed out.

"Yes. That. Of course, they would still perish," Dal Kanik responded, spreading his hands in a gesture of inevitability. "Their fate is sealed."

"Then there's no choice at all," I said.

"Indeed."

Then, I felt the Mist gathering at his command, and I responded in kind.

CHAPTER FIFTY-FIVE

A FATED BATTLE

I'm not special. Not unique. Yet, I'm surrounded by the best of the best. Gala. Alistaris. Even Freddie was strong for a Templar. But me? I'm only a little better than average. And Mira . . . She's so far beyond even those others that she's practically a different, far more evolved species. That scares me.

—Patrick Ward

A sharp tendril of Mist extended from the black-clad mystic, aiming directly for my heart. I slapped it aside with my own Mist control and rocketed forward. As I did, the other mystics and Adjudicators opened fire, filling the fifty-foot-wide corridor with projectiles of all sorts. Meanwhile, Gala erected a portable Mist shield as she and the dozen Dengyts let loose with their own firearms.

It was chaotic.

But there was order to it, too. I could see it all via my Mist senses. And any projectile that came close to me was knocked aside with a subtle influence of Mist. I didn't need armor, but still, I'd covered myself with a layer of protective energy that could rival any Mist shield I'd ever seen.

I wasn't worried about the extras. They couldn't hurt me. Instead, I was entirely focused on the man with the melted-wax face. Because it required every ounce of concentration I could muster just to hold him off.

With gunfire echoing through the corridor, I raced forward. When it became clear that neither of us could gain an advantage via our control of Mist, we clashed in melee combat.

I ducked under his initial sword strike, then threw myself upward with a massive uppercut that connected with his jaw. However, instead of hitting solid bone encased in a thin layer of flesh, I found something more akin to clay, slimy and formless. My fist sank in, and for a moment, I was stuck.

It was just the opening the black-clad mystic needed, and before I could initiate a dodge, there was a glistening sword tearing through the air, aimed at my neck. Judging by the amount of Mist in the blade, my foe clearly intended to end the fight with a single strike. Instinctively, I raised my hand to block, infusing it with Mist.

It hit with undeniable force.

And yet, I denied it.

It should have been unstoppable. My hand—and everything else in the blade's path—should have been cut.

It was not.

Instead, I blocked the strike, even sending the blade rebounding out of control. Shock decorated the pale mystic's malformed visage, and though he recovered quickly, I did so a few seconds earlier. I leaped high, ripping my hand free of his face and connecting with a Mist-infused round kick that sent him stumbling into a few of his own allies.

At the same time, another pair of mystics attacked me—one wielding a spear, the other with a pair of daggers. Each weapon was coated in Mist, which actually worked against them. Without even turning from my fallen—but recovering—foe, I slapped the newcomers' weapons away with thin tendrils of Mist. Governed by a thread of thought I barely even acknowledged, those wisps of Mist were nearly instinctive.

But that didn't make them ineffective.

Indeed, they did their job with aplomb, then snaked out to wrap around the mystics themselves. They tried to fight, but their attempts at resistance were useless. I wrapped them in Mist, then squeezed.

They burst like a pair of balloons filled with viscous red liquid.

I paid them no mind because I was totally focused on the wax-faced mystic who was picking himself up from the ground. I dashed toward him, using a combination of Engage and Teleport that I'd devised on the spot. Mist rushed out of me, but I replaced it a second later by dragging even more from the ambient Mist.

As soon as I reached my opponent, I aimed a side kick at his knee, crumpling it. But to my horror, it snapped back into place a second later. Clearly, his odd malleability wasn't limited to his jaw. He snapped out with his sword, and I couldn't react quickly enough to dodge. Nor could I block it. So, the blade ripped into my side.

But he wasn't rewarded with the expected shower of blood. In fact, my body—made almost entirely of nanites—mended even as his blade passed through me. So, aside from a brief shock, I was entirely unaffected as the blade exited my body. With my Mist senses, I could see that millions of nanites had been destroyed. Yet, that number was barely impactful.

It was also obviously surprising because he stared in shock. Only for a moment, but that was enough.

I punched out with a jab that deformed his jaw. Then, I followed it up with a right hook that knocked it the other way. Finally, I ended the combination by grabbing his mushy head and launching myself upward with a knee that took him directly in the face. My flight didn't stop there, either. Even as he flipped backward, I threw myself forward with an ejection of Mist, pummeling him with a two-handed attack that sent him rocketing toward the floor.

He hit with enough force to flatten his body and dent the plasti-steel floor.

But he managed to roll out of the way to avoid my descending strike. When he picked himself up, his body snapped and plopped back into something resembling his old shape.

At the same time, Gala and the Dengyts had everything they could handle with the other mystics and Adjudicators. Gala was a whirlwind, Ferdinand in one hand and her blade in the other. The Adjudicators couldn't stand against her, and if she caught a mystic alone, they were at just as much of a disadvantage.

Meanwhile, the Dengyts fought completely differently. They almost looked like they teleported around the battlefield, but through my Mist senses, I could tell that they were just engaging some form of stealth, coupling it with a movement type of ability, then racing across the battlefield to attack another target. To mundane senses, it looked like they just disappeared, only to reappear in another location—a perception that wasn't helped by the fact that they all looked almost identical.

It was chaos, and it was hard to appreciate the level of ability they showed.

Gala was an unstoppable juggernaut. The Dengyts were almost impossible to pin down.

And me?

I was everything, all at once.

Tendrils of Mist shot out in every direction, guided by whatever remained of [Multimind]. Some mystics, I outright killed, but for the most part, that would have taken a lot more focus than I could expend on that endeavor. So, I used my Mist control to foul their footing, blunt their senses, and stagger them. It was enough to keep the other mystics under control.

The Adjudicators proved another challenge. I couldn't control norcite, and it was sufficient to block my attempts at Mist manipulation. However, their armor wasn't perfect. It had gaps, most of which were only a single nanite wide. Yet, that was enough to provide an opportunity for exploitation.

It took more than one train of thought, but I managed it all the same. Whole swaths of the black-armored soldiers fell as I flooded their bodies with Mist, exploding them inside their seemingly invulnerable armor.

At the same time, I stalked toward my real opponent.

"I am impressed," he said.

"I'm not."

Then, I resumed my assault, peppering him with attacks. Some were mundane, harnessing my incredibly powerful body to do devastating damage. However, as I fought, I realized that the same principles that allowed me to use Teleport or fly were usable in combat. I didn't use them to move my whole body, though. Instead, I accentuated attacks, pushing against the Mist to add more force to punches, kicks, and knees.

And when he tried to counterattack, I realized that I could simply let his intended attacks pass right through me. Sometimes, I even flickered out of existence for a brief moment, and he hit nothing but air. It was an odd way of fighting, but it was also effective—not only because I avoided any lasting damage, but also because it was clearly frustrating.

Which made things that much easier for me.

He expended great quantities of Mist, but slowly, his efforts grew wilder. Less controlled. It was useless. He couldn't touch me. In fact, as the battle went on, it felt more like I was toying with him than fighting a life-and-death battle. Even when he leveraged the entirety of his Mist against me, it was like throwing a bucket of water into the ocean. He simply was not on my level.

That wasn't to say that he went down easily. He did not. His strange body was impervious to most damage, and he had vast stores of Mist at his disposal. Still, I wore him down, and then, I sharpened my Mist tendrils into points and shoved them through him. He was ripped into pieces beneath my eviscerating efforts.

And just like that, he was dead.

But I wasn't finished. I reached out, grasping the Mist in his core, and dragged it into my own body. I no longer had a real core of my own. When my body had reconstituted itself, it had spread the Mist throughout my form. I absorbed everything he had, becoming far denser than ever before.

And to my surprise, his Mist came with a host of memories.

Dal Kanik was from a mostly aquatic planet, and his odd skeleton was the result of his species having evolved under the immense pressure of ocean depths. He'd overcome that via Mist control, joining the Arbiters of Orion the moment he'd displayed a basic proficiency with Mist.

Since then, he'd slowly climbed the ranks until he was one of the top one hundred mystics in the entire organization.

And now he was dead.

At my hands, no less. I could feel his frustration. His indignation. His pride. It had all counted for nothing, though. He was nothing before me.

Nothing.

Just a collection of flesh and Mist. And I had taken his Mist. Now, he was just lifeless meat.

Suddenly, I realized that the entire battlefield had gone silent. I looked up to see that I was surrounded by a bubble of Mist that no one else could perceive. A few feet away in every direction, a solid wall of bullets, superheated balls of Mist, and other projectiles hovered in place.

Gala was down, lying in a pool of blood. The Dengyts were dead. I could tell that from a mere glance. There were plenty of other bodies all around me. Dozens of Adjudicators and mystics, all fallen. But still yet more were still alive, and all their weapons were aimed at me. Nestled in my bubble of Mist, I couldn't hear their fire. But with every passing moment, another projectile added its weight to the collection around me.

And in the distance, I saw even more Adjudicators, blue-uniformed crew members, and a host of mystics rushing down the corridor in my direction.

I screamed.

The projectiles all reversed course, going back in the direction they'd come. Some of the fire hit home. But the ones who fell from that first volley were the lucky ones. With a thousand tendrils of Mist, I lashed out.

But not in the same way I'd done so before.

Instead, I reversed the polarity of my senses—and my control. The whispers became screams, echoing my own. And when I sent my tendrils of Mist at the Adjudicators, mystics, and crew members, there was nothing that could stop me. I ripped their powerful armor away, then flayed them where they stood.

It happened in seconds. Blood and flesh of all different colors and consistencies painted the walls. Body parts flew in all directions. And their screams—so different from the ones in my mind—joined the chorus.

It only took a few moments before every single person in the corridor was dead.

And I was all alone.

I released my grip on the Mist. Hundreds of bullets fell to the ground with a clatter. None of the blood had reached me. In fact, all around me for a few feet in every direction was entirely spotless. That couldn't be said for the rest of the corridor. The blue-and-gold walls had been stained with every color in the rainbow.

I stood there for a long moment, just staring at the carnage. I hadn't even thought about it. Not consciously. The Mist had simply responded to my need, like it was an instinctive part of me.

In fact, that was how it had been since my body had been destroyed and put back together. It was like I was the Mist, and the Mist was me. I didn't know what that meant, but after only a few more seconds, I recognized that I had another issue.

Gala.

She was still alive, though only barely.

I rushed to her side, dropping to my knees and sliding the last few feet across a blood-slick floor. Once I came to a stop, I reached out with Mist, checking her condition. It only took an instant before I'd hacked into her interface. Fortunately, hers was even more advanced than the one I'd once had installed, and it came with a detailed health readout that characterized her injuries as severe.

She was dying.

I knew it.

But I refused to accept that. So, I shoved my Mist tendrils deep inside of her and commanded them to repair the damage. At first, nothing happened. But then, I remembered the automender I'd used during my first Rift. Buried deep within my mind—or perhaps the nanites—was the memory of how it had worked. At the time, I'd been incapable of understanding it. However, combined with that memory was the ability attached to [Mist-Infused Body], which was capable of repairing all but fatal damage.

Even with those memories and methods, I relied mostly on my desperation and instincts to give it form.

Suddenly, Gala's wounds began to mend. I poured Mist into her, and her flesh fused back together. Broken bones healed. Bullets and other projectiles slid out of her bovine form. And then, after a few more moments, she let out a gasp and shot upright.

"What happened?!" she bellowed.

"You were injured," I answered truthfully. "I healed you."

"How?"

"Same way I do everything else. Mist. Are you okay? Because we still have a job to do," I said.

After Gala checked herself over—apparently, the sudden healing was more than a little disconcerting—she declared herself fit. Unfortunately, all the Dengyts had been killed while I was focused on Dal Kenik, the black-clad mystic. It was a tragedy, but they'd come to *Infinite Conquest* fully prepared to die. So, I shed no tears for them.

"Pick, is everyone in position?" I asked.

It was Alistaris who answered via the Secure Connection we'd established before setting out. He said, "The fleet is poised to launch the moment you bring the blockade down. We will destroy the drones, carving a corridor through which we can reach the world ships."

"Have they arrived?" I asked, striding through the corridor. Gala accompanied me, looking this way and that as she searched for any enemies who might've lived through my onslaught of Mist. There were none.

"They're waiting just outside the range of *Infinite Conquest's* sensors."

"How quickly can they get here?"

"Minutes," he stated. "Are you ready?"

"Give me a few moments," I answered, finally reaching the terminals. I reached out, touching the port. I no longer had the Hand of God or a personal link, but with Mist control, I didn't need them. In seconds, I had infiltrated the system, tearing through the Mistwall so easily that it might as well not have existed.

Suddenly, the entirety of the ship's system was laid bare before me. Unfortunately, I could only look at most of it. The terminals I'd infiltrated weren't connected to *Infinite Conquest*'s overall functions. Instead, they were solely connected to the blockade controls.

With a flick of my mind, I deactivated it.

The moment I did, I became aware of a dozen ships arriving in Earth's orbit. Each one was the size of *Infinite Conquest*. But they were sleeker. With better Mist control. Through the blockade's satellites, I saw them.

Pristine white and shaped like giant wings, they were also decorated with gold filigree. But I didn't need to see anything but their white hulls to know who they were.

"The Templars have arrived," I said.

Then, I became aware of a hundred missiles being launched from each of those ships. Each one was teeming with Mist, telling me that whoever had launched them had some significant modifiers. Even one would rival the explosive power I'd unleashed on the moon. All hundred? That was enough to destroy Earth.

Yet, the planet was not their target.

Instead, the missiles were aimed at *Infinite Conquest*.

CHAPTER FIFTY-SIX

WHISPERS OVERWHELMING

Being the most powerful person on the planet doesn't mean anything if the entire universe is arrayed against you. Sometimes, you're just destined to lose.

—Alistaris Kargat

As Gala shouted something I couldn't be bothered to hear, I acted on instinct. Gathering the Mist around me, I embraced the structure of Teleport. At the same time, I wrapped myself in a protective barrier that, in my panicked state, I hoped would protect me. Then, I flickered out of existence, riding a wave of Mist through the ship's various bulkheads and coming out on the surface of its elaborate blue hull.

But I didn't stop there.

Instead, I threw myself at the missiles, each one brimming with more Mist than I had ever seen concentrated in any munitions. And I tore them apart. Time didn't mean anything to me. Every passing second felt like minutes. Or hours. I knew the cocoon of Mist surrounding me wasn't going to last. Even as I ripped through those missiles, my protections degraded.

And eventually, they were completely sundered.

I couldn't spare the focus necessary to rebuild them. Instead, the entirety of my concentration was squarely on keeping those missiles from finding their way to *Infinite Conquest*.

There were so many, though.

Too many.

Thousands of them, and every one powerful enough to cripple the massive ship. I could feel it.

Yet, I endeavored to protect it—not only to save myself because, after all, I couldn't remain in space for much longer, but also to save Gala. Mostly, though, I wanted to preserve access to the blockade controls because there was a seed of an idea in my mind. I couldn't quite pinpoint the specifics, but I felt certain that there was something there. Something that could save us all.

In any case, just like I couldn't spare the focus to protect myself from the vacuum of space, I couldn't give the idea the thought necessary to bring it to fruition. So, I concentrated on the task at hand, destroying one missile after another. Some, I simply disabled their propulsion systems and sucked the Mist out of their explosives. Others were too complex, and I simply detonated them.

But one by one, I cut the bombardment down.

Meanwhile, I could see the world ships in the distance. They were far enough away that they only looked like gray specs amid the stars, yet I knew them for what they were. At the same time, a fleet of ships had launched from Earth, each one carrying with it thousands of people that represented the hope of humanity's continued existence.

Fortunately, the Templar ships didn't care about them.

I had painted too large of a target on my back for them to ignore. Which was fine. If I was meant to be a distraction, then so be it.

But it was all too much.

I was powerful. Inordinately so. I could do things nobody else in the world—perhaps even the galaxy—could do. Yet, I couldn't be in a thousand places at once, and that deficiency showed itself in my inability to stop all the missiles before they crashed into *Infinite Conquest*.

Some exploded with predictable fury. Fortunately, the ship's defenses were extraordinarily robust, which was likely why the Templar fleet had aimed so much ordnance in its direction. That's what it would take to completely overcome the shields. Other missiles were destroyed by *Infinite Conquest*'s defensive cannons.

But some made it to the hull by activating some sort of countermeasures meant to bore through the shields. They didn't explode, though. Instead, from their fuselages extended a series of metallic arms, which they used to latch on to the fuselage. Then, they breached the hull.

Clearly, the Templars had sent boarding parties.

And now that they were open, I could sense their occupants.

All mystics. All just as powerful as the wax-faced alien I'd killed only a few minutes before. Even as the Templars flooded into the ship, I checked the ships from which they'd come, and I was surprised to see that they hadn't launched any more missiles. So, I wasted no more time in space; instead, I used my new version of Teleport to return whence I had come.

I thudded back to the terminal room, gasping for air with my body half-frozen. Even with my cocoon of Mist, I wasn't nearly as protected from space as I'd thought. With a little time, there was a chance I could improve the process, but time was the one thing I didn't have. After all, there was a small army of powerful Templars racing through the ship.

And I wasn't so naive as to believe Gala could do much against such a force.

So, I looked up, saying, "You should probably go. Find the escape pods. I'm sure a ship this size has plenty. Get back to Earth."

"But—"

I pushed myself to my feet, surging Mist to heal my not-quite-human body. There was even less of the old me left now. Maybe twenty percent human. It was odd to know that I was more Mist than flesh. But there were advantages to that, too. I felt closer to the Mist than ever before. The whispers had grown even louder. I felt that if I inverted my perception, they would become deafening screams.

In seconds, I was back to normal. "Gala, this isn't a fight for you," I said. "I know you're strong. In most battles, you'd be an asset. But in this one, I can't afford to split my focus between protecting you and fighting what's coming."

She clearly wanted to argue. I could see it in her bovine eyes. But I could also see resignation. She knew I was right. And deep down, I think she knew what our separation represented. If she left, there was every chance that she would never see me again. Did I intend to sacrifice myself? No. But in the battle that was coming, we both knew the odds were stacked against me.

With all my power—and I had that in spades—I was still just one person.

"Go."

She sighed, then reached out to grip my shoulder. Her hand was large enough to brush against my neck. "In a lot of ways, I feel like we barely know each other," she said. "But in others, you're like family. Please don't do anything rash."

I knew how difficult it was for someone like her to walk away from a battle. She was a warrior, and an elite one at that. But there was enough of a realist in her to know that she couldn't contribute to what was coming.

For my part, I was glad to see her go. She was one of the few people in the world—or the universe, I supposed—I would count a true friend. She'd helped me almost from the very beginning. But there was more to it than that. Over the years, I'd visited her countless times. Usually, I did so under the pretense of buying ammunition or seeing if she had any new weapons available. The reality of it was that I just liked her company. My uncle had trusted her, and so I had, as well.

So, the goodbye felt incredibly poignant, as much because I had finally admitted how much I cared about the minotaur as because I recognized that my chances of making it through the coming battle grew increasingly slimmer by the passing second.

"Don't do anything stupid," she said.

"I wouldn't be me if I didn't do something stupid, right?"

She just gave me a sad smile. "Seriously. Be careful." Then, she handed me her blade. "Use this. It's better than any of these others."

I took the sword. It felt good in my hand, like an extension of my arm. I looked up into Gala's eyes, and I lied: "I'll be careful."

Careful really wasn't in my nature, and I think she recognized that. But neither of us wanted to acknowledge it.

After that, she took off, and I took a minute to let Patrick know what was going on. He echoed Gala's sentiments, though he seemed far more confident that I'd make it through than she had been. I wanted to share that sentiment, but I knew what was coming. There were hundreds of mystics, each a trained Templar and as powerful as any I'd faced so far. My odds of survival were slim, but I knew that if I didn't make a stand, they would simply reengage the blockade, trapping all of humanity on the surface. To escape, they needed time, and I had vowed to give them just that.

So, I prepared myself as well as I could, pacing back and forth amid the bodies of the Arbiters of Orion I'd just killed. As I did, I continued to listen to the whispers of the Mist. I knew there was something there. I could feel it. I just needed to be more receptive.

I didn't get the chance, though.

Not before the Templars arrived.

They looked so intimidating and heroic, wearing their white robes. Each one radiated a level of might that only served to exacerbate that aura of power. But then again, so did I. For the first time since my body had been rebuilt by the Mist, I let my own aura extend unrestrained. It undulated from my body, wild and vicious, as it responded to the thoughts running rampant in my mind.

It was a fitting reflection of my anger.

Of my indignation.

Of my stubborn refusal to surrender before overwhelming odds.

The most powerful Templar—a bearded alien with red skin—stepped forward on cloven hooves. He wielded a wicked polearm, its blade glistening with barely restrained Mist.

"Mirabelle Braddock," he croaked, his voice sounding like it had come from a demonic frog. "You are hereby ordered to remand yourself into our custody. Otherwise, we will be forced to destroy you."

"As if you don't plan to do that anyway," I said, pacing back and forth. I rolled my shoulders. "That's why you're here, right? You want to enslave me. Or kill me. I'm not going to let that happen."

"Do not force our hand, child."

"I would say the same to you" was my retort.

"You believe you can win. You are mistaken. Surrender and we will save your people," he said. "Give yourself to us and we will—"

"No."

"No?"

"That's what I said," I replied. I pointed my sword in his direction. "You're going to be the first to die, just so you know. I'll rip the Mist from your body, and while you're reeling from the sudden weakness that follows, I will decapitate that pretty red head." I turned to the others. "You all won't be far behind."

He shook his head sadly. "You would sacrifice your world to avoid going with us?"

"It's a decision I've made before," I answered truthfully. I'd been offered the same sort of deal by Nora. It hadn't ended well for her. Besides, this time was different. Even if this red-skinned asshole intended to make good on his promise, there was no way it would be good for humanity. At best, they would be indentured or enslaved and shunted off to some forgotten corner of the universe. At worst, he'd just kill them all anyway.

Because the Templars didn't care about Earth. Truthfully, they didn't care about me, either. Their only driving force was the preservation of their own power. Freddie had made that abundantly clear, and the whispers of the Mist felt like they supported that notion. I couldn't understand them—not yet—but they clearly didn't like the Templars.

I chose to trust that rather than the dubious promises of an alien who'd been sent to kill me.

"You truly do not intend to be reasonable?"

"From my perspective, this is the only reasonable response. But I'll give you a chance. Leave. Go back to your ships and fly away. Leave us to our own devices," I said. "Let humanity board the world ships, and—"

He cocked his head to the side.

That's when I felt it.

The Templar ships hadn't run out of missiles. Because of course they hadn't. Instead, they'd simply redirected their fire. Even from so far away, I could feel the world ships exploding.

I sighed. "You really shouldn't have done that."

He started to say something, but I didn't allow it. Instead, I rocketed forward, using my new version of Teleport to close the distance. At the same time, a thousand Mist tendrils snaked out. Most of them were directed at the red-skinned Templar, but quite a few extended all around me, where they poised to block any attacks the others might aim in my direction.

My Mist tendrils slammed into him, latching on like ephemeral leeches and sucking the Mist right out of him. It came in a flood—more than with any other opponent I'd ever faced. If I'd encountered him even an hour before, I might have struggled.

But with every passing minute, my command of Mist had grown, and the fight against the wax-faced mystic had solidified things in a way no degree of practice ever could. I leveraged that new prowess to my advantage, tearing the red Templar's Mist away in great chunks.

His eyes widened in shock, and he stumbled in weakness.

Then, Gala's sword—gleaming like a blade of pure Mist—descended. It bit into his Mist-deprived neck like it wasn't even there. Black blood flew into the air, staining his pristine white tunic.

His head followed only an instant later.

But committing to that kill opened me up to hundreds of attacks from powerful mystics. Even as I planted my feet and the mystic's head hit the floor, I was buried beneath a barrage of Mist-based attacks. Some were simple blades of Mist. Others gripped my limbs. Still others manifested as various projectiles—some of which looked like arrows or spears, while the rest took the form of simple balls of roiling energy. A good many of them I managed to deflect, but even with my prowess, I couldn't get them all.

The first few didn't do much, but enough hit their mark to send me stumbling. That was the only opening they needed. After all, the Templars were all trained warriors, and they knew how to take advantage of even the slightest slip.

I felt the bite of innumerable blades as they cut into me, one after another. My arm was the first limb severed, but it wasn't the last. In seconds, I'd been sliced into a dozen pieces. They took no chances, and one of the mystics destroyed my head, splattering it into bits of skull and scattered brain.

Yet, just as I had in the ruins of New York, my consciousness refused to surrender to death. Instead, I remained in the atmosphere, a pool of disembodied Mist. The whispers grew louder, and my connection to the Mist escalated. And then, I coalesced.

Even as the Templars congratulated themselves on a job well done, I reformed my body. My bare feet slapped down on the plasti-steel floor, garnering the attention of the suddenly shocked Templars.

"Is that all you got?" I asked flippantly. Then, with a deft control of the ambient Mist, I manifested a glimmering blue blade. It took the form of the old nano-bladed sword I'd used for so many years—appropriate and comfortable in my hand. It shone with the light of uncountable nanites, all working together to infuse it with unmatched power.

The Templars flinched back.

I did not.

With my ever-increasing Mist control, I launched myself forward, flickering from one spot to the next in less than an instant. A moment later, two pieces of Templar—her torso and her legs—went flying in different directions.

That's when the slaughter began.

I didn't even have to use my version of Teleport. Instead, I simply willed myself from one spot to the next, appearing for only so long as it took me to slice a Templar to pieces before moving to the next spot.

In seconds, a dozen of them were dead.

The rest decided that was a good time to run.

Of course, I had no intention of allowing that. They'd come to kill, capture, or enslave me. They'd threatened to kill everyone on Earth. Because of that, I didn't feel the least bit guilty about butchering every last one of them.

Besides, it wasn't even difficult.

Perhaps if I hadn't been so thoroughly trained, I would have struggled. Maybe if I wasn't a veteran of a thousand battles, I would have hesitated. But with the combination of my experience, training, and most of all, my connection to the Mist, the fight couldn't even qualify as a battle. Instead, it was just a slaughter.

And in its wake, I stood amid hundreds of dismembered pieces of alien, my breathing calm and collected, as I basked in the feeling of might.

It wasn't until Patrick contacted me over Secure Connection—which still worked, for some undefinable reason—that I realized that my fight, if could even be called such, was only one small part of the battle.

"Mira, we're struggling here," he said. "If you've got anything else to add, now's a great time to do it."

"The world ships?"

"Gone."

"The Templars?"

"They're turning their attention on us. We're holding on, but not for long. The transports carrying the refugees are going back to Earth," he explained.

I was more powerful than ever, but I couldn't be everywhere at once. I couldn't save them all. I was powerful but impotent.

"I don't know what to do," I admitted.

"The biggest Templar ship is doing something . . ."

"What?"

"I don't know. There's this huge cannon coming out of the . . . Oh . . . Oh no . . ."

"What is it?"

"Alistaris says it's meant to destroy Earth. They . . . I don't know . . ."

"Miss Braddock," came a voice over *Infinite Conquest*'s intercom system. "I know you can hear me. My name is Captain Gradion, of the Arbiters of Orion. You have boarded my ship. You have killed my people. Now, we have brokered a deal with the Templars. With your actions, you have doomed your planet. I hope it was worth it."

A COUNTDOWN TO EXTINCTION

There is freedom in hopelessness born of necessity. Striving toward a goal you think is impossible to reach can sometimes result in miracles.

—Galatira Iamaxis

t's charging up," Patrick said.

"How long?" I asked, racing across the room to one of the terminals. I had no idea what I was going to do, but I needed to figure something out. I didn't need any further explanations to understand that the Templars' cannon was Earth's doom. Perhaps it wouldn't immediately destroy the planet, but it would do enough damage that it probably wouldn't matter.

"Alistaris says a minute. Maybe two at the most. He says it's a mark-seven D-3274. It's going to tear a chunk the size of a continent off the planet," Patrick stated.

I didn't care about the weapon's designation. And if I was honest, the explanation of the cannon's strength wasn't important, either. I could intuit that much on my own.

"You have to get everyone to turn back around," I said. "Send them back to the surface."

"Already on it" was Patrick's response. I could tell he was stressed, probably in battle. *The Leviathan* was no warship, but it was capable enough to hold its own, especially with him at the helm.

I reached the first terminal and slammed a Mist tendril into the machine. A second later, the system was opened to me. However, I belatedly recognized that it was quarantined from the ship, and by a gap I couldn't hope to bridge. I slammed my fist into the wall, denting the blue-painted plasti-steel.

I didn't know what to do.

I didn't know how to save everyone.

After everything, the collective might of the enemies we—no, I—had made was overwhelming and unstoppable. I could kill thousands of Templars. I had slaughtered tens of thousands of Adjudicators and mystics. And yet, it was not enough. One person couldn't fight against the entire universe.

But even as the countdown to Earth's doom progressed, I refused to accept that. I'd overcome worse odds. I had beaten other people I should never have been able to touch. I could save Earth. I just needed to figure out how.

So, I cast my senses outward in a web of Mist tendrils that tore through *Infinite Conquest*. Time felt like it slowed down. And for me, it did. One second lasted whole minutes, at least from my subjective perspective. With that glut of time, I scoured the ship for something—anything—that might give me an edge.

And I found the weapons systems.

While *The Leviathan*—or any of the other vessels in Earth's fleet—was not a warship, *Infinite Conquest* certainly was. And it had all the requisite weapons that designation would suggest. I harnessed them all.

After only a second or two, I aimed and launched every missile. I fired every cannon. I engaged every gun. The result was a barrage of gunfire the Templars couldn't hope to dodge. The first missiles slammed into a powerful shield that dissipated their force with ripples of Mist. However, the slower-moving cannon projectiles never got that far because the swarm of norcite-shielded drones swooped in to intercept them.

Whole swaths of the machines were destroyed in explosions of blue Mist and pieces of metal. However, their sacrifice was effective, and the Templar ship was spared the bulk of the barrage. I tried to fire another, but I was disturbed to find that they wouldn't respond to my commands. I attempted it again and again, but after a few more seconds, I found the culprit responsible for my failure.

The crew of *Infinite Conquest* had destroyed their weapons' firing mechanisms, rendering them useless. I was so furious that I lashed out, killing a few dozen of them with my Mist tendrils. Then, after gathering my wits, I tried to fix the problems.

But for all my talents, I was no engineer.

Perhaps Patrick could have figured it out. Certainly, he could have done something. But me? My talents lay in another direction.

I railed against my own futility, but there was nothing I could do. The weapons were useless. My plan had failed before it had really had a chance to get started. Sure, I'd weakened the Templar ships' shields. And I'd managed to destroy much of the drone fleet. But the huge cannon descending from the ship's belly continued to charge, and the countdown to Earth's destruction persisted.

For a moment, I considered calling for Patrick and escaping. I had tried. I didn't owe Earth any more than that. And besides, what had humanity ever given me? Since my childhood, it had taken everything. First, my mother whose face I could scarcely remember. Then, Jeremiah, who'd died because of an insecure woman's jealousy. But it was more than the people I'd lost. It was the life I'd never gotten to live. I'd been fighting for so long, and all because of humanity's inability to resist alien corruption. Because of their collective inadequacy before the tide of oppression coming their way.

And I was tired of it.

I'd given it my all. I had fought. I had done more than anyone could reasonably expect. Who could blame me for saving myself and leaving it all behind?

But there were two issues with it. One was practical, but the other was more personal.

From a realistic standpoint, I knew the Templars would never let me escape. Perhaps Patrick could manage it. He was talented enough, certainly. But I couldn't believe that the Templars, with all their power, would be incapable of countering a relatively low-level smuggler's skills.

The second—and, if I was honest with myself, more important—issue was that I couldn't stomach losing. The idea of failure was nothing new. I'd experienced enough of it in my life that it wouldn't cripple me. However, the notion of just giving up was anathema to my very ethos. Even if it was necessary for my survival, I didn't think I was capable of admitting defeat and acting accordingly.

So, my mind raced in a thousand different directions as, with every passing second, I searched for some solution. Some way to prevent the Templars from destroying Earth. To keep them from claiming victory.

And then, suddenly, I figured it out.

I had access to one function that could save Earth. I just needed to make it work. So, I dove into the terminal, searching for the blockade controls. Normally, it was intended to keep things in. However, it seemed to me that it would only take a slight adjustment to configure it to keep things out.

The more I thought about it, the more I latched on to the idea. And soon enough, I found the controls and went to work. It was the most difficult bout of hacking I'd ever attempted. Turning the blockade on and off was easy enough, and it was tantamount to flipping a virtual switch. Yet, reversing its function was something else altogether, and accomplishing that feat required me to push into the fundamental framework of the controlling system.

Seconds passed, and even as I toppled one obstacle after another, solving equations and piecing together virtual puzzles, the Templars' weapon continued to charge. My head exploded into pain, and exhaustion gripped my mind.

I pushed through it, shunting my discomfort to another thread of thought I could ignore.

And eventually, I managed it.

Patrick's voice erupted over the Secure Connection: "It's about to fire!"

Indeed, with my Mist senses, I could feel that the thing was nearly charged. I only had a second or two.

I thrust my mind into the underlying foundation of the system, then rearranged things in a way I hoped would accomplish the goal. It wasn't as simple as flipping everything around. Instead, it required me to change a hundred different commands, each one chaining into another.

The weapon fired.

And I finished the job.

The blockade—or shield now—reactivated, but it was too late. The cannon didn't fire a single projectile. Instead, it erupted into a continuous beam that hit Earth with the power of a meteor.

Millions probably died.

But the assault only lasted a second before the shield finished activation. A blue shell of Mist encircled the globe, cutting the beam of destruction off. But it continued to fire. I could feel the Mist being destroyed.

Shields were finite, after all. They could be broken. Overcome. And it seemed that the Templars intended to do just that. The blockade was incredibly powerful. With Earth's weapons, we'd had no chance over breaking it. But the Templars were on a completely different level. They had access to firepower we could only dream about.

And slowly, the shield was overwhelmed.

After almost thirty seconds, it became clear that my gambit was useless. The blockade would soon fall, and Earth would follow.

"Mira . . ."

"I know, Pick."

"What do you want to do?" he asked, even as I sensed the beam melting through the shield.

"I . . . I don't know . . ."

And I didn't. I'd done my best. I had given everything I could. And yet, everyone was still going to die. I was still going to lose.

I wouldn't accept that, though. There swas an argument to be made that I simply couldn't. I wasn't capable of accepting my own failures.

With that fueling my efforts, I drank deep of the Mist, searching for an answer. The problem was power. The shield could hold. There just wasn't enough Mist to keep it going when the beam continuously destroyed the nanites. As I continued to infuse myself with more Mist than I'd ever held before, I felt my body shifting. Whatever humanity I'd maintained—and it wasn't much, after most of my body had been destroyed—retreated before the flood of Mist.

And that's when I realized the answer.

In retrospect, it seemed so obvious. If the blockade needed more power, then I could provide just that. I could be the battery that fueled Earth's saving grace.

So, I pushed the Mist out, funneling it into the terminal. In turn, it raced toward the satellites that controlled the actual blockade. But it wasn't enough. It was too slow. I needed to get closer.

"I hope this works . . ."

"What are you—"

I didn't hear Patrick's retort. Instead, I wrapped myself in Mist, then used my new version of Teleport. But instead of only going a few dozen feet, I passed through the blockade and appeared miles away and next to one of the satellites. I slammed into it, grabbing hold before I bounced off and went spinning into space.

I could feel the vacuum eating at the Mist around me, but I couldn't pay attention to that. Instead, I shoved a tendril into the satellite, then flooded it with my own Mist.

And it worked.

Even as the incomprehensibly dense Mist inside me drained into the satellite, it used it as fuel to keep the blockade active. Now, all I needed to do was keep it going long enough for the ship's weapon to run out of fuel.

Seconds passed, and I actually thought I'd found the solution.

But then, a second ship opened fire—not with the massive cannon of the largest ship but, rather, with more normal munitions. Usually, they would have been inconsequential against a shield of the blockade's power. Yet, with the system already taxed by the huge, world-ending cannon, they started to tip the balance.

The rest of the fleet followed suit.

And once again, Earth's doom loomed large on the horizon as I felt myself being drained at a ridiculously powerful rate. I could do nothing to stop it, either. The moment I let go, the shield would fall, and Earth would be destroyed.

So I clung to the satellite, sinking deeper into the Mist than I ever had before. The whispers roared in my mind, and I felt my body dissipating with every passing second. I screamed into the void, but no sound escaped from between my lips.

Bit by bit, I felt myself being unmade, drained into the blockade's system and used as fuel. The tiny bits of normal flesh broke off, frozen and drifting into space. There was nothing left but the nanites.

With that came power, though. Strength. They replicated at an unreal rate, pouring into the satellite as I pitted my will against the might of a Templar fleet.

And for a while, I held my own.

Yet, the tyranny of power soon reasserted itself. I was strong. But so were they. And they had the benefit of numbers and technology on their side.

I had power on my side, too, though. And as I felt myself draining away, I felt closer to the Mist than ever before. Closer than I thought possible. So close that I had difficulty telling where it stopped and I began. I pushed into that, letting the Mist envelop and infuse my very being.

And I saw.

Everything.

The world—the universe—opened up to me in a way that defied description. The whispers that had become screams were suddenly speaking a language I could understand. And they told me what I needed to hear. They explained that the Mist was both more and less than anyone knew. It wasn't just a series of microscopic machines. It was that, certainly, but it was also a record of everything that had come before. In the Mist was the resting place of everyone who'd ever existed.

Everyone who ever would.

It was everything.

With my eyes finally open, I saw the solution. I knew what I had to do. And yet, I hesitated.

Then, I heard a familiar voice.

"You've become more than I could have ever expected. More than I could have hoped you could be. You are poised to save the world, to pick up the slack where I failed. I started off trying to save people," Jeremiah said, his face shimmering before my inner eye. "I truly did. I wanted to help everyone survive. Somewhere along the way, I lost that. I became bitter. Vengeful. After I lost . . . everything . . . I stopped caring about saving people. I just wanted to kill. I wanted to make the aliens pay."

He shook his head. I wasn't sure if it was really him or if it was just an echo of the man he'd been. But I knew it was real. Maybe it was even whatever passed for a soul.

"Then your mother died. And just . . . I just abandoned everything in favor of a singular mission. Keeping you alive and giving you the tools to survive. In that endeavor, I was successful. You can live. You can keep going. They won't be able to kill you. You feel that, don't you? You're so far past them that you may as well be a goddess.

"You could collect Remy's boy and jet off into the universe, safe and sound."

"But?" I asked, feeling like the world had frozen. Perhaps it had. Or maybe I was functioning at such a high speed that it felt like it.

"But you have a choice. Leave. Survive. Fulfill the purpose that was the subject of my obsession."

"Or?"

"Or you can sacrifice yourself. You feel it, don't you? You can give it everything. You can inhabit this system and protect the world. I don't know how long it'll last, but so long as it does, no one you don't want on Earth will get past you. You will be the world's guardian angel. Its goddess."

He sighed, then rubbed his bald head. That familiar gesture brought tears. I'd never truly processed his death, instead focusing on my vengeful response. That was a mistake.

"But you won't be you. Not in any way that matters. You won't pass on. You won't join me and the others. You'll be stuck in between. A different kind of existence. A fusion of human and Mist. I won't pretend to understand it, but I know you won't be Mira anymore. You might not be anything. Just a collection of nanites with a singular purpose driven by the person you used to be."

"I know."

"You do?"

"I do."

From the moment I'd teleported to the satellite, I'd known what was coming. Maybe not in the forefront of my mind, but somewhere deep down, I knew that protecting Earth would require a sacrifice.

It would require my life.

My Mist.

My soul.

It would take everything. I could feel that as clearly as I'd ever felt anything in my life. I didn't need Jeremiah to confirm it. But his explanation brought everything into focus.

I had done terrible things. I had killed millions. Many of them had deserved it, but hundreds of thousands of innocents had perished by my hand. I'd always wanted to see myself as a good person. I'd justified my actions in a thousand different ways, at least. But those actions condemned me. I was a villain. A selfish person who only ever acted in her own interests. Since the war for Earth's survival had begun, I'd tried to change that. I had resisted the urge to flee, but even that was born of some degree of selfishness.

And this was no different.

If spite drove me to selfless sacrifice, was it still heroism? I wasn't sure. But more than that, I wasn't really concerned with that sort of thing. I never had been. Instead, I was driven by one overriding factor: I refused to let the aliens win.

I would fight to the last second, and if forcing them to retreat in defeat meant that I had to die, then so be it. I was okay with that.

But others likely wouldn't be.

"Pick," I said.

"Whatever you're doing, it's working. I think—"

"Patrick."

"I'm just saying—"

"Just shut up for a second," I said, still using the Secure Connection. "And listen. I don't have much time here. I'm about to do something you probably wouldn't want me to do. But I want you to know that I love you. Meeting you was the one truly good thing that's happened to me since . . . well . . . since forever. Thank you for putting up with me. I know I wasn't always the best partner. I was moody, angry, and selfish. But you made me a better person. I hope . . . I hope you'll miss me, though."

Then, before he could respond, I shut off the Secure Connection. If I had to listen to what he would inevitably say, I would lose my nerve.

"Are you sure?" asked Jeremiah.

I didn't verbalize an answer. Instead, I just gave him a small nod. Then, with my mentor—the man who'd raised me—hanging over my shoulder, I gave myself completely over to the Mist. At first, it was no different than what I'd been doing. But I pushed further, and with every passing second, I diffused into the shield.

At some point, the satellite exploded into a shower of blue sparks. Then the next in the web. They all followed, one by one, but the blockade persisted. Meanwhile, my body dissipated into the Mist, and I merged with the whispers.

They welcomed me with open arms.

But I refused their embrace. Instead, I hovered just out of range, leveraging every ounce of control I could muster to infuse the shield with my essence.

It hurt.

Agony unlike anything I'd ever felt rocketed through the Mist that comprised me. I ignored it, forcing my awareness into the shield. The pain continued to mount until there was nothing else left.

Then, suddenly, it ceased.

And I knew everything.

I felt everything.

I was everything.

It was so enticing. So peaceful.

I resisted the urge to continue down that path. Instead, I kept my goal in mind, letting myself spread out and envelop the Earth. Below me, the blue-and-green ball spun. Above me, space beckoned. A tiny ship—no bigger than an insect—stung me.

I swatted it.

Somewhere in the rapidly receding back of my mind, I was aware of the Templar ship—and the fleet surrounding it—being ripped to pieces by huge torrents of Mist. But it was an academic knowledge. A simple acknowledgment of what had come to pass. I felt nothing, save for satisfaction that I'd accomplished my goal.

That I had fulfilled my purpose.

Then, even that retreated, and whatever remained of Mirabelle Braddock disappeared. In her place was only Earth's protector.

IN THE WAKE OF SACRIFICE

Patrick glanced up at the sky and smiled sadly. It had been a little more than a year since Mira's sacrifice, and the shield around Earth remained as strong as ever. From the planet's surface, it was only visible during the day, and even then, the visual effect was limited to giving the atmosphere a slightly more vivid color palette. Most days, Patrick didn't even notice it at all.

But all it took was one stray thought, and he'd remember that day. Usually, that resulted in tears.

Mira's choice might not have been necessary. There may have been other options. Patrick could barely conceive of the scope of her powers there at the end, so neither he nor anyone else on the planet could truly criticize her decision to sacrifice herself for Earth's protection.

Especially when it had worked.

Since that day, no aliens—save for Alistaris and his people—had been allowed onto Earth's surface. The ones who were already there had been given the option to leave. Patrick wasn't sure if that was the system responding to Mira's shield or if she'd somehow hijacked it for her own use. What was clear, though, was that if the hostile aliens chose to remain past the deadline for evacuation, they met with grisly ends.

Patrick had seen an entire city of aliens who'd had the Mist sucked right out of them. When he had found them, they had been reduced to barely living husks that begged for death. He—along with a squad he'd formed for that very purpose—had obliged. As a result, they'd all been rewarded by the system, gaining quite a lot of progress to their levels.

For the aliens, the message was clear.

Even if they managed to find their way to the surface, they would be used for nothing more than fuel for humanity's progression. And there was nothing any of them could do about it.

As a result, Earth had been largely left to its own devices. Certainly, there were ships hovering just above the shield. For six months, another Templar fleet fired upon the shield in the hopes they could breach it. However, their every attack served only to strengthen it. Even when some obscenely powerful mystic arrived, the results were the same. She had filled the entire atmosphere with lightning and fire, and yet, the shield held against an assault that, according to Gala, was strong enough to destroy the planet.

After that, most of the aliens had departed, leaving only a few in the area to monitor the situation. Because, from what Alistaris and Gala claimed, no one truly believed that Mira was gone. Instead, they thought that she had simply empowered the shield in some way they didn't understand. As such, Earth's enemies were simply biding their time until the power source ran out.

Patrick wasn't sure that day would ever come.

After all, there was a long history of people being used as infinitely recharge-able Mist batteries. The Pacificians had done it, and the universe was full of others who'd gone down that route. It was frowned upon, certainly, but no one ever actually did anything about it. It was a sad commentary on the worth of a sapient soul that it was allowed to continue.

Regardless, that history was why Patrick expected Mira's shield to last indefinitely. That expectation was even further supported by the fact that it seemed to harvest the Mist from any attacks leveled against it, strengthening its structure in the process.

No—the shield would remain.

Fortunately, humanity wasn't trapped by it. If they so desired, people could leave Earth. Patrick had, visiting Earth's closest neighbors. There was no life present, but for that month, the journey as well as the magnificent sights he'd beheld were a nice distraction. More, he'd managed to get a handle on space travel and navigation, which he would need if he ever wanted to travel to any other inhabited planets.

Or perhaps the core systems.

"She's up there, you know," came a familiar voice. Patrick looked back to see Gala standing slightly behind him. She continued, "I can feel her watching over us."

"I can't," Patrick said, feeling tears trace lines down his cheeks. He didn't wipe them away. What was the point? More would just come. It was the same any time he considered Mira's death.

Or transformation, he admitted. She might not have died. There was every chance that some part of her consciousness inhabited the shield. That's what Alistaris and Gala insisted. Yet, that didn't really matter—not in any practical sense. If the person Patrick loved was still alive, she would have reappeared by now. No—her sacrifice might not have been complete, but it was close enough that the distinction didn't matter. Mira was gone. Alive or dead, she was no longer the person Patrick had loved.

"She's up there," Gala insisted. Then, she put her hand on his shoulder, turning him slightly. When he turned around, he saw a large box in her hand. She handed it over, saying, "We found this yesterday when we were retrofitting *The Leviathan*."

Patrick took it, then flipped it over. The cube was made of metal, with a host of esoteric designs on the surface. Other than that, there was a single port meant for a personal link.

"What is it?" he asked.

"A record," Gala stated. "I tried to access it, but it's coded only for you."

"Is it safe?"

Gala shrugged her huge shoulders, saying, "I don't know. I think so, though."

"Why? Do you have any evidence of that?" he asked.

"Just access it," she said. "You'll see."

Patrick sighed. He hated it when people withheld information, but Gala had proved herself a hundred times over. She was a friend, and she only wanted what was best for him. He trusted her.

Still, he wasn't going to access the cube immediately. He wanted privacy for that. So, he asked, "Is the ship ready?"

Gala and a few of the Dengyts had been fitting *The Leviathan* with new and upgraded weaponry they'd built from the harvested wreckage of the alien ships and settlements that had been left behind. Patrick had offered to help, but his class was more suited to working on personal cybernetics.

Gala went on to explain that *The Leviathan*'s upgrades were progressing well and that it would be finished within a month. Other than that, she explained the other efforts to drag humanity forward. Mimicking some of the larger forces in the universe, they'd established schools and other programs meant to efficiently develop children. In addition, they had begun to build a global fleet as well as a fighting force.

Because even if Earth remained protected by the shield, they would eventually want to venture out into the universe. And for that, they would need power.

Real power.

Universal power.

Fortunately, Gala and Alistaris were well equipped to handle that burden. Gala was a former member of one of the most elite fighting forces in the universe, so she knew their training methods as well as the level of gear they would need to be effective. Meanwhile, Alistaris had connections with the Ark Alliance that he could leverage to their advantage. The only thing missing were mystics, though there were bound to be some people who could carry that torch.

They had the tools. Now, they just needed to implement them. It was a process that would take decades. Perhaps even centuries. But that was okay. Mira had given them time. It was up to them to use it wisely.

"What about the wildlings?" asked Patrick. "Are they still acting weird?"

"Yes," Gala said. "All reports suggest that they're far less aggressive."

"Do we know why?"

Gala shook her head. "It might be natural evolution," she stated. "Or maybe it's something Mira did. We have no idea. Maybe the cube will help."

He sighed. "You're going to keep bugging me until I look at it, aren't you?"

"I am."

"Fine. I'll be in my quarters, then," he said.

After that, Patrick made his way through their settlement—even though it was almost a year old, it was still rough around the edges—until he reached his house. Once he was inside, he sat in his favorite chair and pulled his personal link from the port in his artificial arm. Then, he plugged it into the cube.

Scanning . . .
Identity confirmed. Welcome, Patrick Ward. Autoplaying message . . .

"Hey, Pick," came Mira's voice. "I'm using the last bit of my consciousness to put this together for you. I hope you don't mind."

Patrick's throat constricted, and his heart felt like it had skipped a beat.

The message went on: "Mostly, this is a record of what I went through since I got my Nexus Implant. Did you know they record everything? I didn't. Thoughts, emotions—everything. Kind of creepy, if you ask me, but there it is, all the same. I don't know if you have any interest in looking through all of that, but I thought I'd record it, just in case."

"Mira? Are you there?" Patrick asked, hoping that the record was more than it seemed. The fact that it existed at all meant that Mira had survived her sacrifice. But there was no response, dashing his hopes.

Instead, the recording went on, "Mostly, though, I just wanted to say a proper goodbye. I'm sorry, Pick. I didn't set out to do any of this. It's just . . . I didn't know any other way. In retrospect, there's a chance I could have teleported over to the other fleet and killed everyone inside, but that was a temporary measure. There were always going to be more. I think this was the only way to ensure that Earth had a chance. That humanity would survive.

She sighed, continuing, "I'm sorry we couldn't grow old together. I'm sorry we couldn't explore the galaxy. The universe. I wish . . . I wish we'd had more time. I love you. To me, you're the most important person on Earth. In the entire universe. So, survive. Find a way to thrive. You deserve it."

There was a slight pause, then she said, "The shield will last for at least two centuries. More if the idiots keep feeding me Mist. But by the time you hear this, my consciousness will have been absorbed into the Mist. It's all so . . . There's so much more to it all than we ever knew. I don't know if I believe in the afterlife. Maybe these are all just echoes. I might even be one. But I don't think so. Regardless, I want you to understand that I'm going to a better place. I know that probably doesn't help. You're going to be sad no matter what. That's inevitable. But when your time comes, Pick—I just want you to know I'll be waiting for you with open arms. Then, we can be together for all eternity."

Patrick's tears continued to flow.

"Oh, and Pick? Quit moping and get to living."

After that, the message ended, and the record lay out before him. He started it:

"I tore through the alley, ignoring the trash piled against the walls as I clutched my ill-gotten gains to my chest. Behind me . . ."

Patrick settled in to listen to Mira's story, a small but sad smile spreading across his face as he got to hear her voice for a little while longer.

ABOUT THE AUTHOR

Nicholas Searcy is the author of Death: Genesis, Mistrunner, and Path of Dragons, originally released on Royal Road. He enjoys writing, reading, spending time with family, sports, and, of course, a good cup of coffee.

DISCOVER
STORIES UNBOUND

PodiumAudio.com